THE TIES THAT BIND

DCI JOHN DRAKE
BOOK 2

M. R. ARMITAGE

Copyright © M. R. Armitage 2024

M. R. Armitage has asserted his right under the Copyright, Designs and Patents Act, 1988, to be identified as the author of this work.

First published by Zenarch Books in January 2024

All characters, names, places, incidents and storylines, other than those clearly in the public domain, are fictitious and any resemblance to persons living or dead, is entirely coincidental.

All rights reserved. No part of this publication may be reproduced, stored in a retrieval system, or transmitted, in any form or by any means, without the prior permission in writing of the publisher or author.

ISBN: 978-1-7392593-3-4

Find out more about the author and other forthcoming books at:
www.mrarmitage.com

*For my parents,
Richard and Rosemary*

SPOILERS WARNING

This book is the next instalment in an ongoing storyline and there are spoilers throughout regarding the events of Book 1.

If you have not read Book 1, *The Family Man*, I strongly recommend picking up a copy before reading any further.

To find out more, scan the QR code below:

1

The man burst from the ground, the wooden hatch thumping behind him.

He immediately stumbled, and fell to his knees, biting his lip hard to stop himself from crying out in pain. Tasting blood, he willed himself up off the frozen snow-covered ground, his balance made awkward by his tightly bound wrists. He didn't stop to collect himself or understand where he was, or why.

He ran.

He ran towards the only thing that might give him some form of cover. Away from the room, away from the place he'd been held.

The sound of his frantic breathing filled his ears while he scurried towards the line of trees in the distance. His large belly bobbled beneath his awkward, outstretched arms and the snow scrunched beneath him like cotton wool. The one remaining ankle binding hung loose, whipping at his free ankle.

No matter how much he wanted to, he daren't look back, for fear of what may be after him; for fear that his freedom, maybe even his life, would be all too short-lived. He knew moving quietly wasn't an option and it wouldn't have been worth it anyway, not in the enormous field he found himself in. The flat expanse of virgin snow, illuminated by the light of the waxing moon, contrasted starkly with the tall hedges and dry-stone walls. And, unfortunately, himself. His thin red cashmere jumper, jeans and old trainers stood out like a beacon against the snow's stark white glare.

He pushed on for what seemed an eternity, his lungs heaving and chilling from the winter air, his feet pounding the frozen mud and stones. Each step made him painfully aware of his breath, the puffs of frozen air like that of a steam train. But he knew he had the advantage of distance – at least, he hoped he did. He prayed he wouldn't lose his footing on an unseen rock or root, tripping or twisting his ankle and leaving himself at the mercy of whoever had held him in captivity.

Halfway towards the tree line, he was met with screams piercing the darkness. But it hadn't come from just one person. There were . . . *multiple voices*? Were there others out here besides him?

Taking a chance, he slowed down, cocking his head back over his shoulder and stumbling at the shift in balance as he checked for any sign of a pursuer. But all that met his gaze was the tree line amidst the snow and unending darkness of the night. There wasn't anyone there. No shadowy shape in pursuit, no obvious source for the screams.

Slowing further, he took one more haggard breath and slowed to a halt, squatting down and balling his hands into fists against his forehead. He took in a panicked gulp or two of the frozen air and tried his best to get his breath back and make sense of the situation. His heart pounded like a pneumatic drill and, despite him stopping, it didn't show any sign of letting up.

Lights suddenly flashed to his left, out of the corner of his eye, then were gone again just as quickly, followed by more screams echoing around him once more. In his tunnel visioned dash for freedom, he'd not seen that the dry-stone walls and hedging had come to a stop. Instead, a tall, wide-barred metal field gate stood to his side – one which provided no way of him squeezing through the bars or climbing without the full use of his hands. He huffed in frustration, his hopes immediately dashed. However, the gaps in the bars showed him something else, something that was completely alien to his situation. A curious structure of multi-coloured lights spinning in the distance. Schizophrenic patterns flashing as the structure rotated – the direction from which the screams continued to spew forth, he realised. He couldn't believe what he was seeing.

It was a fairground. The backdrop of screams were people on rides, a pendulum stuffed with people whipping through the air.

Where the hell am I?

A sudden, sharp crack sounded from behind.

He froze, his heart leaping into his mouth. His head snapped in every direction like a startled rabbit, eyes bulging in panic.

Run, you fool!

He took off against a backdrop of lights and screams. Another snap sounded, then another. His legs were burning with each stride, his ankles stiff and unyielding.

Just a few more strides, he thought. *You can do it. You need to do it.*

The trees loomed silently overhead; he'd made it. Immediately bundling himself up against a tree trunk, he slid to his knees, spluttering and wheezing, his lungs on fire.

Peering beyond his pathetic hiding place, he discovered his 'wood' was only a small thicket, barely six or seven trees deep. Tears ran down his cheeks at the discovery, the feeling of despair threatening to overwhelm him. He'd have to make another break for it again. He knew it, no matter how much he wanted to curl into a ball and wish it all away.

Inhaling sharply, he summoned his inner strength once more and got to his feet. Darting from one tree to the next, he made his way slowly and carefully through the scant evergreen foliage while cursing the tracks he left, but what could he do? He wasn't Rambo, for fuck's sake.

Snap!

He flinched at the sound, whimpering uncontrollably at how close it was while he hastened on. Icy sweat stung his bulging eyes; he couldn't take much more.

The thicket now firmly behind him, he was immediately beset by more misery: a new expanse of fields, one even bigger than before. The sight made him ground to a halt, his head flitting between the thicket and the woods beyond. He realised the futility of it all. He couldn't keep this up. He was exhausted, his pathetic body failing him.

An owl hooted somewhere while his mind raced. Perhaps he was imagining things? Or they had drugged him? Maybe this was all in his head. Or a bad dream he'd wake up from soon?

No – no, this is real, he rationalised. *You can't forget where you've been.*

He couldn't let this get the better of him. He needed to push, fight on, to not let his captors win.

Digging deep, he spurred himself on for one final push and turned back towards the woods, just in time for his face to meet a clenched fist. His nose crunched beneath the blow. His vision exploded in a sea of white, searing pain as he stumbled back, the blood pouring down his chin. A hand clawed at his mouth to muffle his cries and pull him to the ground. He fought back as best he could, standing his ground. His hands were repeatedly batted away like they were nothing. His attacker laughed, then the beating began, each strike raining down, blow after blow. A vicious hook to his temple finally sent him careering to the ground, the snow filling his bloodied nostrils. Now on the ground, he did what he had feared he'd do all along. He curled up pathetically, and gave in.

The countryside echoed to the sounds of his cries and whimpers at each strike and kick until finally he was silenced.

His attacker dragged the unconscious body towards the woods, the moon shining in the fresh blood amidst the snow.

2

Detective Chief Inspector John Drake took a deep breath, the bedsheet slack in his trembling hand. He stepped up onto the flimsy chair, causing it to wobble under his weight.

It wasn't the first time he'd stood there. But it would be the last. He was certain. This is what it had come to; him standing on a chair in a bedsit, a sheet soon to be hitched over a loft beam and tied round his throat. A man soon to be found with his neck at an unnatural angle, his tongue hanging out, thick and discoloured, piss-stained trousers and a note of apology nearby. *This* is what it had come to. He closed his eyes and a tear ran down his cheek.

It was fair to say the past year had not been kind. The saying, 'Time is a healer' was horseshit. It had been anything but. Time hadn't mended the cracks in his psyche. They'd only deepened, leaving him with the daily agony of waking up to the same circumstances, day in, day out. Becca, *his wife*, was gone. His daughter, Eva, estranged, his family forever shattered. Nothing would change that. Nothing would bring his wife back. Nothing.

Anguish radiated through his body as he stood moments from death. The pain was as raw as the day it had been inflicted, a persistent burn deep within his gut. His thoughts languished in a pain-filled fog. It would all be silenced soon, if he did what was right.

But for now, Drake could still picture it. Picture every moment: the knife tearing through Becca's neck, the blood pulsing from the wound. Her eyes. Those accusing brown eyes tearing at his soul.

Eyes still closed, he flinched as his mind projected the image of his daughter's face bristling with accusation. The moments where he was met with this stare in real life increasingly few and far between since she had moved in with her Aunt Rachel, Becca's sister, in the immediate aftermath of her mother's death. Eva had found herself unwilling and unable to live in the same house as him. The funeral and few meetings since hadn't forged the new connections that he'd yearned for. Instead, they'd only opened up further rifts between them. Her anger towards him, the hatred; those emotions weren't subsiding. If anything, they burned brighter each day.

He clenched his fists, the bedsheet scrunching in his grip. His throat tightened at the thought of his beautiful girl being without her mother, and it was all down to him. His failings. His mistakes: enabling the situation, allowing it to happen. All of it was down to him. Exposing his family like that. Not thinking it through. All the implications of his work that he should have taken more seriously, but hadn't.

Drake took another deep breath while indecipherable music pounded from the flat below, the bass vibrating the floor and chair. He opened his bleary eyes and looked over at the note he had carefully prepared next to his mobile phone. Both were placed on the small bedside table next to a sorry-looking single bed shorn of its bedsheet, the duvet tossed to one side and missing its cover.

He shivered involuntarily, his shirt drenched in sweat, the material clinging to his back. Drake felt ashamed it had come to this, but he remained resolute that his daughter was better off without him. Removing himself permanently from her life meant she could live her life free of burden. There would be an instant lessening of any threat of violence towards her.

There were criminals he had put behind bars, criminals who would think nothing of settling old scores with him on their release. She'd always be a target with him around. The solving of the Family Man case had made him the celebrity detective once again. And it had put him front and centre for all the deranged people who fancied themselves serial killers. He'd received all sorts of threats since, and Eva had received her share of comments at school, messages on social media. There was no hiding from it. Because of him, she'd be unable to live a normal life, right? And why would he wish that upon her for a moment longer? She'd be better off without him. He knew it.

He slung the sheet over the loft beam and knotted it carefully.

She deserved no more pain caused by him and his actions, bar this one irrevocable act.

Wrapping the makeshift noose around his neck, he tightened it as best he could and took another breath.

Just one more step and his mind would be silent.

He stared down at the chair and braced himself.

* * *

Earlier

'Do you know why you're here, Mr Drake?'

Drake glanced up at the woman. 'Yes.'

'And what is the reason? In your own words, if you don't mind.'

The Ties That Bind

It took him a moment to muster up the words. He still didn't like saying it out loud, making it *real*. 'My wife . . . she . . . she died . . . in front of me. She was murdered.'

He shuffled uncomfortably in his seat amidst the sparsely decorated office in Harley Street, central London. The blare of a car horn sliced through the silence. He didn't want to be here, explaining himself to 'professionals' like this. Putting voice to the thoughts running through his head. They weren't for public consumption, nor were they to be analysed.

'I see. And what can you tell me about the incident, Mr Drake?' she asked in a matter-of-fact voice.

Dr Helen Proctor-Reeves sat in a chair opposite him, a ballpoint pen in her hand and a notepad resting on her crossed thigh. Drake placed her in her late fifties, her blonde hair tied back in a styled bun. She wore a rich purple silk shirt that was clearly expensive, along with a black skirt and shoes. Also expensive.

He understood she was one of the more experienced appointed psychologists for the Metropolitan Police, and she had been assigned to him after Detective Chief Superintendent Miller had formally raised concerns for his ongoing wellbeing.

His wellbeing, he thought with a dismissive huff.

It was more likely to be other colleagues who had raised it to his boss, rather than Miller herself wanting to. She knew his way. They'd worked together long enough.

He conceded he had perhaps been a little *belligerent* since the incident, but to push him off on to a shrink didn't sit well with him. He felt he was being managed, with this being the next step on a path to his eventual dismissal. Though, at the moment, he frankly couldn't give a shit if it came to that. Perhaps it would be a blessing in some ways.

Drake further analysed the shrink, and she returned the favour. He could see her assessing him behind that flat look.

Determining what psychological box they could lump him into, what standard course of action she would advise him to take.

'Please, enough with the "Mr Drake". It's John.'

'Okay . . . John. How are you feeling today?'

'How am I *feeling*? I'm feeling that's none of your goddamn business right now. That's how I'm feeling,' he growled, scratching at his stubble in irritation.

'I see,' she said and jotted down a word or two, her face impassive.

The silence continued before she slotted her pen between a sheet of her notepad and clasped her hands together. 'John. Your superior has seen fit to appoint me as your psychologist. You need to be honest and open with me. I am here to help, after all.'

'Help? I don't need any help. I'm not some soft millennial who can't go five minutes without talking about their feelings.'

* * *

Drake froze, one foot off the chair. The thought of Eva's reaction to what he was about to do had slipped back in. It was enough to give him pause, and he teetered on the chair for what seemed to be an eternity.

The sudden realisation served to focus his mind. He zoned in on the mental image of her being told of his death, perhaps even finding him, however unlikely that would have been.

He shook his head. *No, she'll be better off without me.* It would be a relief, a mercy for her and for her future. Wouldn't it? His mind concurred, but the feeling in his gut said otherwise.

Drake lingered, staring blankly at the floor as the music pounded below.

Suddenly, his mobile phone rang, and his mind snapped back

to attention. The obnoxious tone and vibration continuing unabated, contending with the noise of his neighbour.

A picture shone out from the screen. His wife's.

Becca? What? How?

His eyes grew wide from the incredulity at what he was seeing, his heart pounding in his skull. Sweat formed on his brow. It wasn't possible. She was dead.

He squeezed his eyes shut, feeling bewildered and overwhelmed. It had to be his mind playing tricks on him. It had to be. He looked over at the phone again.

It wasn't his dead wife calling after all, but his daughter; it was her image on the screen. Eva had not called in months. It had to be important.

She needed him.

Drake shook his head to regain his senses. His daughter needed him.

She needs me. My daughter needs me.

Hands shaking, he hurriedly unfastened the homemade noose from the loft beam and threw it to the ground in disgust. The chair wobbled at the shift in weight, one leg coming off the floor.

'Shit!' He stood still, sentinel-like. It would be just his luck for him to fall and break his neck. The phone ceased ringing as he clambered down from the chair. Picking it up with shaking hands, he sat on the bed and checked his missed calls. Only there weren't any. Just messages long left unanswered from Miller and Becca's sister, Rachel.

'What? I couldn't have imagined it . . . could I?' he murmured. He knew he wasn't quite in the right frame of mind, but to outright imagine phone calls . . . That wasn't right. That was new. Maybe it was a sign?

A sign that I'm going insane, more like.

3

'Next we have Detective Sergeant Ellie Wilkinson, Specialist Murder Team. Commendation awarded for her selfless display of bravery when assisting an officer in peril.'

Ellie, who'd had a new haircut especially for the occasion (a tapered fade with brown tinting on top) was dressed in full uniform. The clothing felt strangely alien as she rose from her chair at the announcement of her name. As did being met with the rapturous applause of her peers and superiors piled into the conference room for the annual Police Bravery Awards. The truth was, Ellie didn't feel brave. She felt guilty. Guilty, because she hadn't spotted the signs with Andrea Whitman. That it was because of Ellie that Andrea was still out there somewhere, potentially one step away from killing again, having killed her husband and so very nearly her daughter, Cari. And guilty that Cari had been in need of her help and she'd just assumed she was dead. She still couldn't believe the daughter had made it. Ellie maintained the smile on her face, suppressing the frown brought on by her negative thoughts, as she climbed the few stairs to the stage. The stage and massive projection screen spanned the back of the cavernous conference room; her projected face framed by heavy curtains and a few ill-fitting balloons. The flash of cameras from the attending press contingent were doing their best to blind her.

Chief Constable Jarred Burns, who'd sidestepped away from the presentation's lectern, gave her a rigorous handshake when she accepted the framed commendation and thanked her.

'Well done on stopping that bastard, Sergeant. Bloody good job.'

'Thank you, sir.'

He turned to the official photographer, a big corporate smile on his face, and she took his cue to do the same, both gripping the frame and projecting for the camera.

Burns thanked her again, before motioning her off to the side with the other recipients and returning to his place, centre-stage. She felt awkward standing there while the room looked on, as though she was on display, one of the few black faces in a sea of white. An urge to do some sort of inappropriate dance came over her before she brushed the notion aside.

Ellie's smile dropped immediately when she noted a chair still stood empty at one table. She'd hoped her former boss, DCI John Drake, would have been sitting there, perhaps having snuck in late, but he was nowhere to be seen. She'd not seen him or spoken to him properly for nearly six months, and the most recent time had only made her more concerned for him.

Despite the ranking seniority and age difference, they'd formed a friendship and partnership over the course of their sole case together. So, the silence worried her, perhaps more than what came in the aftermath of the Family Man serial killer's detainment. Her boss had always been a little cantankerous in the time she had known him, but the way he had been since his wife's death . . . it had gone beyond that into something 'other'. Besides, she wanted her reluctant mentor and partner back, and where else could she get the experience of working directly with a DCI too?

Since their case together, the work she'd been doing had been mostly uninspiring, administrative stuff to support Drake's peers. Maybe she'd been spoilt, if that was the word, by the Family Man case, but she knew there was more she could be doing. Her impatience was growing by the day.

Ellie nodded to herself. She knew what she had to do: she'd have to raise her concerns about Drake, and that of her own stagnating career, to the boss of the SMT, DCS Laura Miller, in the morning. It couldn't go on.

Surveying the room further, she grinned at the sight of her parents, husband and colleagues, including Miller and DS David Bradfield, who stood clapping, all smiles and proud looks. Barring Miller, of course, who was *almost* nearing a smile. Bradfield, by contrast, was a little overenthusiastic with his whooping and shouting.

After a few more photos as a group, Ellie returned to her seat. Setting down the framed commendation on the table, she turned to her husband. Len, dressed in his smart dark suit, nimbly reached over and caught a teetering wine glass she'd knocked with her elbow.

'Steady!'

'Sorry,' she said, shrugging. She acknowledged her dad on the opposite side of the large circular table. The old man was looking a little worse for wear as he raised his wine glass to her. She turned her attention back to her husband. 'How awkward was that?'

'Awkward? How so? You were great. I'm so proud of you, Ellie,' he said, raising his voice slightly as more incidental award music started playing loudly overhead.

She leant forward. 'Oh well, you know. Just the whole cere-

The Ties That Bind

monial side of it and this bit of paper . . .' She cocked her head at the commendation on the table amidst the wine glasses and table decorations. 'Maybe just ignore me.'

'Come on now, you *earned* that. You've even got the scar to prove it,' he said, taking her hand in his and tracing the scar on her palm with his thumb. The healed skin looked like she had an additional heart line. 'As I've said, I hope you won't be doing that sort of stuff in every case, though. Bella needs her mother to stick around for a few more years yet, and so do I.'

'Yeah, all right. Don't you be going all maudlin on me, now,' she said, taking his hand and giving it a squeeze. 'I expect that was a one off. It's not normal to face that kind of situation day in, day out, is it? Anyway, it's been what . . . nearly twelve months? The other stuff I've been working on since has proved dull by comparison, right? This should be the last time we have to be reminded of it.'

'Okay.' Len glanced around the room before giving her a look. 'Say, do we have to hang around here long, do you think? The night – or late afternoon, in this case – is young.'

She returned his look. 'Why, are you thinking what I'm thinking?'

'If that's "making a run for it", then I'm all ears. I've had enough of watching people I don't know receiving awards.'

'You read my mind!' She laughed. 'Let me just say bye to my parents. I imagine they'll stick around to squeeze a little more free booze out of the establishment.'

He smirked. 'I don't think your mum needs any more, and your dad isn't far behind by the looks of it.'

Ellie had slipped out with her husband, the music dulling to a low thud as she closed the door, when a voice came from behind her.

'Similar thoughts?' the voice said.

Ellie turned to see DCS Miller, leaning up against a wall a little way down the corridor, phone in hand. Her superior wore a full uniform, her mousey grey hair tied back severely as usual, and her shoes looked like they'd been polished to within an inch of their life. But she looked as bored as Ellie felt. She got the impression Miller had never been one for work parties, instead focusing on the work side of work rather than the schmoozing that came with it. But some events were unavoidable, particularly at her rank.

'Sorry, Len. Can you give me a moment? I'll catch up with you outside,' Ellie asked, squeezing his hand.

'Sure, okay. Don't be long.' He nodded at Miller and walked away down the corridor.

Ellie gripped her commendation with both hands and went over to her boss.

'Similar thoughts, indeed,' she sighed.

'I can't say I blame you. I find these sorts of things . . . *tedious*. Besides one of my own detectives being rewarded, of course.'

'Thank you, ma'am.'

Ellie noted her boss looked more worn out than usual, as though there was a great weight upon her shoulders. She wondered if the woman had many friends outside of the few hours she didn't work. Ellie knew she didn't have a husband or any close family to speak of, at least from the gossip in the office.

Miller regarded her in silence, the bags under her eyes appearing to darken while she did so. Ellie felt unnerved, and then just plain uncomfortable as the seconds passed before she broke eye contact and looked around the corridor.

'I understand you've been grumbling,' Miller said, abruptly.

Ellie frowned. 'I'm sorry?'

'Grumbling . . . about your current work. With DI Granger.'

'Ah.'

Shit, she thought. *Who told her that?*

'I'm sorry if it's been reported that way, ma'am.' Ellie gripped her commendation harder. 'I guess I was used to working on a more . . . *equal* footing with Dra—*DCI* Drake. He didn't insist on hierarchy in the way DI Granger does. And he was more "collaborative", shall we say.'

Miller blinked slowly. 'I see. Well, I'm sorry you see it that way. It sounds to me like Drake let you get away with behaviour unbecoming of a DS. I expect you to keep your complaints to yourself in future, rather than bitching to your colleagues outside of SMT.'

She paused, letting her words sink in, before continuing, 'You and I both know you're better than that. DI Granger is well respected, albeit old-fashioned. I expect you to treat him with the respect he is due, even if he isn't part of SMT. You know that we sometimes have to second to CID when there are no appropriate cases for someone of your *limited* experience. They don't work like us, and DCI Collins has everyone he needs for the work we have ongoing.'

'But—'

'No. No "buts". Accept what I'm telling you, Sergeant.'

Ellie felt ashamed at the dressing down, particularly with the stark contrast of the commendation in her hands.

She thought she'd got better at not taking things to heart in the past year, but Miller still had a knack for making her feel small. Perhaps she had got ahead of herself, but it was a big case, if not *the* biggest, that she'd worked on solving. A large part of bringing the Man to justice was owed to her diligence and quick thinking. The Family Man might still be at large if it wasn't for her. She knew now was probably not the best time to argue that point and bit her tongue.

'Sorry, ma'am.' She felt dejected, like a naughty schoolchild. She let her award drop to her side and flexed her free hand.

Miller continued to stare her down before her eyes softened a little. 'However . . .' A glimmer of a smile formed, if only for a second. 'I can understand your behaviour. You're eager to learn and take the progression that comes with that. I get it. I really do.'

Ellie perked up. 'Ma'am?'

'That's why I will do my best to ensure you get a chance to be deployed next – along with a superior, obviously – on anything *interesting* that comes our way. Understood?'

Ellie's heart skipped a beat. Miller still thought favourably of her, despite the feedback she'd received. She must be doing something right, after all.

She beamed. 'Thank you, ma'am. I truly appreciate it. I really do. Thank you.'

'Okay. Now, go and find your husband. I've got places to be.'

'Yes, ma'am . . .' she said, before stopping and turning back. 'Oh, sorry, ma'am, one more thing. I know this may not be my place to say, so excuse me. But have you seen or spoken with DCI Drake recently?'

Miller cocked an eyebrow. 'Yes, why?'

'Is everything okay with him, besides the obvious? I understand he's due back full-time soon, and I haven't seen or heard from him.'

'I'm not going to discuss my DCI's wellbeing with you, DS Wilkinson. You know that's not how it works. It's a private matter.'

'I know, I'm sorry. But I'm worried about him.'

She sometimes took it for granted she was speaking to someone three ranks superior to her, but she couldn't help herself. Bureaucracy was a pet hate of hers. It hindered more than helped more often than not.

'Your concerns are noted. I'll pass it on,' Miller said, ending the conversation.

'Thank you, ma'am.'

God's sake, Ellie, she thought as she hurried towards the exit. *You need to learn when to stop pushing your luck.*

4

Drake looked out over the River Thames from his vantage point on a raised wrought-iron bench. The night was dark and cold, with only a few people in the immediate area. Tourists, he surmised by the phones being used to take pictures of the view. Any locals were scurrying past him, hands stuffed in pockets, shoulders hunched in a bid to stave off the cold.

He heard footsteps come to a halt behind him, followed by a man exhaling loudly.

'John.'

He looked over his shoulder to see his DS David Bradfield staring back at him from a short way below him. 'Dave, thanks for meeting me. I could have come to your neck of the woods in Barndon, you know,' Drake said. He stepped down from the raised bench and shook Dave's hand.

The man seemed older than when Drake had last met up with him. He was sporting a few more wrinkles, and his moustache was turning grey like the remains of his hair. Or perhaps he'd just decided to stop dyeing it. Dave appeared to have been to an event

The Ties That Bind

because he was dressed in a more expensive-looking suit than normal.

'It's no bother, John. Let's get inside, out of the cold, eh?' Dave said, rubbing his hands as they made their way over the road and inside the pub.

On the rare occasions they met outside of work, their choice of pub was always the same. It was an old Edwardian called The Crooked House, known locally as 'The Crook', near to the Putney office that was the primary base of operations for the SMT these days.

The pub was a small and cosy affair; full of comfortable chesterfield sofas, high-back chairs and wooden panelling. It spoke to the heritage of the place. Drake had always enjoyed the large open fireplace, too. It had a proper log-burning fire in the winter months, which illuminated the surroundings of etchings, paintings by long-forgotten artists and the myriad of tatty old books lining the shelved alcoves.

It was welcome in the darker days of early December; the daylight seemingly shortening by the hour each day, and particularly with the snowfall of the last few having brought a freezing chill to the air.

He gave way to a man who came by and threw on another log. 'What can I get you?' Drake asked, raising his voice over the chatter while they waited to catch the barman's attention.

'Just any stout they've got, not too fussy.'

'Gotcha.'

They took their pints to a nearby table, away from most of the noise, and settled in.

'So, is there a reason you weren't at the awards do today?' Dave said, pursing his lips and raising his eyebrows.

Drake shrugged. 'It had completely slipped my mind, if I'm

honest. And even if it hadn't, why would I have gone? That sort of thing isn't me and you know it.'

'Er... maybe because your protégé was receiving a reward for what she did that day?'

Crap, he thought, *even for me lately, that's a pretty shit thing to do.* But what could he say? He couldn't give his actual reasons out for what happened earlier that day. No one wanted to hear his nonsense, nor would he say it out loud. No chance. But his actions earlier in the day *were* part of the reason he'd reached out to Dave. He'd realised, somewhat belatedly, that he needed someone to talk to, to keep him from hitting rock bottom and getting that desperate again. His problem was that the only people he had anything resembling a friendship with were female: his boss, and someone at least twenty years his junior. It made him a little embarrassed unburdening himself to someone of the opposite sex. Which made him feel like a bit of a dinosaur in itself. But truth be told, he felt more of a kinship with Dave these days, with them both having been through the wringer with cases over the years. He'd lost count of his scars, physical or otherwise.

'*Christ*! Now I really do feel bad,' Drake said, dropping his eyes to the table, watching his pint of Guinness as it settled. 'How was it?'

'She did good. I mean, there's not much to it really, going up on stage and what have you, but I was proud of her. We all were. I think she's got quite the career ahead of her – unlike us old bastards.'

'I'll have to speak to her, make my apologies.'

'Yes,' Dave said, supping on his pint before nodding his head. 'You will.'

They sat in silence for a while as only people of a certain age seem to able to do and enjoyed their drinks.

'So what's with you lately?' Dave said, looking him in the eye.

'I know you've had a lot to deal with, but – speaking to you as a mate now, I know you're my ranking officer and all that – John, you've been really out of sorts. It's getting on a few people's wicks.'

He frowned. 'My wife died, Dave. And my daughter has disowned me.'

'Aye, sadly she did, and we're all sorry about that. The times I met Becca . . . she was a fine woman. She didn't deserve what happened. Not her.' He paused, taking a drink. 'I wouldn't wish what had happened to you on my worst enemy. But it *happened*, and you've got your daughter to think about, even if she blames you, as you say she does. She's a kid, it's what kids do. But . . .'

Here it comes.

'John, Becca wouldn't want you behaving the way you've been, would she? This wallowing act, the self-pity you've got going on, it really doesn't become you, mate. You're better than that, and I think you know it. It's been nearly twelve months.'

'Dave—'

'No, let me finish,' Dave said, his eyes set. 'I know you can't really put a time frame on these things, but you're not helping yourself. You need to find a focus again, whether it be work, or something else outside of it, I don't know. But *something* has to pull you out from this mire of shit you've set yourself up in, mate.'

Dave stopped, took another sip of his drink while studying him. 'And, finally . . . I'm here if you need me. Who knows, perhaps we both retire and play golf forever more.'

He finished the last part of his speech with a scrunch of his mouth under his moustache.

'Dave . . .' Drake paused. He wasn't sure what to say. He knew the man was right, knew it in his heart of hearts, but that wasn't enough to switch his mood in an instant. The trauma of the past year was significant. Drake couldn't imagine there being a greater, more challenging time in what life he had left. However, with the events of the day: the pathetic attempt on his own life, the imagined phone call, the subsequent realisation with his daughter . . . Perhaps this could be a turning point? He could try his best to treat it as one.

'Thanks.'

Dave nodded and downed the last of his drink. 'My pleasure, now . . . you getting me another drink or what?' he said, shaking his empty pint glass in Drake's face.

5

Drake woke to the sound of his mobile phone from beneath his duvet. He desperately hoped it was just his imagination playing tricks on him, but the noise persisted. Focusing his bleary eyes, he saw the time on his bedside clock as he made a feeble grab for the phone. He'd overslept.

Swearing under his breath, he answered the phone with a gruff 'DCI Drake', the words catching in his dry throat.

'John, is everything okay?'

It was Miller.

He ran his free hand through his greasy grey hair. Of all the people he didn't want to speak to when he was hungover for the first time in years, his boss was high on the list.

He'd never been one for drinking heavily, even under the significant stress of the last year or during a case. His dad had been diagnosed with cirrhosis of the liver, and it had brought the impact of heavy drinking into sharp focus for Drake.

He sat up and stifled a yawn before responding, his eyes heavy from sleep and his head pounding. 'Er, yeah. Sure is.'

'I need you in my office in an hour.'

'Can't it wait?' he snapped, before wincing at his tone. That was unnecessary. And why did it need to wait? It wasn't like he was busy.

There was silence on the line for an uncomfortable amount of time. 'I'll ask again, is everything okay?'

'Yes . . . yes, it is. I'm sorry, Laura. You just caught me in the middle of something. I didn't mean to snap. I'll be there.'

'Good,' she said, hanging up before he could respond.

Drake groaned and flopped back on the bed. He hadn't expected to be out so late, but Dave had proven to be a good listener to his belly aching, as well as a hardy drinker. It had amazed him the man was still standing after what he'd drunk when they eventually parted ways.

As if on cue, music kicked in from the flat below again, the punch and drone of the bass reverberating through him. It was bad enough he couldn't think straight these days, let alone when subjected to the racket from below as well. The noise made him think of all the times Eva had blasted music in her room, and him running up the stairs to tell her to keep it down. The times when they'd still lived in their home in Barndon.

Since the incident, the house had stood empty for the past twelve months. He'd unwisely stayed on the sofa the very same night his wife had been taken from him after he'd been patched up and SOCO had cleared out. Drake had been unable, and unwilling, to stay anymore after that. He'd left, only going back there once to pick up some essentials and Eva's things that she wanted at her aunts.

He shook the ache of her distance from his mind, sighing as he made his way to the bathroom.

* * *

Tap-tap.

'Yes?' Miller answered, her voice muted by the door to her office.

She looked up as Drake peered in. Miller motioned him over, and he sat down while she finished an email. Her hair was tied back for work as usual and, at first glance, she didn't appear to be in a particularly bad mood. But Drake knew not to assume that the meeting was going to be a positive one. She wasn't easy to read at the best of times, let alone when he wasn't in the best of shape. To battle his dehydration and muzzy head, he'd downed a pint of water before leaving the flat, treating a coffee much the same before entering the building. He was still waiting for some semblance of self to return.

'Right, now you're here . . .' She looked up from her laptop. 'I'll ask again what I asked earlier. John . . . is everything okay?'

He shuffled in his chair, focusing first on the grain of the desk, then on the wall behind her before finally looking her in the eye. He didn't want to admit to anything, but he supposed he'd have to give her the honest answer.

'No, I suppose it's not, and it hasn't been since *that day*. You know that.'

'Well, you look like you've had a bit of a rough night, too. You should look after yourself better, Drake,' she said, staring at him intently with her cold, grey-blue eyes.

He was aware he looked like shit. He'd rushed out without shaving and he knew the bags under his eyes were giving him a hangdog look. He didn't need a further reminder.

'No, I . . . erm, well, yes. I *may* have had a bit to drink with Dave last night. But you know me, Laura, I don't go in for that sort of thing. It's a rare occurrence. Don't put that on me.'

'I wasn't having a go, per se. I'm sure it was good for you to talk to someone outside of your meetings with Dr Proctor-

Reeves, but I've had a few comments from people.' She leant back in her chair, her hands clasped in her lap. 'Colleagues are worried about your welfare, as you know.'

'Look, I'm not going to lie and say things have been plain sailing. I thought I'd been honest with you these past twelve months.' He scratched at his cheek, crossing his leg over his knee. *I'm seeing a damn shrink for you, aren't I? What more can I do?*

Miller leaned forward, her elbows planted on the desk.

'You have, for the most part. But you've been putting on a brave face. I can see what others don't. I've known you for what, twenty-seven years now? Others . . . well, I think they might see your behaviour as a little *erratic*, and just yesterday, not attending those awards for DS Wilkinson.' She raised an eyebrow at him, disapproving.

'That was a pretty shitty move, John, particularly because she is only getting that commendation for putting her life on the line for you and your daughter. She's got a young kid of her own, remember? She could've waited for backup, but she didn't. You might not be here if it wasn't for her. Your daughter could have lost both her parents that day, or you could have lost Eva,' she said pointedly. Miller's mouth had formed a tight line, her frown deepening further.

Drake scratched again at his stubble. 'I know. Dave pointed this all out to me last night. I'm sorry. It completely slipped my mind. I was preoccupied – *am* preoccupied. But that's what these meetings with the doctor you've assigned me will tease out. That's the purpose of all that, isn't it? So I get my shit together. So I can pretend none of it happened, am I right?'

She shook her head, taking on a look of tired exasperation. He wasn't surprised she was exasperated. Even *he* thought he was exasperating.

'John, I'm not saying—'

Her phone rang.

'I've got to answer this. Excuse me.'

'Yes, ma'am,' he said, sardonically.

Again, with the lack of respect, he thought, *fuck's sake, what's the matter with you?*

His behaviour, as Dave pointed out over the sea of drinks the previous evening, had been shit. Dave had been blunt in telling him he shouldn't even have a job right now. He'd found out that Miller had been pulling all sorts of strings to keep him after his extended bereavement and compassionate leave period. At least that's what Dave said he'd heard.

She'd had to lean heavily on his past record: the people he'd put away, his rank. She'd had to defend the no shows, lack of effort, constant wallowing, laziness and general unpleasantness he exuded. It had weighed heavily on those he worked with. That Dave, a detective sergeant, knew what Miller had done for him, showed that even his sergeants and constables were growing fed up with him. The gossiping and complaining were chipping away at his once good standing on the force. He had to get his shit together. Now.

'. . . Okay, thanks, I'll send someone down immediately,' Miller said, finishing her call and pinching her brow.

'All okay?'

'No. A body's been found in Barnet, in an area of woodland called Folly Brook,' she said. The frown from earlier was deeper, nearly obscuring her eyes completely.

'And? What's that got to do with us? You slinging us out there for anything or anyone that's died these days?'

'No, John. But now you mention it, I'll bring it up – our remit is changing and I'm going to be using you as the test bed for it, whether you like it or not,' she said, showing how tenuous his position now was.

'I want you to go out there and assess the scene, like a triage of sorts. This will be the norm now after we get a call in from Response. Response will be getting a direct line to us, depending on certain thresholds and capacity limits that they're informed of. If they flag anything, and you get there and deem it's for us, we'll sort it out. If you suspect it's the usual sort of crap when you get there – domestics, one-offs etc – then we'll sling it off to CID for them to deal with. And CID will extend the same courtesy to us when the ball's in their court. Like before, but just not as often. CID are close to breaking point and my superiors have tasked me with taking on some of the burden in whatever way possible.'

'What, for every murder in London? You've got to be kidding me.'

'No, just those that will have been flagged as suspect in the first place. Think of yourself as second-line support, after Response – and not just London, the whole country if we're in the area. CID can't be spending days on it before passing it on. You know how this works.'

'This sounds shit.'

'It is shit. But that's the way of the world now, and you know it.'

He sighed; it sounded like busy work. Not what they should deal with in SMT. They were a team of twenty at last count. Surely they were stretched enough themselves?

The other DCI in the team, Collins, had his hands full, while the few more experienced inspectors that could take on a Senior Investigating Officer role had little capacity, either. This wasn't even considering the serial murders they dealt with, the stress getting the better of most who joined. The staff turnover was becoming infamous.

'Is this coming from above even your pay grade?'

'Yes, and I've been getting it in the neck for months now with you not pulling your weight.' Drake cringed inwardly at that comment, as Miller went on. 'Things were tight before, but this, well, it's next-level *shit*. They want us to be in ten places at once for two-thirds of the budget.'

He gripped the arms of the chair. 'That's just not possible, let alone sustainable.'

'I know, John, and – as you know full well – things are getting worse out there, not better. For every "Family Man" you take off the streets, there's another psycho waiting in the wings.'

They were both silent for a moment before Miller added, 'John, you need to realise it's not just you that's been affected by what happened last year. DS Wilkinson hasn't been working with us for a while now, as you've not been up to mentoring her. A few weeks on one case with you wasn't sufficient. She needs more experience before being left to her own devices.'

He grunted his agreement, but burned with shame.

'We'll continue our conversation another time. I want you there ASAP.'

Drake stood. 'Okay, give me the address and I'll check it out.'

'Here you go.'

'I'm sure it'll be nothing,' he said, giving Miller a forced smile and closing the door behind him.

6

Drake grimaced as he drove down the single-file country lane towards Folly Brook. There'd been a flurry of snow the previous evening to top off the heavier snowfall two nights back. It meant most of the untouched greenery in the areas he passed remained covered and frozen. Though he didn't expect it to last, what with it being London, it wasn't nearly as cold now. The roads he'd used were already a mass of dirty slush, and the country lane was party to several similarly slushy tyre tracks. He turned his nose up at the thought of walking through it all in his shoes.

He hoped no one would be driving in the other direction. Drake was not in the mood for having to reverse half a mile or riding up an embankment and undoubtedly getting his car stuck in the undergrowth. He wasn't even sure if he'd taken the right turning, the satnav on his phone having hit a GPS black spot earlier on. The built-in car one had died a few months earlier still. He huffed irritably at life's little challenges.

The hope that the scene would be a case for him had been running through his mind on the journey over. Dave had been right. He needed something as a focus, and what was better placed to do that in his world than a murder? It would be challenging after what had happened before, but he needed to turn anything coming his way now into a positive. He needed to look forwards and turn his life around, for his daughter's sake, if nothing else. She was all that mattered.

It turned out his gamble had paid off. Spotting what must have been the initial response vehicle ahead and a Scene of Crime Officers' van, Drake pulled over. He wouldn't have had any other option either way. The road ended soon after with a metal gate.

He sat for a time in his car, taking three deep breaths and attempting to centre himself. The trick from an old marriage counsellor still seemed to do the job and help bring some modicum of focus, but it had been less effective this past year. And it hadn't been intended for someone who'd had one too many drinks the previous evening.

An unusual sight in a field just over from his road took his attention, something he wasn't expecting: a fairground. Drake watched while a huge Ferris wheel was disassembled. A large lorry, partially obscured, was being used by fairground workers to steadily store the rides collapsible frame in sections. He was still focused on the sight when a knock interrupted him.

'DCI Drake?' came a voice, then another knock on the window. A blonde female officer in her mid-to-late twenties was peering at him. She was wearing a black overcoat and a blue blouse, not typical for an attending Police Constable. He'd not been told of any detectives having been at the scene already. That was why he was here, after all. Drake indicated he was getting out of the car, and she backed off as he opened the door to an icy wind.

'Yep, I've come to take a look at the body. And you are?' he said, moving to the front of his car, adjusting his coat as he went.

'DC Gemma Chambers, I was first on scene with another

chap you'll meet. We got a call from a member of the public,' she said quietly. She offered her hand, which he met with a firm shake. He noticed her shoes were caked in slush and mud.

He frowned, pulling his coat in around him as the wind bit again, realising his own shoes would meet a similar fate soon. 'DC? How's a Detective Constable already here?'

She paused. 'Ah, well, I was doing a ride along for the day with the Response team. I'm pretty new, so it's part of my training to get experience of other departments. It's proving to be quite eventful.'

'I see. Quite the morning already then.'

She nodded. 'Er, yes. Something like that.'

'Dog walker?'

'I'm sorry?' The DC said, a look of confusion on her face.

'Was it a dog walker that found the body? You said, "member of the public"?' He arched an eyebrow, more out of bemusement than irritation.

'Oh . . . yes, sorry. Apologies, I'm a little shaken up by it all. Only the third body I've seen, you see.'

'You never quite get used to it, I'm afraid.'

She looked down. 'So I've heard. Guess it depends how often you see them too, eh?'

'Yes.' He nodded. 'So, you were saying? Dog walker?'

'Yes, a young couple called it in. Their usual route every few days, apparently. Found the body – a male – in the woods a hundred metres or so from here.' She pointed toward the larger tree line further up in the field. 'Their collie was still barking when we got here fifteen minutes later. Traffic was shit.'

He surveyed his surroundings through narrowed eyes, not seeing any other viable entrance from where he was standing. 'No one else came by that you saw? They didn't see anyone on their walk?'

'No, not that I'm aware of.' She shrugged. 'You can ask them yourself, though. I took their details before they left. They were in shock and wanted to go home.'

Drake pursed his lips; his preference would have been to talk to them while they were still here if he'd had the chance. He chose not to mention it, or recommend she should have kept them around for longer. He needed to be on his best behaviour and it may not be his case, after all. Nothing to show it was for him just yet.

'How long has it been since you received the call?'

She looked at her watch. 'An hour . . . maybe an hour and fifteen, max. SOCO turned up soon after I validated it and called it in. My partner for the day is at the scene with her now.'

'Her?' he asked, crossing his arms to keep warm. His wool overcoat was failing miserably.

'Yeah, just some SOCO whose name I can't remember.' The DC scratched her head. 'She got here about ten minutes ago with her colleague.'

'Okay, let's get on over there.'

'Sure. Follow me.'

* * *

Drake followed Chambers, paying attention to his surroundings as they went. The snow flurry from the previous evening had been heavy, but he hoped it would prove not to have been heavy enough to hide any tracks that could be in or around the surrounding area. The way the weather was in England, if they weren't quick, they could lose any that may have been made. Even lose any sign of where the perpetrator and victim came from. He made a mental note to be careful on the periphery of the scene and asked the young DC to do the same. Her head bobbed in agreement while they walked.

Despite working in London, and living relatively nearby for most of his adult life, it always surprised him when he went to areas like Folly Brook. The area made him feel like he was out in the countryside in the Cotswolds, or near his old home in Barndon, encased by farmer's fields and woods. Not Greater London, with its skyscrapers and office buildings, a never-ending sea of grey impersonal buildings crowding out the buildings of old.

The clouds hung heavy while they clung to the narrow path at the edge of the field, orbiting a thicket as they went. His feet felt damp, the sodden melange somehow oozing into his shoes, and Drake grimaced in disgust.

It wasn't long before he spotted figures in the distance, near the edge of what had to be the wood proper, the woodland appearing denser and more compact than what they'd just passed. A male SOCO was messing around with setting up a white tent in the distance. The PC that Chambers must have come over with and a shorter SOCO remained at the edge of the woods in her white overalls. There were no obvious signs of a crime scene yet. He assumed the examiners had moved off to the fringes to prepare properly after their preliminary photos.

Chambers gave her colleague a wave. The man was of medium build, with a thick brow and small eyes. He was wearing the usual high-vis police officer's jacket, but had substituted his standard-issue hat for a beanie to stave off the wind. Drake jealously eyed up the thick gloves the man was wearing while stuffing his hands back into his pockets.

'PC Adam Mewton, this is DCI Drake.'

'Sir,' Mewton acknowledged. 'Nasty business. We've tried our best not to disturb anything, but had to do some checks, just to be on the safe side. And the SOCO has done some "preliminary work". Her words, not mine.'

'Not obvious he was dead to you?'

'You'll see, sir.'

'Okay,' he said, before issuing some instructions: 'Right, Mewton, stay here. Chambers, I want you to scout out the surrounding area while I take a look. Obviously, it goes without saying that you're not to let anyone else near. Mewton, if you get a chance, try to cordon off the perimeter as best you can. Can you do that for me?'

'Yes, sir.'

'Oh and one last question,' Drake said, turning back towards Mewton. 'From which direction did you approach the body, so I can do the same?'

'We all came from the left side as you face it. The couple said they did the same. I made sure I didn't step on anything. I just touched his neck to check for a pulse. That's all, I swear,' PC Mewton said, his eyes wide.

'Okay.' Drake gave the man a thin smile, and made his way towards the SOCO with the tent. He requisitioned a pair of shoe coverings before requesting a few minutes alone so he could understand what he was dealing with. The SOCO, looking a little green around the gills, appeared all too happy to oblige.

It can't be that bad, he thought. *Surely.*

He looked up once more at the sky before entering the woods. He still felt off. Maybe it was just a combination of his dulled senses from the previous evening and a sense of the unknown at what lay before him. He looked at his shoes as he walked, hoping the shoe coverings wouldn't send him onto his arse from the lack of grip. On a more positive note, they might stave off further damp seeping into his shoes, at least.

Rounding a large oak at the side of the woods, he soon

spotted a set of what appeared to be drag marks. He approached carefully before crouching to study them. Their path was defined by the remains of a thin layer of slush which had infiltrated the edge of the woods, smearing along the frozen ground.

Drake tracked the fading marks slowly with his eyes, leading him to their eventual end point.

A half-naked body bound to a tree.

His eyes narrowed at the sight.

Hmmm.

He stood, his knees feeling stiff as he continued his careful walk. He cocked his head to one side as he took a wide-angled approach from the left, being careful where he stepped while he took in the scene before him.

The body of a large, overweight man was sitting with his back against the tree, his legs splayed in front of him and a frayed rope trailing from the left ankle. The victim's arms were flopped by his sides; one hand balled into a loose fist, the other open with the palm facing outwards and another binding hung from the wrist. This one appeared to have been cut cleanly.

He was bare-chested, and had been tightly bound to the tree by several ropes. Or possibly it was one long length, wrapped multiple times round both the tree and the victim. Drake wasn't sure yet. The tightness of the binding had made the man's large belly bulge protrude further beneath the rope, making Drake think of a strung beef brisket. The head was slumped forwards and completely wrapped in black duct tape, apart from some areas where tufts of brown hair poked through.

There was hardly any snow around the body. It was surrounded by sporadic patches of grass and vegetation, frosted and thin. The exposed ground appeared smeared and frozen with a few darkened areas of footfall. There didn't seem to be any discernible prints that could be lifted. The dog had likely scampered all about the place and messed up whatever may have been left in the mud. Drake would follow his path out when he was done, either way, just to be safe. He hoped to God the SOCO team was better than the last one he'd dealt with on the Family Man case.

Drake knelt beside the body. A faint odour of death hung over the scene, but nowhere near as bad as normal. He suspected the contents of the man's bowels had emptied and frozen in his trousers, which had gone some way to dampening the smell.

The man's skin was a patchwork of blue, black and purple from the severe beating he'd appeared to have endured to his chest. Drake assumed his head, once the tape had been removed at the lab, would be much the same.

The body was also streaked with dried blood that had run down from the head and gagged mouth. Rivulets trailed from the victim's neck to the waistband of his trousers, and ended in a smattering on the ground between his legs.

Drake pulled some gloves from a coat pocket and put them on, the cold latex cooling down the little warmth he'd built up in his hands.

He put two fingers beneath the man's chin and lifted it delicately so it faced forwards.

What the . . . ? Is that glass in his mouth?

Sharp fragments had pierced the duct tape around the man's mouth. The cool daylight reflected off the specks that weren't caked with blood. It seemed likely whoever had done this had forcibly fed the man glass before wrapping his head in duct tape and beating him to death. But was that before or after they had tied him to the tree?

Drake checked the man's chest for footprints, which would show he'd likely been stamped on from a prone position before being tied up. There were scuffs, but nothing clear cut. They may have kicked him while tied up. He'd also have to figure out whether it was actually at this site that the main attack took place.

Something else for the pathologist to look at after unwrapping their main present, he thought.

He lowered the man's head and inspected the bindings, which looked to be a blue nylon rope, nothing out of the ordinary. The killer had used several different lengths, judging by the various knots scattered about, at least four by his count. Perhaps this showed a lack of experience or confidence in their ability to keep the victim from breaking free? He made a mental note to get the knots examined. If there were any unusual variants, it could show someone with a naval or military background or similar.

Drake was getting the feeling this might be up SMT's street. This kind of death was not typical of day-to-day London killings. They had subjected the man to torture, and while that wasn't completely unheard of in some areas of London, it still wasn't the norm. His gut was telling him something was off about this, and the sooner the forensic pathologist got to work, the better. He wouldn't be passing this off to CID just yet.

Even so, he needed more.

'DCI Drake!'

His head snapped toward the voice. It sounded urgent. He spotted the blonde DC waving at him from the start of the drag marks.

'I've found another one.'

7

'You what?' Drake shouted back, squinting at the light that had broken through the clouds. He couldn't have heard her right, could he?

'I've found another one. Another body!' she said. Chambers sounded as though she was on the verge of tears.

Interesting.

'Wait right there!'

Drake shuffled back along the path he had taken and shoved his gloved hands in his pockets as he approached the flustered DC.

'Tell me what you saw,' he said, feeling strangely irritated by the woman. It could be the remnants of the hangover, the effort of proper work coming to the fore, or both. He wasn't sure.

'I was checking the surrounding area like you wanted, and spotted similar drag marks in the snow to that guy over there. It was a little harder to spot, as the snow's already melting – don't get how, I'm bloody freezing.' She pointed over toward more woods, before stopping and trying to catch her breath, her hands gripping her thighs.

'Easy . . . just slow down. Take a moment,' Drake put a hand on her shoulder in a weak display of support.

'It's okay. I'm sorry, I ran back here . . . and by the way, now that's *four* bodies since I've been on the detective career path,' she said, forcing a weak laugh. She took a moment to compose herself. 'So, anyway, I followed the tracks. They started further out in the open ground than this one, and it wasn't long before I found a woman in a similar state.'

'How far?'

'Not far, about fifty meters or so in that direction, at a guess.'

All he could see beyond their position were more trees, open fields and some marks where the detective had run and walked. She must have walked on for a time to get there before spotting anything.

A male SOCO made his presence known just before they headed off. He was wearing a blue mask now. 'Are you finished?' the man asked, intense grey eyes peering back at them.

Drake nodded, irritated at being interrupted. 'Yes, for now, but you're going to need to get more of your colleagues down here. There's another crime scene. We're going to go over there now and check it out.'

His eyes widened with surprise. 'Shit, really? You're kidding me?'

'Nope.' Drake turned his back on the man and motioned for Chambers to proceed ahead to the crime scene.

She led him on a short walk to the start of the next set of tracks, partially obscured by the recent snowfall. The DC was right; it *was* much like before. Though these scuff marks were on the larger side, and more intermittent, as though the killer had stopped often whilst dragging the body. Or perhaps the victim put up more of a fight?

They tracked through the steps that Chambers had made previously and soon came to another natural opening in the woods. Another victim was tied up against the first large, mature tree within. The walkers evidently had spoken the truth and hadn't come from this direction. It was pristine, barring his colleagues' tracks.

He took a deep breath through his nose and pursed his lips. 'Stay here for a minute while I take a closer look.'

'You don't need to ask me twice,' she said, crossing her arms and rubbing her sides.

'You're going to have to develop a stronger stomach if you're going to stick at being a detective, you know?' he remarked, glancing back at her.

The DC's eyes dropped. 'Yeah, I suppose you're right.'

He made his way over to the body, noting that the MO was like that of the male victim. The woman was also semi-naked, and in a similar state to the male victim. In contrast to the man, she was olive-skinned to his paler complexion, but their bodies bore the same battered and bruised patterns. A binding at the wrist that had been cut or broken, blue rope under her breasts and around the tree, ensuring she couldn't escape her fate.

But there was one stark difference that Drake could see. Her head was not bound in black duct tape like the first victim. If there were other potential differences, her long brown hair obscured them from his position.

Drake moved in, frowning as he went; he still couldn't make out what had happened to her. Absently, he reached into his coat pocket before realising he still had his gloves on and lifted her head by the chin, exposing her face.

The victim's mouth had been sewn shut.

Drake winced at the sight and examined her face further. He

noted the dried blood that caked her swollen and shredded lips. The thick black threads, keeping her mouth from opening more than a quarter of an inch. Razor sharp glass fragments protruding, in places, piercing the skin; in others, stretching it grotesquely. The woman's eyes were open, the milky death stare peering out through the strands of her matted, bloody hair. Her face had been left battered and bruised, her eyelids swollen. It corroborated his thoughts that they had beaten the first victim about the head, too.

What the hell is going on here? He thought. *Why the variation with the mouth? What does this signify?*

A thousand and one thoughts ran through his mind as he crouched, his breath fogging the cool winter air. If he wasn't completely convinced before that this was work for SMT, then this fresh addition was certainly leading him down that path. What would cause someone to inflict such a deliberate and cruel death? And to two people in quick succession?

'John?' a voice said, so close it felt like their breath was in his ear.

Becca?

The familiar voice shook him from his thoughts. He flinched; no-one was there.

'DCI Drake?'

He blinked a few times and looked back to see Chambers stepping delicately towards him. It was her all along.

What is the matter with you, man?

'Yes?' he said, feeling bewildered.

'Another van's pulled up. Looks like it's SOCO for our lady here.'

'Okay, thanks. Go and explain the situation to them, would you? This scene's more preserved than the others. Inform them of that, please. I need to make a phone call.' He got back to his feet.

'Got it.' She proceeded back the way they came, the crunching of snow and slush under her feet growing fainter. Drake made his way back to the field slowly behind her.

The sky had started to clear, blue sky peeking through the dispersing clouds. It was turning into a bright winter's day. A stark contrast to what he'd just witnessed, though it wouldn't be long before the darkness won and closed in once more.

Drake checked his phone, surprised to find it had a signal, before dialling Miller's number.

'John? How is it?'

'Bad, Laura. There are two victims here, not just the one as originally reported,' he said, looking back towards the location of the female victim.

He heard Miller sigh. 'Not clear cut for CID?'

'No, 'fraid not. There's brutality here I've not seen in a while. It appears to have been well planned; organised, *calculated*, but personal somehow. Like it wasn't just some thugs, you know?'

'Damn it!' Drake heard her thump something. 'That's all we need.'

'I'm sorry, Boss.'

'No, it's not your fault. Shit, it's not my fault either. We should just be getting on with finding who did this. Budgets and staff utilisation shouldn't even be entering the equation.'

His mouth formed a thin line. 'You're right.'

'Okay, so, tell me what you need,' she asked, her voice flat once again.

'Initially . . . I need a DS, depending on what else comes of this; from the pathology, who the victims are, etc. Then I may need more. For now, I think we both know of a sergeant that's knocking about the place, eh?'

The line was silent for a moment, and Drake heard what he thought was a small sigh of resignation.

'Okay, get DS Wilkinson down there now.'
'You got it.'
He smiled, ending the call.

8

Ellie leant back in the banged up old office chair and let out a yawn, stretching her arms out in an exaggerated display of boredom. She blinked slowly, trying to maintain focus on the task at hand. Failing miserably, she looked around the bustling office, taking it all in. The place was a potent mix of phone calls and chatter between colleagues. Some teams were stashed away in conference rooms, paper plastered to the glass and whiteboards, but most had to make do in the open plan pen she was in.

Her current task of filing reports was something she'd never enjoyed. Who did? But particularly when it involved reporting back on the lack of success of door-to-door canvasing, the weak leads not panning out. Busy work was never her forte.

Ellie thought back to her conversation with Miller the previous day. She was worried that one day she'd push a superior too far. That it would be the end of her stint in the SMT, and she'd be back in uniform with Response before the end of the week. She didn't want that, no chance.

'Bored, DS Wilkinson?' DI Granger observed, standing over her desk and sounding as irritable as ever. The man was bald, with a hooked nose and gaunt face. There was a strange, cruel air about him and he gave the impression he thought he was better than everyone.

'No, sir. Sorry, I was just taking a moment.'

'I see.' He sat on the edge of her desk and cupped his hands in his lap. 'I can always have you helping on the phone enquiries, if this is too much for you.'

Ellie didn't like the continual undercurrent of irritation he had with her, like she'd wronged him somehow, and this was before she'd grumbled. Shit, it was *because* of how he treated her she'd started saying what she had. Some people just weren't meant to work together.

'That won't be necessary, sir.' She forced a smile. 'I'll have these done today, and then maybe we could look at getting me more involved in the case?'

He sneered. 'Don't get ahead of yourself. This isn't your beloved SMT. We don't just let you do what you want here.'

'I wasn't saying that, sir. I was only hoping I could have a more... *active* role, I guess.'

He peered at her with his dead eyes. 'There's no I in Team, Wilkinson. You'd do well to remember that.'

That phrase... really? What a dickhead, she thought, mentally rolling her eyes.

'Sir, I... I mean, "we"—'

DI Granger watched her squirm as her mobile started ringing on her desk.

DCI Drake displayed on the screen.

'There you go. You better answer that. Get some practice in for tomorrow.'

Ellie ignored him and answered.

'Drake? How are—'

'Ellie, save the pleasantries. I need you down here ASAP. Can you do that for me?'

Ellie looked up at Granger, who was still looming over her as she spoke. She felt his breath and shuddered.

'Erm . . . I'm working on a case with DI Granger's team at the moment. I'm not sure I can drop what I'm doing, just like that,' she said, the disappointment plain in her voice.

'Ellie, I don't have time for you to argue the finer details with me. I'm this DI Granger's superior, what I say goes. Got it?'

'Okay, just one second. I'll ask.'

She turned to Granger, trying her best to be professional, but secretly hoping he'd lose it. She knew Drake would get the upper hand. He could be quite persuasive, irrespective of rank.

'Sir, DCI Drake has requested me to join him on something he's working on as soon as possible. Do you approve?'

'What? No, I don't approve. Give me the phone, Sergeant. Now,' he demanded, thrusting his hand out angrily for the phone. The surrounding desks grew progressively quieter as they listened in to the impending confrontation.

'Okay.' She handed him the phone and strained her ears to tune in to what her old boss would say to Granger's refusal.

'DCI Drake, what's this about wanting to take DS Wilkinson? She's not available.'

In a matter of seconds, Ellie saw the colour drain from the man's face in response to the indecipherable shouting on the other end of the line.

'I . . . see. I see,' the man stuttered. 'Right. Okay.'

DI Granger passed the phone back and swallowed heavily as she took it.

'You're free to go. He wants to speak to you,' he said, pursing his lips.

'Thank you, sir.' Her heart leaping in her chest. She could

barely contain her excitement as DI Granger headed back to his corner desk.

'Drake, so, what's going on?'

'I need you to get across to Folly Brook. It's near Barnet. Get here as soon as you can. We may have a case kicking off and I understand you're bored.'

She beamed. 'You don't know the half of it. I'm on my way. Send me the address.'

'Will do,' he said, hanging up.

She stuffed her phone in her jacket pocket and gathered the rest of her things. She spotted DI Granger glaring at her from his desk, met his gaze, and smiled.

9

"Ellie, where are you?"

Ellie read the text message just as brake lights came on in her periphery, causing her to simultaneously slam on the brakes and fling her phone into the passenger seat.

Stuck in this damned traffic, she huffed, *that's what.*

She'd always detested London traffic. And now she had more reason, having had at least two near-death encounters with cars and cyclists on the way over. In normal circumstances, she'd be suppressing a fit of rage by now. But she felt strangely energised by the impending crime scene, so she took all the surrounding road rage in her stride as best she could. She was intrigued to see what lay ahead of her, partly because of Drake's customary lack of elaboration.

Ah crap, Len and Bella.

It was her day for collecting her daughter from school. She'd need to call on Len yet again, and she could already imagine his unbridled joy at that bit of news. She made another grab for her phone just in time for the traffic to start moving, leading her to chucking the device on the passenger seat for the second time in as many minutes. This pattern continued until finally she pulled up behind the final of three SOCO vans. Hers was the last in a long line of vehicles, the hubbub of a working crime scene in action.

Finally parked, she sent the text to her husband. A brisk wintry blast beset her as she opened the door before slamming it closed once again, remembering she had a scarf on the backseat. She grabbed it and wrapped it around herself tightly, the yellow sparking off her sombre black overcoat.

Braving the door once more, Ellie surveyed her surroundings and took a deep breath to steel herself. It had just gone half two in the afternoon. There'd only be an hour or so more of daylight, so she'd have to get up to speed with what was going on quickly. She wondered about the severity of what she was about to witness, about what would require this many officers on site. It had to be something big, it just had to be.

Ellie showed her credentials to the PCs at the taped-off entrance, a roughly hewn wooden gate that had seen better days, and made her way up to the scene. She spotted Drake talking to a few SOCOs in the distance.

Trudging through the remains of the well-trodden snow, she marvelled at the number of trees ahead shorn of their leaves and standing bare amidst the evergreen foliage. She loved this time of year.

'Drake!'

Ellie started waving – perhaps a little too enthusiastically, in hindsight – as she approached.

'Nice of you to show up, Ellie,' he said. The man sounded tired as he raised an eyebrow at her arrival.

Close up, Drake did look worn out, more so than when she'd last seen him, and she hadn't thought that was possible. The man's blue eyes were sunken, bags upon bags slung beneath them.

And he looked gaunt, his hawkish features more exaggerated, the pallid skin taut across his cheekbones. He had always had the tired detective look down to a tee before, but he used to have a little more weight on him. Not anymore.

'All right, traffic was *bad*. You realise you made me drive through central London in the middle of the afternoon, right? What do you want me to say?' she said, pulling a face, trying to tease something from him.

He peered at her. 'Okay, well, thank you for coming as soon as you could.'

He took her to one side as a SOCO came past.

'So, what've we got?' she said, keeping her voice down.

'Two bodies. A male and female, similar treatment on the whole, but two different methods with the heads.' He looked skyward, a frown set on his face.

'The heads? What? Are they decapitated or something?'

'Nothing like that. The male victim has his head wrapped in black duct tape, whereas the female had her mouth sewn shut. The killer fed both what appears to be shards of glass prior to that happening, then beat them to death. That's my initial take.' He paused. 'I'm expecting that the pathologist will find a lot of internal haemorrhaging to be the primary cause of death. Perhaps asphyxiation because of the blood. By the looks of them, they might have been here for at least one day. It's a little harder to tell with this sodding weather.'

She winced at the description; she could see why he'd waited to tell her until he was with her. 'Jesus Christ, so you're thinking this sounds like an SMT sort of case, eh?'

'I think so, yes.'

'And what better duo to face it than the mighty Drake and Ellie? I like your thinking.' She beamed excitedly.

'Ellie . . .'

'Sorry Chief, getting carried away again. Just excited, you know?' She took stock of her surroundings. 'So . . . Where are the bodies, then? I presume they're behind you, in those woods.'

She tiptoed as she peered over his shoulder. 'Are they together, or—?'

'No, the woman's body is nearby, east of here.' He pointed toward a returning SOCO. 'They've pitched all the tents they need to preserve the crime scene and keep it from public view. Not that they could get past the cordon, anyway – I'll let you take a look, and you can report back what you think, okay?'

She nodded. 'Sounds like a plan.'

* * *

Ellie finished up her inspection of the second victim as the sun was setting. She'd made sure to move out of the way whenever a SOCO needed a particular shot of the body and surrounding area. Floor panels and lighting had been set up within the tent, leading to the victim's stitched features looking particularly brutal in the artificial light. The panels were damp from people traipsing in from the thawing and overworked snow. And she was desperate not to slip and fall onto any potential evidence, or, God forbid, victim. It was just the sort of thing that would happen to her on her second SMT case proper and with that in mind, she had taken no chances.

She physically shuddered at the thought of both victim's last moments; they were nasty ways to go. The thought of the mess the glass must have made internally, the feeling of glass slicing through and puncturing flesh. She wondered what would drive someone to inflict injuries in such a way, while the difference in methods left her puzzled. It felt as if they had subjected the woman to a more calculated assault, but by contrast, the male was possibly rushed. If so, why?

Ellie was still thinking it through as she made her way back. Nearing the drag marks of the first victim, she looked out over the southern end of the field, at the buildings far off on the horizon where normal life continued unabated.

Still lost in thought, she slipped on a patch of black ice, hidden amidst the mud. 'Ah, fuck!'

The expletive echoed around the field as she hit the ground. She scrambled to her feet in the vain hope that no one had noticed. Scowling, she knew the echo had probably put paid to that hope. She grimaced at the throb coming from her right shoulder.

Ellie brushed at her coat, tutting at the mess she'd made of it, her hand skimming off a thin layer of dirty wet snow. She was still studying the mess she'd made of the ground when something caught her eye to the south. Something some distance from the final drag mark at the edge of the trees; it was out in the open, but more obfuscated by the retreating snow slush beyond the cover of the trees.

Squinting, she saw what appeared to be a large imprint in the patchy thaw and several indentations preceding it. She carefully trailed a path around it, making sure she wasn't stepping in anything before pulling out her phone and turning on its torch function in the hope it might highlight some more detail in the dusk.

Sure enough, it looked like something had occurred toward the other end of the field, away from the woods. Perhaps where the victim was beaten? Or maybe he fell as he was being led to the woods?

'Ellie? What're you doing? Spotted something?' Drake called as he approached from the direction of the first victim.

She turned her attention back to the south. 'I don't know. I think it might be where he or she was prior to being taken into the woods? What do you think?'

Drake pulled out a small, more powerful torch from inside his overcoat and shone it on the area.

'Mmm, you may be right. Looks like this was covered more by the snowfall than the rest,' he said, looking deep in thought as he walked closer. He shone the torch around the edges of the feint prints. The narrowing impression of a toe of a shoe pointed toward the woods behind them, where the two victims had met their fate.

His eyes lit up. 'Ellie, there's a trail leading away from here.' He pointed in the direction of a small wooded area. 'It's coming from that direction. From that . . . whatever it's called.'

'Thicket?' Ellie offered.

'Yes, that.'

'Not much of an outdoorsy person, eh, Boss?'

Drake scowled and ignored her comment, before starting towards the direction of the thicket. He was moving gingerly, being careful not to step in anything as he went, his shoes coverings clearly agitating him.

She followed suit.

Drake stopped. 'You see that? There's blood in that large patch.'

He shone the torch on the patch; the light cutting through the murk. The crimson had leeched into the surrounding snow, but was definitely still there.

She nodded. 'Shit. Let's see what else there is ahead.'

Her heart was thumping by the time they reached the thicket. The increasingly slushy steps gave way to frozen ground and a lesser set of scuff marks.

Drake stopped and pondered for a moment. 'It looks like it continues back through here, Ellie. Here's hoping it will lead us to something more than a few specks of blood, eh?'

He looked up at the sky. 'Keep an eye out. It's getting dark, and we don't want to miss anything. I'm not having us waste time coming back again. Time is critical with cases like these, if it's what I suspect.'

'Okay, Chief, no worries.'

She flashed her weaker phone light at a set of scuffed prints by a tree.

'And bring a better torch in future, please? Outdoors scenes need a little more than a poxy phone light,' he said, expressionless.

He's not in the best of moods, she thought. *Even for him.*

Ellie shrugged. 'Sorry, Drake. Was in a rush, I didn't give it a thought.'

He grunted and delved further into the thicket.

She couldn't see anything obvious from her vantage point. Nothing dropped on the ground, nothing out of the ordinary shouting out at her. Just trees, and the victim's shoe marks – what she assumed to be the victim's shoes, anyway.

'You see this?' Drake gestured to her to look at a tree trunk.

She stepped over to where he was. 'See what? I can't see anything.'

'It looks like someone stopped here and slid down the tree. See how the moss is all smooth there? And the marks on the ground? Like something, or someone, slid down it?'

She stuck out her bottom lip and nodded in agreement. 'Now you've pointed it out, yeah . . . you're right.'

Drake carried on hypothesising about the victim's last movements. 'I'm guessing that he might have stopped here for a moment, or hid here? Perhaps he was being chased, and he was hiding? But then I can't see other footprints near his, or out toward the woods where he died. There's nothing for a second person, victim or otherwise. Curious.'

He continued surveying the surroundings, not looking happy with what he was seeing.

'Beats me at the moment, Chief. We may never know. This damn snow is melting, and with it, any traces of footfall at this rate.' Ellie pulled her coat in around her as she navigated Drake's position by the tree, avoiding the few footprints that may survive the impending night. An icy gust blew through, making the trees creak as it passed. The darkness was closing in, and with it, the temperature was dropping.

'Drake, I'm going to continue on for a bit, while there's still something to go on.'

'Okay, I'll follow in a moment,' he said, turning his flashlight back on the area surrounding the scuffed tree.

Ellie made her way through the last remnants of the thicket, the sun casting a final glare on the horizon. Its orange hue cut through the stripped branches as it was slowly engulfed by the night. She observed a few further marks while she continued on, but nothing that jumped out at her, or looked different from what came before. However, there was still a trail, and that buoyed her enough; it would have to lead to something. It had to. The male was too big, too unfit-looking to have come far, particularly if he was being chased. Whatever he had been running from, it had to have originated from close by.

The faint marks trailed out once more into the more defined, hard-packed snow of the field. The weather hadn't tampered with her evidence so much here.

'Good. Now where did you come from, big guy?' she murmured.

Ellie continued following the trail, the single set of tracks flattening out at irregular intervals. With her newly acquired bush skills, she figured the man must have stopped to catch his breath before soldiering on, likely terrified.

Following the trail further, she finally spotted the source of the man's fear.

10

Drake frowned as he considered his surroundings. Why not stop here and hide? What drove you on? Did you see something . . . or someone?

He stood, deep in thought, for a minute or two. Despite the grim subject matter, he was enjoying getting his mind back in gear, focusing on something other than his own problems for a change. The events of the flat the previous day seemed a distant memory for now. He hoped it stayed that way. But he knew it wouldn't. He'd have to face those demons again . . . soon.

'Drake!' Ellie's voice echoed.

He looked up in the direction she'd gone, glimpsing a yellow scarf through the trees and fleeting light. 'What is it?'

'Can you come here? I think I might have found the source . . . What this guy was running from.'

The source?

'On my way. Stay there.'

Drake made his way through and saw Ellie in the distance, several yards deeper into the frozen farmer's field. He couldn't see what she was speaking of; there was only darkness now the sun had fled.

He continued gingerly stepping towards her, using her footprints as paving stones.

'Do you see?' Not waiting for him to answer, she pointed. 'Over there. Maybe turn off your light for a moment to help your eyes adjust.'

Drake turned it off and squinted in the direction she was pointing, his eyes slowly acclimatising to the darkness. There was the silhouette of a large building at the end of the farmer's field, barely visible beyond a set of trees whose leaves were unaffected by the bite of winter.

He grunted his approval. 'Good spot, Ellie. We'll make a scout of you yet.'

'So, what should we do?' she asked, ignoring his comment.

'Well, "we" won't be doing anything.' He gestured toward the crime scenes, lit up like a Christmas tree. 'You'll be going back and letting SOCO know that I'm going off to check out a lead in this direction. Then you can hurry back and be my backup.'

She frowned. 'Isn't that against protocol, leaving you? It's not something I would have done back in my Response days, Chief.'

'But this isn't your old role, Ellie. And I'm telling you, it'll be okay,' he said, his breath freezing in the dropping temperatures. 'I suspect whoever did this is long gone by now, and we'll need SOCO over here sooner rather than later. All right?'

'Boss—'

'Just do it, Sergeant,' he snapped.

'Okay, sir,' she replied, pursing her lips.

Drake stood and watched her leave, the sound of her foot coverings swishing in the sodden grass slush growing ever fainter. Before long, she had disappeared into the thicket.

He let out a sigh and followed the trail towards the silhouette.

He knew he'd been a little selfish. While it *was* a good idea to let the crime scene guys know where their lead investigator had gone, he could have just phoned it in. But he wanted to have the place to himself for a bit, to give him some time to think, even if it was only for a few minutes. He felt like a rusty old engine, being tinkered with and brought slowly back to life.

Slowly rounding the trees which had obscured most of the building, Drake could see now what it was as it came into full view.

The dark outline was that of a pub. The remains of one, in this case; the shadow of an empty free-standing signpost loomed high in the overgrown gravel car park. Drake could make out a main road over the wall next to the padlocked alleyway door that led to the front. Dry stone walls and hedges of the farmer's field protruded from the crumbling remains of the pub's rear boundary. It was like the breached wall of a fort brought down by a hard-fought medieval siege, bricks strewn about in the undergrowth.

Drake switched his torch back on and scoured the area before progressing any further. The beam cut through the darkness, highlighting the years of decay and neglect that had befallen the building. The roof had seen better days; there was a hole in the slates by a chimney that appeared to be teetering on the verge of collapse, the flashing peeling away and hanging loose. The brickwork was also failing. Damp and weeds had taken hold, while most of the windows were long since smashed or boarded up. The peeling paint of the sign to the side of the pub read *The Dog and Thistle*, minus a few long-lost letters.

Putting his attention – and his light – back on the trail, he crunched along the slushy gravel and followed the marks, soon discovering the source; an open void. The hole was set a foot away from the main building and opened directly into the ground, framed by two wood hatch doors. The beer cellar.

'Jackpot,' he murmured.

Drake made his way cautiously over to the gaping hole. His nerves were not what they used to be since the events of the last year, and he didn't want to startle any intruders, despite his earlier comments to Ellie. You never knew what might happen.

A car sped by, a beam of light passing over the building in tandem with the thrum of an engine. Then it was silent once more.

Drake called down. 'Hello?'

'Hello?' he repeated. 'Police. If there's anyone down there, now would be the time to come up. No funny business, or I'll beat the living shit out of you.'

Silence.

'Really, Boss? Is that how you approach potential suspects these days?'

The voice made Drake jump. He turned to see Ellie behind him at the edge of the carpark, her eyes shining in the light of the flashlight and a big grin on her face.

'*Christ*! Ellie, don't do that. Seriously. I'm getting old. Do you want a dead DCI on your record?'

'Sorry, Chief, couldn't resist.' She chuckled, turning her attention to the cellar hatch. 'What're we looking at here?'

'A potential place where the victims were held is my thinking so far. The tracks lead straight to it. I reckon they were holed up down there. Who knows for how long?'

'Exciting.'

He saw she was buzzing. In truth, he was too. But he needed to be level-headed.

'Yes, but imagine being down there against your will with no idea what's going to happen to you or if you'll ever see daylight again.'

'Okay, okay, puts it into perspective, I suppose.'

'Mmm.'

Drake realised he had to get used to Ellie's ways again. He'd not been exposed to her sense of humour for a while. He knew it was more of a shield, a way of her coping with stressful situations, or the anticipation of what lay ahead. It was how many people coped with their line of work.

'So, would you like me to do the honours, Chief?'

'No, I'll take point. You follow. Be ready to grab anyone who might slip past me,' he said, looking back at her with a flick of his flashlight.

She nodded. 'You got it. Been a while since I've rugby tackled anyone to the ground.'

The comment reminded Drake of her brutal takedown of The Family Man the previous year, smashing the killer to the ground and giving them a vital few seconds. The memory stirred up a lot of unwanted feelings. He shook the memory from his mind and steeled himself.

'Right, let's do this. I'll shout when it's good to come down.'

'Roger, Roger.'

Ignoring the *Airplane* quote, Drake took a deep breath. *Right, here goes.*

He cast his flashlight into the hatch, the light highlighting the rickety and rotten-looking wooden stairs. A rough concrete floor lay at the foot of the steps. He gripped the left side of the handrail and took a tentative step down into the darkness. The stairs seemed firm enough, so he tentatively took another, leaving the solid ground of the carpark. He'd need to go a little further down before he could get a good view of the cellar.

Another step. The stair let out a creak in protest, not dissimilar to the chair in his old study. He rolled his eyes and shone the light around the room further.

He could make out the bottoms of a few steel kegs and a sheet of metal, presumably used as a ramp for them.

'See anything, Chief?' Ellie whispered from above. 'You're going pretty slow.'

'I'm just taking my time, that's all. It's not a race. Take note,' he said, feeling a little jittery, admittedly. It wasn't a daily activity for him to be going into the bowels of derelict pubs where people had been kept against their will.

Adrenaline coursed through him. His head was level with the hatch now, so he bent in, and took the last couple of steps.

There was a sudden scurrying in the far end of the room, out of the corner of his eye. He snapped his flashlight at the movement. The shape let out a screeching squeak. He saw it burrow into something piled by a pillar to his right.

He perched at the entrance and scanned around the cellar with his torch. There were more steel beer kegs, with all the relevant connections still in place, lined up neatly against the whitewashed, dirty walls. Cobwebs and grime caked the corners and upper reaches of the cellar. A rusty air conditioning unit was piped in to his left, with a supporting foundation post. The concrete floor was caked in leaves, mud and detritus: plastic bottles, food wrappings and some old clothes.

Drake flashed his light through the gaps in the stairway behind him, and was semi-relieved to find it, too, was empty with only more rubbish and filth piled in heaps against the sloping back wall and corners.

SOCO is going to have a field day with this, he thought.

He cast the torch back on the post where he'd seen the rat. The floor at the base looked roughed up, as though someone had spent some time there. He recalled the binding around the man's ankle and wrists. Surely they hadn't been substantial enough to resist being pulled against the post? Unless the victims were being watched and hadn't the opportunity? Or maybe the supports were unstable?

'Ellie,' he called up. 'Looks like you won't be tackling anything but rats today, I'm afraid.' He shone his torch on the steps. 'Come on down.'

She stepped down heavily behind him. The stairs creaked under the pressure, but didn't give way. 'What we got, Boss?'

'Lots of shit, rats, and what looks like the location our guys were being held.' He shone the torch toward the pole supports.

'Urgh, what a grim place to be holed up. It bloody stinks,' she said, turning up her nose. He hadn't paid attention, his senses focused on his surroundings, but now she mentioned it . . . there was a bit of a stench.

He grunted in agreement. 'Yeah, something like that.'

Ellie wandered over to the pile by the post on the right side of the room.

'Ellie, don't—'

'Holy shit!' Ellie squealed, almost jumping out of her skin as the rat bolted from its hiding place, screeching as it ran up and out of the cellar.

'Thanks for the warning,' she hissed. Her eyes were as wide as saucers, and Drake couldn't help smirking. 'I did say there were rats, Sergeant.'

'Oh God. Is that what I think it is?' Ellie gestured at the pile.

'Yep. That's the literal shit I mentioned.'

'Jesus,' she said, bringing her hand to her nose. 'Whoever did this treated them like animals.'

He looked over at the other post. A similar situation appeared to have played out there.

'But how did they escape? They can't have been able to loosen their restraints themselves and open a door – which, I'm guessing, had been bolted shut at some point?'

'Inside and out, by the looks of it.'

'Huh?' Ellie looked at him.

'The hatch, there's a bolt on the inside and on the outside too.'

Ellie frowned. 'That's weird. Why would you have a bolt on the inside when there's no other exit up and into the pub directly?'

'Something to ponder, I'm sure.'

He moved around the side of the stairs and crouched down to get a better look at the rubbish at the back, which was bundled away from the main area of the room. Ellie continued her survey of the main area, tapping on the kegs, which returned a hollow sound.

Drake frowned as his torch caught a glint of something in amongst the rubbish.

'Ellie, I think there's something back here. Can you cast your light this way while I try to reach it? The wall slopes really steeply here.'

'Okay.' She turned, shining her torch on the area he indicated.

Drake got down on his knees, the concrete digging in roughly as he clambered forwards on all fours before remembering he needed gloves. He awkwardly pulled a pair from his pocket and pulled them on.

'Just a little more . . .' He strained as he reached for the object.

Brushing the corner of the object with his fingers, he worked it free slightly, and rotated it a little towards him.

'Gotcha,' he said triumphantly.

The object felt soft, like leather. He gripped the corner and pulled it towards him before examining it.

It was a black leather wallet, with metal lettering adorning the front: *A. L.*

'Ah! Is there anything to ID them? What's inside?' Ellie asked excitedly.

Drake flipped it open. A number of cards were inside, and a five-pound note. He pulled out a UK driver's licence and shone his light on it. A solemn overweight man looked back at him, short brown hair, thick glasses and a badly shaped beard.

'*Alex Ludner*,' he read out. 'Looks like we may have got our duct tape man.'

11

It was early evening, and the crime scene was lit up like a Christmas tree as the driver and passenger doors of Drake's Audi slammed shut. He'd spotted the media huddle forming down the lane, the reporters setting up, the cameramen sorting their lighting rig. He didn't fancy becoming the face of the investigation, at least not yet.

The car was damp and fogged up, much to his annoyance, so he started the engine and fiddled with the heating controls. Soon the fans revved up, and he was met with a loud continuous roar as the hot air fought to thaw the chill of the car.

'Give it a few minutes. The car's getting old, but it should sort out the temperature in here soon enough,' Drake said, rubbing his hands together.

'If it's all the same to you, I'll keep my scarf on for now. It's frickin' freezing,' Ellie said, shivering as she wrapped her arms around herself.

After they'd cased the rest of the old pub, they found there was nothing more of note that they could highlight to SOCO. It appeared likely the suspect had kept the cellar as their sole base of operations. He'd handed over the wallet and ID, and they'd photographed and tagged it, but not before he had taken a photo or two of his own. After a few SOCO-related mistakes on The Family Man case the previous year, Drake wasn't taking chances anymore. They could label him a control freak if they wanted, he could label them incompetent. He was happy for it to go both ways.

'We'll need to get some checks run on who this Alex Ludner guy is. Get a profile together. See if it might help identify the female. Perhaps they knew each other. Friends, partner maybe?' Ellie offered.

'Yes, but—'

Tap, tap.

Drake turned to see the misted image of Chambers knocking on his car window. He wound down the fogged-up window and peered out.

'Yes, Gemma?'

'Sir,' she said, bending down to meet his gaze. She looked frozen. 'Just to let you know I'm off now. Uniform has got the place under lock and key for the night.'

'Thank you, Constable. Appreciate your help today. Good job on finding the second victim, particularly while we still had some daylight on our side.'

'Thank you, sir. Will you need me . . . you know, after today, for any of this?' she asked, cocking her head toward the crime scene.

'No, I guess your superior will tell you that you can get on with your training. Is that all?'

'N-no, I mean, yes . . . sir. Thank you for today,' she said, giving a weak smile before she stood and left, allowing the full brunt of an icy gust to blow into the car.

'Shit.' Drake pushed the button to get the window up. The

electronic whine going on forever before it finally closed, dampening the noise of the investigation going on outside.

He scratched his stubble and turned back towards Ellie. 'Anyway, as I was going to say, the ID . . . seems a bit of an oversight by our killer to leave something like that lying around, don't you think?'

He fiddled with the console to turn the heater down. The noise was agitating him, but at least the heat was beginning to work its magic, the fogged windows giving way to the sight of police vehicles and mud in the darkness.

'I guess so, but perhaps things hadn't gone according to plan? Maybe that accounts for why this Ludner chap had a different method applied to him?'

He drummed a finger on the steering wheel. 'Perhaps. And if it's their first time committing a crime – particularly something as overtly vicious as this – then that sets off all sorts of emotions. And, with there being no sight of the woman's belongings as well, we've some work to do on that front. I'm thinking we may need to get some additional resource on this.' He sighed, before adding, 'if there's budget.'

'Bring in Dave, maybe?'

'I don't think so. I'm thinking we may need more. He's not long for the job, remember? This differs from The Family Man case – we're starting from scratch here. We don't know what we're dealing with. There could be a third out there for all we know.' He sighed. 'I'll float it by Miller, see what she makes of it.'

'Sounds like a plan, si—Drake,' she corrected herself. Clearly Ellie remembered he didn't like being addressed as 'sir' by someone he worked with closely. Particularly someone who had saved him and his daughter.

Shit, I should say something about her award, shouldn't I? He gripped the steering wheel tightly in his right hand.

'Ellie, I wanted to say . . . I'm sorry.'

'Huh, sir—Drake, bah! Fuck's sake!' She raged at herself.

He smirked and raised his eyebrows, but said nothing. The uncomfortable silence continued amidst the billowing of the heater.

Finally, he sniffed and spoke. 'I'm sorry for yesterday. I wasn't there for your award ceremony. That was wrong of me. I apologise. It's not an excuse, but I wasn't . . .' He hesitated for an uncomfortable length of time again. 'I wasn't in the best frame of *mind*.'

'Drake, you don't have to. It's okay. I understand. Really, I do. You've had the sort of year I wouldn't wish on anyone. What happened to your wife was . . . it was awful. I know we've not spoken much, if at all, this past year, but I care. I want to help, I mean that.'

'Yeah.' He paused again, refusing to bring up *her* image in his mind, composing himself. 'Nevertheless, you saved Eva. I'll never be able to repay you for that. Because of you, we locked away that bastard for good.'

Samuel Barrows, known more widely as *The Family Man* serial killer, had been the making and breaking of Drake. Twenty years prior, he'd thought he'd done the world a service by apprehending someone he rightly believed was 'the Man'. A man he'd thought was long dead and buried. But he wasn't dead. Samuel had deceived Drake, leading to the Man killing indiscriminately for the past twenty years right under his nose, and his wife had been the killer's last victim.

They'd stopped him, and Barrows was locked away for good. But the deception so many years ago had allowed the Man to change his MO. As a result, they were still identifying and cataloguing his victims; much like Samuel had done when he'd butchered them. He'd held on to victims' belongings as keepsakes. Jewellery, identification, clothing, you name it.

Drake understood there had been *sixty-three* positive identifications. Men and women of varying ages, ethnicities and backgrounds. Sixty-three people who would never see loved ones again, and Drake knew it was because of him.

He should have known. He could have acted, could have stopped him. It tore at him. The same way it tore at him that the Man was in prison, alive and revelling in their discoveries. Even with there being no chance of release, the thought of Samuel still drawing breath burned Drake's very soul. His daughter without a mother, he without his beloved Becca.

Ellie spoke, breaking the silence. 'Talking of The Family Man . . . I don't want to dredge this up too much, but there are still no leads on the whereabouts of Andrea Whitman.'

'I know.'

'Oh?'

'Yes, I've been doing what I can off the record to trace her. But, there's literally nothing. I can't fathom how someone could just disappear so suddenly, so *completely*. A woman that disturbed has to have left a trail. She's not of sound mind. You wouldn't be some kind of Houdini in that state. There has to be some kind of explanation.'

'Yeah.' Ellie replied, downbeat.

He knew she still felt accountable for what happened that day, for not having spotted the signs. But how was she to know Andrea had butchered her husband and almost killed her own daughter, somehow mimicking the Family Man's vicious methods?

'How's the daughter doing now? Honestly, I still can't believe she's even alive. I genuinely thought she was dead,' she asked, a look of hope in her eyes.

'Cari? She's still unable to speak, despite them having repaired the damage to her vocal cords,' Drake said. The thought of his daughter's best friend Cari reminded him that his own daughter was barely speaking to him. 'Eva's not said much, but she is worried about her friend's mental health. She should be talking now apparently, but she appears unable or unwilling to. She's traumatised.'

'Poor kid.'

'Mmm.'

Cari Whitman didn't have any other family. She'd lost her dad, and her mum had disappeared in the space of one evening. Despite her continued anger towards him, holding Drake responsible for her mum's death, Eva had begged for him or Rachel to take her in. But he'd barely been in a state to look after himself, let alone take on another family's traumatised kid.

Once again, Becca's sister, Rachel, had come to the rescue, looking after Cari when she'd been discharged from the hospital. The same hospital that Cari's mother had vanished from.

Drake took a sharp intake of breath. 'So, anyway . . . in future, you win another award . . . I'll be there, all right? We got a deal?'

She smiled. 'Yes, Boss. Thank you. Anyway, you didn't miss much. Just a load of white men and women congratulating themselves, mostly.'

'Hey, I hope Miller and co didn't fall into that category?' he said, cocking his eyebrow at her.

She shrugged. 'No, but I felt like I stood out a bit, even in this day and age.'

'Sorry to hear that. Here's hoping for the future, eh?'

'Amen to that.'

12

Drake arrived back in Putney just before midnight. He was relieved to be nearly back. It had been a long and tedious journey; though snow never lasted long in the south-east, particularly in London, it had ground everything to a halt all the same. There'd been traffic as far as the eye could see, the roads a mess of slush and dirt. The continual stop-start while he drudged on drove him to distraction. His destination was the SMT offices, which were located near the Thames, not far from New Scotland Yard. It was around thirty minutes away as the crow flies.

London was a city that never slept, even more so around Christmas time, evidenced by people still stumbling around in clothes not meant for the time of year. Bright red Christmas hats, full-on Santa costumes, Santa's *not-so-little* helpers, the works. There were still hordes of Christmas parties on the lookout for their next pub before last orders. Gaggles of women tottered across roads, followed by men stumbling and looking back for their mates. A few slips kept him darkly entertained while he drove.

Drake pulled into the staff entrance for the office block

located in a side street off the main road. The plate recognition gate opened as he approached, clattering and screeching for an interminably long time.

He stole one of the last precious few spaces in the tiny car park. He hoped Ellie wouldn't be far behind. It was torturous trying to park in London at the best of times, let alone in this sort of weather.

Soon after, the rickety lift – metal coffin on a string would be more apt, Drake always thought – had climbed to the top floors of the dilapidated building. The place had been taken on at great expense many years before his time. Miller and he had often speculated about where that 'great expense' had really been incurred.

The office space appeared to have run aground years before the police took it over. Old fabric desk dividers were torn and falling off. Worn grey carpet tiles were missing in places, revealing the chipboard beneath. Coffee stains were more frequent than not, while a few buckets had sprung up in the last few weeks, peppering the corridors to catch whatever liquid came through the ceiling. It seemed that winter had finally breached their miserable locale.

Given the time of night, few desk lamps remained on. The main lights weren't used past mid-evening – some cost-saving exercise or another – but those that were punctuated the darkness with an ominous glow. Here or there, a face was lit up by the pale blue-white flicker of a laptop screen or monitor, but precious little else pierced the gloom.

Drake spotted Miller's office light was on. He struggled to remember the last time he'd been in the office when the lights were off. If she wasn't dealing with the press or her few superiors, she was nearly always there.

He poked his head round the door, seeing her standing and looking out over the cityscape. Her reflection showed a woman

The Ties That Bind

deep in thought; and not of the good kind, by the looks of it. The pressure of the job and her responsibility were never far from her mind.

'Laura,' he volunteered, softly rapping on the door.

'Oh, John. You're back.' She turned, barely glancing at him, and took a seat behind her desk.

Drake took one of two seats on the other side, not offering anything in response other than a tired exhalation. His boss leant forwards, steepling her fingers under her lower lip. He noted the circles under her eyes. He daren't imagine what his were like right now; Drake didn't like how he looked these days, how the past year had aged him.

'So, what have you got for me?' she asked. Her voice was low and wearily expectant.

'I'm sorry to say it's not looking good, Laura,' he sighed, shifting in his seat. 'Two murders, evidence of kidnapping and imprisonment – for how long, who knows at this point – and one victim potentially identified. We found the man's wallet in the cellar we believe they were held in. I'll have confirmation tomorrow, all being well. The other is a Jane Doe.'

'I see. Good work in locating the ID, at least it's something. Makes a change, comparatively speaking.'

Drake knew she was referring to The Family Man case. There'd been no actionable evidence at any of those crime scenes. She was right, at least it was *something* with this one. But it didn't make him feel any more at ease, given the violence on display.

She continued: 'Any idea why the MO was what it was? Why the force feeding of the glass?'

'I think that's pretty simple to theorise,' he said, interlocking his fingers and leaning forward slightly, keeping his voice low, despite the lack of an audience. 'In short, I believe he, or she, wanted them to suffer. To me it feels as though it was personal, that this person *knew* the victims and was exacting a revenge of sorts. I'm hoping the coroner will give us more to go on when they examine them. Maybe what the glass was once part of. I think that will go some way to explaining it, *if* we're lucky.' He paused, doubting himself. 'But it's just a theory. You know how it goes with these things, ten per cent investigative nous, ninety per cent luck.'

Miller leant back in her chair and looked out the window. 'Okay. Well, keep it to yourself for now. I've tried to find whatever resource I can to allow you and DS Wilkinson more time to focus on the main thrust of the case. Needless to say, I need you to get it done and dusted sooner rather than later. I don't want this turning into another case spanning decades.' She turned back and looked him in the eye. 'And I don't think you do, either.'

He grimaced at the remark but held his tongue, taking a deep breath before he said anything he later regretted.

'No argument there,' he replied through gritted teeth.

His boss, and former partner, had a tendency to be a little blunt. The case 'spanning decades' had resulted in the death of his wife, for God's sake. And she was just as culpable as he was in the initial investigation all those years ago. Drake recalled her not putting in the same hours as he had.

He buried his thoughts. 'So, who or what do you have in mind, ma'am?'

'I've already selected them for you. Believe me when I say the talent pool is mighty thin these days. But I've pulled a few strings and got you . . .' She looked down at her notes: 'DI Andrew Melwood, DS Luka Strauss, and DC Gemma Chambers.'

'Is that it? I thought you wanted this done and dusted, Laura?' he said, letting his earlier thoughts get the better of him. He immediately regretted it. He wasn't in any position to be getting surly with his boss.

She gave him a hard stare. 'This is what I can afford to give you, John. Take it, or leave it.'

'I guess I'm going to have to take it then.'

'Good. And John . . . I know you're having a tough time of it. It seems never-ending for you, and I get it.'

'But . . . ?'

'Don't ever speak to me like that again. You're walking a thin line as it is – I'm getting it in the neck, and I can't be having the same from my team too. Particularly after all the leeway I've given you these last few years. It's not just this past year . . . got it?'

The hard stare had turned into one of her withering looks.

'Laura, I'm sorry. I get it. I'm trying here. I'll do better,' he said, cowed by her words. He felt weak and stupid, and suddenly overwhelmed.

'Good. Now, report back to me when you have something more concrete.' She took out her phone and begun tapping on it, turning away from him in a show of dismissal.

'Got it.'

* * *

'All good with DCS Miller, Chief?' Ellie said, her voice coming from the corridor connecting to the metal coffin.

Yeah, peachy.

Drake stopped in his tracks, giving her a thin smile as she caught up. 'Yes. Sounds as though we'll be getting a few more hands on deck from tomorrow.'

'Good news! Though got to admit it'll be strange, I'm not used to that with you. Only had Dave part-time in the past. Is he tagging along?'

'No, not this time. We've got a DI, DS and DC – and a

partridge in a pear tree. Slim pickings apparently, so I hope they're up to scratch.'

'Who are they?'

'DI Andrew Melwood, DS Luka Strauss and DC Gemma Chambers. The DC is the woman that spoke to me while we were in my car earlier, the one that discovered the second victim. Only joined a while ago, supposedly,' he said, before looking at Ellie pointedly. 'So, going to need a bit of extra attention, I suspect.'

She sighed. 'All right, I take the hint. Will do.'

'I don't know anything about the other two, not had the pleasure.'

'Me neither. As long as DI Melwood isn't like that DI Granger you spoke to today, I'll be happy.'

'Can't pick 'em, Ellie. Just got to do your best,' he said, before adding with a smirk: 'Not everyone's as good a boss as me.'

She nodded in mock knowing. 'Ain't that a fact, Chief.'

'Right, I order you to get some rest. I suspect tomorrow's going to be a big day for both of us.'

She frowned. 'But I only just got here.'

'Ellie . . .'

'Okay, okay. I don't need telling twice,' she said, smiling and turning back the way she came.

* * *

Drake sat at his desk, mired in thought; he'd been staring at the sole picture of Becca and Eva that marked the desk as his own, when he looked up and realised he was alone. He must have lost track of time. It was silent, the office still; what few remaining lights were off. The stillness exuded a sudden strange feeling of dislocation. Shaking the cobwebs from his mind, he stood and collected his things before making for the exit.

Rounding the final darkened corner, a sudden wave of disorientation hit him. It was like he was being pulled through an airless room and out the other side, causing his chest to tighten instantly. The sensation stopped him in his tracks. His briefcase and coat dropped to the ground, and Drake felt like he was going to collapse at any moment.

He brought his hand to his chest as he scrambled for the closest wall, his breathing becoming more and more ragged. It took all of his strength to stop himself from slumping to the floor. Instead, he managed to prop himself against a wall with his hands on his knees, his heart pounding in his ears.

Then the thoughts and feelings bombarded him. They came at him as though a door to a room containing it all had burst open, leaving his suppressed anxiety free to engulf him: Becca pleading, Eva screaming at him. The Family Man cackling as he slit his wife's throat. His wife's funeral, his mother's death, murders from years ago, assaults, chases and injuries. The images rose to the surface and faded as soon as they emerged, becoming an intangible blur as they ran through his mind.

Drake felt as though he was going to pass out. Sweat poured off him as he tried to rein it all back in once more.

'No... No... stop... STOP!' he shouted, panic-stricken.

He braced himself against the wall for what seemed like an eternity. Then, just as suddenly as it had appeared, the feeling was gone. His chest loosened, the scramble of his mind coming to a halt. His ragged breaths were becoming slow and deep, his heart rate normalising as the disorientation cleared, like an ocean after a storm.

Drake looked up to see if anyone had rushed to see what was going on, running his hand through his hair. To his relief, the immediate vicinity was still empty, though his hand returned slick with sweat.

What was that? Jesus, was that a panic attack?

'What's the bloody matter with you?' he murmured, scrubbing at his face.

Taking a few steps, another feeling suddenly flooded him. This time, it was one of anger, rising from deep in his gut. He turned and punched the thinly plastered stud wall, an indentation appearing beneath his blow. He struck it again, then again and again, the sound of his rage and frustration pouring out amidst the flurry of blows. A bloody smear formed on the plaster beneath his onslaught before, finally, it caved in.

Drake collected himself, grimacing at his bloody knuckles, before calmly picking up his coat and briefcase. Without a sound, he continued on to the lift, leaving the hole in his wake.

13

Ellie pulled up near her house in Harrow, northwest London. The stillness of the street was strangely discomforting. The bare pollarded trees loomed overhead, the backdrop of the moon against the houses lining the road. She closed her eyes and took a minute to reset herself after what she'd seen that day, returning to normal life.

Lately she'd been quick to leave work and quick to get in the house, the drudgery of her day-to-day having become increasingly depressing. Until Drake's call earlier that day, that was. But now she was feeling the pull of the investigation, the need to be out and working the case. It excited her, but the familiar feeling of being repelled by it was there too. The awkward sense of guilt that she should be excited by what had befallen those poor people, that she was learning and benefiting from their deaths.

I really need to learn to distance myself more, she thought. *The sooner the better, please.*

Ellie remained in the car for a moment longer before exiting. The crunch of gritting salt greeted her as she walked the short distance to her house. A set of lights were fixed over the entrance and a *Santa stop here* sign stood unlit in a large flowerpot.

'Only me,' Ellie called in a low voice, closing her front door.

She felt comforted by the warmth as she took off her coat and scarf, hanging them together by the door before kicking off her shoes. The mid-terrace's hallway was softly lit by the living room and kitchen doorways leading off from it. She grimaced slightly at the sight of the garish purple, silver and gold tinsel hung from the walls for Bella's benefit.

Ellie walked through to the living room. An overloaded and oversized Christmas tree, nearly scraping the ceiling, stood stuffed in the corner by the bay window. More tinsel was making itself known, garishly accenting the myriad of family pictures they had on the wall. Bella on the swings, Len with his parents, Ellie with hers and Ellie with her recent award.

The dining area took up the back of the room, framed by an open archway. Len was sitting at the table wearing the thick, black glasses he used primarily for work. He looked up in greeting, surrounded by work paraphernalia: laptop, notepad, various files, as well as a glass of red wine and a half-empty bottle. Her husband had a darkly handsome, angular face. His hair faded to cover the fact he was slowly going bald, much to his annoyance. Though she liked it, she gently teased him about it anyway.

'Hey, how'd it go?' He took off his glasses and placed them on the table, giving her a look of concern.

Ellie slumped down on the dining chair closest to him and let out a tired sigh. 'Not great. What we found was pretty nasty and has all the hallmarks of one of our *special* cases,' she said, making an air quotes gesture with her fingers.

Len shut his laptop before neatly piling his notes on top of it. 'So you're going to be rammed again, right? Today's not just a one off?'

She yawned, blinking a few times. 'Yeah, I'm sorry. I'm afraid so, babe. Might be very busy for the foreseeable.'

'Come on, don't be sorry. It's the nature of the job. You've been crying out for a case such as this. Your other work was driving you crazy.'

She knew that her proper work as part of the SMT got to him a little, despite his words to the contrary, but he was onboard with it and as supportive as he could be. He was *still* relieved (and it had been well over a year now) that she wasn't out night after night on shift work in Response, getting into all kinds of scrapes and situations with the general crime population, like the old days.

But he had blown his top at the close call she'd had with The Family Man case. Her hand still bore the scars of the knife slash that could have been her neck or face, the new skin a few shades lighter. She'd had to reassure him it wasn't always going to be like that. But she wasn't a fortune teller. It was hard to predict what could and couldn't happen when dealing with the psychopaths she was learning to take on.

He still raised concerns occasionally that what happened to Drake and his family could happen to them, that Bella could be hurt or worse. She'd vowed it would never be the case, but she knew she had no evidence to back up her claim.

'Thanks, you know that means a lot to me. Don't forget that.'

He smiled and picked up the bottle of malbec, gesturing to her.

'No, I'm okay, thanks. Did you collect Bella okay? Sorry for dumping that on you at the last minute.'

'Yeah, all fine. I just had to shift a few things around and work late, as you can see.' He gestured to his work. 'But yes, she behaved herself. She asked when you were coming home and was a little upset not to see you. But she's starting to understand the reasons it happens sometimes – it's scary how much she's grown.'

'Thank you, and God, tell me about it. Soon she'll be picking us up.' She yawned again involuntarily. 'I'm sorry, but I'm going to have to make a move for bed. I'm knackered, and Drake wants me in early doors tomorrow. You coming?'

'Yeah, let me just pack this up,' he said, reaching over the table for a few stray post-it notes and a coffee cup. 'Oh, did you get a call today, by the way?'

She gave him an inquisitive look. 'A call? No.'

'Yeah, a man called the house, asking if you were in. He said he needed to speak with you.'

'Was it Drake? DI Granger?'

'No . . . No. He didn't give a name. It was a quick call, sounded like he was in a hurry. I gave him your work mobile number. I hope that was okay?'

She pulled out her phone and had a look for any missed calls. She didn't see any. 'Yeah, sure, thank you. Must've missed it. Weird, they'd call the house phone – who does that these days?' She shrugged. 'Guess I didn't have any signal in that damn field.'

'No worries. Now, let's see if we can get upstairs without waking the little terror.'

Ellie quietly opened the door of her daughter's bedroom to see the pink room dimly illuminated with a nightlight. She smiled at the sight of Bella bundled up tightly in her duvet, a cloud of fluffy unruly hair poking out and her thumb in her mouth.

She couldn't believe her little girl was five years old already. As Len had said, it was scary where the time went.

She felt a hand on her shoulder.

'You're really playing with fire now. She's fine. Come on, let's get to bed,' he whispered.

'Okay. I can't help myself, you know?'

She pulled the door up without fully closing it.

Once they'd left the room, Bella opened her eyes and pulled out an action man from under her pillow.

Its head was bound in black duct tape.

14

Drake exited his car and looked up at the morning's oppressive grey skies. The car park was as empty as when he'd come out from the office for some sleep. He looked down at his watch and understood why. It had only just gone six in the morning.

He felt like shit, groaning out loud while he stretched. He glanced back at the reason for his ill-feeling: his makeshift bedroom in the back seat of his car. It had felt like a good idea at the time, but his back clearly thought otherwise.

He still couldn't bring himself to spend a moment more in that flat than he had to. The place where he'd nearly done the unspeakable. In the cold light of day, Drake felt a degree of shame and guilt that he'd not felt since his wife's death. Nearly taking the 'easy' way out and leaving Eva to face the consequences? It was pathetic, and it certainly wasn't him. He could get through this, he knew he could, and he didn't need a shrink telling him what to think and feel either. He growled at the thought of yet another appointment later that day.

Drake noticed the crumpled mess that was his shirt in the reflection of his car window. He could use his dark suit jacket to cover some of the shame, but not all. He pulled yesterday's blue tie out of his pocket and hastily knotted it to hide a further few of the crinkles. Nothing he could do about his suit trousers, but he was sure the creases would work themselves out eventually. Maybe.

He nursed his right hand, flinching slightly when he ran his fingers over his knuckles.

I'll be fine, he reasoned to himself. *That was a one off.*

With a yawn, he snatched his dark grey woollen overcoat and old briefcase (which was becoming more of a glorified laptop bag these days, despite his protestations) from the passenger seat and made his way inside.

Taking the coffin up to the main office, he ignored the hole in the wall and stopped for a minute or two in the kitchenette. He made quick work of the cup of foul-tasting machine coffee from the vending machine – which still used beige plastic cups, reminiscent of the nineties. He grabbed another, despite the taste, and set about locating the investigation room that SMT had stolen in a land grab in the preceding months.

The room, which he suspected was once an oversized utility cupboard, was tucked away down a labyrinthine mix of corridors. If he remembered correctly, there *was* a literal broom cupboard within that he might have to make use of as SIO. Drake's shoes echoed on the corridor floor until finally, he found the unassuming room.

Drake tried the door, but it wouldn't budge. The long handle gave a pained squeak as he pulled it down and pushed again. He gave the door a puzzled look. It wasn't usually locked. Come to think of it, he didn't think it *could* be locked. Putting his cup of suspect brown liquid and briefcase down, he gave the door another try. It still wouldn't budge.

'What the hell?' he muttered. Deciding to give it the strong-arm treatment, Drake put his shoulder against the door and shoved until it gave way, banging off the wall with a satisfying *thwack* and judder.

I need to stop abusing this building. It's getting out of hand.

He grunted with satisfaction as he surveyed the moderately sized room from the doorway. His memory was correct. A separate room led off from a doorway in the corner.

That'll be mine for the foreseeable, he mused.

The main room contained several worn-out whiteboards which took up the wall at the far end. A mess of grey and blue marks remained, the result of permanent markers having been used by accident and rubbed off again with cleaning fluid, with little success. A couple of wheeled swivel whiteboards were available too, shoved out of the way in the corner. Fabric pin boards covered the remaining wall estate amidst a scattering of chairs, computers, desks and power points.

Drake dreaded to think what cases had been pinned up in here, what horrors had been carried out on the victims, the crime scene photos staring back at the investigating officers for the months and years this room had seen use. He knew his team would probably push to use software to track the case, but he still preferred having it up and in front of them, too. He wheeled out one board. Drake wasn't ready to give up on the physical world just yet.

* * *

He hadn't long settled into his residence in the Senior Investigating Officer cupboard at the back of the main investigation room, his briefcase emptied of his laptop, notes, and papers when he heard movement and peered out.

He spotted the familiar outline of DC Chambers, checking

out her new home, her back to him. She was probably judging the state of it as much as he was, even as someone new to the job. It wasn't a professional marvel, and she clearly knew it as much as he did by the look on her face as she turned.

Away from the cold weather clothing and distraction of the previous day, he noted her delicate features, waif-like and brittle. Her timid nature seemed more apparent than before. It was a strange quality for a detective.

He coughed.

'Oh! DCI Drake, sir, good to see you again,' she said, seeing him step out of the office space. 'Looks like this case will be an on-the-job training for me, after all, then?' she blurted.

'Indeed. I wasn't expecting anyone for a while yet. You're keen – good to see you're taking advantage of the chance we're giving you.'

'Well, I live locally, so . . . ' She paused, catching her breath and concentrating on her words before speaking in her unusually quiet manner. 'I wanted to give a good impression. I'm here to learn. Clearly, you're a good teacher, based on that DS Wilkinson you worked with. Her getting all those awards and such.'

'Yes . . . well. Flattery will get you nowhere,' he said flatly.

She seemed taken aback.

'How about you go and get a coffee, while we wait for the others to arrive, eh?' he offered, knowing how bad the coffee was and immediately feeling guilty for suggesting the experience to her.

'Oh . . . okay. I'll do that,' she said, seeming grateful to get out of the awkward conversation.

* * *

Drake had made quick work of putting up the few details of the case on to a whiteboard, writing up the dates, general times and particulars of the circumstances in which Alex Ludner and the mystery female were found. Photos and names would follow as they worked, with elements replaced or removed as they progressed. He'd nearly finished by the time the man he assumed to be DI Andrew Melwood made an appearance with a knock on the battered door. Chambers followed him in, a pained expression on her face and a beige cup in hand.

Drake's presumption was down to how the man carried himself. He looked to be in his mid-to-late forties, tall – two to three inches past six feet – with an arrogant air about him and eyes that appeared slightly too wide for his face. He had the look of someone who was permanently on edge. His grey hair was slicked back on top like someone who had watched one too many episodes of *Peaky Blinders* or *Boardwalk Empire*, the sides graded down to the skin. He wore a light grey waistcoat, suit jacket and trousers.

'DCI Drake?' Melwood offered.

'Yes. DI Melwood, I take it? Or . . .' – he couldn't resist demeaning him – 'DS Luka Strauss, maybe?'

It worked. The man struggled to contain himself at the slight.

Melwood's eyes bulged further. 'It's *DI* Andrew Melwood, thank you.'

'Right, got it. Good to meet you,' he said, offering his hand and receiving a clammy, limp shake.

'You too. So, should we get started?' Melwood asked, taking a seat and leaning back on an armless office chair that had seen better days before putting his hands behind his head. Chambers made for a chair nearby, steering clear of the new man in the room.

'We'll give it a few more minutes for DS Wilkinson and DS Strauss. Have you two met before?' Drake asked.

'No, don't think I've had the pleasure,' Melwood said.

Chambers frowned, looking put out. 'We have. You ran a small session on crime scene investigation a few weeks back. I found it most interesting.'

'Oh, really? Are you sure?'

'Yes, sir.'

'Oh. It must have been a large class.'

'There were four of us.'

'I see. I—' Melwood began, as Ellie entered the room.

'Sorry, I'm late, Drake. Traffic was a nightmare, yet again,' she sighed, plonking down her bag on the nearest desk and pulling up a chair that was languishing against a nearby wall. She felt like a welcome whirlwind after the preceding few minutes.

Melwood piped up. 'Err, excuse me, DS Wilkinson, isn't it? You know you're not supposed to interrupt those superior to you, right?'

Drake rolled his eyes. Is this really what he'd have to be dealing with? He wasn't in the mood for this kind of crap. Miller wasn't kidding when she said the resource was a little *thin* on the ground, if this was what was available.

'Okay. Enough of that,' he snapped. 'I'd suggest we get going. We've got an initial lead that needs following up. The pathologist working on the victims today, which I hope will give us more information and—'

There was a noise at the door as a man rushed in, out of breath and sweating.

'I'm sorry, I'm so sorry I'm late.'

DS Luka Strauss fell into one of the few remaining chairs. The man had a subtle German accent, but his overall appearance was decidedly not in keeping with the German stereotype. He was looking unkempt, with scruffy stubble punctuating his face. He was not composed in the slightest and appeared to have terrible timekeeping. A confusing mix for someone who'd made the rank of detective sergeant and particularly one that was seconded to SMT.

Strauss attempted to tidy his unruly brown hair, brushing it back with his hand. Then tried to smarten himself up, swiping at some mud on his suit trousers, but making it worse.

'The damn bus broke down, and then the bloody tube station was closed. I had to run the rest of the way. Apologies, sir.'

'You made it, Strauss. That's what matters,' Drake said, trying not to smile.

'Thank you for the understanding, sir.'

Despite appearances, and in contrast with his superior, something Melwood would undoubtedly point out any second now, Drake had a hunch Strauss might work well for him.

Strauss pulled a laptop from his bag and lifted the lid.

'Please, and this goes for all of you,' Drake said, looking around the room. 'We're probably going to be working together for a while, so call me Drake when it's just us. Okay? I don't have time for this hierarchical bullshit.'

He stressed the last part, deliberately not looking at Melwood and catching Ellie smirking at him.

He continued: 'Now, I hope you've been given some of the details and have digested it all before getting here today, but here's where we're at . . .'

Describing the details of the case to the small audience of frowning faces, Drake stuck the pictures he had printed to the whiteboard beneath areas marked for each person. A big question mark hovered above the second victim, her stitched and torn mouth stark in the artificial light of the office.

'*Scheiße.*' Strauss grimaced. 'Going to need a strong stomach for this case, aren't we?'

'Indeed,' Melwood said, cocking an eyebrow in Strauss' direction. 'Whoever's doing this hasn't the makings of a pleasant fellow.'

'It wasn't the nicest of discoveries for me, I have to say.' Chambers said in a low voice from the back.

'Don't worry. It gets easier,' Ellie offered.

Chambers nodded uncertainly. 'Doesn't feel that way, but I'll take your word for it.' Her eyes dropped to her hands in her lap and she resumed picking at a cuticle.

'Why the variation in MO between the two bodies, Drake?' Melwood probed. 'Any ideas yet?'

'None so far. Hoping that this will become clearer once we've got a better picture of the victims' backgrounds, who they associated with, the usual. We need some results of what the glass was, and any significance related to that. You know the drill, I'm sure.'

'Certainly. I like a challenge,' the DI said, scratching the back of his neck.

'That's good to hear. I'm suspecting this will be one. And Melwood?'

He stopped scratching. 'Yes, Drake?'

'I'm assigning you to lead on background and the day-to-day management of information to any other support we may get related to the case. Relay anything you find to DS Wilkinson and myself.' Drake pointed with the whiteboard pen at Strauss and Chambers. 'As well as you and you to digging into their backgrounds with Melwood. See if you can get a positive match on the female, and what links they may have to each other, if any. Pull up anything and everything you can, no matter how insignificant it may seem.' He paused. 'Oh, and Chambers?'

'Yes?' she said, looking up from her lap again.

'Please, don't be afraid to ask questions. I'm sure Melwood and Strauss will be happy to help. Don't waste the opportunity to learn from these two, eh?' he stated, staring at the men in turn.

Melwood remained expressionless, but Strauss smiled and nodded.

She smiled meekly. 'Thank you. I'll do my best, sir.'

Drake paced the room. He was getting a feel for the team, and felt a little more confident than he had at the start of their meeting.

'If *any* case critical information is discovered by *any* of you, you are to let me know immediately. Is that understood?'

'Yes, Drake,' the room said in unison.

'And Melwood . . .'

'Yep?'

'You'll be the front for the media from now on, too.'

Melwood turned his nose up, his reluctance obvious, knowing what it would entail. 'Got it.'

He noticed Ellie was trying her best not to bound out of her chair and get going. She'd always been impulsive on their previous case together. He suspected the year since they'd last done any serious work together had built up a lot of energy, which he would have to direct accordingly.

'Good. Now, depending on what comes up, I want us to meet here at this time every day, all right? And for today, until we really get to the bones of this case, I want you to all reconvene with me later this afternoon, too. I will want to hear all that you've found out about this Alex Ludner and our Jane Doe. Meanwhile, Ellie and I are going to attend the post-mortem and see what's what.'

He breathed in heavily.

The work starts now.

'Now, get to it.'

15

'Er . . . Drake?' Ellie called, nearly losing him by the turn of the corridor.

He stopped and waited, pulling on his overcoat while she closed the door and caught up with him.

'Just to let you know, I've . . .'

Impatience radiated from him as she thought of a less wimpish way to let him know a tiny detail she'd kept from him.

'Out with it, Ellie. I've not got all day – we've not got all day,' he amended, scratching absentmindedly at his stubble. He looked rough, Ellie thought, as though he'd slept in his clothes. His skin was sallow, and she noticed his knuckles were grazed.

I hope he's okay?

'I've, it's just . . . I've not been to a post-mortem before, okay? The thought of it freaks me out. All that . . . *stuff*.' She flapped her hands around. 'It's really grim, isn't it?'

He gave her an unimpressed look. 'You're kidding, right?'

'N-no, I'm not, seriously,' she said, looking down at her feet. She felt like an embarrassed school kid.

Drake pursed his lips. 'Well, I'm sorry, Ellie, but you're going to have to attend one sometime, and now's as good a time as any.'

She really didn't like the idea of seeing the bodies opened up. It was going to be messy, even if they hadn't been subjected to all that glass and the beating. Her mind's eye conjured up images of the intestines she'd seen at her first scene with Drake. She had to stop herself from gagging.

'Will you hold my hand?' she joked.

'Oh, sweet Jesus,' Drake rolled his eyes and strode off.

'Okay, okay.'

She followed him down to the car park.

* * *

They'd made it across Wandsworth to the pathology offices by Queen Mary's hospital in surprisingly good time. The place had been sold by the institute several years ago and was now used primarily for post-mortems in cases such as theirs. The building was decidedly drab from the outside, all tatty cladding and aged brickwork. She hoped it wasn't the same inside.

Ellie savoured her last breath of fresh air before they plunged into its depressing reception, her hopes immediately crushed. She'd never liked hospitals, even buildings repurposed from one it turned out. The smell of years of strong disinfectant still hung heavy in the air. She hoped to God that the smell didn't linger on her clothes when they left.

Drake notified the receptionist that they were there to see a Dr Kulkarni, a name that he hadn't mentioned to Ellie before they'd arrived. She imagined a small Asian lady would soon welcome them through, and, a minute later, it appeared she wasn't far off the mark. Though she was taller than Ellie by a couple of inches, making her five foot eight inches or thereabouts (much to her irrational disappointment). And had a remarkably cheerful disposition for someone in the habit of poking around dead bodies in various states of decomposition.

'Ah, the illustrious DCI Drake makes an appearance for the first time in I-don't-know-how long,' she said, greeting him. 'How are you?'

Ellie liked how her voice was very particular and enunciative. The pathologist was in her late forties to early fifties, obviously Indian, with a pleasant oval face and long, rich dark hair down past her shoulders.

'And who is this?' she asked, pulling off a latex glove and holding out her hand.

'Ellie Wilkinson – DS Ellie Wilkinson. Nice to meet you.' Ellie shook her hand. 'Though not sure I'm looking forward to the rest of the visit, if I'm being honest,' she said, before hurriedly adding: 'No offence.'

Dr Kulkarni laughed. 'None taken at all, and please, call me Tanv – short for Tanvi.'

'Okay, Tanv. I might even break out the "Dr K", if I'm feeling playful.' Ellie winked.

'Steady on,' Drake interjected, impatiently. 'Anyway, Tanv, how's it looking? Are you ready for us? You don't mind both of us coming along for the ride, do you?'

'No, no, not at all,' she replied, smiling warmly. 'Will make a change. People don't come down here too often. Can't understand why.'

'Great.'

Ellie may have been imagining things, but she sensed the good doctor may have a slight crush on her boss.

Tanv led them through a sterile-looking lab and a set of key card-locked double doors into the room where the bodies had been laid prone on stainless steel post-mortem tables covered by white sheets. A series of X-rays adorned a wall, it appeared she'd got to processing the bodies a little before they arrived. The images showed the sheer quantity of shards that had been forced into the deceased. Smaller crushed nuggets were intermingled with more visible larger shards, with some appearing lighter or darker, depending on the density. Some smaller pieces had made their way into the victim's stomachs, whereas others were lodged in place in the mouth or the throat.

The steel tables were punctuated with drainage holes, which made Ellie's mind wander to places she didn't want to go. A slew of tools, contraptions, weighing and recording equipment were contained in and around the working area. They all appeared to be polished to such a standard that they appeared brand-new. The tiled walls and floor were absolutely spotless, too. Tanv's assistant, whose back was turned, was standing in a set of scrubs and what appeared to be a surgical mask, tinkering with something on the other side of the room. She could make out gloved hands arranging some equipment.

Dr Kulkarni caught Ellie admiring the woman's handiwork. 'Yes, I know. Bit of a clean freak, if I'm being honest. My assistant, Graham, is also to thank for it. I'm probably bordering on actual OCD,' she remarked dryly.

'It appears so. Very impressive,' Ellie said, trying her best to mask her distaste for the smell of disinfectant. It had mingled with the stench of blood and death that was seemingly impregnated into the very fabric of the room.

Get it together, Ellie. It's about to get much worse.

'I'll just be a moment. I need to get ready,' Tanv said, retiring to a side room.

Tanv was out of earshot, when Drake, a frown on his face, asked: 'Are you okay, Ellie?'

'I'll be fine. I'm sure there's nothing to worry about.'

There *was* something to worry about, though. She felt terrible, and they'd not even started yet. Her mind kept running through the images and, it was becoming overwhelming.

'I thought I recognised that voice.'

They both looked up. The statement originated from the direction of Tanv's assistant, who was walking in their direction with a tray of equipment.

'And you are?' Drake said.

'Oh, sorry.' The man put down the tray on a trolley and removed his surgical mask.

It was Reynolds, his wide mouth and thin lips giving him the same creepy quality as when they'd last seen him up in Haworth, Yorkshire. Reynolds had been the temporary lead SOCO that had worked with them on the first new Family Man killing case all those months ago. The same man who Drake blamed for missing key facts in the case and taking his merry time getting them the information they'd so desperately needed.

'You,' Drake replied through gritted teeth.

'How are you both? Long time, no see. I hope the last year has treated you well?' he said, smiling at them both.

'No.' Drake said before Ellie had a chance to respond.

'Oh, I'm so sorry. That was crass of me. That man killed your wife, didn't he? My condolences.'

Ellie saw Drake take a deep breath, his lips tightening. She sensed he was just about to blow his top and give Reynolds both barrels when Tanv came back into the room. She'd tied her hair up and contained it within a surgical cap and now wore a surgical mask, complete with an apron and clear thin-framed glasses.

'Oh, my apologies. This is Graham Reynolds, my new pathology assistant.'

'We've met,' Drake said, stony-faced.

'Oh, small world!' She clapped, the gloves dampening the sound somewhat.

Reynolds smiled. 'Indeed. These two have caught me! When you saw me last, I was in the process of moving down here to gain my qualifications to become the next great Dr Kulkarni, and now here I am. It looks like monstrous crimes are following me around.'

Drake looked like he was about to explode.

'*Okay*. Well, are you both ready to start?' Ellie asked, forcing a smile despite her prejudices about what they were about to witness.

* * *

Drake and Ellie, decked out in white surgical overalls, stood and watched as Dr Kulkarni peeled back the sheet to reveal the bloated, naked body of Alex Ludner. His head remained wrapped in the pierced mess of black duct tape, while his upper body was marked by bruises and the onset of lividity, along with a great many streams of dried blood from his brutal beating. Ellie winced at the contusions and puncture marks littering the man. Several awkward points stretched and strained the skin on his neck, like it would pierce the skin at any moment.

Dr Kulkarni recorded her findings using a microphone that stopped and started recording at the touch of a button. Each press detailing the specifics of his condition, aided by the details of his driver's licence, which had divulged his age as forty-six.

'Hmmm, we need to determine whether this is all just our victim's blood, or if our killer's blood may have mingled with it. Who's to say they weren't cut in the process?' Tanv noted.

Drake nodded. 'Indeed.'

Seeing nothing else of note beyond the obvious head impairment, Tanv unceremoniously pulled back the sheet to reveal more bruising and lividity to the chest, tree trunk legs, swollen ankles and feet.

'So, detectives, what do you make of this?' She beckoned them over for a closer look and pointed at a mark just below his hip. It was circular in shape, an outer ring with no mark on the inside, like a form of skin branding.

'How long ago do we think this was done, Tanv?' Drake asked.

'It's certainly not recent, so you can discount it from having happened at your scene.' Tanv said, taking pictures using a camera with a light ring. It's unusual, I guess, but I've seen weirder things in my time.'

Sometime later, after documenting the rest of the body, the doctor was ready to start on the head, having taken copious photos beforehand. Her methodical nature impressed Ellie, though the jingle of the camera between each shot was beginning to irritate her.

While Tanv searched for a suitable end to the duct tape, Ellie felt a sudden excitement building in her chest. This was the moment where they could find out what the glass was. Hell, a glass map to the killer would be handy right now.

Kulkarni gripped a rough end of the duct tape while Reynolds held the head still. She pulled gently, not having much luck with it coming away, as the many layers were proving tricky. She picked up a pair of surgical scissors. 'I'm going to have to cut into the tape. Is that okay with you?'

At Drake's nod, she cut into the black tape and began her slow and steady progress. The silence was occasionally punctuated with the clatter of grass fragments hitting the surface of the table. She paused her work to collect them carefully in a kidney-shaped metallic bowl as a makeshift repository.

Soon there was only tape remaining around his eyes and mouth. His cheeks weren't a pretty sight, looking much the same as his neck.

Ellie peered at Tanv's collection. There was a scattering of clear glass, but curiously, there were small amounts of blood-smeared blue, red, orange and green too.

'What do you make of that, Chief?'

Drake gave a slight movement of his head, but said nothing, remaining engrossed in what was going on.

Stained glass? she thought. *A window, perhaps? Broken bottles? Or something else?*

'Right, this may not be pretty,' Tanv said, looking directly at Ellie. 'I'll begin removing the last pieces of tape now.'

Using a scalpel, she prised the mangled tape away from the man's mouth. The glass had savaged his lips. Much like his cheeks, cuts and small fleshy chunks and bits of skin came away with the tape.

Alex Ludner's mouth was full to the brim with sharp shards. Glass protruded like he'd taken mouthfuls of popcorn and stuffed himself to capacity. The thought of being beaten with that amount of glass in your mouth and no way to get rid of it or even breathe properly made Ellie wince.

The tape was removed from the man's eyes, revealing a pair of bloodshot and bulbous eyes with clouded corneas. He appeared to be in a state of permanent pain, even in death. The death stare coupled with his mouth fit to bursting was repulsive.

'Are you going to remove all that now? I feel like we need to give the guy a break,' Ellie said.

'All in good time, Sergeant.'

Tanv brought out a bowl for the remaining volume of glass, along with a pair of long tweezers. 'No need to hold the head now, Graham. I think we're clear.'

Graham took the receptacle and held it for her. She used the tweezers to remove a multitude of shards and nuggets from Alex Ludner's mouth, placing them carefully in the bowl. Some were well over three inches and covered in dried bloody streaks.

Eventually she'd removed so many that the man's mouth could close naturally.

'There we go,' she said. 'That's as many as I can get without cracking him open at this stage. We've got a veritable jigsaw puzzle here, as it is.'

Ellie saw Drake focused on the bowl containing the shards of glass. She wanted to piece all the different colours and shapes, and she could sense he was itching to as well.

Tanv opened the man's mouth one more time, using a torch to shine into the cavity.

'Oh, hang on, what's this . . .'

'What? What is it?' Drake demanded.

'Patience, Drake.' Tanv frowned as she twisted her head and hand into a position to retrieve something.

She pulled out the object and squinted at it under a light. 'It looks like photographic paper or an actual polaroid, unless I'm mistaken,' she noted. 'One second while I make a few notes, then I'll smooth it out for you.'

After speaking into her mic, she brought it to a table and ushered them over. She turned on a lamp and worked on unscrewing the photo.

'What is that?' Ellie queried as the pathologist continued working on it.

'Is that . . . Is that a picture of a *room*?' Drake said, looking at Ellie in surprise.

16

A photograph of a room? Why the hell would anyone stuff a picture of a room inside someone's mouth and beat them to death? Was it a way for the killer to really make it personal to the victim somehow? Maybe an attempt to lead their investigation astray, or perhaps even a breadcrumb for them to follow?

Drake focused on the picture, trying to make out what the killer could be trying to tell him. Just looking at it made his eyes strain, the aesthetic reminding him of polaroids from 60s and 70s America with their soft focus and brown and orange interiors. The sepia hue of it all.

The image was painfully, frustratingly blurred, as though someone had taken it in a rush, or the shutter speed had been set for too long. There were also seams, cracks and stains where it had been screwed up and shoved down the man's throat, which obfuscated the subject somewhat. But it was a picture of a room they were looking at, that much was clear.

The room in the photo was dirty-looking and barren. A single-sized metal bed frame and mattress on one side, with an undefined blurry shape on it. The photo had been taken from near floor-level, making it hard to make out more than that. To the left side of the picture was a small log burner or stove, similar to the ones that peppered sitting rooms up and down the country these days. In the centre was a smear, likely a figure, mid-motion and completely undefined to Drake's eyes. A brown and white blur of movement. Possibly mid-movement to someone or something?

'Can anyone make out what that is?' he said, pointing at the centre of the picture.

'Beats me, Chief. I'd say it was a person for sure, but, male or female? And what they were doing? Your guess is as good as mine,' Ellie replied, her voice giving away her frustration at another vague clue.

Tanv nodded. 'I'll echo DS Wilkinson's thoughts. I'm not even sure if an expert could undo the damage and sharpen up the subject to a level that could prove useful to you.'

'Don't say that, Tanv. I don't want my blood pressure going any higher than it already is, thanks,' he said, and pursed his lips.

'Sorry, Drake, but that's my view,' she said, straightening up from leaning on the table. 'Also, I'm sorry, but we need to continue with the post-mortem. There's still the woman to work on. There'll be more time for analysing the evidence later.'

'Oh, sure, Doc. In the meantime, though, can your *assistant* please ensure we get copies of the photo as soon as possible?' he asked, glaring at Reynolds. 'Send them to DS Wilkinson and I. We'll pass them on to the rest of the team once we've given them some context.'

'Of course.' Tanv cast a glance in Reynolds' direction. 'Graham, would you do the honours?'

'Yep.' Reynolds picked up another camera and made his way to the table, averting his gaze from Drake.

Drake motioned for Ellie to follow him back to where Alex

Ludner lay, ignoring the former SOCO. He watched as the doctor continued her work while the digital chiming of the second camera went on in the background.

Tanv made fast work of cracking open the man's chest, noting his fractured and broken ribs before trimming away at the rib cage with a pair of rib shears. She went on with expertly removing his internal organs: examining, weighing and photographing them using a plinth and various measuring instruments.

Drake could see Ellie's face pale slightly as the pathologist cut, dissected and massaged the man's organs, her gloves increasingly covered in fluids as she went on. Before long, she'd started dissecting the man's neck, peeling back layer after layer of tissue and muscle to expose his oesophagus and the glass lodged within. Drake admired her handiwork.

Drake mentally gambled on the cause of death being asphyxiation as per the previous day, and Tanv deemed him the winner when she said as much. Though she was keen to stress that if he'd had a passageway with which to breathe, he would have died soon after from massive internal haemorrhaging and asphyxiation, essentially drowning in his own blood.

'Grim.' Ellie observed.

'You've got that right. Whoever did this needs to be stopped, and stopped fast.' His mouth down-turned in disgust.

'Good thing we're on the case, eh?' she said, coughing from the smell of the man's bodily fluids and holding her nose.

'You may want to turn away here. Some people find this part particularly off-putting. Heaven knows why.' Tanv said, making quick work of shaving the man's head and readying herself to access the man's skull and brain.

Ellie's eyes widened at the realisation of what was about to happen, audibly gagging and turning away at the sound of saw biting skull.

The Ties That Bind

* * *

Soon after, and much to Ellie's visible relief, Dr Kulkarni turned her attention to the second victim, their Jane Doe. The rough stitching seemed even harsher from where the blood had drained away from her extremities, her lips blue. The dark stitches contrasting sharply against the increasingly pale, near translucent olive skin.

'Well, this should be simpler, at least,' Tanv said jovially.

Ellie grimaced in response.

Drake was worried the doctor was going the way of Ellie, making light of even the darkest of situations. But he supposed she had a right. Such was her job, working on the dead, day in, day out. He was sure they'd be fast friends in time.

During the slight break, Graham Reynolds had made his way back over to assist with his boss's work.

Drake grumbled to himself; he had no time for the man. Somehow, Reynolds had advanced as a 'professional' despite his mistakes and incompetencies. He'd cost them time, possibly even lives on the Family Man case. Perhaps even his wife's life. Drake felt as if failure was being rewarded somehow. He realised he might be seen as irrational, his recent experiences clouding his judgement, but there was just something about the man that had always seemed off.

Drake batted away the images of his wife from his mind for the hundredth time that day and tried to focus.

The pathologist started her inspection, noting there was no identity as yet. She estimated the woman to be a similar age to the man, no more than mid-forties. There seemed to be no unique features that were of note to the investigation, besides her mouth stitching.

She pulled back the sheet covering the body, then paused and frowned, the only part of her expression he could make out due to her mask and glasses. 'Drake, I think you may have got your first link.'

'What? What do you mean?'

'The woman also has this sort of branded mark beneath her hip bone.' She pointed with her gloved finger. 'See, here?'

'Shit, you're right. What the hell could that signify? Have you seen that before? Two bodies, with a symbol like that?'

'Never.'

'Could be that they were together after all, maybe some sort of ritualistic shit that they were into? Some misguided coupling through scarring?' Ellie suggested.

'Hmm, one to highlight to the team.' Drake said, nodding at Ellie.

He saw Reynolds working at a computer out of the corner of his eye. The man appeared to be mid-uploading of the photos he requested.

Could it be that I may actually get something in time from the man? Good lord.

They stood back as the pathologist took more photos and made more notes on the condition of the body, before finally back to focus on her head.

'Okay, so I'm just going to unknot one end and go from there,' she said, in a matter-of-fact manner, as though she unstitched people's mouths on a daily basis.

'Would it not be better just to cut one end?' Ellie asked.

'It may come to that, but I want to preserve it in one piece as best I can for now.'

The pathologist began working on the bulbous knot to her left and soon worked the ends free. Taking the end, Tanv threaded the thick thread out of the wounds, the lips and surrounding skin quivering and puckering grotesquely. Finished, she handed them to Reynolds for cataloguing.

'Right, more glass work. Let me see if there's an accompanying picture secreted in her throat too,' she mused. 'Chance would be a fine thing.'

Tanv worked methodically, the woman's cheeks and face becoming less contorted the more she unpacked. There appeared to be less glass this time round.

'Right,' she said, sounding satisfied. 'Now, let's see what else may be in there.'

Once again, she used a torch to shine some light in the cavity.

'Looks like you're out of luck, detectives. No picture here.' She tilted her head in the other victim's direction. 'Looks like your man there was a one off.'

'You sure?'

'No, Drake, I was just saying it to piss you off,' she deadpanned. 'I said there was nothing there, and there's nothing there. Okay?'

'All right, all right. Nothing meant by it, Tanv.'

'Good.'

'Are you thinking there'll be much more to this one than the first?' Ellie asked the doctor.

'Not looking that way to me at the moment.'

Drake suspected she was right. The female victim felt almost secondary somehow, but the actual sewing of her mouth felt more controlled. It was like the killer was in a different mindset. Perhaps the male victim had provoked or caused the killer additional problems, perhaps the order was the other way round and he was second? There had to be something more to this. But Drake was at a loss right now.

'Could you estimate time of death for each victim yet, Tanv?' he asked

'They had only been in situ since the previous evening, from what we can tell. And based on all the usual factors, it would appear likely they died within an hour of each other. Either way, do you think there's really any pertinence to that? Will it matter if he was first, or she was? I suspect the answer is "No" in the grand scheme of things, don't you?'

'Fair point. Ever thought about becoming a detective?'

She winked. 'No. Doesn't pay enough.'

'Another fair point.'

Ellie piped up. 'Tanv, while you continue your work . . . can we take a further look at the glass? Perhaps try to rearrange it somehow?'

'As long as you keep it to that table there, then you can try it. Don't directly touch any of the particularly bloodied ones – remember to put some gloves on first too. You handle it or lose any of it and I'll kill you myself.'

Ellie raised her eyebrows and inched away from the pathologist.

Given Tanv's penchant for cleanliness, Drake wasn't sure if she was joking.

'Got it! Death by pathologist if mishandled,' Ellie said. She took two sets of gloves from the nearby dispenser, handing one to Drake, who made a face as he fiddled with putting them on.

Reynolds spoke up. 'One second, please, before you start on that.'

He grabbed the bowl containing Alex Ludner's glass and took it to the side table Tanv had indicated. He then took a lipped tray from a cupboard, and emptied the glass carefully onto it.

'There, more surface area. That way, it's less likely to go off the edge and you can spread it more.'

Ellie nodded at his patronising comment. Drake felt she wasn't the man's biggest fan, either. *Good.*

He tried to ignore the cracking and wet noises coming from behind them as Tanv worked on the woman, and focused on the task at hand.

'Okay.' Drake picked up one of the larger shards of glass, doing his best not to touch the dried blood smeared on the edge and tip and held it up to the light. He continued picking up further pieces, one by one. 'Pieces appear largely flat, not curved or shaped like a glass bottle. So, we could be looking at what? Some sort of stained-glass window? Like a church window, perhaps?'

Ellie nodded. 'It seems that way.'

'Let's see if any of them look like they go together.'

They started work, treating the glass like pieces of a jigsaw. They sorted through the shapes carefully, mostly focusing on the shards rather than the nuggets and collecting the colours. But nothing was really coming together as they worked; in front of them lay a jumbled-up mess of saliva and blood-stained clear, red, blue, green and orange glass pieces.

Drake pondered. 'Hmm, if this is from a stained-glass window, we'll be missing the adjoining lead pieces to bring the segments together, right? Without those, we may never get the right shape for each section.'

'Don't say that, Boss. You're knocking my hopes here.'

'Just being a realist. We may need a stained-glass expert, if there is such a thing for this sort of scenario. Perhaps they could figure out what the image could be? Thought I imagine they'd have to work from the image, which sort of defeats the bloody object, eh?'

'Or it could just be a dead end for now.' Ellie's face fell.

'Or that—' His phone interrupted him, the ringing seeming rudely loud in the environment they were in.

There was an agitated 'You going to answer that?' from Tanv as he scrambled for this phone.

It was Becca's sister, Rachel.

What could she want? He thought. *Has something happened to Eva?*

He frowned and made for the exit. 'Ellie, you carry on here, and meet me outside if you feel that there's nothing more to be seen here, like me,' he said, turning to Tanv. 'Thank you, Tanv, I've got to take this. May not be back. Appreciate your work.' She nodded at him and shooed him away with a bloodied glove as he hurried out the door.

17

'Rachel? What is it? Is Eva okay? Has something happened?' Drake burst through the fire exit, his heart pounding in his chest. Cold air swirled around him as the white noise from an industrial fan unit drowned out the call. He paced further away, the sound dimming.

If anything's happened to her—

'What was that . . . ? John? Hi? Whatever. In answer to the question I heard, nothing's wrong. Don't worry, she's fine.'

He exhaled loudly in relief. He ran his free hand through his hair, the thin strands greasy and unwashed.

'Ah, Jesus. Thank God for that. I never hear from you, so expected the worst.'

'Yeah, sorry, work . . . you of all people should know,' she retorted bitterly.

'Did you call to make me feel like crap? If so, too late. I already feel terrible.'

'Aww, poor you. You think I give a damn how you feel, John? Need I remind you that because of you, my sister is *dead*. I couldn't give a flying fuck what you feel,' she hissed down the phone.

'Yeah, don't I know it? So come on, is this about you and me, or Eva? If it's Eva, we should at least try to be civil.' He tried to remain calm. She could really rile him up with her snide tone. But he always felt strangely conflicted because, as well as being the spitting image of his wife, she also *sounded* incredibly similar. However, that was where the similarities ended.

'Well, as you may *not* have noticed – you being you and all – Christmas is just round the corner. You thought about – I don't know – seeing your teenage daughter, perhaps? The girl I look after on your behalf? Maybe doing something with her on Christmas Day, huh?'

Truth was, it hadn't occurred to him. He felt the familiar pang of guilt in his chest.

Drake continued running his hand through his hair. A ginger cat leapt onto the fence behind him as he tried to think of the words to say, to make things better, more reasonable at least.

'Of course I had,' he lied. 'I just hadn't thought of how it would work. Becca was murdered in our house, so I can't imagine Eva would want to spend Christmas there. And this shitty flat I'm staying in is no place for her.'

'I don't want you in my house, John.'

'I know that,' he snapped. 'But I can't see any other alternative, can you? I'm surprised she'd even want to see me anyway, judging by the past few times. Why the change of heart?'

'She's not having a change of heart. This is me trying to do the right thing by her, despite my own thoughts and feelings. She's your daughter, and my niece.'

'I see. Can I speak to her?' He leaned against a wall.

'No, now's not a good time. She's not having a good day. Her medication has made her feel ill – you know, the meds she's on because of the depression caused by you. She hardly sleeps, and when she does, she wakes up screaming, John. Her friend ain't much better either, even if she is mute.'

Drake squeezed his eyes shut and squatted down against the wall, trying to hold back tears. He'd thought Eva was off all that now. The medication was supposed to have only been something to get her through the initial pain of it all. Eva had lied to him, he realised. Even though she hated him, she'd still spared him the thought of her own pain. Even now.

'I need to see her. You know it's the only way to resolve this.'

He heard Rachel sigh loudly. 'Fine. Okay. But not today, all right?'

'Okay then, when?'

'Tomorrow evening for dinner? You're buying.'

'Done.'

She hung up the phone.

Drake remained squatted against the wall in silence, his fists balled against his forehead as he tried to suppress the rage building deep in his gut.

18

'Everything all right?' Ellie asked, poking her head around the corner.

'Oh yeah, everything's just great,' Drake snapped, still hunched against the wall.

He wondered how long he'd been out there. It was hard to tell. He was in the midst of some sort of brain fog, he realised, his senses dulled. Standing, he tore off the surgical gown before disposing of it in a nearby bin and walked towards the building's fire exit. Ellie followed suit without a word. He knew she'd learned quickly when and when not to press him.

'Anything more I should know about from the postmortems?' he asked as they neared the reception.

'No, nothing more came of it,' she said, nearly bumping into him as he slowed his pace to let someone pass. 'I asked Dr Kulkarni to put together the reports and send them over personally, though,' she went on. 'We both know that "Graham" is inept. Still seems weird hearing his first name.'

'Good idea.' His voice and their footsteps echoed along the polished corridor.

He tapped on the glass of the door leading to the main reception, and the receptionist buzzed them through.

Ellie let out an exaggerated sigh of relief as they exited back out into the fresh air proper.

'Glad to be out of there, Drake. That was not pleasant, and the *smell* . . .' she said, sniffing the arm of her dark suit jacket. Drake noticed that she wasn't in plain clothes to the same level that she normally was. A suit and shirt wasn't her normal attire.

'Why the more formal look?' he said, ducking into his car.

'I suspected you might treat me to a post-mortem today, so didn't want any of my nicer clothes tainted by god knows what.'

'I see.' He gave a light huff of amusement.

Navigating the early afternoon London traffic caused Drake untold consternation. But, having finally made it back to the office and back to a priority parking space that was now earmarked for him as the SIO, he was relieved. That relief didn't last long when he realised his next appointment with the psychologist had started ten minutes ago.

That's the last thing I need right now.

He didn't take in what Ellie was saying as he got out of the car, locking it hurriedly as he made his way to the building entrance.

'. . . Drake, you okay?' Came her voice from back by the car.

'Yeah, sorry,' he said as she caught up to him with a look of concern on her face. 'Got somewhere to be. You okay with relaying what we've found so far to the team, if they're about?'

'Of course. You going to be gone long?'

He looked at his watch, not really understanding why that would give him a sign of how long he'd be. He knew the time; he knew the session was going to be an hour of his life he wouldn't get back.

'Not long, maybe an hour, if that. I'll come straight to the investigation room, soon as I can.'

'Got it.'

* * *

Drake paced through the tangle of twists and turns the building offered until finally coming across a set of nondescript rooms. In order to remain discreet for the occupants, and particularly an occupant of his seniority, there were no signs to advertise their true purpose.

He burst into the new room they were going to be using without knocking, causing the psychologist to look up from her temporary desk with a start.

'Sorry—'

'Do you usually burst into rooms like that?' She questioned, interrupting his apology.

'No?'

She gave Drake a half-smile. 'I see, well . . . please, sit down. Make yourself comfortable.'

He moved over to the dilapidated chair she'd pointed to, low-backed with cheap oak arms and a brown fabric cover that had seen years of use. The prominent springs poking into his arse soon confirmed the level of use when he sat down. Other than the other arse probe of a chair opposite him, the rest of the room was sparse, containing the basic desk at which she sat, her laptop and a box of tissues (for him?) along with an errant set of old phone handsets in the corner of the room in a makeshift pile. It reminded him of dreary, old conference rooms and it depressed him. Surely not what she wanted him to feel when coming to one of their meetings? Not that it was much of a stretch for him to feel that way anyway, he supposed.

Dr Proctor-Reeves got up from the desk and sat in the chair opposite him before crossing her legs and resting her notebook on her lap. She remained silent.

He broke the deadlock finally. 'So, you won't reprimand me for being, what . . .' he looked at his watch, 'fifteen minutes late?'

She tilted her head. 'No, DCI Drake, I won't. It's your time. It's not for me to reprimand you for being late.'

'Is this some reverse psychology trick? Are you saying I should reprimand myself, if anything? Is that it?'

'No, not at all.'

'Okay, then what should we be doing?'

'What would you like to do?'

I've not got time for this.

Drake gripped the arms of the chair tightly, his knuckles slowly turning white, his jaw set.

'What would you suggest? You're the psychologist, after all.'

'Okay,' she said, setting one hand on top of the other, maintaining a neutral look. 'Let's start simple. How are you feeling today?'

'How am I feeling? I've just had to watch a pathologist take apart two murder victims, piece by piece. How do you think I feel? I'm not feeling elated. I can tell you that for free.'

'Sounds like a difficult, though necessary, part of your job. A task you've experienced before? Why don't you tell me how you *feel* and we can try to understand?'

He paused in an attempt to maintain his composure. A clock ticked in the background somewhere behind him. 'Okay.'

'How about you close your eyes, take a few deep breaths, and tell me what springs to mind? No suppression on my account, please. I want honesty.'

He entertained her suggestion and closed his eyes, a slight

ringing in his ears the only sound which could be tinnitus for all he knew.

They sat in silence. Drake took a deep breath while focusing on the sensation.

Within moments, a familiar image flashed in his mind: Becca bleeding out in their kitchen. He breathed out, his hands gripping the chair.

Second inhalation; and more images: her ribs cracking, blood gushing from a slit throat. Drake winced and exhaled, his eyes quivering as he struggled to keep them closed.

Third and final breath: his mind cloaked in darkness before a memory of Eva's screaming echoed inside his head.

He exhaled, catching his breath and doing his best not to cough.

'What do you feel?' She queried in the psycho-analytical sort of way that aggravated him.

'I . . . I don't want to say.'

She probed further. 'What do you think that means?'

'That I'm not . . . that I'm not ready to say?'

'Perhaps. But, try. If not for me, then try for yourself.'

'Okay,' he said, taking a moment more. 'I feel . . . I feel *nothing*.'

He felt a niggling twitch at the corner of his eye.

'Really? Nothing at all, John?'

He noted the use of his first name, the disapproving tone that she must have mistakenly let through her veneer. He opened his eyes and saw her writing something in her notebook. She looked up.

'And why do you think you feel nothing?'

He stood up. This was not helping him. If he wanted to be prodded and probed, then she should save it for a time when he wasn't up to his neck in death. This wasn't right.

'I've not got time for this, Doc.'

She gestured calmly towards the chair. 'John . . . Drake. Please, sit.'

He sighed and sat down again. 'Okay, but if this is going to go the way I think it's going to go, then I'm out of here.'

'So, why do you feel these feelings of . . .' she looked down at her notes, 'essentially emptiness?'

'I didn't say emptiness. I said nothing. There's a difference.'

His mind flitted back to the previous evening, and the morning before that: the half-hearted attempt on his own life. The panic attack. The wall . . . the anger.

I can't mention any of that, he thought. *She'll recommend to Miller I'm put on leave, or worse. I'm on my last chance. I can't let it jeopardise the case, I can't let it jeopardise me.*

He remained silent, unsure of what to say.

'Drake, do you think you're purposefully punishing yourself? That you feel you need to, perhaps . . . *atone* for what happened? Is this why you're not being forthcoming with me?'

'What? No.'

She's probably on to something there.

'Right.' She snapped her notebook shut and placed her pen on top. 'Okay, I think that will be all for now. Next time – and there *will* be a next time – I expect you to be more open with me. You're holding back, and you know it. I may be here to listen, but I have my limits and patience, and there's only so much I can do with those that don't want to be helped. Remember, it's not just your mental health that is at stake here.'

'And you think saying that is going to help?' he snapped, his irritation getting the better of him. 'You think that sort of pressure is going to aid this . . . charade?'

Her eyes narrowed ever so slightly. 'No, but maybe it will help bring a certain element of . . . focus.'

She stood and opened the door for him.

19

I learnt about punishment from a young age.

From that time, that period, everything had changed. Nothing was quite so simple anymore, quite so . . . *carefree*. I wasn't sure why it had happened or how it came to be, but it had happened all the same.

It was just something I had to deal with.

And dealt with it, I did. As best I could, day after day, night after odious night.

Nobody should have to deal with what I had to and *how* I had to. Nobody.

I struggled through, though – boy, how I struggled.

And persevered.

I still do.

Despite it being over now, the memories, the pain . . . they all remain. They're not going anywhere.

But it is different now. For that, I am thankful, but also . . . also *angry*. So, *so* angry.

Their punishment is due.

It is only fair.

20

Ellie sat and drank her coffee while observing her new teammates from the corner of the room. There was a nice hubbub of activity between the core team, amidst the coming and going of various analysts and support teams directed by DI Melwood. The three seemed a curious bunch, not misfits, perhaps, but certainly not people she could see working a typical CID job. Melwood, with his apparent knack for rubbing people the wrong way; it surprised her he'd got to Inspector rank with that quality in this day and age. Strauss, with his particular brand of self-assuredness, blunt nature and apparent dislike of small talk. And finally, Chambers, with her quiet inexperience and nervous nature.

Ellie couldn't shake the feeling that the high-on-ups might have dumped them on Miller and Drake as a means of keeping Miller quiet. Also, Miller giving her the earliest 'opportunity' that came up. The word could mean the complete opposite these days. Pulling a ragtag bunch together was a strange thing to do considering the severity of the crimes, but it was how it was done in SMT – Specialist in name, but haphazard in nature this past year. She got the impression they were permanently scrounging for resource rather than being sought. Other than her own application a year earlier, the gossip king, Dave, had told her there'd been few other applicants since. Perhaps what had happened with Drake had put people off?

In her mind, the police weren't exactly experts at decision-making these days and the less said about the top brass, the better. Bunch of snide brown nosers and boot lickers, more akin to politicians than proper police. Say what the public wants to hear to the camera. Reel off empty promise after empty promise, then disappear to a different team – *opportunity* – when the stats show up their screw ups.

Ellie scrunched her nose, tutting to herself at the notion.

'Good stuff, cheers,' Melwood said to someone on his mobile, scribbling notes on a piece of paper, his leg crossed over his knee. 'Excellent . . . right . . . let me know the address as soon as you can.'

He finished his phone call just as Drake entered the room with a beleaguered look etched on his face. Ellie had to admit she was getting more worried about him again; there was something bothering him, she knew it. He'd worn the same expression when she'd last worked with him.

Why? she pondered. *I know things haven't been great, but still.*

'Ah . . . Drake, just in time,' Melwood said, leaning back in his chair, his elbow now resting on the desk. 'I've got a few developments for you.'

'Let's hear it. I'm in need of some good news, Inspector,' Drake half-muttered, appearing distracted.

Chambers turned to hear the news, reaching over and tapping a headphone-clad Strauss on the shoulder. He took them off, but the music continued to blare out, before he realised and stopped it.

'What? Oh, sorry,' he said, shrugging his shoulders as Melwood and Drake glared at him.

Melwood got up and walked to the whiteboard, now populated with placeholders for the photos that would be coming in from Dr Kulkarni. He snapped up a whiteboard pen and started writing while he spoke.

'Alex Ludner, we now know works – or worked – at a supermarket up in Acton. He's got no direct family left to inform, just some distant cousins that live up in Newcastle. No marriages, divorces. No priors – he's basically as dull as dishwater. Nothing from the preliminary checks jumps out to give an indication of why this happened. He's worked at the same supermarket for over ten years.' Melwood underlined *No priors* on the board.

'Okay. And—' Drake started.

'Sorry, sir, just to add to that . . .' Strauss piped up.

Ellie winced; this could go one of two ways with Drake when someone interrupted him. Strauss realised what he'd done, stopped and waited for Drake's word.

'Go on, Sergeant.'

'Okay.' Strauss said. 'I've done some digging around the old pub where the victims were held. The owner died a couple of years ago. It's all dragging on in probate at the moment, so nothing seems of use from that angle. I'll do some more digging, but there doesn't seem to be any link to Alex Ludner directly at this stage.'

He cocked his head at the whiteboard. 'Obviously, I'll do another pass once we get the ID on that female. We've coordinated some uniforms to knock on doors in the surrounding area too, but with that location . . . there won't be much to go on, in my opinion.'

'Good, Strauss. Nice work, Melwood,' Drake said, nodding in their directions.

Ellie noticed the mound of beige coffee cups nearly spilling over from the bin. The smell of shit coffee made her strangely thirsty.

She shook the thought from her head, listening while Drake picked up where he left off. 'Do we have a contact at his work that we could speak to if there's no immediate family? We need to get a bead on what this guy was like, whether he was into anything unusual,' her boss said, reeling thoughts off out loud. 'They could point us toward a workmate perhaps, someone he may have confided in?'

Strauss had been bobbing his head as Drake had reeled off his thoughts. 'One step ahead of you, Drake. Just waiting on the details now for his boss.'

'Sod a home visit. Let's just get on over to the store after we're done here. Phone ahead to see if whoever we need to talk to is still on shift.'

I hope that's where I come in.

Melwood raised his eyebrows. 'Sure thing, sounds like a plan.'

'Chambers?' Drake looked over at the blonde DC, who didn't look up in response. 'Gemma?'

'Oh! Erm, sorry! N-no, nothing from my end just yet. I'm drawing blanks on the woman so far.'

'Okay, well, keep pursuing that. We need to figure out her part in this sooner rather than later. I don't want to wait on DNA. She may not be on the system, anyway.'

Ellie watched him scratch the back of his head, his mouth a thin line.

'Check the latest missing persons' reports, anything that might lead us to identifying her. That goes for all of you if you are stuck for something urgent to do, okay? And someone look into the marks she and Alex have on their hips, I trust you've read the report despite the lack of photos just yet. Perhaps that might lead us somewhere. Speaking of which, we should have those photos now, surely?'

'Yes, sir. They've literally just come through now. I'll get those up on the whiteboard soon.' Strauss confirmed, the sound of a printer whirring into life in the background.

Ellie beat Strauss to it and grabbed the print outs, placing them on the board. The strange circular scarring, the bloodied glass shards laid out on a tray for Alex Ludner, the second for the Jane Doe. Bruised and battered faces minus duct tape and stitching juxtaposed the covered face shots from earlier.

Her stomach roiled at the memory of Tanv placing the Jane Doe's brain on a stand for recording purposes. It made her head feel funny, like her brain was telling her not to think of doing the same any time soon. At least Drake hadn't been there to see that. She was already embarrassed at her behaviour, and the images had reminded her of it again when she least expected it.

Chambers put up the last picture, looking green about the gills. She mumbled something about a phone call, and hurriedly left the room.

Ellie had to admit she was glad she wasn't on the grunt work like Chambers. She'd had her fill these past few months. Visiting the store with Drake would be next on the cards. She always enjoyed the interviews, the potential for discovery always a pull.

'This polaroid then, eh?' Melwood nodded in its direction, having sat down again. 'What do you guys think of it? It's hard to make out, isn't it? Photographer's clearly got no sense of what makes a good composition.'

Ellie posited. 'Perhaps it was taken by accident?'

'Yes, perhaps the camera was dropped, and it went off?' Strauss concurred.

'All possible theories,' Drake said. 'Can we get someone with some image manipulation ability on that? Strauss, you're a bit of a techie, I hear?'

'Think it might be pretty tough to get anything out of it, but I've got the file on my computer. I could have a play. May need something a bit more powerful than this *scheiß* laptop, though,' he said. He seeming excited, his eyes lighting up at the prospect.

Ellie smiled to herself at his use of the German word for shit. If she didn't know his name, she wouldn't have guessed he was from there. The man must have lived in England for a long time. In her experience, most people who moved to England sounded American when they spoke English, mostly because they'd picked it up from films and television series. She'd need to interrogate him about it, she decided. She was nosy like that.

'Okay. Melwood, give me the details of this shop, and I'll go over there with Ellie,' Drake said. 'Give me the guy's home address too, and we'll stop by there afterwards. One more thing, can you do some digging around this glass? Maybe we could bring someone in who knows a thing or two about it. Might be a long shot, but what else can we do?'

Melwood scratched at his knee. 'Sure thing, I'll get on that now. Drake, I would like to go out in the field a bit myself at some point, you know.'

'Thanks, Melwood,' Drake said, putting down the whiteboard pen and ignoring his comment. 'As ever, let me know of any developments.'

Everyone nodded and turned back to the screens.

Ellie grabbed her suit jacket off the back of the chair and got a whiff of hospital, causing her to screw her nose up in disgust.

Bloody hospitals.

21

Drake pulled up a seat in the modest office on the top floor of the supermarket. The floor appeared to be reserved for staff, with an office canteen and dining area, meeting rooms, and other such things necessary for the day-to-day operations. He didn't pay it much mind. The building was just a faceless store, not anything like the old village shop back in Barndon run by the Jacksons. He understood the local shop was still closed since the incident that occurred there. He batted the encroaching memories from his mind. He didn't need more of that today.

Alex Ludner's boss, an aging, rotund blonde woman introduced as Clare Baker, plopped herself down in the chair on the other side of the desk, her large frame clad in a green uniform scrunching under the chair arms. She panted as she turned to face him properly and leant forwards, causing her dappled, fleshy cleavage to rest on the desk's surface. He could imagine her feet not reaching the floor beneath.

Ellie brought a chair round, back to front and sat with her arms leant on the top. This seemed to make the large woman nervous, judging by her eyes flitting between the two of them. The skin beneath her nose displayed a light sheen of sweat.

Ellie started, 'Thank you for making some time for us at such short notice, Mrs Baker.'

'It's *Miss* Baker,' the woman said curtly. Her small eyes narrowed, almost being engulfed by her cheeks. 'And I'm afraid I can't be long. We've got stock-take today. I need to be keeping things going, it being the damn Christmas season and all. We've been a man short for a few days now.'

'About that,' Drake said.

'Mmm?'

'Do you have an employee by the name of Alex Ludner?'

'Yes, why? Oh.' Suddenly it dawned on her why two detectives were in her office. Her eyes bulged. 'What has he done? Is he? Oh . . .'

'I'm afraid he's died.' Drake said, the words sounding blunter than he intended, but her manner aggravated him. Or was it that anyone he spoke to lately aggravated him? He flexed his hand beneath the desk.

'Oh my . . . erm, has his family been informed?'

Drake rested his other hand on the desk. 'He doesn't have any close family that we know of. Unless you'd like to correct us?'

'No – no, I'm not sure either. I didn't really know him. I'll check with HR when I get a minute.'

'He worked with you for over ten years, didn't he?' Ellie jumped in.

'Well, yes, but that doesn't mean we were best buddies, does it? He was just a man who showed up to work, did it – sometimes better than other times, mind – and went home again. It's a supermarket, not a pub,' she added snidely. 'We don't just sit and chat all day.'

The woman picked up a pen and started fiddling with it, passing it back and forth between her hands.

'So, what was he like?' Drake asked.

She shrugged. 'Just like . . . I don't know . . . quiet with most people. He seemed distant and in his own world.'

'You say *most* people,' Ellie pressed. 'Were there people he was more open and friendly with?'

Drake gave Ellie a look, which she ignored.

'Just another guy, Liam. They worked some nights together, other shifts. Guess they had to be pally, working that amount of time together.'

Ellie smiled. 'Unlike you guys.'

'Yes, unlike us. I'm his boss, and I don't make a habit of fraternising with staff,' she said, turning her nose up.

'Is Liam in today?'

'Why?'

'Obviously we'd like to speak with him.'

'As I said, I'm short-staffed—'

Drake clenched a fist under the table. He didn't have time for this.

'I don't think you quite understand. We're not *asking* you; we're *telling* you.' He seethed. 'This is a murder investigation. It's more important than whatever shit you've got going on with bloody stock. Okay?'

The woman's face turned puce in an instant, her mouth hanging open as though she'd never been spoken to that way in her entire life. She stuttered a few nonsensical words before finally forming a sentence. 'I'll put a call out for him over the tannoy now.' She squeaked.

'Good.'

He saw Ellie looking at him as if she was giving him a mental high-five.

The Ties That Bind

* * *

The woman put a call out over the supermarket's tannoy system and within a few minutes there was a knock on the thin door. Clare yanked on the handle and a man, presumably Liam, stuck his head round. He was a short man with a receding blonde hair line in his early thirties, wearing a stained green uniform. He reminded Drake of a blonde Oompa Loompa.

'Oh,' he said, seeing Drake and Ellie. 'What's this all about?'

Clare told him as he moved past her and sat down across from Drake and Ellie.

Still standing at the door, the woman announced, 'If you don't mind, I'm going to get on.' She pointed a finger in the man's direction. 'You come get me if I'm needed, all right? And hurry up about it.'

'Okay,' he said, his voice flat. The man's mood had dropped the moment his boss had blurted out what had happened to his friend.

Liam sat in the chair, playing with his hands, and stared at the floor. 'So, how did he die?'

'We can't give out that information right now.'

'Okay.' The man looked up, a light going on in his head. 'Wait, was that the one on the news? In those farmer's fields, by the woods in Barnet?'

'It was,' Drake said.

'Shit.' The man let out a dejected sigh, looking anywhere but at either of them.

'Did he ever have a reason to go there or that area, Liam?'

'No, not that I know of. Sorry. We're not *that* close. I just work with the guy – I didn't ever really see him outside of work. Besides, that's nowhere near where he lived in Acton, is it?' Liam shrugged. 'North London . . . Dunno why he'd go there.'

Despite the lack of new leads, the man was irritating Drake less than his boss. He seemed genuine enough, however this was getting them nowhere. Perhaps the victim's house would rustle up something for them. Still, Drake supposed he wasn't in this role for it to be easy and straight-forward.

He tried a new angle. 'Did Alex ever speak to you, perhaps about an incident that happened in the past, or a relationship with a partner that may have ended messily?'

The man sat and wiped his nose with his sleeve as he appeared to strain for any sort of memory.

'No, I can't remember anything.'

'Are you positive?' Ellie asked.

'Hmmm, no. I'm not, to be honest,' he said, appearing to strain harder. 'He was a private guy, you know? He never had a girlfriend in the time I knew him. Just played games on his computer and watched films on the weekend, I think. Sorry.'

Suddenly, a memory must have bubbled up to the surface of the man's brain. 'Oh! Actually, he mentioned some girl that he was with a few times, like, before he started working here. He lost his job soon after they broke up, apparently. Then he was here. He fucking hated working here . . .' He paused, suddenly embarrassed. 'Oh, sorry for swearing, heh.'

Ellie's eyes lit up at the response, her voice picking up pace. 'Can you tell us anything about her? What she looked like? What her name was, you know?'

'Hmmm . . .' He paused once again, sat in deep thought for a moment.

Drake could picture Ellie wanting to leap across the table and give him a good shake.

Finally, he shook his head. 'No, sorry. I don't think he ever actually said. Just that he was cut up about it.'

Maybe it's this Jane Doe of ours, Drake thought.

'Well, if you remember anything at all, please call us, okay?' Drake jotted down his mobile number and passed it to Liam, who nodded.

'You got it. Please find whoever did this. For Alex.'

22

Drake wished he had a car where he could just whack on the blues and twos. The image of lights and sirens blaring while he skimmed through all the accursed traffic bogging them down warmed his soul. Darkness had descended on the city, turning it into a sea of lights; cars, buses and vans of all descriptions, all pissing out pollution. London doing its bit for global warming, day after day.

He thought back to his time in the pub with Dave a few days prior, and yearned to be back there again. Maybe he would later. He needed some time to think. Funny that prior to the recent events, time was all he'd had.

'What's funny, Chief?' Ellie asked.

'Oh, nothing,' he said, strangely embarrassed. He must have chuckled out loud without realising. 'So, you enjoying being in the Drake-mobile again?'

'The . . . *Drake*-mobile? Really? You been on the sauce?' she said, then turned to him. 'Wait, should you be driving?'

'What? Come on . . . it's a glorious name, you'll see. It'll stick.'

'I thought I was supposed to be the silly one here?'

He winked at her. 'What can I say? I have my moments.'

Distinctly daft moment out of the way, it dawned on him he couldn't remember the last time he'd seen his daughter, and even longer since he'd seen her laugh or smile. Drake's momentary lift in mood took a marked dip. Maybe tomorrow evening's dinner at Rachel's would be a start of some sort? He had to have hope, however futile it may be.

'Here we go,' Ellie said as the traffic started moving again.

Drake weaved in and out of the traffic until, finally, they reached a street like many others in London. Though this one wore its rundown heart on its sleeve a little more than most.

'That's the one. Just there, beyond that bus stop.' Ellie confirmed from the details on her phone.

'Maybe I should just employ you as my navigator from now on. Might save me a few quid getting this piece of shit satnav fixed,' he mused.

Ellie mumbled a response, but he was too absorbed in what lay before him. Drake turned his nose up at the area. Flattened and mangled cardboard grocery boxes littered the dimly lit street, courtesy of the large commercial bins overflowing near a closed fruit and veg seller. The suspect stains (not unlike dog shit) and other miscellaneous litter, cluttered the pavements in front of the later Georgian terraces. The houses all looked in desperate need of sprucing up with some paint and masonry work at a bare minimum.

Drake moved to step out of the car, manoeuvring carefully over some stale vomit. London, the city that keeps on giving until you puke your guts up, he thought.

'Ah, home sweet home.' Ellie said, breathing in the air theatrically.

'What?' Drake cast an eye at her.

'This street, it's similar to mine. Just without all the literal and figurative crap lying around.'

'Oh, I see.'

Seeing the surrounding destitution, Drake suddenly had an urge for his quaint home on the outskirts of Barndon, Oxfordshire. The place his wife had died. The urge wore off immediately.

'Okay, so, he's the first-floor flat,' Ellie noted.

'Indeed.'

Drake opened the rusted gate. Brushing past the overgrown, waist-height weeds growing throughout their victim's front path and feeding into their neighbours. He noticed a light on in the ground-floor window.

At least we'll only have one door to get through if someone's in.

He noted the entryway had the faint smell of cat piss as he buzzed for the ground-floor flat. No one answered.

Drake sighed, his blood beginning to simmer. 'Come on, I don't have time for this.'

He buzzed again, and again . . . and again. Finally, a woman answered with an agitated, 'What!'

'Police. Let us in, please.'

'Oh, come on, you don't expect me to believe that, do you? Sod off.'

Drake rolled his eyes. 'We'll put our ID against your window.'

'Okay.'

He gestured for Ellie to do it. She leant down, plucking out her wallet and pressing it up against the glass.

A young girl pushed the curtain aside, squinting before making a face and disappearing. The door buzzed like a half-dead wasp and the door opened.

Drake entered the junk mail-ridden hallway and was soon confronted by the woman from the intercom. She wore an oversized white t-shirt with a stunned-looking cat and a rainbow on it, her dark hair tied up in a bun, and she seemed flustered.

'What's this about?'

'Does Alex Ludner live here?' He kept his agitation off, his game face on.

'Yeah, he's the next one up. What's he done?'

'He's not done anything. He's dead.'

The girl looked shocked. 'Oh!'

'Indeed.'

'Hang on . . . He didn't die in there, did he?' She pointed up at the ceiling.

'What? No. How would we know he'd died otherwise?'

'He might have done what those guys on Facebook and stuff have done, live-streamed their suicides.'

Drake looked at her in disbelief. 'That is *not* what happened.'

He looked back at Ellie. Her game face remained intact.

'You wouldn't happen to have a spare key or know of whom to contact for one?' She popped her head round Drake's frame to ask the question.

'Don't think he had anyone to give one to. He was a lonely sort of guy. Kept to himself. Been here much longer than I have. He had to ask me to take one – the landlord here is a right dick.'

'Please, can you retrieve it for us?'

'Sure. Does this mean I'll have a new neighbour soon?'

'No idea,' Ellie said, before Drake could snap at the selfish question.

The girl brought back the key and handed it to him.

'So, er . . . when did he die?'

'Two to three days ago, we believe.'

The girl looked taken aback. 'Really? Are you sure?'

'Yes. We're sure.' He pursed his lips.

'Oh,' she said, looking distressed. 'It's just that I heard some footsteps up there yesterday. Thin ceilings, and all that.'

Drake's eyes went wide, and he met Ellie's gaze. She looked fit to burst.

Turning his attention back to the young girl, he put out a reassuring hand and kept his voice low. 'Okay. Get back in your flat now or leave the premises, please. Is there anyone on the top floor too?'

'Shit! Okay, okay . . . no, it's vacant at the mo,' she whispered.

The girl disappeared back into her flat, the sound of frantic locking and bolting coming from her door.

'Drake, this might mean—'

'I imagine they're long gone by now, but best to err on the side of caution, eh?'

'Right.'

He wondered what had driven the killer to make a post-murder house call. Had they left evidence behind? Something that belonged to them? Drake needed to find out, and standing around wasn't going to answer anything.

'I'm going up.' He started on the stairs.

'Drake, we should really call in backup for this type of thing. We don't know if he's armed or what.'

'I know, I know. Just trust me, okay?'

Ellie sighed. 'Okay, but I'm coming with you.'

'No, you're not. You're staying here in case someone makes a run for it.'

'Drake—'

'Just do it, please. That's an order.'

He started making his way up, leaving an agitated Ellie to guard the base of the stairs.

He squeezed past a bike on the landing, dark marks on the surrounding walls. The general state of the place would have driven him crazy if he lived there. It reminded him of a flat he once owned. Becca had detested it, and he'd soon had to change his ways.

Rounding the banister, he saw the door to the flat a couple of steps ahead on his left. Whoever had entered or left had appeared to have at least closed the door behind them.

Drake strained his ears as he climbed the final couple of steps, listening for any telltale sounds as he approached the door, ensuring his shadow wouldn't be obvious to whoever could be inside.

There was only silence.

He reached over and put the key in the lock. He turned it carefully, wincing at the solid click. Pushing it open gently, thankful it didn't creak, he was greeted with nothing but the dim stillness of the flat. A kitchen lay directly ahead of him, lit only by the faint glow of a digital cooker clock, and a street lamp cast a faint sliver of light onto the lounge carpet through a gap in the curtains to his right. He'd noticed the curtains were drawn when they'd approached the house, but whether that had been done by the victim or the killer was anyone's guess.

Drake put his head around the door, scouting the rest of the hallway. There was the dingy light of a lamp in the bedroom, with a part-made bed in view.

He flicked his head back to the lounge, double checking for anyone or anything. His heart started beating faster. Should he go further, or heed Ellie's advice and wait for backup?

Before Drake had a chance to make that decision, the sound of someone barrelling towards him came from the direction of the bedroom. The door slammed into the side of his head, knocking him off balance.

'Drake!' Ellie shouted upon hearing the bang.

He let out a pained groan as the assailant shoved him out into the hallway. The back of his head slammed against the wall with a dull thud and he fell to the ground. Drake shot an arm out, grabbing a leg momentarily before it shook free, and the person bolted.

'Ellie! Grab them!'

All he could hear was the muffled sounds of a scuffle as he groggily clambered back to his feet and skirted round the landing banister and to the stairs.

He took the corner just in time to see someone in a hooded top barge past Ellie. The impact sent her cartwheeling backwards down the stairs in a tangle of limbs before the assailant made their escape running out and onto the street.

She appeared uninjured, made apparent by her scrambling to her feet and running after him before Drake had time to react.

'Ellie, no! Jesus Christ, *stop!*'

He pelted down the stairs as fast as he could, his legs feeling like jelly as he part-stumbled, part-ran to the gate of the property. His head darted around, spotting Ellie running up the road into the darkness, another faint figure beyond her.

'Jesus, stop!' Drake turned and pursued them both, pounding the street but gaining no ground. He was struggling to keep up, but Ellie appeared to be closing in. The assailant barged past a young couple as they walked their dog. Taking a few more strides before clambering up and over the barbed fence of a power substation and then again over the side, somehow seemingly unscathed.

Ellie stopped, realising the danger, and came to a halt, resting her hands on her knees to regain her breath as Drake caught up to her.

'Argh! Fucking bollocks!' she ranted, her voice catching through laboured breaths. He noticed she had a carpet burn on the top of her hand, otherwise she appeared remarkably fine. 'You saw, though, right? I can't go jumping into one of those areas – I don't want to get fried or shredded on the top of that fence. God knows how they did it.'

'No, you don't. Seriously,' he said. Trying to get his own breath back, he ran his hand over the back of his head, checking for anything out of the ordinary. He was relieved to find he wasn't bleeding.

'You okay?' he asked. 'You took quite a tumble on those stairs back there.'

'No, I'm good. Must have landed just right. You?'

'Yeah, think I'm okay, just a bruised ego. Did you get a look at them?'

'No. Whoever it was, they were wearing a face mask and had a hood up. I'd say it was someone skinny, white judging by their forehead. Could be male, maybe female though, didn't get a good enough look. Can't say for sure. Damn it!' She stood up, glaring at the electrical substation fence.

'We should get back to the house. Maybe we disturbed them in the middle of something.' He panted, still struggling to catch his breath. He was getting too old for chasing murderers.

* * *

'You two sure you're police?' The girl from the ground floor mocked as they made their way back inside.

'Go back inside your flat, now.' Drake shouted at her.

'Okay, okay.' She put her hands up and closed the door behind her.

'You were remarkably polite, Boss,' Ellie remarked with a pained smile.

They spent a good deal of time surveying the rooms. The lounge lights were now on, revealing their victim as something of a slob. Clothes hung on a clothes rack beside a desk, with a desktop computer and monitor dominating one side of the room, while a large flat-screen television blocked out the window. There were some dead plants, and the floor was seeded with food crumbs, empty cans of beer and soft-drinks. Nothing screamed 'This is why I am dead' to Drake. Just a single guy, living what seemed to be a solitary existence. It was strange. The place was so impersonal, there were no photos of family, or friends, nor of any activities. There were a few shelves full of films and video game cases, which would all need to be checked by SOCO, but otherwise, nothing.

The bedroom where Drake assumed the assailant came from wasn't remarkable, either. Condoms in a bedside drawer, underwear and clothes, the usual.

Was the intruder looking for something and didn't find it? Or did they find something and got it past them in the struggle? Drake couldn't tell. There appeared to be nothing left for them, nothing even close to similar to the glass or the photograph for them to find.

'Nothing jumping out at you, Ellie?' He called from the bedroom.

'Nothing. And nothing literally either, thankfully,' she answered distractedly from the kitchen. She still sounded aggravated at the outcome of her encounter.

'Back in the old days, I would have caught that fucker,' he heard her mutter as he went back to the lounge. Drake was unsure if she intended for him to hear it or not.

'You and me both,' he said, sighing to himself.

'What?'

'Nothing.'

He studied the desktop computer tower case.

No photos, nothing particularly personal about the place. We never found his phone either.

Liam had said that he played games and watched films in his downtime. Perhaps everything personal to him was on his computer?

Drake studied the computer tower further and rotated it. He didn't feel any resistance from cabling. It wasn't plugged in. In fact, *all* the cables had been detached. Curious.

He pulled on some gloves from his coat pocket, then carefully took hold of the desktop case, unscrewing the thumbscrews with his fingers and removing the side cover.

'Ellie,' he called.

'Yeah? What—'

'Gotcha.'

The hard drives appeared to be missing from the case. No solid-state drives, no old-fashioned hard drives. Nothing. Just a void where they should be.

'My thinking is whatever was personal to this guy was on that hard drive. And whoever we came across, came back for it.'

'Shit,' she said, studying the case before looking up at him.

'Yeah. Shit.'

23

Ellie rotated her shoulder gingerly in the bathroom back at headquarters. The tussle and fall on the stairs had left her feeling sorer than she expected now the adrenaline had worn off. She was still pissed at not having caught whoever it was, and no doubt would be until they caught the bastard. Still, on the bright side, she'd not broken her neck.

Thinking back on all the times she'd pursued suspects down alleyways, through gardens and over fences, she realised she'd actually enjoyed the thrill of confrontation. Though there were exceptions... She ran a finger over her scarred palm.

Melwood had followed the same thought process regarding potential injuries when she and Drake had arrived back in the office, egos bruised. They'd passed on their developments to the team. They'd spent time wondering what could have been on the hard drive that was worth risking going back for. Strauss, in particular, had wondered why the intruder would go back multiple times, if the girl on the ground floor was to be believed?

* * *

The Ties That Bind

Ellie had been staring at the strip lighting, lost in thought, for who knows how long, when Melwood brought her back to her senses with a jolt.

'Okay,' Melwood boomed, making a show of looking at his watch. 'We've kicked off a few fresh lines of enquiry and have a few things to wait on. What say we all go to the pub, eh? First rounds on me?' He followed up the theatrics with an excited rub of his hands.

Perhaps she'd been mistaken, having marked him down as being a guy that wasn't a team player, just one of the over-promoted yes men she disliked. Maybe he wasn't all bad? There was only one way to find out.

The rest of the core team had met Melwood's proposal with a resounding silence. Drake was sitting in the small cupboard, now known as the SIO office, so may not have heard, but Strauss and Chambers looked less than enthusiastic.

Well, if they're not going to rise to it, then I will. She thought. *For the good of the team, and all that.*

'Sounds good, Melwood. Where were you thinking?'

'The Crook, naturally? Best pub in our neck of the woods.'

She smiled. 'What do you think, guys?'

'I guess one wouldn't hurt,' Strauss answered. He closed the laptop and stuffed it in his rucksack. 'They better still have a few decent beers on tap, none of that lager crap.'

'Chambers? Come on. You been before?'

She spun her chair in Ellie's direction, Chamber's sporting the face of someone feeling under pressure. 'No, I've not actually . . . but, erm . . . sure, okay. Why not?'

'Drake?' she called through, waggling her hand like she was holding a glass. 'Pint?'

He got up from the desk and squeezed through back into the

main room. Same world-weary expression as earlier in the day. The expression soon changed when she repeated the question and he smiled, seeming genuinely pleased. 'Sure, let me just wrap up here, and we'll get on over. You could all do with a breather. I'll see if Dave's in the area too, would be good to see him.'

* * *

On the journey over, Ellie had kept Chambers company while Melwood talked shop with Drake and Strauss. She noted Strauss hadn't really joined in much, whereas Drake seemed to be genuinely engaged with whatever the Inspector had been waffling about, much to her surprise.

Chambers spoke mainly of her brother and sister, and how they'd all set to working in London in wildly differing careers. Ellie had failed to stop herself from talking about Bella, despite doing her best. She knew that waffling on about your own kids could get on people's nerves, but she couldn't help herself, and the conversation had been stilted. She was finding Chambers hard to gee up and awkward silences were not Ellie's strong point. Some people just didn't work that way, she supposed.

Soon after, they'd all ploughed into The Crook, pulling their coats off at the wall of heat that greeted them. Crowds lined the bar and spilled out onto the various tables, inside and out. Melwood grabbed a low-set table just as a group was leaving, throwing his coat to lay claim just ahead of an irritated-looking man. It seemed the DI had a knack for rubbing just about anyone the wrong way.

The group made themselves comfortable. Drake plopped down on one of the old-fashioned armchairs supported by a series of near-flat cushions, while Chambers sat on a low sofa which nearly swallowed her whole. Strauss joined her and nearly vanished into it as well, his knees nearly coming up higher than his head. Considering their experience, Ellie opted for a sturdier chair near Drake, though it towered over everyone, despite her comparatively short-stature.

Melwood remained standing and rubbed his hands together. 'Right, what we having?'

Everyone gave a preference, and he left to bother a barman. Strauss struggled out of the sofa to help, leaving the three of them at the table.

'So, how'd you find it today, Gemma?' Ellie asked, speaking over the table and the din.

'Yeah, it's pretty full on, I guess,' she said, trying her best to be heard.

'Pretty big opportunity for you, I'd say.' Ellie immediately cringed at herself for saying her least favourite word.

'Yeah, something like that.' Chambers looked down at her hands.

Ellie gave her best, most encouraging smile. 'Give it time, you'll warm to it,' she said. 'I think you've landed with a good bunch of guys for such a nasty case, but let me know if you need anything. I'm happy to help.'

'Thank you.' Chambers smiled meekly in return and clasped her hands in her lap.

Drake leaned over to speak to Chambers, and Ellie looked round the pub. She realised it had been a while since she'd been out for work drinks. Her life was taken up by work and family these days, and having the younger woman around almost made her miss her old single life. The late nights, the seemingly never-ending stamina. Out all night, working all day. The opposite when Response shifts called for it. Looking back on that period, she didn't know how she did it.

She soon spotted DS Bradfield entering the pub and scouting

for them. Ellie was always pleased to see him, having first worked with him on the Family Man case. He was easy to work with and they had a similar sense of humour – probably not a good thing for their colleagues when they were together, she suspected.

'Dave!' She called through the noise, waving when she failed to get his attention.

'Ellie! Ah, it's been so long.'

'Come on . . . it's been, what, a couple of days?'

'Yeah. Too long. Not won any more awards in that time, I hope?' he smirked. Or at least, she thought he did. Lately, his greying moustache was starting to overpower his face.

She cupped her hand to his ear. 'Get to the bar. Melwood – if you know him – is still ordering, and it's on him. Grey hair, looks like someone from London in the early 1900s, can't miss him.'

'I like your thinking. Seen him around, though I've not worked with him personally,' Dave said, before winking and disappearing into the throng.

The night wore on, and a few more drinks than expected were sunk. Dave and Drake had moved onto whisky, which Ellie turned her nose up at. Even Strauss and Chambers seemed to have loosened up slightly, though Strauss had been nursing the same pint for most of the night.

Her belly was warm and her cheeks flushed, but the first pangs of sleep were hitting all the same. She checked her watch; it was nearing closing. She'd have to get a taxi at this rate.

'So, how're you finding it, Strauss? Or is it Luka?'

'Either's fine.' He produced a faint smile.

'What made you join this merry branch of the Met?' she asked, not having to speak quite so loudly now a few people had left the pub.

His eyes dropped for a moment while he considered the question. She was slowly cottoning on to the fact he wasn't one for blurting out the first thing that came to mind. 'Just what happened when I was young, you know?'

She didn't know, but she let him continue. 'I had a pretty tough upbringing because of it, and I felt like I wanted to make a real difference to everyday people. Keeping the really savage criminals inside locked away – for good, if I had my way. Some things I saw growing up were . . . difficult to deal with,' he said, his eyes fixed on something past Ellie.

She found the answer strangely intense.

'What was it that happened, if you don't mind me asking?'

'Oh . . .' he said, sounding markedly German all of a sudden while he considered his answer. 'My parents died in a car crash. I survived and got placed in a children's home, then fostered out many, many times. Didn't get the best of treatment. I was a bit of a . . . difficult child, shall we say. But who wouldn't be?'

'Luka, I'm so sorry. That was rude of me to ask.'

'No, it's okay,' he said, producing a sad smile.

'Was that in Germany?'

'No, here. Soon after we got citizenship.'

'Did you move back?'

'Nope, no-one to move back to. No one that mattered anyway,' he said, staring into his pint, his messy hair flopping forwards into his eyes. He brushed it aside. 'Now I just catch bad guys. Pretty good at the tech side of things too, probably why I was brought on. I hear our SIO isn't that way inclined.'

'Yes, something like that,' she said, chuckling. 'He's still keen on paper and practical methods. Hence the whiteboard and a gazillion printouts rather than the software we could be using.'

Chambers broke off her conversation with Dave, who promptly vanished into the melee at the bar, and shuffled over to them from her side of the sofa.

'Mind if I butt in? What are you guys talking about?' She

said, seeming more energetic for the first time since she'd known her.

'Oh, just work.' Ellie smiled, taking another glug of her pint. 'Getting to know the gang?'

'Oh yes. Dave is a funny guy, isn't he?' Chamber's cheeks were decidedly flushed. 'Shame he's retiring soon-ish.'

Ellie still wished that he wasn't, but she'd do her best to keep in touch with him all the same. Good people were hard to come by. She found that more and more, the older she got.

She looked over at him at the bar. He seemed older at a distance. The wrinkles around his eyes and his neck more pronounced. Her heart sank a little.

Melwood jumped in.

'Sorry to interrupt. You guys want another?' he gestured with a tumbler. He'd joined in with Dave and Drake on the whiskies and seemed to be all the worse for it.

'No, no, I'm good, thanks,' Ellie said. 'I'll probably have to make a move soon. Going to need to get a taxi home. Any more nights like this without seeing my daughter to bed and Len will be signing the divorce papers.'

'Heh, well, you'll be in good company then,' he slurred. 'I got divorced six months ago. Can only see my son at weekends. Shit, eh?'

'Oh, that's so crap. I'm sorry.'

'What for? It is what it is. My own fault. I'll deal with it, make it right. Just not right now,' he said, the sadness in his eyes belying his cocksure response.

Well, I'm certainly getting to know people this evening...

'I think I'll pass too. Got to drive. My car's been sitting in the office carpark for so many days now, they'll tow it,' Strauss commented. Ellie thought he was cracking a joke, but his straight face said otherwise. 'Can I give you a lift home?'

'Oh, would you? That'd be great. Thanks.' She beamed. Ellie couldn't face paying for a taxi all the way across London, and the tube would be a slog at this time of night. She wasn't even sure if the District or Piccadilly lines would be open, such was the frequency with which she drove.

'Are you sure I can't convince you guys to stay? Feel like I'm only just getting to know you,' Melwood said, contorting his face in an exaggerated demonstration of sadness.

The Melwood personality switch was slightly unnerving. It was nice that he'd let his hair down, but maybe it was a little too much for a first night with the team.

Is that what being recently divorced does to someone? She thought of what Len would be like if they ever split. She couldn't even imagine it – she daren't. Unless he cheated on her, then she'd have his balls over a barbecue pit faster than he could say 'Sorry'.

Ellie chuckled malevolently to herself at the thought while gathering up her coat.

'You okay to leave now?' she asked Strauss.

'Yeah, sure,' he said, and gathered his things.

She made her way over to Drake.

'Be careful.' She let her concern show on her face. 'You shouldn't drink too much. You got knocked on the back of the head pretty badly this afternoon.'

He smiled at her. He wasn't drunk, but he seemed merry enough.

'What are you, my mum?' He laughed. 'Don't you worry about me. I'd worry about him, though,' he said, pointing in Melwood's direction. 'That's a man trying to make up for something.'

Even half-pissed, he's still got an eye for things.

'Don't ever change, Chief.'

'Not planning on it,' Drake smirked.

* * *

'That's the one,' Ellie said, pointing at the house. 'Thanks so much for the lift. I hope it's not too far out of your way.'

The ride had been surprisingly free of awkwardness, even with a few prolonged silences. Ellie decided against probing further into what he'd told her in the pub.

'A little, but what're teammates for? I sleep little these days, so it's something to do, you know?'

'Fair enough. Thanks, buddy.'

Strauss nodded, and she clambered out of the car, the fresh air hitting her and making her head spin. Perhaps she'd had a little more than she expected, after all.

Ellie waved off her new colleague and carried out her usual ritual of creeping through the gate and bypassing the door as stealthily as she could. There was no light tonight. The house stood shrouded in the night's gloom. Kicking off her shoes, she crept to the kitchen to grab a glass of water and steady herself before daring to creep upstairs. Settling back in the lounge, she let out a quiet, satisfied sigh and reclined further into the sofa.

Her phone started buzzing. When she glanced over at it, she saw a withheld number.

She snatched it up. 'Hello?'

'It's me.' The voice was low and strangely distorted, like a crackling vinyl.

Ellie remembered Len's message about a man trying to get a hold of her, but was struggling to remember if he'd told her a name. 'Yes, who is this?'

'Don't pretend you don't remember me.'

'No, I'm sorry. I don't recognise your voice. Who is this?'

Distorted laughter emanated from the phone. 'You will soon.'

'What do—'
The line went dead.

24

Ellie woke to the rare sight of light streaming through a crack in the curtains. The near constant grey skies of recent weeks had made her question whether they would ever leave. She yawned, her mouth gaping while she fought the desperate desire to have a few more minutes in bed. Perhaps it was moonlight, and she had a few more hours to claim as her own? Sadly, looking at the clock, she discovered it was the opposite. She was running late.

Her brain scrambled into gear, the memory of the crank call immediately making an unwelcome return.

She heard Len in the hallway. 'Len, did you get any more phone calls looking for me since the previous one?' she called.

He poked his head round the door. He looked exhausted in the half-light. What could be making him so tired?

'No, nothing. Sorry, love,' he said, flatly.

'Are you sure? Not just saying that to make me feel better, are you?' she said, pulling back the duvet cover and dragging herself to her feet.

'No, nothing, I swear . . . why?' Len pushed the door open

and entered the room, looking as handsome as ever in a dark grey suit and dark blue tie. Ready to go to work, taking Bella to primary school on the way as usual.

'Just got a crank call last night when I got in, is all. Not something that happens to me. Was a little creeped out by it, if I'm honest.'

'Must have been pretty bad if it's rattled you. You're made of stern stuff.' He frowned. 'I take it they withheld the number?'

'Yeah, annoyingly,' she said, pulling herself to the edge of the bed.

'Hmmm. Well, just don't get into a conversation, if any more calls come in. I'm sure they'll get bored soon enough. Imagine it's probably just kids randomly entering numbers,' he said, not moving from the doorway.

'Yeah, you're right. They didn't mention my name or anything, so probably just a weirdo chancer.'

Len cocked his head at the hallway. 'You want to say bye to Bella? We'll be off soon.'

'Argh, why didn't you wake me? Of course, I do. I'll just hop in the shower quick,' she said, hurriedly stripping off her pyjamas.

He shrugged. 'You were beat. I thought you could do with a few mins more.'

'Normally yes, but not right now.'

'Sorry.' A look of agitation flashed across his face.

'Len—'

'Go get ready, love,' he said, and left her to it.

* * *

Ellie ambled down the stairs, smiling as her daughter ran towards her.

'Mummy!' Bella cheered.

Ellie had managed to get ready for work in record time and was pleased not to be wearing a work suit for the day or smelling of death. Instead, she'd opted for her favourite of a turtleneck and high-waist black jeans.

'Hey, how's my little munchkin today?' Ellie knelt to give her a squeeze and received a face full of hair for her efforts. Her daughter had bunched her hair in two uneven, bushy black pigtails.

'Ooooh, look at your hair. So fancy.'

'Is this your doing?' she whispered in Len's direction; her eyes wide as she beheld one bushel.

'No, she wanted it. I left her to it. God forbid I get in the way of my ladies and their hair,' he joked.

She turned back to Bella, hoping the school wouldn't kick off at her when she was next in.

'Do you like it?' Bella squeaked, putting her hands behind her back and looking coy as she waited for her mum's opinion.

'Yes, sweetie, it's lovely. Let's get your coat on and get you to school.'

'Okay.'

Ellie grabbed her black trench coat and Bella's purple and pink coat for her, snuggling her daughter into it and pulling a face before opening the front door. She figured she'd grab breakfast on the way, despite the protestation of her stomach.

Looking out the door, the sight of someone who looked near identical to Strauss surprised her, rushing behind a car across the road opposite her front gate. At least, she thought it was him. The messy hair seemed remarkably similar.

'Luka?' she murmured, frowning as she dashed to the gate and looked out on the street. She couldn't see any sign of anyone in either direction. The man had vanished.

'Len, did you see a man just then? Messy hair?' she asked, gesticulating back at the road with a thumb.

'No, love, I didn't,' he said, ushering Bella out of the house.

Ellie turned back towards the road. *Who the hell was that, then?*

25

Ellie grabbed a cup of brown dishwater from the office vending machine and took a moment amidst the sea of ringing phones and endless chatter, official and otherwise.

Was that really Strauss at her house, or was she still on edge from the phone call?

'Ellie, it's you!' A familiar voice, one with a familiar Scottish lilt and one she'd not heard in a long time. 'Sorry, I should say *DS Wilkinson* these days, eh?'

She turned to see the beaming face of the newly appointed Inspector Phoebe Elgin in one of the many doorways to the kitchenette. She appeared to have gained a few pounds, as well as a few crow's feet around the eyes since they'd last worked together in her early Response days. Elgin's greying hair was tied back in a severe ponytail, perhaps a little too tightly. The look reminded Ellie of a Scottish version of Miller.

Ellie's eyes lit up, and she smiled, her face a picture of surprise. 'Wow, Elgin. Long time no speak. What brings you to our neck of the woods?'

'Oh, just been summoned for a briefing. Leading a team now, you know?'

'Yes, I'd heard on the grapevine.' She leant back on the counter and put her coffee down. 'Sorry, I know just texting a "well done" was a little lame of me, but it's been pretty hectic these last few days.'

'It's okay. I understand my old apprentice may get a little busy from time to time,' she said. 'How's the family keeping?'

'Oh, they're good, thank you. Bella's a little terror and getting bigger by the day. And you? Anyone on the scene?' she winked.

The inspector's face dropped at the question. 'No, just me again. You know how it is with me.'

'Balls, sorry to hear that.'

Ellie didn't know what to say. She never had done. Her former partner and mentor had always had a tricky time in the man department. It reminded Ellie of the times she'd had to listen to Elgin talk about it, sitting in their patrol car, with nowhere to escape to. The endless dates, the endless list of mishaps, constantly choosing the wrong sort of man and it inevitably blowing up in her face.

'Ah ha, DS Wilkinson. You okay?' The voice of Andrew Melwood blared in the small kitchenette. She was being assaulted from all angles. 'I thought you only drank a little last night? Must have had a bit more than I thought if you're drinking this shite.'

She turned to see Melwood standing in the other doorway. The man had dark circles under his eyes, white stubble forming on his chin, and was still in the previous day's clothes.

Her old boss saw this as an opportunity to leave, ignoring the loud DI and raising her eyebrows at Ellie.

'I'll see you soon, Ellie. Don't be a stranger, you hear?'

'I won't. Speak soon. Drink perhaps?'

'Sounds great. You've got my number,' Elgin said, waving at Ellie and giving Melwood a friendly nod as she turned and left.

'How are you feeling today, sir?' Ellie turned towards him, ignoring his question about her.

'Come on, you don't need to be formal with me, Ellie. We're friends now, eh? You know all my dirty secrets – and who was *that*, dare I ask?' he said, before giving her a sly wink.

Not out of choice, she thought. *And you can leave her well alone, thanks.*

She could smell the stale alcohol from where she was standing. He must have ended up an absolute wreck last night. Ellie hoped Drake and Dave didn't go to the same extreme. She didn't fancy working with a hungover Drake for the day. He had his moments at the best of times, let alone post-drinking session. Come to think of it, she hadn't taken him for a heavy drinker. Perhaps not even a drinker at all, for that matter.

'In answer to your question, pretty . . . *pretty* rough,' Melwood continued, judging the coffee cup in his hand with disgust. 'But, nothing a cup of the devil's coffee won't solve. This stuff really is complete and utter swill.'

Ellie nodded. 'Something we can agree on, for sure.'

'Drake's in the investigation room, by the way. We've got some developments you'll be wanting to hear.'

'Oh?'

'Get on in there; you'll see.' Melwood cast an arm back toward the investigation room.

* * *

'Ah, DS Wilkinson, nice of you to join us,' Drake said, his finger pointing at the whiteboard. He seemed to be suffering no ill-effects of the previous evening. But she'd never seen him with a hangover, so perhaps he hid it well. She couldn't be one hundred per cent sure, but she thought he was once again in the same clothes. Maybe he just had more than one set?

'Sorry. Was just getting a coffee,' she said, taking her coat off and slinging it over a nearby chair before sitting down to listen to the discoveries.

'If that's what you can call it. I was just getting started, so I'll start over,' he said, raising his eyebrows and scrubbing at his stubbled cheek. 'In short, we've got a match on the system for the second victim, a Sofia Machado, forty years of age. We had her for low-level dealing several years ago, so we have her home address, and it looks like she'd been working in a cafe since her last arrest, no other priors. We've cross-referenced it with our other records and she has a brother, Rodrigo. Both parents are deceased, and other family is based in Lisbon. We've got someone on the case with informing them once we've spoken with the brother. Don't want him disappearing before we've spoken with him.'

'And that's where we come in?' Ellie suggested.

'Precisely. We'll swing by the brother after casing her flat. See if there's anything there relating to Alex Ludner or anyone else. Maybe we'll get some information on whom she's been kicking around with, something that would shed more light on this damn mess.'

He picked up a cup and took a sip. 'And well done to Chambers for resolving the mystery surrounding her with Dr Kulkarni's help,' he said, nodding in her direction.

'Thank you, sir.' The woman's cheeks turned a deep shade of red.

Drake walked to Strauss' laptop. 'Any luck with the photo?'

'I'm having trouble getting anything from it,' Strauss told him. 'There's not much to work with, sorry. Will probably need to get it over to people dedicated to that sort of thing for a second try. But I doubt they'll have much luck either.'

Drake sighed. 'Mmm. Thanks for trying.'

Ellie's eyes followed him as he started pacing the room. 'This photo . . . it *has* to be related to Alex and Sofia somehow. Did they have a room like that at one point? Did something occur there? Were they directly involved? What is the meaning? Why use it?'

'Only one way to find out,' Melwood offered, startling her. Ellie hadn't seen – or smelt – the DI in the room. He'd somehow turned into a master thief in a matter of minutes. She hadn't quite figured the man out. She certainly wasn't sure if she could trust him fully. Her trust was something that had to be earned, even if Melwood was her superior.

She selfishly hoped that she would not have to work directly with anyone but Drake on the day-to-day. Ellie wanted to learn more from him. Their time together on her first case had been all too brief, given the magnitude of it and with him being out of action so soon after.

She noticed Drake rubbing the palm of his hand with his thumb. The wound where the Family Man's knife had gone straight through, pale and ugly. He'd required therapy on it to gain a full range of movement again. It must be an awful reminder, not that he needed one.

Ellie shuddered inwardly at how he must suffer. He'd never struck her as someone who let go easily, if ever. She recalled their conversation the day after the incident. Drake's complete devastation, the magnitude of what had happened to him and his daughter. The shock of discovering what Andrea Whitman had done to her own family because of The Family Man's twisted influence.

Andrea's actions still repulsed Ellie to this day, despite learning of the long, difficult history of mental illness that had plagued her. Her husband, Ben, had ultimately paid the price for burying his head in the sand about the severity of her illness. Ellie maintained to this day that watching the videos of the killings must have triggered her somehow. A sickening example of the dangers of the internet in the wrong hands, and the impact it was having on society.

Drake concurred with Melwood's sentiment about hard work. 'Indeed: investigate, investigate, investigate. Nose to the grindstone.'

'Yep.' Melwood nodded, pursing his lips and folding his arms.

Drake looked over at her. 'Okay, Ellie, you're with me. Let's go.'

26

The winter sun continued unabated as they drove under a graffiti-ridden bridge and on to the series of flats that were their target: a property on the outskirts of Seven Sisters near Tottenham. Ellie always enjoyed the days where the skies were a striking sea of blue, barely a cloud around and with a bite to the air. She'd never been a fan of summer, particularly working in it in full uniform. The country wasn't built for it, and neither was she. Air conditioning was next to non-existent in homes. This was her in her element.

'How're you feeling, Chief? Good night after I left?' She smirked.

'Yes, it was nice to be out,' he said, avoiding her question. 'Dave's been a good mate over the years. We'll need to give him a proper send off when the time comes.'

'Oh, for sure. Whatever you decide, I'm there with bells on.'

'Glad to hear it. He's rather fond of you.'

'And me, him,' she said, smiling in Drake's direction before concentrating on the road ahead.

Ellie noted the car had a strangely musty smell to it that

hadn't been there the other day. She was still wondering what it was when she felt the car accelerate. Drake had taken advantage of a large red bus having pulled over to its next stop. The road ahead was now unusually clear. They steamed past row after row of trees, standing bare against the sky and people spilling out from the Seven Sisters underground station. Dilapidated shops and a seemingly endless parade of takeaways and cafes went by in a blur.

'Did Melwood embarrass himself at all?' she said, ending the silence.

'Ellie, don't be too quick to judge. He's been having a hard time of it recently, what with his divorce and all. Explains a little as to why he is the way he is. Probably feels that work is the only thing he has a modicum of control over. I think we can all relate to that at times, don't you?'

Ellie felt a sting of shame. Her words now sounded childish to her ears. She forgot their age difference sometimes, and even with a child of her own, she knew she could be a little lacking in empathy if she didn't particularly like someone. She decided the best course of action was to keep quiet and focused on the satnav app on her phone.

A few minutes later, they'd nearly arrived at the ground-floor flat. The place was in a slightly rundown area, something that was becoming increasingly common due to the direction the government's policies were taking.

'There.' She pointed. 'Over there on the left. There's a spot we can park up, then it's just a short walk.'

'Got it.' Drake pulled slowly into a space in a cul-de-sac. 'Let's see if we have more luck this time, eh?' He raised his eyebrows and glanced in her direction as he undid his seatbelt.

'Don't fancy another case of "Let's see if the stairs kill her or not", you mean?'

'Quite.' Drake agreed, rubbing the bump on the back of his head.

They walked toward the flat, Ellie looking at her phone occasionally for guidance. It saddened her how much she relied on it these days.

The litter strewn street rattled with empty crisp packets and other mess, much the same as the previous afternoon's destination. Though this time there was the sight of a soiled mattress and a heavily-dented washing machine in their path. A dog barked continuously in the distance somewhere. As likely to have resulted from being holed up all day in a flat, Ellie suspected, rather than from having warned someone away from its territory. Bass pumped from a nearby car as it sped past on an opposing street before fading quickly.

'Okay, the directions say to take a left at the washing machine, before reaching our destination next to the pile of sticky porno magazines.'

'Hilarious,' Drake sighed.

'I try. Seriously, we are here, though. It's just there.' She pointed at the dilapidated building. It must have been a house before being converted into flats, or maisonettes. There was an entry to the ground floor at the front, and a separate entry to the first floor in the rear, the configuration continuing along a row of five houses in total.

The property's curtains were drawn, closed to the tiny plot of overgrown grass, which was nearing waist-level. The meagre foot-high fence encircling it lay broken. A fractured plant pot by Sofia's front door and the energy utility cupboard to the right, peeling blue paint included, completed its homely feel.

'Dare we knock? I'm not sure which of us is more prepared to be knocked over at this stage,' she said.

'I'll do it. Don't worry.'

She took a position behind him as he knocked forcefully on the door. Obviously, there would be no answer. There was no one alive who owned the property.

The door opened a crack, and a bleary-eyed, familiar face looked back.

'Yeah? What?' A scruffy man answered.

Surprising.

A near replica of the stitched woman's face peered back at them, albeit with more masculine features, fewer stitches and a deeper olive-skinned complexion. It had to be Rodrigo, the brother.

'Are you Rodrigo?'

'It's Rodri, and yeah, why? What's my sister done now?' Rodri asked. A strong cockney accent played on the words, 'sister' and 'now'.

'Can we come in?' Drake asked.

'Suppose you can, yeah. Going to have to 'scuse the mess though, she's not been back for a bit. And I've been staying for a while. My place was flooded by a fuckin' numpty that lives above me, leaving his damn bath on. Can you believe it?'

'Sorry to hear that, Mr Machado,' Ellie said.

'It's Rodri. As I said,' the man glared back at them through half-open eyes.

'All right. Sure.'

He led them into a dark mess of a living room. The glare of a television with a computer game on pause highlighted the various beer cans strewn around the living room and on the coffee table. A blanket hung half off the sofa's front.

Rodri opened the hooped curtains with a *schhhing*, the increase in light causing Ellie to shield her eyes for a moment. Sadly, the light did nothing to spruce up the miserable, filth-encrusted room.

'Take a seat. Don't both need to stand, do ya? You're making me nervous, like.' He plonked himself down in the only armchair, sinking into it much like Chambers on the sofa the previous evening. The thought made Ellie think she should have brought the woman along. In her place, Ellie knew she would have found the experience useful.

Drake and Ellie sat on the edge of the sofa, not wanting to slide into whatever could be secreted in the cracks. She cringed as the sofa made a strange crunching noise regardless.

Ellie prepared herself to deliver the message about Sofia. She'd spoken to relatives of the deceased many times, and informing them was never easy. It wasn't a part of the job she enjoyed. Selfishly, it always made her glad that it wasn't her or her family that it had happened to.

'Mr Machado,' she started. 'I'm sorry to inform you, but your sister passed away recently.'

The man's face was immediately crestfallen. 'W – what? Sorry?'

'Your sis—' Ellie started.

'I know what you said.' He snapped, his face hardening in an instant. 'Sofia, it just had to happen, didn't it? Just had to happen to you; you poor, stupid *Garota*. Fuck,' he muttered to himself, half in Portuguese. He was obviously distressed, but Ellie noted the anger undercutting it.

She sat in silence, while Drake looked ahead, unmoved.

'Mr Machado . . . Rodri. I'm sorry to have to use this time to ask questions, but really, we need some understanding as to why someone would want to harm your sister.'

'Harm? What? Someone killed her? Is that what you're saying?'

'Yes.'

'Mr Machado,' Drake interrupted. 'Would you mind if I took a look in your sister's bedroom, please?'

'Er, yeah, sure, whatever. Down the hall and on the right.' Rodri said, with a cursory wave of his hand.

Ellie guessed she was on her own, then.

* * *

Drake left Ellie to her lines of enquiry. He didn't feel the man had anything special to say. Truth was, it had made him uncomfortable seeing someone's reaction to the death of a loved one more than it had ever done previously. The guy hadn't reacted all that badly compared to some he'd attended, but Drake still needed the excuse. Maybe the alcohol of the previous evening was messing with him more than he thought, that or the lack of sleep again. He felt a sudden well-timed twinge in his back to remind him the car wasn't doing him any good.

Hopefully, there would be something useful in the dead woman's room. Perhaps something that could clarify this butchery, give him some kind of lead, *anything*. He spotted the door at the end of the corridor, passing a crooked slogan hanging on the wall. *Home sweet home.*

Heh, he snorted to himself. *Who're you kidding?*

The door felt flimsy, as though any force would cause it to fall off its hinges. Gently pushing it, Drake hit some unexpected resistance. He donned a pair of latex gloves and poked his head round the door, spotting a bundle of clothes clogging its path. The curtains were blocking most of the natural light in the room, giving it a melancholy atmosphere.

Pushing his way further in, Drake flicked the light switch for the room. The miserable light cast from the naked bulb overhead bathed the room in a stark hue, doing little to ease the depressing feel of the place. Instead, it provided a warts and all view of a bare, stained mattress on a cheap bed frame. The bed took up most of the space, the duvet hanging off at the opposing end to him. A smell of damp hung strong in the air. He traced the source to a corner of the ceiling, black and spotted with mould.

He sighed as he took in the sorry surroundings. It reminded him of his own flat, the one he was avoiding; the emptiness, the lack of personality, the 'I'm just existing' feel of it. A void. A deep, black, desolate hole. All it was missing was the same grotty kitchenette.

Drake gave his head a shake and brought himself back, taking another step towards the bed frame to peer over it. The step knocked something beneath the bed, an object clinking from the impact.

He moved back, a frown on his face while he felt around for his small torch, eventually pointing the light at the source of the sound: a dark brown and blue shoebox.

He pulled it out from under the bed, the weight not that much more than if it was empty, and placed it on the edge of the bed. Lifting the lid provided him with the sight of someone familiar smiling back at him. Two people, actually. Sofia Machado and Alex Ludner. Sitting on a bench in a park, smiling at the camera; using a selfie stick, judging by the reflection in Alex's sunglasses.

Bingo. That's more like it. Drake's eyes lit up. *So they were together. Finally, a link.*

He picked up the picture, revealing more beneath, sexual in nature and clearly of the two of them. Drake turned his nose up at the sight, trying to gloss over the sordid images while he continued rummaging. Finally, he found the source of the sound. Two rings, simple gold bands.

He held one of them up to the phone light between his thumb and index finger. No etchings, nothing of any personal meaning from what he could see. Same for the other. And, if they'd not been together for years, as Alex's colleague, Liam, had claimed, then why would she still have this collection in the first place? Maybe a memento, such as those rings... but intimate photos? Seemed unusual.

Turning his attention to the photos again, Drake flipped over each photo in turn to see if there were any notes on the back, maybe a place name or a date. He cast the last one down in disgust. Nothing.

Give me a bloody break.

Still, there was now a definitive connection between the two of them. That was something, and it implied the killings were not random. Were they revenge? Who was the third party at play here? A jealous ex, or wannabe lover? They had no one else in the frame so far.

* * *

'Nothing at all. Are you sure? Please take your time,' Ellie said.

Soon after her boss had left the room, the man had broken down, the realisation that his sister was gone and he would never see her again finally hitting home. Also, that he was going to be homeless. Ellie was wondering which of the two he was more upset about when Drake re-entered, holding something.

'Do you know this man?' He thrust it unceremoniously under the brother's nose.

Rodri snatched it from Drake. He considered it, sniffing loudly, the sound of phlegm catching in his throat. 'Yeah, think that was an old boyfriend from years back... Alex? Alexis? Something like that. Anyway, weird prick. Only met him a couple a...'

He sniffed again and swallowed grotesquely, '. . . times. There was something off about him.'

'Care to elaborate?'

Rodri hesitated, his eyes flicking between the photo and Drake. 'No. It was just a feeling, and like, the way he carried himself. If that makes sense?'

Drake pushed on. 'Clear as mud. Come on, Rodri . . . help us help your sister.'

'I haven't anything to tell, mate. That's all I got. All right?' He looked down at his feet and skimmed the photo across the floor to Ellie's feet. She picked it up and saw a selfie of Sofia and Alex smiling back at her.

Ellie sensed that the man was holding back somehow, but what, and why, she wasn't sure.

Drake's eyes darkened with a look of anger Ellie hadn't seen before.

'Listen, you little shit. Your sister is dead, got it? Whatever you're not telling us – so help me God – you better spill soon, or I'll have you,' he snarled, bending down into Rodri's space. His face was no more than an inch or two away from him.

Drake jabbed a finger at the man's forehead. 'This isn't about you and your pathetic existence. More people could die. Do you want that on your hands? Do you, huh? I know I don't, so tell me what you know . . . now!'

Before she could react, the man jumped to his feet, squaring up to Drake, even though Rodri was considerably smaller. He shouted and shoved at him, but he might as well have been pushing a concrete post for all the difference it made. Drake stood his ground as Ellie dived between them, pushing Rodri away.

'Stop, just stop!' she said, appealing more to Drake than Rodri.

'Oh, assaulting a police officer, eh?' Drake sneered.

The Ties That Bind

The man backed down, realising what he'd done. 'Fuck! I'm sorry, I shouldn't have done that. I'm sorry . . . I'm sorry.' He gibbered. 'I know nothing though, I swear. My sister's dead. Give me a break! I'll be bloody homeless now.'

'You better be telling the truth,' Drake spat. 'Otherwise, I'll be back for you, and there'll be no one here to stop me next time.'

With that, Drake stormed off, kicking the living room door on his way out and leaving a bewildered Ellie in his wake.

27

'Chief . . .! Wait up . . .! *John!*' Ellie called, catching up with him as he strode towards the car, carrying the shoebox under his arm. 'What was that back there?'

Drake didn't know himself, if he was being honest. He'd seen the man was holding back, and he just saw red. He'd not been able to control it. Not even during the worst moments in his marriage had he lost his cool in the ways he had been recently.

He'd always been the calm one, the one that tried to keep it together, because he knew blowing his top wouldn't achieve anything other than more shouting, particularly when they'd had Eva. He hadn't wanted her to pick up on that kind of behaviour. But in the last few minutes, his mind had seemed to clear, as though the outburst had blown away the remnants of his brain fog.

He took in the cool air, noticing the dog on the estate had since stopped its interminable barking.

'Are you okay?' Ellie asked, putting a hand on his shoulder and causing him to stop.

'I'm okay. I just . . . he was holding back, you saw that, right?' he stressed, continuing towards the car.

She spoke in a low voice. 'I did, but that's no reason to behave like that. We'll be no better than the people we're trying to catch if we go off like that at everyone we come across. I shouldn't be needing to tell you that, Boss.'

'You're right. Of course, you're right. I'd be saying the same,' Drake conceded. He shifted the shoebox of photos under his left arm. Despite the clarity afforded by the outburst, he wished he hadn't given Ellie a glimpse into his current state of mind. He'd done a good enough job of keeping up the walls until that moment. But the anger was always there lately, on the periphery.

'He'll have done a runner soon enough.'

'I got his mobile number, and he told me his original address, so let's hope that's not the case, eh?' she said before setting her eyes on the box he was carrying. 'What's that?'

'Oh, just a further set of the Sofia and Alex show. These aren't for her brother to see. To be fair, I don't really want to see them myself again either.' He set the box down on the boot of the car while he searched his pockets for his car keys.

'What like this one?' she said, pulling the photo of the couple from her pocket. 'We can't just be taking stuff from him.'

'These . . . they're not quite so "child-friendly", put it that way,' Drake nodded at the picture in her hand. 'You got permission for that?'

'Yes.' She cottoned on to what he was saying. 'So we'll count it as *general* permission, eh?'

He winked. 'Got it in one. It was part of the same collection, after all.'

* * *

Drake pulled into the long, winding driveway, the slow crunch of gravel audible as the car crept past the gated frontage. Rachel Drayton and her wife, Anna, lived on the outskirts of Oxford, relatively near Barndon. The location was ideal for giving Eva, and her best friend, Cari Whitman, continuity for school. He knew he was fortunate that his wife's sister was so well off. Eva would likely have run away by now if they'd lived under the same roof.

Rachel was a prosecution lawyer. Several high-profile cases had accelerated what was always destined to be a bright career. The lawyer, as well as being blessed with the same attractive features as her sister, had a searing intelligence (much like that of his wife) and didn't suffer fools gladly. Perfect for working in the legal world. Not so much when he was on the receiving end of her grief.

Drake stopped before rounding the corner of the drive to the house proper, turning the engine off and cloaking himself in the car's darkness. He needed time to steel himself for the evening ahead. The familiar throb in his head had intensified as the day wore on, with case developments having stalled again after corroborating the victims' relationship. His continual lack of progress was really driving his headache. The fleeting clarity he'd gained had faded, the morose once again in place.

Impeccable timing, as always. He drummed the steering wheel in the half-light.

Drake peered out of the driver's side window. The clear sky of the day had remained, allowing the stars to shine unabated, helped undoubtedly by the lack of London light pollution. The moonlight shone through too, giving shape to the surrounding undergrowth, the manicured driveway and its tree line.

He did his usual – now failing – routine when under significant stress, one after the other.

First breath cycle: Becca bleeding out played in his mind's eye.

Second exhalation: Eva's screaming for her mother, flashing before him.

Third time: silence and the inky, bottomless dark.

Drake kept his eyes closed, the black void making him think back to when he was young and begging his mother not to turn the light off. One of the few lasting memories he had of her.

One of these days, the reminders of the past years would become too much and he'd be back in that flat. The image of the room and loft beam, chair beneath it, was now firmly front and centre in his mind.

Tap, tap.

The noise startled him, as did the face at the window. Becca. He squeezed his eyes shut in shock, his heart suddenly racing.

It couldn't be.

He opened them again. Rachel was staring back at him, the usual look of irritation on her face.

'Are you coming in or what?' she said, her voice muffled through the glass separating them.

He feigned a smile and gave her the thumbs up, starting the engine. He pulled away, and she walked ahead, the car inching slowly towards the house and Drake's daughter.

28

Drake looked across at Eva amidst the strained silence of the dinner. Her head remained down, focused on taking the smallest of bites of the Indian takeaway that he'd ordered in. She'd not once looked him in the eye; or maybe she had, and he'd been looking away in shame.

He already wanted to suppress the memory of the awkward conversation that had ensued about what to eat. Eva hadn't been interested at all, and Rachel had needed to coax her into giving a preference. Then there had been the long, silent wait for it to arrive.

Once they'd sat down to eat, Rachel and Anna had sat opposite each other at the end of the dining table, trying their best not to intrude. The meal had been punctuated with awkward, well-intentioned conversation by Anna. She was short in stature, with medium-length red hair, and one of the few who saw Rachel's good side. There had to be one for Anna to have married her, right?

Drake could count on one hand the number of times he'd heard Rachel laugh, with ninety per cent of those coming at their wedding a few years prior. He remembered their first dance together and how happy Anna seemed with her. Even back then, Rachel had never been Drake's biggest fan, despite understanding more than most why his work had been so consuming of his time and his energy. She never commiserated with him, giving him short shrift on more than one occasion.

Cari sat mute next to Anna, and he next to her, while Eva was made to sit opposite him in the large, opulent dining room. The room, rather disturbingly, reminded him of the crime scene from the Family Man case up in Haworth. All rich green painted walls, white cornicing and white linen which he'd since splattered curry on. Naturally, high-backed chairs were in situ too.

Drake's eye twitched at the mental image of the Cartwright family: the blood-soaked tablecloth, the dead bodies tied to the chairs . . . Rachel's Christmas decorations seemed morbidly out of place. He was getting fed up with the litany of terrible memories.

Eva looked older than when he'd last seen her; not the bright sixteen-year-old she should be, her birthday having come and gone without fanfare at her insistence, a couple of weeks prior. Her jet-black hair was well past her shoulders now; she resembled Becca far more than him the older she got. She'd also become painfully thin in the past year, her face drawn, and he noted the prominent bones of her wrists. Whether that was down to him or the medication, he wasn't sure.

Her deep brown eyes flitted up for a split second, catching his before immediately dropping once more. A quiet anger radiated from her.

'I'm finished. Can I be excused, Aunt Rachel?' she asked, her soft voice piercing the silence, though barely a whisper.

'No. We're not finished, and you're certainly not either.'

'You can't make me eat.'

'Do you think your mum would like to see how thin you've become? Huh? Do you?' Rachel snapped back.

'Don't say that. You know that's not fair,' Eva murmured, cowed by her aunt.

Is this what it was like when he wasn't around? It's no wonder Eva hadn't improved any, being got at like a naughty school child.

Rachel ran her napkin over her mouth before putting it on the table in a show of irritation. 'Life's not fair, young lady. You should know that better than most.'

'Rachel . . .' Anna interjected, taking hold of her wife's hand. 'Give the girl a break. She's probably feeling overwhelmed right now.'

Drake looked sideways at Cari. The girl was still sat in her own perpetual silence, finishing the last of her food. With her hair tucked behind her ear, he could see the makings of the ugly slash across her throat. He snapped his eyes back on Eva, not wanting a reminder of what the Whitman girl had lived through.

'Eva, do as your aunt asks, please,' he added softly, immediately regretting doing so.

'You . . .! Don't you dare tell me what to do! You don't have the right anymore,' Eva seethed, her voice doubling in volume. She slammed her cutlery down on the plate, pushing the plate away from her and storming from the room despite Rachel's ensuing protests.

Drake winced, his heart sinking. Her words still wounded him more than any knife could. Remaining silent, he took a moment before meeting Rachel's venomous gaze.

She'd picked up the discarded napkin and was toying with it beneath her whitened knuckles. 'You need to sort this, and soon. It's becoming intolerable, John. I won't stand for it much longer.'

Anna kept quiet amidst their back and forth, while Cari

continued eating as though nothing was happening in front of her, slowly working her knife and fork.

'What do you want me to do, eh? She's clearly not ready,' he remonstrated.

'She never will be if you keep tip-toeing round her like a damn coward. She's your daughter, for Christ's sake,' she snapped. She slapped the napkin down on the table once more and gave him a look of disgust.

Drake supposed she was right on some level. Perhaps it was time that he tried a different approach. What had distance done but drive a bigger gap between him and his daughter? They had mended nothing, no bridges had been built. Just a desperate gulf of nothingness where a father and daughter relationship should be. Becca would be turning in her grave.

'Talk to her, that's all I ask. If not for yourself, how about for us, your family? It's what *my* sister would have wanted. Not to have this dragging on, week after week, month after month.'

The way she spoke of Becca incessantly was riling him. It was unfair, beating him with it every time she spoke to him. Reminding him of what happened, time after time.

'Don't you justify everything with your sister's name, Rachel – just don't. I won't have it anymore,' he said. 'I get it. She was your sister, but she was my *wife* for twenty *years*.' He slammed the table with his scarred fist. 'Where were you in that time, eh? Following your career. We saw you, what . . . once a year? And you think you can treat me like this?'

Rachel tried to retort, but he spoke over her.

'What do you think this is? Hmmm?' He pointed at his scarred palm. 'And this!' He unbuttoned his shirt and pulled it to one side, showing the large slash of scarring across his upper arm. 'You think I don't understand how it feels? I was fucking there – I saw it all happen. *Me.* Not you. I see it day after day, in my dreams, in my waking hours. Whenever I close my eyes.'

Cari shrunk into her seat. Her hand moving to her own scar at her throat.

'John, I—'

'No, Rachel. No. I'm not interested, I—'

'Sp . . .' came a faint whisper. 'Spe . . .'

Drake looked to see if Eva had entered the room again. She wasn't there.

He realised where the noise was coming from. Turning to her, he met Cari's eyes, and saw the tears rolling down her cheeks.

'Spe . . . Spe . . . Speak . . . to . . . *her,*' Cari rasped.

29

Ellie strolled into The Crook, realising she'd been in the pub twice in as many days now. She was worried it was going to become a habit. The bar staff might even recognise her, which was sort of cool in its own way. She could be like a cowboy from the old western films of the fifties and sixties, the bartender sliding a shot of whisky to her at the slightest of nods.

She'd taken up Elgin on her drinks offer sooner rather than later. The guilt of unintentionally ignoring her old boss and partner for so long had nagged at her since their meeting. Drake leaving for a personal matter meant the opportunity had presented itself.

The newly appointed inspector had been grateful for the quick call. She hadn't fancied a night of small talk with her peers, apparently.

Ellie ordered glasses of wine (sadly, not whisky) for them both and sat down to wait at a small table tucked away next to the spent fireplace. She was pleased to see the place wasn't quite so busy this time round, so she'd actually be able to talk at a normal level.

She was busy wondering whether her old boss would turn up at all when Elgin finally appeared at the entrance. The inspector had let her hair down since leaving the office and had changed out of her uniform into a plain green top and a pair of blue jeans. She was never one for fancy dressing, even if she'd had the time.

'Ellie, well, this was unexpected,' she said, sitting down with a sigh of satisfaction. Another when she picked up the glass of wine.

'Yeah, sorry about us getting cut off earlier. The DI that you saw is a bit of a lout at times. Hearts in the right place, though. I suspect.'

'Is he single?' Elgin said, giving her the eye.

'Phoebe!'

She laughed. 'Come on, I don't meet many fellas these days. I wants me an inspector, no more sergeants. Show me the money!'

Elgin had a history with several sergeants. She'd been burnt by her many failed relationships, and it affected her confidence. Dating apps the way they were too . . . Ellie was just relieved she was off the market with Len. Even the thought of those apps made her shudder. Also, the thought of Melwood in that way . . . another shudder followed.

'He's going through a divorce by the sounds of it, not something you'd want to touch right now.'

'Right now? So, in future then? Beggars can't be choosers at my age,' she smirked.

'Erm . . .' Ellie took a large gulp of her white wine, spluttering slightly at the harshness hitting the back of her throat.

Elgin gave her an inquisitive look. 'So come on, what's this big case of yours?'

'A couple of murders happened up in Barnet in the fields there. I'm not sure I can say much more than that right now.'

'Come on, Ellie. It's me you're talking to.'

'I'm not sure.' Ellie didn't like Elgin pressing her. Why was she so interested suddenly?

'You can tell me.'

'No.'

'Go on, what was it like?'

'I said *no*, Phoebe,' she snapped.

Elgin thrust her hands up in a sign of mock surrender. 'Guess I'm not your boss anymore. Can't force these things out of you.'

'Fortunately,' Ellie said, smiling to lighten the mood again.

Elgin returned the smile. 'Anyway, how's Len – and Bella? Bet she's growing up to be a little troublemaker, like her mother.'

The remark felt slightly barbed. But Ellie did her best to ignore it.

'She's doing well, thank you. She started at school, and is making friends. I still find it hard to leave her at the school gate, though.'

'Oh, I bet.'

Ellie took another gulp of her wine. She was wishing she hadn't agreed to come. This was going to be hard work, and she didn't quite understand why.

30

Drake peered over the banister at the top of the stairs, gripping it tightly. The ornate chandelier shone in the entranceway, a circular table aligning with it at ground level, the cold, hard floor beneath. He considered the distance, unwelcome thoughts entering his mind; of how falling from this position would surely break his neck. He shook them away.

There had been a time when he was jealous of where his sister-in-law lived, the extravagance her career had afforded her compared to that of his own wage. Now, he just felt nothing. They were all baubles and trinkets, nothing of substance. Nothing resembling love and family. Maybe that was why Eva had become increasingly distant.

Rather than returning to him, perhaps she was taking on Rachel's strength of personality, becoming more and more like her and less like Becca. Harsh, cold and clinical – unforgiving even. He sorely hoped not. He was probably just looking for someone to blame, he realised. His sister-in-law was an easy target. Much easier than himself. He was driving her away. *He* was prolonging the situation, not easing his daughter's feelings of loss. Him. No-one else.

Drake turned, hearing familiar music thrum softly through the hard oak door of Eva's bedroom. For a moment, he was back at their old house, wanting to come in and ask her how her day had been. Becca cooking downstairs. Eva listening to music too loudly, avoiding her homework. It made him realise for the first time in a long while how much he missed his downtime. Listening to old records, watching the films of his younger years. Sharing his music with his daughter.

He knocked gently on the door, probably not hard enough to be heard over the music. He recognised *The Cure,* just as it was abruptly turned down.

'What?' Came an indignant voice.

'It's me,' he said, his voice catching. 'Can we . . . can we talk, please?'

A pause. 'You can. Doesn't mean I'll listen to you.'

'Can I come in, at least?'

He took the silence to mean 'yes', and slowly entered the room.

The room was twice the size of her old one and seemingly twice as dark. Eva was sitting on her bed, her back up against the wall. Her phone was cast to one side, a laptop resting on her lap. When she'd moved to her aunt's, she'd taken her desk and most of her belongings with her. The furniture looked diminutive in the sizeable space. Drake noted the family photo on her bedside table. The silver-framed photo usually showed Eva when she was just two years old, alongside him and Becca. He'd since been carefully folded out of the picture, Becca now holding sole ownership of their child, the brown backing support of the frame in place of him. Drake's heart dropped.

He gestured to her desk chair. 'May I sit?'

'You were already going to, so why ask?' Eva snapped.

He pulled it out and sat, the chair creaking beneath his weight.

'Eva . . . please, don't be like that.'

'Like what?'

He spoke plainly. 'Angry.'

'Why not?'

She had a point; she had every right to be angry. She had him as a father, her mother had died, and her best friend had been savaged. And Eva was being actively and cruelly bullied at school for having a dead mother and living with her lesbian aunt. Even in this day and age of understanding and education on mental health and all its pitfalls, teenagers could be so callous when they chose to be.

'Because, while I understand the need to be angry, it's not helping you up here, is it?' he said, pointing to his temple.

Eva put her laptop to one side and brought her knees up to her chest. She stared straight at him, her eyes devoid of any feeling that he could detect.

'God, don't be so patronising. Do I look like I want to be psychoanalysed by you, of all people? I've had enough of that with the therapist at school and the doctor who started me on this medication. Let alone my arsehole of a dad, the one who caused all this in the first place.'

Her words stung. They always did.

'I could say any number of things and you wouldn't accept any of it. I realise that, Eva,' he told her. 'If I was given the chance to swap places with your mother, I would, in a heartbeat. She would be here, and I would be gone. You'd be happy.'

Her face twisted. 'But you won't have that chance, and you'll still be here. She'll still be dead. That . . . *thing* is still alive in prison. You couldn't even kill him. I hate you for that.'

'Eva—'

'No. I know you're hoping that things will change. That if you give me space, I'll despise you less. That I will come round and things will go back to "normal" . . . but that's not going to happen.'

'Eva, I can't go round killing people. No matter what they did and no matter how much I would want to.'

'Not even for her?' She turned her nose up at him in disgust. 'Not even for Mum?'

'That's not how it works, and you know it.'

'I don't care how it works. I care about my mother being dead, because of you and your fucking work. The argument that day, I heard it. When that *man* started killing again, I heard how you twisted her into making you take that case.'

'What?'

She looked pleased at his reaction. 'Yeah, you didn't realise. I listened to the whole thing.'

'Then you know that's not true, Eva. I said I'd steer clear of it. That I'd turned it down, that I refused to take it on, for both of your sakes. For my sake.'

She sighed at him. 'That's bullshit. You forget, I might be a little girl to you, but I've grown up, I've had to. I know bullshit when I see it and when I *hear* it. You work with criminals every day. You know how to twist things, how to twist people.'

'Eva, that's simply not true.'

Was it true? Now, hearing how Eva described it, he wasn't sure anymore. Had he really meant it, or had he always hoped that Becca would let him work on the Family Man case? He didn't think he'd manipulated Becca, not consciously . . . but had he? He couldn't say for sure. So much time had passed, and he'd compartmentalised the whole sorry saga. But Eva wasn't thinking straight, either. She couldn't be right, could she?

She snarled at him. 'So just because you say it isn't, it can't be true? I'm the one that's lying? Way to go, *Dad*. I can see why that man killed her. You're a shit negotiator.'

'Eva, please, we've been through this. We have to find a way through. I love you. You're all I have left.'

'That's a shame for you then, as I don't love you. I never will again. You're dead to me. Now, fuck off. I don't want to see you again.'

The words crushed him. There was no feeling there. She didn't look upset or sad. There were no tears, just a flat statement. It was chilling.

'Eva . . .' he said.

'Do you want me to get Aunt Rachel to throw you out?'

'But it's nearly Christmas. I want to spend time with you.' He pleaded feebly. Was he actually about to lose whatever he had left of his relationship with her?

She huffed in disgust. 'Christmas? You think I give a shit about Christmas? You really are an idiot.'

'Eva . . .' he pleaded again, reaching out to her.

'Get. Out!' she shrieked.

'You heard her, John,' Rachel said from the doorway.

He backed out of the room. This wasn't helping anyone.

'If you think this means I'll keep looking after her for much longer, you're mistaken.' His sister-in-law hissed as he edged past her.

'What's that supposed to mean?' he said, pulling up the door to his daughter's room.

'You know exactly what it means. Now, do as she says. Fuck off and don't come back until you're done with whatever the hell is going on with you,' she said, her voice like a vat of acid. 'And be quick about it. I don't want her or her friend here in the new year, you hear—'

Drake started walking away, raising his hand dismissively. 'I *really* don't have time for your shit, Rachel. Not now.'

Shaking his head in disgust, he slammed the door behind him.

31

Drake drove back to the office. His ears ringing, the silence deafening. He squeezed the steering wheel as his blood pressure rose, the leather creaking under his grip. He wouldn't give up on Eva, he wouldn't. She was his everything.

Drake remembered the day she was born. He'd received the news from Becca's worried mother that her waters had broken, a month prematurely. He'd rushed down to the hospital. He'd been mid-case naturally, but that hadn't mattered for once. The potent mix of being terrified and so, so excited meant he couldn't keep still on the drive over.

Then pessimism had taken over. He'd convinced himself that something was going to go wrong. That Becca would lose too much blood, that the baby would become trapped or tangled in the umbilical cord, that he would be left without a wife or a child. It was completely ridiculous of him, but he couldn't help it. That was how his mind had been conditioned. His mother had great difficulty with him, so why wouldn't Becca have difficulty? It was an illogical pattern of thought. Thankfully, his worries had been for nothing. Despite being premature, Eva was born with no serious conditions. She was monitored for just over a week before they could take her home. His family was safe. His family was complete. Not anymore.

The next thing he knew, he was waiting for the interminable gate to open to their headquarters. He frowned, realising he couldn't recall much of the journey once he'd left Rachel's driveway. He pondered her words. How she could threaten to dump Eva on the street. What was wrong with her?

Drake pinched his eyebrows and rubbed his face with both hands, trying to revive himself for the work ahead. It wasn't working.

He got out of his car and saw Miller coming from the other direction.

Come on, not now, he thought. *Any time but now. Please.*

He turned back towards the car, hurrying with his keys.

'John.' The Detective Chief Superintendent's voice was as flat as ever.

Drake froze. He squeezed his eyes shut and took a deep breath before opening them again as he turned to greet her, forcing a smile.

'Boss. Dare I ask how it goes in the ivory tower?'

She ignored his sarcasm. 'Is there any progress?'

'As of now, we're developing a picture.'

Her eyes narrowed. 'That's not what I asked. Is there any progress?'

He looked up at the sky. A plane was flying overhead, low enough for him to hear the roar of the engine. 'We've established that there is a link between the two victims. They were together many years ago. There are photos proving it.'

'Any motive?'

Drake could barely hear her as the plane passed. Finally, the sound dissipated into the distance. 'Not yet,' he said. 'No motive, no reason for the viciousness of the killings, or the glass. Or indeed, the photo.'

'Drake, we've got to nail the bastard quickly. The media have got hold of the MO. They've started calling him the "Stained Glass Killer."'

'What a name.' He sighed. 'Look, Laura, you know I'm doing my best here.'

Again, she ignored him. 'How's the team, the additional resource?'

'They're working well. An odd bunch. Where did you get them?'

She paused. 'They were the only ones willing and able to join.'

'What? So, they're not actually official SMT resource?'

'Strauss is, but the other two, no. Chambers, obviously not. And Melwood . . .' she hesitated. 'Let's just say Melwood's in a similar position to you.'

That set his hackles rising. 'Oh? What does that mean?'

She stared at him, the way only she could. 'Difficulties outside of work, motivational issues.'

'Motivational issues? Come on, Laura. Give me a break.'

'I'm not getting into this with you, Drake. I'd like to leave the right side of midnight for once.'

Drake felt an immense pressure in his chest at her words. He was losing what little support he had left with her after all these years. All the time they'd worked together. All the people they'd put away.

'Is it your bosses, Laura?' he pressed. 'Is that it?'

'That, and . . . I can't keep this up, Drake. You need to be back to your old self, and you need to be *on it*. I can ill afford my DCI turning up every day as though he's not been home.' She looked him up and down, and shook her head. 'You look terrible, and you're clearly not sleeping. You have responsibilities, John, and you're not setting the right example . . . Not anymore. Sort it.'

He was at a loss for words.

'Now, I have to be going. Please, if there are any developments, let me know immediately. I shouldn't be hearing things second-hand.'

'Second-hand?'

'Yes.' She didn't elaborate. 'The media are on this one as I've said, and we can't afford to make any mistakes, so do your best. I know what that can be, and *this* . . .' She pointed at him, '. . . This is not it.'

He grimaced. 'Okay. Understood.'

* * *

'Chief,' Ellie greeted him in the corridor, giving a tired smile. The light from the incident room cast a shadow behind her. 'You okay? I'm sorry to say, but you look like shit.'

Was there something in the water this evening? Was everyone going to be grinding him down? His daughter, his sister-in-law, his boss . . . his colleague?

'Thanks, Ellie. A pleasure as always. Not to be childish, but you're not looking so hot yourself,' he said, raising his eyebrows.

'Tell me about it. I've been racking my brain about this damn case ever since we got back and you left. Well, that and a quick drink with my old boss,' she said, looking guilty. 'I promised Len I'd be back soon, but I feel like there's something staring us right in the face and it's nagging at me.'

'I can relate to that feeling,' Drake commiserated. He motioned to go past her and into the incident room. 'Got to go with your gut. Review everything, then review everything again. It'll come.'

'I getcha.' Ellie nodded, her face sombre.

Strauss was focused on a computer record of some kind on his laptop screen. He closed it as they entered the room, looking strangely shifty. 'Oh, hello. I thought it was just going to be me working late.'

Drake figured the man had been in a rush on the first day of the investigation and he'd not readied himself, but it seemed the messy hair and unshaven look was just that: his 'look'. He shouldn't be one to comment, he supposed, his current bedtime ritual being a car and his hands being the iron for his shirt. Drake knew he had to go home soon or move. It was becoming ridiculous, particularly now, with Miller noticing and someone apparently feeding her information.

The two large monitors Strauss was using to extend his laptop screen showed images of the scanned shoebox photos recovered from Sofia's flat.

Drake frowned, intending to ask what Strauss was looking at on the screen he'd so hastily closed when Ellie stood in his way and took him aside into the SIO office. The room was uncomfortably small, particularly for two. She closed the door behind her and looked him straight in the eye.

'John, are you okay?' she asked him. 'I know you're not one to shit rainbows on a daily basis and considering your circumstances, fair enough, but there's something more. You can tell me to go fuck myself if I'm barking up the wrong tree. I won't be offended.'

'No, I understand. I—'

'Guys!' Strauss cried. 'Come here, I think I've spotted something.'

Drake's heart leapt. He lived for moments like these. Could the man have cracked it?

He barged past Ellie and over to the DS, secretly pleased that their conversation had ended so abruptly. He wasn't in the mood to face up her observations just then.

'What is it?' he peered at the screens, turning his nose up at the images of the sex acts displayed.

'Do you see what I see?'

'I'm not sure what's in these photos can be *unseen*, to be honest,' Ellie said.

'No, ignore the two of them. Look at these elements of the images.'

Drake looked past Alex Ludner's hip, and the back of Sofia's head, and spotted an old wood burner.

'Is that . . . ?'

'Uh, huh. Now look at this one.' Strauss said, pointing at the other screen.

A battered metal bed frame was in the background beyond the back of Sofia's pre-occupied head. A single mattress was there, and a shape covered by something brown. He couldn't make out what was under it, the image once again part blurry, part shoddy photography.

Strauss looked up at them, clearly pleased with himself. He clasped his hands behind his head and leaned back in his chair, a look of triumph on his patchy, stubbled face. 'It's the same room as the one in the photo. The one we found in Alex's throat.'

'Hell yeah!' Ellie pumped her fist.

'Great work, Luka. I'm glad you could see past it all and spot that,' Drake said. 'But what does this mean for us?'

'I think it means these people were involved in something they shouldn't have been,' Strauss replied. 'And that whoever is seeking revenge has unfinished business. Because I've not shown you the best part yet. I was . . . saving the best till last, shall we say?'

'Oh?'

'The man in some of the photos. It's not Alex. There's no

circular scarring mark on his hip, and his body shape is all wrong. See here?' Strauss brought up another picture.

'You're right.'

'And I had to work some of my magic on this one, but you see here?' He pointed at the corner of the photo. 'Alex is sitting to the side here. See, there's the mark on his hip. He's in the room with Sofia and this other man, but not taking part directly.'

'Also,' Ellie piped up, 'Who's actually taking the photos in some of these? It can't be Sofia or the mystery man, *or* Alex in that one.'

'Indeed. But we were always expecting more, right? That's why we're involved.' Drake pointed out.

'Correct, but we couldn't say for sure, could we? But now . . .' Strauss looked up at them both from his desk.

'What're you saying, Luka? Besides, there being evidence of some sleazy orgy?'

Strauss looked at them both once again. 'I'm saying, it's more than likely, whoever is doing this isn't finished. Not by a long shot.'

32

Punishment was just something I grew accustomed to.

The way it was administered... the time it took.

It could just happen at the drop of a hat. None of it made sense to me.

If only it was routine, then I could have braced for it. Steeled myself, made it *bearable*.

But it hadn't been. It never was.

I dreamt about the day it would stop. About the day I would be free from it.

But when that day came... The punishment didn't stop. It just became... different.

A different sort of pain. One of memories and feelings and, for me, one of loss.

The days turned to weeks, turned to months, until, before long, *years* had passed.

Still, the pain never subsided.

The way I'd been treated.

And the feeling of loss, *utter* loss, never left me. It never would.

Not while they still drew breath.

33

'You're back late,' Len greeted her in the hallway as she closed the door quietly behind her. Ellie had made a conscious effort to leave soon after the discovery with the photos, but even so, it was still close to midnight. She knew that even though he wouldn't explicitly say so, he would be disappointed in her. Ellie thought it best not to tell him about the drink she'd had with her old boss. She could still taste the cheap wine in the back of her throat. Why had it been so awkward?

He pointed into the lounge. 'She's asleep. She wanted to wait up for you now that school has finished for Christmas. But made me promise not to take her up to her room until you'd come home. I think she's tiring of me reading her bedtime stories rather than her mother.'

The last comment cut Ellie deeply. She knew she'd not been around as much these past months, even with the easier work before now. She didn't think he was being spiteful, just honest. Being a mother and having a career in her field was hard work. She'd try harder, for their sake. There were too many broken marriages in the police force, and she didn't want to add to that statistic.

'I'm sorry,' she said, looking sheepish. 'I really don't want to be having to rely on you so much. You know that, right?'

He smiled and nodded. It didn't ease her concern, but it would have to do.

'Work okay?' she asked, though she'd never really fully understood the ins and outs of his finance role.

'Yeah, though my new project is leading me in a direction I'm not keen on. Need to raise it with my boss, and you know that's always a fun conversation,' Len said, making a face.

'Do what you think is best. You always do. I've got your back, like you've got mine.'

'Thanks. But I don't think I want to have your back on some of the shit you have going down.'

'True.' She smiled and wrapped her arms around him. 'Nor me on some of yours. It would go right over my head.'

Ellie gave him a long hug, breathing in his scent. 'Take me to the little monster, would you? I think we need to get her to bed and then I really need to get *you* to bed,' she chuckled as she turned him around, tapping him on his bum when they crept into the lounge.

Bella was cosied up on their comically large grey sofa, sandwiched between two white fluffy cushions. Ellie's heart skipped a beat at the imagery. She was such a sweet girl.

'Hey . . .' she whispered, manoeuvring into position to scoop her daughter up. 'Let's get you up to bed.'

Ellie picked her up. She noted her daughter was getting heavier as she shifted the girl's weight a little. Maybe taking her upstairs could be an exercise in future?

Len kissed the little girl's forehead and left Ellie to take her upstairs while he worked at putting his laptop and books away.

The Ties That Bind

'I'll be up soon,' he whispered.

Ellie navigated the stairs without a peep from her daughter and cracked open the door to her bedroom. Len must have been up already; he'd put on her nightlight and pulled back the covers of her unicorn bed, her latest phase.

She put Bella to bed and pulled the covers up, looking at her daughter as she slept.

What would I do without you?

Bella stirred again, this time opening her eyes. 'Mummy?'

'Go to sleep, honey. That's an order,' she said, stroking her forehead with a finger.

'Stay?'

Ellie smiled. 'Just for a little while, okay?' She grabbed both ends of the pillow and squished Bella's face, making her daughter giggle.

Ellie's hand knocked at something hard. Curious, she reached around under the pillow gently, not wanting to rouse Bella more than she had to. She took hold of the object and drew it out carefully, like she was pulling out a wooden block from a game of Jenga.

A pair of legs and a lower torso revealed itself.

Bella stirred, saw her mother through drowsy eyes, and giggled fitfully before drifting to sleep once again.

Ellie tugged on the rest of the doll, revealing the shoulders and head.

A head bound in black duct tape.

Ellie's eyes went wide with shock. *What the actual hell! This can't be real. How did she get this?*

She took the doll and hurried out into the hallway, pulling up the door behind her and turning on the hall light.

'Ellie? You okay?' Len asked, coming out of their bedroom and seeing her with the doll. 'Er, what is that?'

'Did you give her this? Have you seen this before?'

'No, I didn't. I mean, I haven't. Slow down. What's going on? Why does she have an Action Man toy?'

'It's not just that,' she hissed, keeping her voice down.

Len frowned. 'Why is its head covered in duct tape? Sort of a creepy thing to do, isn't it?'

She stared at him. 'Precisely! Holy shit.'

'Okay, you're weirding me out a little now. What's going on?'

'Let's go downstairs. I'll explain,' she said, still stressing out. She suddenly realised, 'Len, you've locked all the doors, right? No windows open anywhere?'

'Yes, everything's locked up tight. It's December, Ellie.' He said, giving her a searching look. 'Seriously, you're freaking me out a little. What's up?'

Ellie led him down to the living room. She switched on a side lamp, hissing at him to keep the main light off as he went to turn it on. 'We don't want to draw attention.'

'What? Why?' he asked as they sat down on the sofa.

'Someone could be watching.'

'*Watching?* What!'

'Okay, see this doll?' she said, holding it up to him. 'It's head is wrapped in the same tape as the person in this case I'm working on. The *murder* enquiry.'

'What . . . ? Holy . . . We have to call the police, Ellie. We have to call them now.' He got up from the sofa and stared down at her.

'I know, I know. I'm just . . . how did Bella get this? How long has she had it for?'

Ellie looked down at the creepy naked doll again.

'I told you, I don't know. It's the first time I've seen it. I wouldn't keep this sort of thing from you, would I?' His face was a picture of concern while he went about making sure the curtains were closed tight.

She was concerned, too. More than concerned, frightened. Her family was in danger; some psychopath was watching them. Stalking her. Stalking *her daughter.*

Wait, she thought. *That means Bella has seen the person who did this.*

Another thought dawned on her. 'Holy shit, Len. Was that what those withheld calls were about? It must be the same people. The same person has been calling me! It has to be.'

He paced the room. 'Okay. What did they say exactly?'

'That I should "remember them." That I will soon know who they are.'

'You didn't think that was important?' he snapped.

'No! How was I to know? You said so yourself, it could have just been kids,' she retorted. Though she realised now it had seemed too sinister to be a kid's prank call. How could she have been so foolish? She realised that this was bigger than her now, and she needed to get help.

'Len, call this number.' She passed him her phone, the speed dial on Drake's number. 'I need to speak to Bella. Understand how she got a hold of this . . . this *thing*.'

'Who is it? What do I say?'

'It's Drake. Tell him precisely what's going on – he'll know what to do.'

She took the doll back upstairs with her, opening Bella's door as she heard Len start speaking to someone downstairs on the phone, blurting out what had happened. She wasn't used to hearing him sound panicked.

Ellie looked at her daughter, feeling now a semblance of what Drake must have felt, must *still* be feeling. Her family was in danger. Her daughter in harm's way. She couldn't comprehend it.

She *daren't*. She felt so exposed, so defenceless. So useless. How could this have happened?

She knelt down beside her. 'Bella, honey,' she said, keeping her voice low so as not to startle her. She put a hand to her shoulder, the girl's eyes shut tight. 'Bella, I need you to wake up, please.'

The girl stirred, 'Mummy?' she said, her voice groggy, her eyes still closed. The nightlight casting stars and moons over her face.

'Bella, I need you to answer a question. A serious one. But remember you're not in any trouble, okay?' Ellie assured her, stroking her head.

'Okay.' Bella's voice was still full of sleep as she opened her eyes.

'Where did you get this, please? Did someone give it to you?' she said, holding the Action Man by its feet in front of her.

'Oh, him.' She giggled. 'Yes, the nice man did.'

'A nice man. That's good. Why was he nice?'

Ellie's mind was spinning. Thinking of a killer interacting with her daughter.

'He smiled at me, and said I was good at skipping.'

'Okay. Where was this, honey?'

'At school, in the playground. I was playing with my friends.'

'Does he work there, Bella?'

'I don't know,' she said, scrunching her nose up. 'Your face looks funny, Mummy.'

'Why don't you know if he works there or not, honey?' Ellie tried to keep Bella focused.

'He gave me my present through the fence.'

Damn it, so he doesn't work there. Of course, that would be too easy.

Ellie took hold of her daughter's hand with her free one, giving it a squeeze. 'What else did he say to you? Can you remember for me?'

'Erm . . .' Bella brought her finger to her face. 'I don't know. Are you angry with me?'

'No, Bella, but this is *really* important. Try to remember. He said you were good at skipping. Anything else?'

'No, erm . . . just "Hello, Bella". And he gave me that.' She pouted, pointing at the doll still in Ellie's hand. 'Mummy, I'm tired.'

How does he know her name? Oh, my God. She pushed down her resurgent feelings of panic. 'You're doing great, honey.'

Bella's eyes suddenly lit up. 'Oh! The man said something, I remember!'

'What? What did he say?' Ellie held her breath.

'He said he'd see me soon and give me another present.' The little girl smiled. 'I like presents.'

34

Drake was mid-yawn when he pulled up just before two in the morning. His tired eyes fixed on the sight of a response vehicle, lights off, parked a few cars ahead on the street. He exited to the ticking sound of the now lifeless engine, the noise punctuating the still residential street.

The drive over had been an anxious one, mixed with a smattering of confusion. He couldn't believe what he'd heard. Why would Ellie's daughter have such a thing handed to her? How would the killer know her? Know her family? It made little sense. What was her significance to the newly coined *Stained Glass Killer*?

He'd got the call on his way out from the office, having finally decided to go back to his damn flat. He'd still been reeling from the events of the evening; his daughter, the photos . . . and now this.

Making his way to Ellie's house, the moon shining brightly, Drake realised he'd never actually been there before. She was right. It was a nicer version of the other places they'd been visiting recently. All well-tended gardens, streets free of rubbish, and not an errant pile of dog shit in sight.

He spotted a police officer leaving her house while he took in his surroundings.

'Evening, sir. DCI Drake, I'm guessing?' the officer asked at his approach.

'Got it in one, er . . . ?'

'PC Stretton,' he offered. Stretton seemed far too awake considering the time of night. 'Got here about thirty minutes ago. Not often I get a call from you lot for protection.'

'No, quite.' Drake replied. He motioned to get past.

'Don't mind me, I'll just stand here for now. Shout if you need me.'

Drake grunted his version of 'thanks' as he walked up to the front door and knocked lightly. He saw movement through the glass half-circle at eye level and Ellie answered. She looked worn out and fearful, something he couldn't recall having seen before. He didn't like it.

'Ellie, I came as soon as I could,' he said. 'How the hell is this possible?'

She sighed. 'I don't know, Drake. I'm at a loss.'

She moved aside to let him in. He was immediately taken aback by the sheer amount of Christmas decorations that were on display. They really had gone to town with the tinsel.

'Chief?'

He stepped inside while she hurriedly closed the door behind him, bolting it.

'Show me this . . . thing your daughter has.'

Ellie took him through to the living room. An enormous Christmas tree stood in the corner, while three stockings hung over the small fireplace opposite the sofa. Photos arranged on the mantlepiece. A man smiling back, along with a beautiful little girl and Ellie. Drake's heart ached for his family.

'Len's upstairs with Bella. Obviously, she doesn't understand what's going on. And to be honest, that makes two of us,' she said, before correcting herself, 'Three of us, I mean. Len doesn't get it either. He's spitting feathers. Worried about someone harming me and Bella . . .' She tailed off, realising the situation she was describing and the person she was talking to.

'I'd be rattled too, if I were him.' Drake pointed at the doll on the coffee table. 'So, is this it?'

He edged round the table and sat down in the middle of the sofa.

'Yes . . .' Ellie perched next to him.

Drake pulled some gloves from this pocket. 'Please don't handle it any more. I've only got this pair left. We'll need to get it analysed as soon as possible for any latent prints. Will need some from your family to discount them too, though I imagine our man will have been careful.'

He put them on while Ellie talked. 'I need to ask Bella soon if she can remember what he looked like. I didn't want to push too much. Drake, this guy knows her name – it wasn't a random encounter. He didn't just hand it to anyone. He meant for me to see. Maybe, for us.'

'Indeed, but why? To what end?' Drake examined the Action Man figure.

The doll appeared worn, well used; possibly second-hand, perhaps from a charity shop or similar. It was a peachy pink colour and completely naked. The rough duct tape had been wrapped around its head several times, making the head bulbous and much larger than it should be. It reminded Drake of an ugly modern take on a voodoo doll minus pins.

He put it down. 'We have to take this as a threat to you and your family, Ellie,' he stated. 'We'll ensure that there's someone on the property, day and night until we catch this bastard.'

'Thanks, Boss. Not sure how much better that makes me feel, all things considered, but thanks,' she said, putting on a weak smile.

'Do we know how long she's had it? It must have been soon after the first kills, right?'

'That's another question I'll have to ask her when she's ready. She's tired. She's five, remember?'

'Of course, handle it however you need to. But we'll need every scrap of detail we can get from her. I'm sorry.'

'I—'

Drake's phone started ringing, the vibration going off in his breast coat pocket. Then Ellie's started ringing as well.

Curious.

They looked at each other for a split second before each answering.

'Are you sure?' Drake asked, as Melwood gave him the details, his stomach churning.

'Jesus,' Ellie said in response to whoever had called her.

Drake couldn't believe it.

There had been another killing.

35

Drake picked up DI Melwood on the way to the crime scene. The man looked like he was a few sheets to the wind and could have done with some more time in the shower, followed by a strong coffee. Somehow, he actually looked more down and out than Drake did, which took him by surprise. His thoughts must have been plain to see, as Melwood felt the need to justify it on many occasions throughout the car journey.

'I'd only just gone to sleep when I got the call' and 'I'd had a few pints and nodded off' and so on and so forth. Drake didn't really care. He understood how the man was feeling. He didn't know the details, nor did he want to, but he understood. The man had effectively lost access to his son for his extra marital flings and his drinking. It seemed pretty dramatic for the custody to have drawn in the wife's favour to that extent. It left Drake with the feeling that the DI wasn't being entirely honest with what else had gone on behind closed doors.

Either way, he needed all the help he could get right now, and it wouldn't have been right to have Ellie along for the ride. He'd left her at home with her family, where they'd be safe. Drake felt a protectiveness over her that was nearly akin to that of his own daughter. It may be irrational, but with having so few people in his life that he cared about, it felt right. She had saved his daughter's life, and he would do what he could to look after her and her family in return.

'Still waiting on positive IDs and details about the homeowners, Drake. Strauss said we'd see why when we got there,' Melwood said, fiddling with his phone. He'd put the seat as far back as it would go and there was a not-so-subtle smell of alcohol, mixed with mint. Drake did his best to ignore it.

'Anyone in situ yet?' Drake asked, glancing at the DI. His tired eyes feeling like they'd fall out of their sockets if he didn't get some proper rest soon.

'Yeah, that's how they knew to get in touch with us. Your pathologist buddy, Dr Kulkarni, took one look and requested you, apparently. Called me when they couldn't get through to you,' Melwood said. He sounded somewhat bitter, as though he was disappointed his name hadn't been foremost in her mind.

'I hope it isn't a multiple this time,' Drake growled. 'I'm not enjoying having all these deaths on our hands. The longer this goes on, the more culpable we are.' He rubbed his face with his free hand. 'This is on us.'

Melwood sighed. 'There's only so much we can do, Drake. You know this, a man of your *experience*.'

Drake's hackles raised; the man still had a knack of getting under his skin. 'My experience doesn't mean shit when people are dying on my watch. Doesn't it get to you?'

Melwood shrugged and remained silent, only speaking again to tell Drake which direction to take next. He was on satnav duty in Ellie's absence.

They soon pulled up to a house at the end of a street, distanced slightly (and oddly, to Drake's mind) from the remaining ones. The house across the street had been demolished, but the land hadn't been built on yet, and the neighbouring houses were arranged as though the developers had started a new row of terraces at a fresh starting point. It left a curious gap of a few metres between their subject's house and the actual street.

The street was swamped with police cars, SOCO vans, ambulances and Drake's personal favourite, the media. How were they getting their tip offs so soon?

'Have you notified Chambers and Strauss?' he asked.

'Yeah, they were on their way when you grabbed me. Strauss was the one that called Ellie. Didn't she say?'

'No, she's distracted right now, as you can imagine.'

Melwood coughed like he was about to hack up a lung. 'Sorry . . . yeah, can't get my head around why she's receiving our killer's attention. It was a bloke, right? The one that gave her daughter the thing?'

Drake nodded. 'Indeed. Passed it through the fence of her school. Shameless.'

'Crap. If that had been my son . . .' Melwood said. He scratched his shaved temple, the usually slick hair splayed and messy.

'Yeah.' Nothing more was needed.

'Urgh, hate the media, 'specially now with this headache kicking in,' Melwood groaned, slicking his hair back in the sun visor mirror. The sight of the media turning and rushing towards their car made them both grimace.

'Amen to that,' Drake scowled, exiting the car to a flood of blinding cameras.

36

When Drake entered the house, a pervasive, acrid smell immediately greeted him, as though someone had had a bonfire nearby. It made his eyes water while he sized up the crime scene, a bitterness building in the back of his throat.

A SOCO was standing near the stairs, fiddling with some equipment. Drake tapped him on the shoulder, asking for a set of overalls for him and Melwood. The man went off to get some while Drake continued to study his surroundings from the front door.

It was quite unremarkable. A few doorways leading, presumably, to a front room or living room and a back-room dining area. Kitchen at the end of the hall, stairs directly to his left leading up to a small landing and a couple of bedrooms, likely an upstairs bathroom. The walls were all a bland magnolia colour, with similar off-white carpets.

Drake spotted a picture on the wall. A familiar pudgy face stared back at him, only this time in a happier frame of mind. It was Clare Baker, the manager from the supermarket. The woman was holding a champagne glass in a toast with a friend. The two were dressed up as though they were at the races, large comical-looking hats adorning their heads. Ascot, he assumed, not knowing much more about horse racing beyond Ascot and . . . Aintree, was it?

'Isn't that . . . ?' Melwood said, pointing at the photo.

Drake nodded. 'Indeed. God knows why, but she must be the next victim.'

'The plot thickens.' Melwood clenched his jaw as the SOCO man returned with the collection of overalls, masks and shoe coverings.

'The scene's out back. Follow the hallway, through the back room – you can't miss it.'

Drake hoped not. It wasn't like they were on a country estate and had to track through a myriad of maze-like corridors.

'Okay, thanks.' He balanced on one leg as he got the shoe coverings on. Melwood did the same, leaning on the doorframe and hopping awkwardly. Melwood still appeared a little unsteady on his feet. Drake secretly hoped that the media could see the man's non-acrobatic display from their vantage point.

'Ready?' he asked, cocking an eyebrow at the struggling DI.

'You go on, I'll be a minute with this blasted thing, and the damn smell is making me woozy.'

Smiling to himself, Drake continued through to the back room. A sofa was shoved up against the wall to his left, a television on the wall opposite. A small, white circular dining table with a fake flower arrangement stood in the corner closest to him. More photos displayed on the wall to the right side provided further confirmation of the manager's appreciation for the high life and a few drinks.

Through the large floor to ceiling patio doors, spreading the width of the room, was where the main hive of activity seemed concentrated. Tents had been pitched and flood lamps installed, giving SOCO the lighting and privacy needed to work away from the prying eyes of the neighbouring properties and the media.

The closer to the garden Drake got, the stronger the smell became. It was now truly pungent, sticking in the back of his throat, despite the mask.

He carefully edged past a SOCO towards the doors to see if the scene became clearer, the corners of his eyes beginning to water again. He stepped out, people making way for him amidst the scattering of numbered markers where the edge of the paved ground met the grass. Drake could see the signs of a struggle, muddied heel marks directing him down to the business end of the scene.

A black wrought-iron table and two overturned similar chairs were splayed nearby at the corner of the patio, making it apparent the victim had been sitting there prior to what had happened. A free-standing overhead patio light and heater combination was still in place. The heater throbbed an angry red but gave off a welcome warmth all the same.

Strauss and Chambers stood to one side of the table, using the crime scene stepping plates to avoid trampling the table area. They were deep in discussion, which stopped when Chambers saw him entering the garden.

'Sir, glad you're here.' Chambers paced over to him, stepping off the last plate. 'I'm sorry, but I didn't want to go down there until you'd arrived. The *smell*...'

'You're going to have to toughen up, Gemma,' Drake told her. 'There might be worse to come.'

'Sorry, sir. These deaths are racking up quickly for me.'

'Don't be sorry, you've just got to push through it. You'll get there.' He looked over at Strauss. 'I've got some more ideas for potential leads, Strauss.'

The man came over, acknowledging him in his usual formal manner.

'Okay, point me in the direction, and I'll check it out, sir.'

'Thanks. Now that this woman, Clare Baker, is involved somehow, I want you to focus on her background. It can't be a coincidence that she and Alex worked at the same place.' Drake peered over his mask with tired eyes. 'She said at the time she didn't "fraternise" with her staff, but perhaps they had a secret fling, or there was something else there. Give it a shake for me, would you?'

'Of course,' Strauss nodded. 'Once I get back to the office, I'll look into it.'

'Good man.'

Drake left them and ventured towards the scene proper, using another series of stepping plates. In what was strangely perfect timing, the crowd moved off to the sides to work on various activities as he approached, affording him a full view of the scene in all its macabre, grotesque detail.

His heart sank. Before him were *two* bodies stood tied to a pole, their arms bound behind them. The man's head leaning forwards in death, the woman's featureless screaming face pointed up towards the sky.

The ground around them lay charred and scorched, likely from the splashing of an accelerant, he smelt petrol. A few overhanging trees concealing the garden had been partially burned or singed, but their surroundings were largely intact.

Drake had always hated investigating murders where the victims had burned. The mental imagery and the leftovers were haunting. He couldn't imagine the sounds that the neighbours may have heard, the intensity of the flames.

He stepped closer.

The corpse he presumed to be Clare Baker because of its wide, short frame was fixed in a perpetual scream. Her face and hair had burned away, revealing prominent teeth, the empty eye sockets pointing skywards. A length of wire had kept her head in place at the forehead, as had her body and legs. The wire had embedded itself into her ample flesh, and the intensity of the heat had charred her muscles to where she was locked in position, likely until decomposition eventually had its way. The sight, even for him, was difficult. Drake felt a pang of guilt for chastising Chambers.

He turned his focus to the male.

His proximity to Clare Baker's body exaggerated the mystery man's height. He was likely around six feet, but that was the only discernible feature he had left. Parts of his skull were visible through the remnants of a blackened scalp. Drake was glad he couldn't see the face from where he was standing, as unlike Clare, the man appeared to have had no restraint around his neck or head to keep him in place.

'Grim, isn't it?' Dr Kulkarni interjected from behind, breaking his concentration.

Drake's mouth formed a thin line beneath his mask. 'That's one word for it, Doc.'

'Our friend appears to enjoy his line of work. From my initial findings, it appears there had been a struggle beforehand, up by those overturned chairs,' Tanv said, pointing back towards the patio.

'The victims were probably subdued, then dragged, as evidenced by the heel marks, to our current location,' she continued. 'They were lashed to this pole here. I believe it's a rotary washing pole – would you believe it? That's one way of drying things. And I also believe the woman's eyes were forcibly removed prior to her death . . . oh, and can you see here?'

'I don't want to but, okay.' Drake said, grimacing as she pointed into the woman's mouth.

'I believe her tongue was also removed.'

'What? Jesus!' Tongue removal at a crime scene was becoming much too regular for Drake's liking. He breathed in. 'And the man?'

'Well, you're not going to like this one, being male and all,' he detected a hint of a smile behind her mask.

'Why?'

'His penis and testicles were removed, too.'

'What? You're shitting me?' he said, incredulous. The mind boggled as to why that was necessary, but also why *any* of the scene was necessary. It was complete overkill.

'No.'

He sighed, wanting to scratch the back of his neck, but the hooded overall was stopping him. 'How do you know? Didn't they burn away with the rest of their features? Anything else? His ears, perhaps his toes, for God's sake.'

'Nope, just his eyes as well.'

'Oh, good.'

'And the reason we know this is because they're in a pile over there.' Tanv pointed nonchalantly at a blood-streaked and spattered fence panel. 'The SGK – better than Stained Glass Killer, if you ask me – plucked all the bits they needed and just threw them at that fence panel. Like they were bowling at a cricket match or something.'

'I'm running out of expletives here, Tanv,' Drake said, his stomach roiling. Must be getting sensitive in his old age, he thought. The old him wouldn't have batted an eyelid, and might have even been fascinated by the method behind the madness.

'I know, right?' she remarked. He couldn't help but smirk slightly. It was like having a posh, medically-trained version of

Ellie there with him. 'And the fire crew didn't even have to extinguish them. It went out before they really started disintegrating. Fortunate for us, really. We'd have been left with less than this. Must have been going for a good hour or two, though before it went out of its own accord.'

Drake was going to reply when he heard the click of a camera behind him.

'Sorry, could you . . . could you move please, Drake?' The muffled voice of Graham Reynolds requested. He turned to see the man clutching a camera. His eyes didn't appear as apologetic as the voice.

'What a scene, eh?' Reynolds remarked excitedly.

Drake didn't say a word, stepping onto another panel next to Tanv. He wasn't excited by death; just disgusted, angry and determined.

'What's he doing here?' he muttered into Tanv's ear.

'He's my assistant. Why wouldn't he be here?' she whispered, trying to keep her voice low. 'Do I detect you dislike him? Should it offend me you don't like my colleagues?'

'You detect right, Tanv.'

'Grow up,' she hissed.

'You would react the same way if you'd had the shit experience I've had with him,' he retorted.

'Well, people have to learn from their mistakes, Drake. If we shat on everyone who made a mistake, we wouldn't have much of a police force now, would we? Where would you be?'

'Ouch.' He winced as the barb struck home.

'Sorry. Here, have one of my rare apologies.'

'Erm, thanks?'

She stopped just short of poking him in his side with a gloved finger. 'No problem.'

'Sorry, sorry I'm late.' Melwood made a song and dance of his approach, holding his hands up as he stepped from plate to plate. He clearly hadn't taken in the view with Reynolds in the way taking photos. Then he realised what he was seeing.

'Holy shit.' Melwood started retching, the sound making Drake curl up his face in disgust. The remnants of alcohol were clearly not helping the man's cause.

'Seriously, Drake. We need to stop this and stop this now. This . . . this is just sick,' Melwood declared between retches.

'Thanks for that insight, DI Melwood. I believe you're right,' Tanv remarked and turned back to Drake.

'Last point for you – much like the other killings, we've recovered bugger all personal effects. No wallet, mobile phones, nothing. The SGK must have taken them. Really makes me wonder how you found that wallet in the cellar.'

'Not surprising, is it? Makes our task harder. Perhaps there was something on their phones linking them to this "SGK", as you call them.'

'Indeed, but make sure your team check on the phone towers. Maybe they didn't switch them off?'

'Thanks, Detective,' Drake acknowledged Tanv with more than a modicum of sarcasm.

'I deserved that.' She nodded, then gave a short clap of her hands. 'Okay, I've got to get back to the lab to prep for this. Do either of you need me for anything more?'

Drake couldn't think of anything, and left her to collect her things before she made her way back up and into the house. The mood dampened considerably on Tanv's exit. SOCO made moves to start the rest of their work before they took the bodies down to the lab.

'The burning . . .' Drake thought out loud. 'What could that signify? We've had a severe beating, and now something akin to a modern day burning at the stake . . .'

'Witches? They burned witches at the stake.' Melwood offered.

Strauss and Chambers came down and joined them at the sides of the main awning. Chambers' eyes looked anywhere but at the crispy duo, whereas Strauss appeared unaffected.

'Right. And they were burned. Why?'

'Because they were different? They were . . . feared?' Melwood suggested.

'They were never actually witches, though, obviously,' Strauss interjected. 'People burned them because they didn't like the women's behaviour, and other dubious reasons. There was no scientific proof to back up they were what they were accused of. It was ludicrous.'

Drake thought long and hard, to the point where the rest of the team looked uncomfortable. 'So, if we add in the initial revenge angle, this killer's twisted thought process . . . Does this mean these two weren't what people thought?'

'Possibly? Might be a stretch though, Drake. Perhaps this killer isn't as clever as you think he is. And what about the beatings at the first scene?' Melwood pointed out.

'True, but the first killings could relate to something entirely different. More of a brutal, hands-on punishment, perhaps?' Drake turned to Strauss, his gloved hands steepled. 'I can't stress this enough. We really need you to double down on Clare Baker while we figure out who our mystery man is.'

'On it, sir, as said. I won't let you down.'

Drake nodded. 'Thank you. Now all, try your best to go home when you're done here and get some bloody sleep. A busy day ahead. That's an order.'

37

Ellie, frustrated by the last few day's developments, was crawling up the walls. She'd felt like a prisoner in her own home, her family chained to the house as though they'd committed some unspeakable crime. It was a strange situation, one she hadn't experienced before and never wanted to again. Having a police officer stationed at their door was proving more disconcerting than she could ever have imagined. It served in making her more worried, not less.

She sighed as she stroked Bella's hair. The girl was asleep next to her on the sofa, the Christmas lights from the tree slowly changing colour and pattern, glowing then fading. Ellie had felt herself nodding off at points, despite her best efforts.

Len had done his utmost to work from home, but he was finding the situation all too distracting and stressful. She felt for him, having this situation thrust upon him. He'd admitted feeling helpless, and she'd tried to allay his fears as best she could, but it was hard when she felt precisely the same.

With Bella, she'd had to pretend it was all part of a Christmas game. She'd found it fun for the first day, but she was acting up now. The chat with her about the man at the playground fence hadn't got them anywhere useful in the end. All Bella been able to tell them was that he was nice, white, and had brown hair and a beard, which narrowed it down by precisely . . . nothing. Why couldn't he have had purple hair and been seven feet tall? That would have shortened their odds dramatically. The ridiculous thought made her sigh. She really wasn't thinking straight. She was itching to get back out with the team.

'You okay, love?' Len said, handing her a cup of coffee and sitting on her free side.

She looked over at him with tired eyes. 'No, I don't think I am.'

'Me neither. I want it to end already. Can't they just catch him red-handed somewhere, so we can be done with this? Surely there has to be some kind of lead? It can't always be like this?'

'Sadly not, it rarely works that way. It's not something we go about telling the public, but unless the murderers are complete amateurs – which isn't something I deal with in my team anyway – it's usually down to luck mixed with a bit of intuition that gets them in the end.'

She stopped to take a sip of her coffee, which was still much too hot for her liking. 'But the more people involved with the killer, the more likely there are to be elements beyond their control too. Like with the previous case Drake and I had together. We'd likely still be no closer to catching that guy if it hadn't been for his idiot of a son complicating matters for him.'

'You're not filling me with confidence, Ellie.'

'Sorry, on a bit of a downer. I feel like I should be doing something.'

He put down his glasses on the coffee table and looked at her. 'Then *go do* something. I mean it. We're safe here with your police buddies. Go do your thing.'

Her heart leapt in her chest, but it was immediately coupled with a feeling of selfishness. 'Not so sure that's a good idea. I don't like leaving either of you here. I couldn't forgive myself if something were to happen to you.'

'We'll be okay. You're doing us more harm than good at the moment with all your worrying and pacing about the place,' he said with a tired smile. She appreciated his attempt to lighten the mood.

'I don't know . . .'

'Ellie, I promise. I'll call you if anything changes. We'll be fine. Go.'

'I'd like to put it on record that I'm not happy about this, but okay . . . fine. I'll go in for a few hours, and that's it. Then I'm back.'

'Good,' he said, kissing her forehead.

* * *

Ellie pulled herself together, got dressed into something resembling a work outfit – dark jumper, shirt underneath, smarter than usual trousers – and grabbed a lift with her details shift changeover at the house. It was only mid-afternoon, but the light had already drawn in, the sun low on the horizon.

PC Asif Malik, a friendly guy with a thick London accent and a comical-looking thin chinstrap beard, had clearly been bored senseless by his watch detail. He tried to strike up a conversation with her on the drive back. She engaged with it occasionally, but he took the hint after glimpsing the pictures she'd brought up on her phone. His eyes widening as he locked them back on the road ahead. Ellie had received a slew of photos and documents detailing the post-mortem from Strauss after she'd told Drake she was coming in.

He really knows how to spoil a girl, she thought. *Sending me dark shit like this.*

The post-mortem report for the supermarket manager and the mystery man had made for grim reading. Something she was privately pleased she'd not had to attend. The photos were more than enough. The thought of being there and breathing them in? That was a step too far.

The crispy-looking man, in particular, had added some additional challenges with identification. From what she understood, they would use both DNA and dental records too, should that fail.

Both victims had died through a combination of thermal shock leading to a heart attack and suffocation from the fire damage to their lungs. It had been difficult to determine, though; the damage had been so great.

Ellie cringed at Tanv's details of the post-mortems; the eyes being plucked out, the tongue too in Clare Baker's case, and the man's penis. Particularly as the good doctor didn't believe this would have killed them outright or knocked them unconscious. Plus, even if they had been, the fire had soon woken them up for their few, short agonising moments left on this earth.

She shuddered. It also transpired that once again the SGK had left a photo, this time in Clare's throat, but disappointingly damaged beyond repair. Only charred fragments remained, with no chance of divining what the picture was of.

Was that his intention? To taunt them with thoughts of 'what if'? Or had he wanted it to survive the fire for them to see?

Nothing from the house pointed them toward their killer and her stalker. Yet again, he was an enigma.

An enigma that was threatening her family.

38

Ellie entered the SMT incident room to a barrage of noise. If she'd not heard the content of what they were saying, she would have assumed they were excited to see her. However, it was a discovery that had got Melwood, Chambers and Strauss excited, the team clamouring around Strauss' workstation. She spotted Drake looking out from his office to see what all the fuss was about.

'There I was, thinking this was a welcoming party,' she offered.

'Sorry, not this time, Wilkinson,' Melwood replied excitedly. 'Strauss here appears to have found something quite significant.'

'Well, go on, tell us then,' Drake demanded. Ellie noted he was finally wearing some different clothes this time. It made a remarkable difference to the man's appearance, but he still looked a more than a little stressed, to put it lightly.

'Okay, so,' Strauss started, his voice clipped. 'I was looking over the bank records I've got for Alex, and now our latest victim, Clare Baker. It took a lot of digging, but I think I've found something a little . . . *curious.*'

'Okay.' Drake said, clearly wanting the man to hurry.

'There are several unreferenced payments to Clare Baker around ten years ago, around the time that he was with Sofia,' Strauss continued. 'They're quite irregular, but consistent in their values. A thousand, one month. Then a few months later again, then just a couple of weeks. Then they stop altogether and I don't see any interaction again.'

Melwood butted in impatiently. 'Right, but what could the significance be?'

Strauss threw his hands up. 'I don't know. Just telling you what I've found – I don't have all the answers, sir.'

'It shows there's a link there, at least?' Chambers piped up from the back.

'Indeed,' Drake said. 'Strauss, has she got any other payments for a similar amount coming in from anyone else in that time frame, or any time thereafter?'

'I'll have to continue looking. I stopped as soon as I got to this.'

'Maybe he was paying her for this sex party stuff Alex and Sofia seem to be a part of?' Ellie offered.

'Yes, maybe.' Strauss said, looking up at her from his laptop. 'But we've no evidence of Clare in the photos, and her house didn't appear to have a room similar to the one in the pictures, but you weren't to know that.'

She punched her palm in frustration. 'True . . . shit.' She paused for a moment. 'But we don't have evidence to the contrary just yet, do we? They could have been away somewhere for the weekend. She may be the person taking the photos?'

'Good point,' Strauss conceded.

'So, what we're getting at here is that each person is linked, which shows these aren't random killings, at least,' Drake said.

'Which is certainly not nothing, even if it feels that way. We need to figure out the pattern.'

Ellie enjoyed seeing him be this positive. Or was it because he was clutching at straws and making the best of a bad situation?

'So, what now?' she asked.

'Woah, woah, sorry. That's not everything I've found about Clare.' Strauss put his hand up to stop anyone else from interjecting. 'As Melwood and Drake are aware, I've done some more digging into Clare's family situation, and Chambers and I spoke with a few neighbours today. They told us some things, and I wanted to see if I could corroborate any of it.'

He stopped to take a quick swig of coffee, running his hand through his tangled mane. 'From what I've been told, though she was never married, she wasn't just some single woman barbecued in her own garden. Before moving to her current address, she lived with another man for several years. He's been referred to as Gregory or Greg, depending on who we spoke to. I still need to see what I can find regarding her address records. Maybe I can shed some light on that. Maybe it means something?'

'Exactly. She could have been with this Gregory when all those payments were made.' Melwood said, propping his elbows on the desk he'd commandeered during the chat. 'I like where this is going. We're not out of options just yet.'

'Indeed. Keep doing what you're doing, Strauss,' Drake told him.

'Thank you, sir.'

* * *

Drake sighed irritably at Dr Helen Proctor-Reeves. He was fast tiring of these sessions; the incessant prodding and poking into his private life was getting beyond the pale.

He'd attempted to clean up his act since his encounter with Miller a few days before. He'd gone out and bought some fresh shirts, gone to a hotel to have some sleep. He'd even ironed his suit as best he could to at least try to give off the air of someone who had a home they were happy to go to. But going back to the flat was still something he couldn't bring himself to do. He'd been toying with the idea of ditching it entirely and moving back to his actual house. But each time the idea ended with his thoughts of Becca, her dying in that blasted kitchen.

'John.' Dr Proctor-Reeves looked directly at him across the same dilapidated office as before. She'd bought some flowers, white lilies, to brighten the place up, but the smell was overpowering. Maybe that was what the tissues were really for.

'Sorry, what?' he said, his mind foggy.

'You zoned out. Are you okay?'

'Erm . . . yes, sorry. Where were we?'

She tapped her pen on her notebook. 'Your daughter, Eva.'

'Oh . . . yes.' He did his best to keep any emotion out of his voice. What was it with him not being able to open up to her? Drake knew she wouldn't be able to help him. He was a lost cause; he knew that, but what if she could help him and his relationship with his daughter, if nothing else? That would be something, right? He had to try; he was running out of options.

'Well, she . . . ' He looked down at the floor, ashamed to say what he had to say to a woman, likely a mother herself. 'She doesn't live with me anymore. Hasn't for nearly a year now, even though I'm her only parent. She can't bear to look at me, let alone be in the same room as me.'

'I see. Why?'

'You know why,' he snapped.

'I want to hear why you think this is the case?'

'Well, obviously because she believes I was the person who

brought a killer to our doorstep. The way she talks, how she acts around me. I might as well have killed Becca myself. She detests me. It doesn't take a genius to understand that, does it?' he said, looking down at his hands and rubbing them together slowly.

'Do you think she has good reason to think that way?'

'I . . .' He paused. He'd started speaking before he'd really thought it through.

The psychologist gave him a slight smile and tilted her head. 'John, it seems you're taking your daughter's thoughts and feelings as your own. You need to give yourself a break. You're not taking a step back here and rationalising what you're doing to yourself.'

That somehow piqued his interest. 'How do you mean?'

'It may well ultimately be your fault. It's not for me to say it is, or for me to relieve you of that burden,' she said, adjusting her seating position. 'But this is the line of work you're in. The pressure can be intense, and you walk a dangerous line with the criminals you are involved with.

'I see,' Drake saw where she was going, but he couldn't quite accept it.

'Your daughter, Eva. She's grieving, lashing out. She's going for the person who went through the experience with her, as there is *no one else*. Her mother is dead. Her father is not in her life every day. She is festering, and what you have said of the aunt, well, she doesn't appear to be helping, rather fanning the flames of her resentment. Your wife was her sister, after all.'

Drake huffed to himself. *She's got that right, at least.*

'You're not there for her each day to work through her pain,' the doctor continued. 'You've taken what you thought was the right step, but you've taken it too far.'

'So, what are you saying? Or is that "not for you to say" either?'

'You got it, John. This is for you to figure out and for me to listen.'

'This isn't helping me.'

'Really? We've made some progress. You wouldn't have dreamed of talking about your daughter when we first started, right?'

He shifted in his seat. 'I guess. But you're not telling me anything I don't know, beyond repetition and those bloody mindfulness techniques earlier on.'

She smiled at him. 'If that's what you believe, then that's what you believe.'

Drake felt his anger surging, not at the doctor, but at himself. Why couldn't he do right by Eva? Even though it was almost Christmas, a time she had so loved in the past, he still couldn't get through to her. What would it take? What would he have to do?

The doctor's insights made his mind spin and his throat suddenly felt dry.

What she's been through . . . she's not a bloody kid anymore. Can't you see that?

He flexed his hands. He needed to leave before it got any worse, before he said or did something he truly regretted. Drake couldn't have her reporting him to Miller.

The thought stopped his mind spinning, bringing a sudden cold clarity. 'Okay, sounds like we're on to something. You're right, Doc,' he said, forcing a smile.

'That's great to hear—'

His phone rang, causing Proctor-Reeves to stop, her eyebrows raising at the interruption.

Drake rummaged around in his pockets before realising he'd set it on the doctor's desk to his side. He stood and snagged it. It was Melwood.

'Sorry, I have to take this.' He grabbed the phone, moving for the door as he answered.

'We've finally ID'ed the man, Drake.'

'And?' He barked down the phone.

'It's . . . well, it's one of us.'

'What do you mean, one of us?'

'It's a police officer, Drake.'

39

Drake burst into the room. The room went silent, everyone turning to see the commotion.

'He's one of us? A detective? Still in service, retired? What?'

Melwood frowned. 'You didn't give me a chance to say before hanging up.'

Drake stood stony-faced and waited for an answer.

The DI made a face. 'It's a beat sergeant, man by the name of Peter Matthews.'

'Can't say I've heard the name,' Drake said, aghast at one of their own being burned alive. 'Did anyone know him?'

They all shook their heads.

'Not me, Drake,' Melwood said.

'Suppose that's not saying much, is it? That we don't know him? There's *how* many police officers?' Ellie remarked.

He calmed a little, the initial shock wearing off. 'Well, yes . . .'

'Anyway, as I was saying, before the door nearly fell off its hinges,' Strauss went on, 'The man was a loner. There's no history of a family life. His parents died a long time ago. Been on the police force for thirty years last year. *Was* close to having the option to retire. Nothing really of note, he did his job. Run of the mill.'

'What a way to go out,' Ellie said.

'Indeed.' Drake had been half-expecting some fire-related pun from her for a second, but realised she probably wasn't in that sort of mood.

Strauss pulled up the man's picture. Unsurprisingly, it bore no real resemblance to the shell of a man he came across at Clare Baker's address. He was bald, long faced, ruddy complexion, wore glasses and kept a short grey beard. The sergeant could have been any of the police officers Drake had walked past or shared a moment of small talk with.

'So, Strauss.' Drake scratched his cheek while he dished more orders out to the German. 'Needless to say, I need you and Chambers to work your magic on this, all right? Find out everything you can on him, see if his details pop up alongside any of our other victims. Maybe he was involved in this sex business somehow.'

'Melwood, keep this from the press as long as you can. We don't want it being known this SGK is a damn cop killer too.'

'Will do. We can't be letting our own be butchered on our doorstep, Drake. It isn't on.' Melwood frowned. 'Why're you immediately treating our colleague as a suspect, near enough?'

'We really don't know what we're dealing with here. I get it, but don't immediately jump to his defence.'

'Yes, but—'

'Just get on with doing what you can, Inspector. Don't give the guy preferential treatment, distant colleague or otherwise. You more than most should know we need to keep our minds open. Notify any distant next of kin, if we find any.'

'Fine,' Melwood said, turning his nose up at the dressing down and busy work.

Drake knew he was probably overreacting, the man pressing his buttons as per usual. But the news of more deaths, Ellie being threatened and now having a murderer reclassified as a cop killer . . . the pressure was going to build on Miller and him. A vein at his temple throbbed. This needed solving, and solving fast. Four bodies, and it had barely been a week. He needed to do better.

* * *

'Thanks for the lift, Chief,' Ellie looked over and smiled at him, the stark glare of the overhead light casting shadows on her face.

'You're a lucky woman, Ellie,' Dave remarked from the back seat before leaning forwards and clapping Drake on the shoulder. 'Your boss is not one for the chauffeur service. I think I can count on one hand the number of times he dropped me off somewhere.'

Drake huffed. 'I don't think that's true, but I'll let it slide – as I'm your superior, I have the prerogative to do so.'

The lift he'd offered wasn't completely without ulterior motives. He had wanted to stick around for a while, checking out the surrounding area for anything untoward. Drake didn't feel comfortable not having done so since the incident. Dave had tagged along, likely for the same reason, but had also suggested that they both go for a drink after dropping her. It was going to become a habit if he wasn't careful. Drake hadn't drunk this much in twenty years, let alone a week. But it kept him away from the flat and that could only be a good thing.

'Okay, well, it's been fun, both. Appreciate it. Appreciate it more if we catch the bastard soon though, yeah?' she said, before adding with a smirk. 'Not sure how long I can sustain these protection officers' tea supply on my wages.'

Drake and Dave nodded solemnly.

'See you.' Ellie got out of the car, leaving the door open for Dave to jump in the front. She waved back at them both. Drake watched her walk across the road and into the house, greeting the stationed PC as she did so.

'I want to kill whoever threatened her little girl, John,' Dave said, settling into his seat as her front door closed, his face set in a frown.

'You and me both,' Drake said.

'This is all a little close to the bone for you right now, isn't it?'

The overhead cabin light went off, the darkness masking the frown that had formed from his friend's comment. Drake gripped the steering wheel; he didn't want to get into it. Not after today. 'Something like that. But she's a colleague and a friend too, irrespective of what happened to me.'

'Aye, that she is,' the man nodded. 'Do me a favour, would you?'

'What?'

'When I'm retired, keep her out of trouble, okay?'

'Are we talking about the same woman here?' Drake smirked. 'She's the one that creates it.'

'Yes, but she follows you, John. She looks up to you. Don't forget that.'

'What's brought this on?'

'Old age, I suppose – not that you're *that* far behind me. That and the police officer that was murdered brought it all home a bit for me. The world's a messed-up place, and I'm tired of seeing beneath the facade day in, day out. The cruelty man inflicts upon man . . . it's wearing, you know?'

'Mmm.' Drake knew all too well what he meant.

'I think finally it may have worn *me* down, John.'

Dave sounded like the weight of the world was on his shoulders, and Drake cocked an eyebrow at him. 'And here I was thinking you were trying to make me feel better.'

'Oh, you? You're a lost cause,' Dave's moustache twitched.

They sat in silence in the darkness, watching the street. A mangy fox ran out into the road, grabbing something in its jaws before disappearing behind a car.

'How's Eva doing? You both reconciled yet?'

Drake's heart sank. 'I'd rather not talk about it.'

'Not talking about it doesn't make it go away – you know that, John. Ignore her comments and get her home. She needs to be with her dad.'

He'd had it up to here with people telling him what to do. 'Dave, I—'

Drake stopped mid-sentence, spotting something in the darkness. He leant forward, peering out of the car. It was gone the next second, but he could have sworn he'd seen something disappearing over the back of the small fence, a house or two down from Ellie's.

'John, what is it?'

'I think there's someone looking to case Ellie's house,' he said, his voice locked in concentration.

Dave's eyes sparked. 'What? Where? You're just being paranoid, surely?'

'No,' he hissed. 'They've just climbed into the back garden of one of those houses. It looks like they're going to approach Ellie's.'

Dave grabbed Drake's wrist, hard as he went for the door handle. 'Call for backup, now.'

'Not yet. I don't want to startle the little shit.'

He opened his car door and made his way out into the cold of the night.

'John!' Dave hissed, muttering 'For God's sake' under his breath while he undid his seatbelt.

Drake closed the door silently and crossed the road on his approach to the house. He stayed close to the front walls of the houses, ensuring he kept out of the line of sight where the person had scaled the fence.

Crouching as he got closer to Ellie's gate, he flashed his ID at the officer guarding the entrance. The PC was a short, round man, not unlike Dave, but younger and without the moustache. Drake couldn't imagine him jumping a fence in a hurry.

He gestured to the officer to keep quiet, putting his finger to his lips.

'Get some more people down here now – I think I've seen someone. And do it *quietly*.' He made a point of gesturing in a downward motion with his hands to hammer it home.

'What! I've not seen anyone?'

'Next few properties along, you weren't to know.'

Drake left the man to make the call.

'John, stop!' Dave hissed behind him.

'No, I've got to catch the bastard.'

Dave shook his head. 'Chasing these guys is a young man's game,' he said.

Drake waved a hand behind him, not looking back. 'Just keep watch here. I'll flush him out.'

He crept to the gateway a couple of doors down. The fence was only around four feet wide, and about six feet high, recently installed. He pushed on it, and it held firm. Likely why the guard hadn't heard the person jump on it. Drake knew he'd scaled worse in his time.

A crash came from the back of the property.

Shit.

Taking a deep breath, he heaved himself up and over the fence into the darkness.

40

'Hello?' Ellie called, 'I'm back. Len?' She shut the door behind her. Removing her coat, she could hear the soft thrum of Christmas music coming from the lounge. If this had been any other day and any other circumstance, she would have felt more comforted by it than she did. An image from the Family Man case sprung into her mind, her family dead at their dining table.

'Mummy!' Bella spotted Ellie poking her head round the door, and Ellie felt a wave of relief wash over her.

'Here she is,' Ellie smiled, grunting as Bella barrelled into her for a hug.

Her little girl looked up at her, a worried look on her face. 'I thought you left me!' she pouted.

'I'd never do that to my little monster,' she said, heaving her daughter up and into her arms.

She giggled. 'I'm not a monster!'

'Everything okay on the western front?' Ellie looked over at Len, a laptop open in front of him, reading glasses propped on the end of his nose.

'Nothing to report, sir!' Len said, producing an elaborate salute from the dining table.

'That's a relief, at least.'

'Not a good afternoon, evening . . . or whatever?'

'Not the best. I'll tell you about it later when I've tucked this little madam up in bed.' She poked her tongue out at Bella.

'I—'

Crash!

It sounded like it came from the back garden.

'What the! What the hell was that?' Len said, starting up from the table.

Ellie bundled Bella over to him, her heart pounding in her chest. 'Take Bella, Len. Take Bella and get out of the house, now!'

Len nodded and whispered a quick 'I love you' before rushing for the front door. He looked back for a moment, wordlessly pleading for her to be careful, and disappeared from the doorway.

Ellie went into the kitchen and took a medium-sized kitchen knife from the knife block. Her movements suddenly seemed much too loud. Taking a deep breath, she flicked on the outside light before carefully opening the door, knife in hand.

* * *

Drake hurried down the unlit path. It opened out into a small garden with a shed at the end, dormant flower beds lining either side of the stretch of grass. Whoever the intruder was, he couldn't see them now. They must have hopped a fence or two closer to Ellie's place.

Standing in a flowerbed at the front of the dark garden, he peered over the fence. The next garden was also empty, but the one after . . . a panel seemed to be missing in the darkness's haze, over in the far corner.

He vaulted the first one without issue, impressing himself with his apparent agility before struggling on the next. The fence gave a significant wobble as he pulled himself over before his coat snagged on the top as he landed. Drake pulled it free and turned to look at the gap he'd spotted at the far end.

He froze at the sight before him, his heart propelling into his mouth. The man he'd spotted was lying on the ground, the missing fence panel now laying broken on Ellie's patch. It must have buckled under him when he attempted to climb it. But why was the man still on the ground? Was he giving it time before moving, hoping no one had heard? Or had he hurt himself?

The thoughts flashed through Drake's mind while he crossed to the fence opposite, blocking the main exit to the front of the property. He kept himself steady and tried to ensure there was no chance of the man getting round him like at Alex's flat. Midmove, a spotlight came on behind him, illuminating both him and the mystery stalker. The man's eyes locked on him instantly, shining in the light before he deftly clambered back to his feet and ran into Ellie's garden. He did so just as another light came on, this time on Ellie's side.

'Stop right there,' he shouted, knowing the man would do nothing of the sort.

'Drake, what's going on?' Ellie's voice sounded panicked as light flooded the back of her house. 'What the . . . stay where you are!'

Drake rounded the flattened fence panel, seeing the man's back as he ran to the edge of the garden plot, preparing to vault over another fence. He was taking a few steps back to make a run at it. If Drake didn't act now, their would-be killer would elude them once again.

'Stop!' *I'm not letting this bastard get away, not this time.*

Drake lunged at the man with all his might, slamming him

into a concrete fence post. The stalker toppled to the ground, momentarily stunned, before trying to scramble back to his feet. Drake grabbed him from behind, locking his arms around the man's neck, constraining him in a headlock and dragging him to his feet.

He squeezed hard. Much harder than he should have done.

The man choked, scrabbling at Drake's arms and face, attempting to scratch him into letting him go. His legs kicked out feebly beneath him as he wheezed.

Drake tightened his grip further. His blood thumped in his ears, the vein at his temple throbbing from the exertion. The stalker let out a series of pained noises as he struggled further, each attempt becoming weaker.

Images of the dead flashed through Drake's mind: his wife, the victims in the woods, the scorched remains at the house.

'Drake! What're you doing? Stop!' Ellie cried.

He was unaware of where she was as he carried on. He could feel the man losing any fight he had left in him. *Not going anywhere now, are you, eh? You little bastard.*

'John! He's had enough, stop!'

Drake felt Ellie grab his shoulder. He snapped out of it, letting the man drop to the ground. He erupted with a pained gasp and continued to choke on the floor, coughing and spluttering as Ellie looked at Drake, the shock in her eyes plain to see.

'John . . .' She threw the knife away and checked the man on the ground.

The stalker tried to speak, but nothing came. He dry heaved and retched, putting his arm out in a show of surrender.

'Stop, please . . . stop. I'm sorry, okay. Whatever you think I've done, I'm sorry!' The man pleaded between gasps, tears and drool streaming down his face and chin. 'You could have killed me!'

The would-be killer was well built, with a shock of blonde

hair. He was wearing dark jeans and a black cable knit jumper, mud now smeared on both from his fall. There wasn't the look of a serial killer about him, but then he had just nearly had the life choked out of him by a berserker detective.

'Backup's on its way. Is everything okay out here?' The constable said, finally emerging from the kitchen.

Drake looked down at the man, who was still struggling.

'We're going to cuff you and then we'll talk,' Drake told him.

41

Drake couldn't believe what he was hearing. Soon after detaining him, they had taken the trespasser to Wandsworth police station so they could carry out an interview. The man had remained silent on the car journey, wedged between Ellie and Drake. The local police had taken the prints and samples needed before they had led him down to the interview room in which they now sat.

The room was bleak, a construct of bare concrete cinderblock walls with room for a table and four chairs. Interview recording apparatus was laid out on the table. The black eye of a camera was watching from the corner of the room, with a viewing mirror for anyone to observe from the room next door.

Melwood stood poised behind the glass, doing precisely that along with Chambers, but Strauss was nowhere to be seen. Drake and Ellie presided over the man in front of him. The man now purported to be Robert Spencer.

'I'm not sure how many more ways I can say it, officers . . . I was looking for my damn cat. The fence breaks, and the next thing I know, there's a man staring at me. I run for it, then nearly have the life choked out of me, and here we are,' he said, looking about the room.

The man was exhibiting an unusual coolness, Drake thought. In his experience, people were usually jittery in an interview room when confronted by two detectives. It was only natural even if you had done nothing wrong. It wasn't something the average person would ever experience. The man had waved his right to representation, arguing he had nothing to hide, which could itself be a smokescreen, of course.

Drake grimaced at the Spencer man's description of the choke hold encounter. He'd perhaps got a *little* carried away. The moment was still a blur to him, his rage coming to the surface so quickly. He hadn't meant to use such force and for so long, not really. But this man's story was bullshit: a bloody *cat*. Come on . . . though it was almost pathetic enough to be true, Drake supposed.

'If you were looking for your cat, wouldn't you have knocked on a few neighbours' doors? And particularly the one whose fence you scaled?'

Robert leant on the table, putting his hands out as he attempted to reason with them. He was calm, always calm, his hair hanging over his right eye and a prominent slash of scarring on his forehead. 'I didn't think they were in. There were no lights on.'

'And what about the officer standing at the gate a few houses along?'

'What policeman? I didn't see one.'

'Now you're testing my patience. You mean to tell me you didn't see a policeman in a fluorescent jacket standing a few doors down from the property you scaled, after looking for signs of life in the house?'

The Ties That Bind

'No. Why would I lie?' Robert threw his hands up in the air, but he didn't seem to be as frustrated as the action implied.

'Maybe because you were running around in the dark in people's gardens looking for an imaginary cat?' Ellie said.

Robert sighed. 'Look, please check the local neighbourhood apps. I registered him at the vets when I bought him a few years ago. He's gone missing. I only live a few streets away. It's not all that suspicious, surely? What is this?'

'Why didn't you say this when you saw me?'

'What would you do if you'd just broken someone's fence and there's a weird man staring at you?'

'We're asking the questions here. Answer me.'

He sighed again. 'I was scared. Realised it didn't look great. I knew I'd taken a chance, you know, and it was stupid. But I just wanted my little buddy back home.'

'Where were you on Tuesday 12th December, between the hours of six in the evening and midnight?' Ellie asked. That was the timeframe for when Clare Baker and PS Peter Matthews had been killed.

'I was working late.'

'What do you do?'

'I'm a developer, IT development.' He looked at Drake, who gave no reaction. 'Look, what is this? What's this got to do with me breaking a fence?'

'So, you were working, until . . . when?' Ellie asked, jotting down some notes.

'Erm . . .' Robert looked up at the ceiling while he considered his answer. 'It was about ten o'clock, I think. I went straight home, then found my cat wasn't there.'

'Anyone who can corroborate that?'

'The receptionist had gone by then, but, probably . . . probably one of the cleaners, yeah. I think there's probably CCTV or cameras somewhere and there'd *definitely* be an entry logged for my access card at the bare minimum.'

Shit. Maybe he really was doing what he said he was. Drake felt deflated.

There was a knock at the door and Melwood appeared, a frown on his face.

'DCI Drake, do you have a moment?'

Drake cocked an eyebrow at the DI. 'We're in the middle of—'

'Now, please.'

'Okay.' Drake got up from his chair, irritated by how it was all going. Something was niggling him about Robert, but he couldn't quite place it. It reminded him of the feeling you got when you were out shopping and forgot the one item you needed most.

Ellie suspended the interview while he followed Melwood into the room where the rest of the team were. While they'd been interviewing Robert, Strauss had turned up, looking dishevelled and bleary-eyed. Drake realised it was now nearing one in the morning. It appeared time flew by when you were scaling fences of an evening.

Chambers looked as tired as he felt, dark circles under her eyes. She turned away from studying the would-be stalker through the one-way glass and gave him a weak smile.

'We might have something for you, Drake,' she told him. 'Perhaps it could give a bit more background to the guy in front of you.'

'Okay . . . spit it out.'

'Strauss here says he knows this guy,' Melwood said, nodding at the sergeant.

'Oh?'

Strauss nodded. 'I think he was at the same children's home I was in for a brief time. Spoke to him a couple of times, only his name wasn't Robert, I swear. I think it was Jack something. Sorry, I can't remember the surname, but it's been so long – surprised I even remembered the first name.'

'Okay, but wouldn't he have been adopted, perhaps given a new name? How old were you both?'

'I was thirteen. I think he was similar . . . maybe younger? But it was definitely him. He's got a scar on his forehead, right? He was nice to me back then when the others weren't, with me being from another country. It made me stand out to them,' he said, his demeanour not hiding how he felt about his childhood.

'Okay. Well, I can try to surprise him with that information, see if it unsettles him, or sets him off-balance.'

'Sure.'

'Oh, and Drake?'

'Yep?' His hand resting on the door handle, hoping it was obvious that his impatience was coming through in waves.

'Have you thought about showing his picture to Ellie's daughter, maybe? Perhaps that'll put him in the frame. Funnily enough, this cat business doesn't wash with us,' Melwood said, rolling his eyes.

'One step ahead of you, Inspector.'

'Oh?'

'Yes, Ellie's on it. She's going to check with her in the morning. Can't go expecting a five-year-old to be reliable at this time of night.'

Melwood nodded. 'Good stuff.'

Drake peered in Strauss' direction. 'Strauss, I expect you'll be checking in on this guy, finding out what you can, seeing if you can corroborate everything that comes out of this guy's mouth, yeah? Check on the CCTV, access card etc. We've got a little longer with him than normal, this being a murder investigation.

But I'd like it resolved sooner rather than later if it's nothing more than a case of an idiot getting in our way.'

'On it, sir.'

The image of Miller coming down on him like a ton of bricks about wasting time and resource was not one he savoured, particularly after their last discussion. The thought of who it was that had been feeding her information behind his back popped into his head. It made him uneasy, as though the people in this room weren't on his side as much as he thought.

'Thank you, Sergeant.'

He returned to the interview room, setting a hand on Ellie's shoulder as he picked up where they'd left off.

'It's been brought to my attention that you were in a children's home when you were a teenager. Is that correct?'

'Yes,' Robert immediately looked uncomfortable. 'But what has that got to do with anything? Does that somehow make me a criminal?'

That touched a nerve, didn't it? 'No, but apparently your name was Jack, back then. Is this true?'

'Huh? No, that's not right. You can check it out if you want . . . It was actually Tom, but I never liked it, so I changed it when I left care. No crime in that, is there?'

'No, there's not.'

'Can I ask a question?'

'Yes.'

'When can I leave, please?'

'You're being held until we say you can leave, Mr Spencer.' Drake pursed his lips. This interview wasn't getting them anywhere.

'What! On what grounds?'

'On the grounds that you're under suspicion in a murder investigation and threatening a police officer, that's what.' Ellie jumped in. She seemed to enjoy the threat of the statement a little too much.

'What! But I've only damaged a bloody fence. I'll pay for that. Just tell me how much . . . please, this is crazy. Check the cameras, the access, anything. I don't understand!' He pleaded, becoming more animated than he had for the entire interview.

Drake smiled. *Not so cool now, are you?* 'If what you say is true, then you have nothing to worry about, do you, Mr Spencer?'

42

Drake climbed the stairs to his flat, the lift having long given up the ghost. He felt exhausted, and not just from the sheer number of steps. Subjecting himself to this place of misery was the last thing he wanted to do, but it was also necessary.

It was the place where he'd had so many dark thoughts after his wife's murder. Where he'd contemplated the unthinkable, where he might have put an end to the incessant noise in his head once and for all. He was pleased that he was somewhat past that now; at least, he thought he was. But what had happened that evening had made it clear something else was growing inside of him in place of the emptiness, in place of that drab hopelessness. Perhaps something worse. Something he may have no control over, something . . . rotten.

Drake rifled around in his pockets for the keys, hearing the perpetual dull thud of bass from the person below. It was past three in the morning; he didn't understand how someone could still be playing music. What the hell could they be doing at this hour?

Finally finding his key, he was greeted with the familiar musty smell of the flat. The space was just as he left it, microwave food trays discarded on the side, unwashed clothes in random piles. The loft beam looming large, the weak chair below it.

He locked the door behind him, turning on a bedside lamp before collapsing into the solitary stained armchair. What he would give for a sofa right now. He sighed and looked around the flat through heavy eyes. He felt like a mere shell of a man, almost completely broken.

* * *

Drake crept towards the muffled sounds coming from the living room ahead. A light framed the door in the darkness of Ellie's house. He couldn't tell whether the sound was human or animal. Whatever it was, it sounded like it was in a state of distress.

'Ellie? You there?' he said, calling out.

Drake's voice echoed around the house. There was no reply. He continued to make his way forwards, edging closer to the door. The sounds were becoming more panicked the closer he got, more intense.

Suddenly, a beam of light shone down on him and a pool of liquid began forming on the floor beneath his feet. He looked at his hands and saw them running red with blood.

'What the—'

An unseen force shoved him into the living room. Drake careered forwards, slamming his head into the wall across the room, leaving him in a tangled heap. Dazed, he looked up, seeing three figures on the sofa, their heads wrapped in duct tape, shards of glass spilling forth from their split mouths as they writhed in pain.

It was Ellie and her family.

'Ellie! I—'

In an instant, he was on fire, the smoke choking him as his clothes burned. He was screaming as the flames licked at his flesh.

*　*　*

'Whoa!' Drake woke himself with a start. His throat felt constricted as he tried to breathe, his legs and arms still tingling from the imaginary flames.

The bed slowly came into focus in front of him, the continued noise reverberating beneath his feet.

He was in the flat. In the armchair. He must have collapsed into sleep.

Drake's breathing slowed as he acclimatised, the adrenaline ebbing from his system. He ran his hand through his sweat sodden hair, the movement making him feel his shirt sticking to his back.

He wrinkled his nose in disgust. He hadn't had a recurrence of the dream in weeks, and certainly not like *that*. But it was always guaranteed to work its magic, leaving him wringing wet. He looked at his watch. It was just after five. He'd be unable to sleep again. Drake knew how it worked.

Standing up from the armchair, he made to go to the bathroom to shower and get ready for another day.

Still the bass pounded: *Thump, thump, thump.*

He gripped the edge of the bathroom sink and looked into the mirror. Blood-shot eyes looked back at him. He barely recognised himself. The flat wouldn't get the better of him. Not this time. No.

Thump, thump, thump.

Drake splashed cool water on his face, attempting to quell whatever it was taking hold. But the fire in the pit of his stomach was being stoked, not dampened.

Thump, thump, thump.
He closed his eyes, breathing deeply.
It wasn't helping. His chest tightened.
Thump, thump, thump.
He saw red.

* * *

Bang, bang!
Drake slammed his fist on the door.
No answer.
He pounded on the door once again.
He continued, not caring if it woke everyone in the damn block. He was getting an answer, and he was getting it now, come hell or high-water.

'What!' Came a cocky youthful voice through the door.

'Turn that damn racket down! Now!' Drake demanded.

'No.'

Even with the door between them, he could sense the man's sneer.

'Turn. It. Down. Now.'

'Are you deaf?' The man uttered a mocking snort.

'Right, open the door. I'm a police officer – and so help me God, I'll have you for this, you little shit,' Drake said through gritted teeth. He squeezed his hands together, his knuckles turning white in seconds as a vein pulsed in his temple.

'Woah, okay. A po-lice officer, eh? Well, shit. Better get scared now, had I?'

Drake took a deep breath. His mouth bunched into a thin line as he felt his blood pressure rising further than he thought possible.

'I'm warning you.'

'Yeah, and what?'

'If you don't open this damn door by the time I've counted to five, I'm going to break it down.'

'Give it a rest, old man.'

'One.'

'Yeah, whatever.'

'Two. Three. *Four*,' he growled.

'You're so full of shit—'

'Five!'

Drake took a step back from the door, then kicked it with all the strength he could muster. A panel gave a little, but it didn't burst open as he'd hoped. He felt the shock reverberate up his leg.

'Jesus, man. What the hell!'

He tried again, kicking at the same spot. This time, the door frame split against the strain. But still didn't give.

'Okay, okay. Fuck!'

He heard a rattle of a lock, and it opened. A gangly Asian man, no more than twenty-five, with a bright red dyed quiff stood in front of him in a white vest and black jogging bottoms.

Drake flew in before the man said another word, grabbing him by the throat and shoving him up against the wall. His thumb began pressing on the man's Adam's apple as he gasped and wriggled against his grip.

'What the hell are you doing?' the man gargled.

Drake snarled. 'What am I doing? What are *you* doing? It's like five in the morning. Turn the fucking music down, or I am going to beat the living shit out of you, you hear me?'

He croaked. 'Okay, okay. I will, I promise. I'm sorry!'

'Good. And you won't do it again, right? *Right?*' Drake spat, pointing his finger at the man's part-open eye.

'N-no, I won't! Just stop, okay?' A tear ran down the man's cheek as he continued to squirm.

'And if you so much as breathe a word of this to anyone, I'll be back. And I won't be so forgiving next time. You got that?' Drake hissed into the man's ear.

'Okay, I'm sorry. I mean it, I won't do it again. Seriously, man!'

'That's more like it,' Drake said with a snide smile, letting go of him. 'There was no need for it to come to this now, was there?'

'No – no, sir. Are you really a police officer?'

Drake flashed his ID, not long enough for the man to catch a full look.

'Fuck.'

'Fuck, indeed.' He tapped the man on the cheek with an open palm and left the man to close the door.

Drake went back upstairs without looking back. Surprisingly, no one had come out to see what the commotion was. He loved Londoners sometimes, keeping to themselves no matter what happened. But he knew he'd taken it a step too far. The behaviour was so unlike him. Using his position to intimidate a member of the public in that way . . . no matter how shitty they were. It was unforgivable.

Drake smiled.

43

As nights go, it had been another difficult one for Ellie. Not just because of having a stranger trespass in her garden, but seeing Drake act the way he had, the way he had choked that man. The look in his eyes had frightened her. It wasn't like him. Why hadn't he stopped?

She sighed to herself on the journey into the office. Another overcast day wasn't helping to perk her up, and her eyelids drifted closed while the previous evening's argument with Len played on her mind. It had happened once she'd returned home for a few hours' rest, the initial interview with the cat whisperer having since finished. The respite she so desperately wanted certainly hadn't come in the end.

She understood his concerns, understood his reasoning. What she didn't understand was his requirement that they uproot Bella and take her to stay with his parents for a few days. He rationalised it would be safer, that she'd see it as a holiday for her. Ellie rationalised back that it was a moving of the goal posts, a way in which SGK would have more ammunition to play with. He could threaten Len's family, do them harm too. It wasn't out of the realms of possibility, and she didn't want more people involved in this than there needed to be. It was enough just having his and Bella's lives in the crosshairs, let alone his elderly parents, too.

In the end, she'd had to relent. She never was one for arguments with her husband, neither of them were really. It wasn't in their nature. And to top it off, she still needed to understand why she was being targeted in the first place. She'd been wracking her brain for days, but nothing was floating to the surface, nothing was biting, nothing taking hold. She just plain didn't *get it*. What could she possibly have done to warrant such attention?

Ellie made the request to PC Malik for them to be moved to the new address. He'd been hesitant but understood once she'd mentioned bringing Drake into the picture (though he'd feel the same as her, no doubt) and he quickly got the approval from his boss. They'd move later that day, when she was back home.

And speaking with Bella that morning, her high hopes had been dashed almost immediately. Any optimism she'd had of Bella fingering Robert as the man who was at her daughter's school was gone. When Ellie had asked her again what the man at the fence looked like, she'd given a completely different description to the previous one. Before it was brown hair and a beard, and now he was black hair and no beard. Ellie was crestfallen. The initial answer didn't bode well, and that concern came to bear when she'd then shown her the photo of Robert Spencer. This was of a blonde man, and she couldn't even say categorically then, either. She'd given a shake of her head, and a heart-breaking, 'I'm sorry, Mummy. Are you angry?' as a response.

Ellie was at a loss.

* * *

'Ellie's here,' she heard Chambers say as she entered the room. They were crowded around Strauss' laptop. It seemed to be a common theme lately, as he was doing a lot of the legwork. She dreaded to think where'd they be without him while she put her coat down on a nearby chair. Ellie scouted the place for her boss, but Drake didn't seem to have made an appearance yet. She hoped he was okay. Maybe getting a good night's sleep finally.

'Hey, anything since last night? Anything we can use against our cat man? Please tell me yes?'

'Still working on that, but found some more relating to our dead fellow officer.' Melwood said, as though he'd been the one digging. 'Turns out he wasn't sending money to Clare Baker like Alex Ludner was. Perhaps he was getting his kicks pro *bono*,' he snickered.

Melwood laboured the poor joke further. 'Get it . . . ? bone . . .' At the silence from the team, he groaned. 'Never mind.'

'You okay there, Inspector?' Ellie asked. She was surprised someone other than her was making jokes, and even more surprised that someone was Melwood.

The man coughed and moved on. 'There's nothing we can find that directly links Peter Matthews to Clare. It's frustrating. Clare's neighbours haven't come up with anything regarding sightings of him, recent visits, nothing.'

'Anything back from the lab – maybe latent prints, etc?'

'Nothing more than the obvious. Chambers? Mind calling them?' Melwood asked over his shoulder.

'Yeah, sure.' Chambers moved to a chair. 'I'll get on that now.'

Ellie spent the next few hours looking through outputs from the door-to-door enquiries that Strauss and the supporting teams had made. It made for dull and frustrating reading. She re-

reviewed the evidence that they'd put together so far, which irritated her even more... And where was Drake?

Hard drive: missing. Stained glass: inconclusive. Scar marks on Alex and Sofia: likely inconsequential. What were the deposits to Clare's account really meant for? Was it really for some strange swinger sex party games? It seemed sillier the more she thought of it.

She wheeled her chair over to Strauss.

'You know, I still can't believe you knew that guy from when you were young.'

'Indeed, coincidence is an incredible thing,' he murmured, not taking his eyes off his screen.

'Must bring back memories.'

'Not really. I choose not to remember it,' he said, keeping his voice low. 'I'd not have mentioned it at all if I didn't think it might pressure him somehow. Didn't seem to work, though.'

'Did he have any brothers or sisters?'

'None that I saw. They took him away soon after I was put there. It all seemed to happen so quickly. One night he was there, then the next morning he was gone.'

'Bit odd, him leaving in the night?'

Strauss shrugged. 'I choose not to think about those times.'

Sore subject. Ellie thought.

Chambers finished another of the endless number of checkup calls they'd tasked her with as Drake finally walked in the door. He was looking brighter than he had done in a while, Ellie thought. Not exactly a spring in his step, but that was never Drake's way, anyway. He'd even put on an entirely different suit, same dark grey as always, but the cut was different.

Chambers started speaking, 'Guys, a small update. Dr Kulkarni found something relating to those rings that the boss found in the shoebox of smut. Turns out they're the same size as the scarring on Alex and Sofia's hips. They . . . well, it appears they *branded* themselves with one of them.' Chambers' face reddened as she described it, glancing at them all.

Ellie recalled the rings that Drake had found in the shoebox. Why brand themselves? To somehow signify their relationship? The relationship that ended soon after those deposits were made? It made little sense.

Drake spoke, 'Unless everyone has those marks, I don't think they're a cause for much excite—'

Strauss swung his chair round, his arm in the air. 'Sorry to interrupt, sir. I've just received an email attachment from Ellie's daughter's school. They have CCTV footage of the playground from that day.'

Ellie's eyes lit up. 'What! Bring it up, let's see it.'

'Just a moment, I'll put it on the big screens.'

Strauss fiddled on his laptop before bringing the media player up on to one of the larger monitors. There on the screens was a still image of her little girl. A strange feeling roiled in her gut.

'These are good quality images, surprising actually. They're filmed in something bordering HD resolution, so we *should* get a view of the guy,' Strauss said. The glare of the screen cast shadows on his face while he toyed with the laptop.

Ellie had to admit, they did appear to be surprisingly good quality compared to some of the crap CCTV she'd had to deal with over the years, though it was still hard to make out defining facial features.

There was her daughter, mid-walk to a metal fence. A figure in the middle-distance. The camera was much closer than she was expecting. Her stomach roiled again at the sight.

'Well, play it then,' Drake said.

'Oh, yes.'

Strauss pressed play and Bella continued her hesitant walk to the fence in silence, looking back to see if anyone had seen her. The recording had no audio. The person was crouched down, wearing a black hooded sweatshirt, similar to the style of the suspect she'd chased from Alex's flat. Ellie squinted at the footage; the team hushed. As Bella drew closer, the man at the fence pulled his hood down and held out his hand.

Her heart skipped a beat as she saw he had short, dark brown or black hair – he wasn't blonde. He wasn't Robert Spencer.

Shit.

'Great,' Melwood exhaled, leaning back in his chair and slapping his hands on the arms. 'Now what?'

'Hang on, steady now. This may mean nothing. Maybe there's two of them? We need to get the office CCTV and get his access details back before we set the man free,' she countered.

'It's not looking good though, is it, DS Wilkinson?' Melwood retorted. 'He freely gave us that information. He'd only do that if he knew for sure he couldn't be held accountable and that he wasn't at the crime scene.'

Ellie really wished their roles were reversed, and he wasn't her senior. She wanted to tell Melwood to button it and shut up. It wasn't over until all the evidence was available to them, was it? There might be something that they were missing. Robert could have made a mistake amidst his cockiness. He had to have done.

Not long after Ellie had aired her hopes regarding Robert's alibi, Strauss received a call and another email attachment of a video recording. There were records of Robert on CCTV at his office.

Strauss brought up the images. The man's face stared back at them through the camera lens, a slight smile, almost like he was mocking them.

He hadn't made a mistake, his account tallied up.

Ellie's face dropped at the news. Robert Spencer couldn't have killed them.

44

Ellie's mind was in a funk as she closed the front door of her in-laws, with Len and Bella safely inside. She still couldn't believe they'd had to let their one and only suspect go. That his alibi was *that* watertight. There had to be something. There *had* to be. It was just too much of a coincidence him being there. It made little sense.

Either way, she hadn't enjoyed delivering that bit of news to the man when they'd brought him out. Drake's face wasn't giving away much at the time, but she knew it was eating away at him, too. His jaw had been set so tight, she thought it had been wired shut. Not even a full twenty-four hours and their supposed best lead was walking free.

She went over to Dave, who was leaning on the boot of his car at the end of the driveway. He was making a show of admiring the in-laws' house.

It was understandable. The detached property was set back from the road on a quiet private cul-de-sac on the outskirts of Chalfont St. Peter. Len's parents had bought it in the early seventies, and they'd sat back and watched the value rise and rise. Ellie daren't ask what it was worth for fear of her head exploding.

Len's parents were retirees. His mother, Iris, was sadly wheelchair bound because of advanced arthritis, and his dad, George, had taken early retirement to look after her. When, or if, his parents thought it was time to sell, they'd rake in the cash. She wasn't even sure how many rooms it had.

Ellie gave Dave a tired smile as she approached. 'Thank you for driving us. I don't think I could have stomached getting through all that traffic myself. Not after the complete washout that today has been,' she said despondently.

'No problem. I know you'd have done the same if the shoe was on the other foot. Not that I'd want a killer on my tail, you understand,' he said, folding his arms.

'No, I get it.' She drummed a metallic beat on the boot of the car with the tips of her fingers. 'You sure you don't want to come inside? Bella's taken a shine to the man with the moustache.'

'No, no. I'll be going soon. Just wanted to make sure you were safe. Drake phoned to ask me to do it as well, so I had two reasons to be here.'

'Oh? Where is he?'

'Taking a few much-needed hours away from it all, apparently.'

'Strange, I thought he would have told me.'

'He's not one for admitting supposed weakness. You know that, Ellie.'

Her eyes dropped. 'True. He doesn't seem in a good way lately, more so than normal.'

'I'm glad it's not just me that thinks so. Not much we can do though, just have to be there for him.' Dave took a deep breath. 'He has to find his own way.'

'Yeah.' Ellie chose not to tell him about the incident with

Robert Spencer or with the Portuguese brother of Sofia. It wouldn't cause Dave anything but worry.

A squad car pulled up and PC Asif Malik jumped out, smiling at the sight of Ellie.

'Right, that's my cue to leave,' she remarked.

'Oh, okay. Well . . . have a good night.' Dave said. 'Tonight will be calmer, I'm sure of it.'

Ellie smiled and left, waving at the PC as she hotfooted it back up the drive and into the house.

Dave got back in his car, but didn't make a move to leave.

45

'Your parents seemed anxious. Understandably,' Ellie said, immediately regretting how snide the words had sounded.

'Yeah . . . well, I didn't think it was a good idea to have us holed up where a crazy guy knows where we live, Ellie.' Len reasoned.

They were cooped up in Len's parents' spacious second sitting room. The room was on the ground floor at the other end of the house, far away from where the in-laws had retired for the night. Her mother-in-law's condition meant she struggled to use stairs.

Ellie stretched out on the rich purple L-shape sofa, her feet just about reaching her husband who lay on the chaise longue end. A large television sat on a stand flanked by two towering floor-standing speakers, with a record player nearby and an oak shelving unit housing a substantial number of vinyl. She'd always felt jealous of the collection. Ellie had had little time to listen to music lately, or watch any films, and she found the thought mildly depressing.

The Ties That Bind

Bella was upstairs, away from the heated voices, and, importantly, away from any potential harm.

Ellie usually enjoyed visiting Len's parents. They were a kindly couple, one that she aspired to emulate the older she got. She admired the gentle humour still existing between them. A humour that had been missing from her relationship with Len since the events of the last few days.

She picked at the fluff on a cushion as she spoke, trying not to get agitated by their situation. 'There's nothing to say that he doesn't know about this place, or that he won't have followed us, Len.'

'But he'll be less familiar with it, so less confident, I reckon, even if that was the case. We'll be okay.'

'I wish I had *your* confidence,' Ellie said, feeling his reasoning was naïve. But she supposed she had to give his way a chance.

'Just trust me on this, love,' he said, massaging the arch of her foot with a thumb through her ankle socks. The action only served to annoy her rather than soothe her.

'You don't think I want to? I want for this to all be over, Len. I don't want to be targeted like this. It's not right.'

'Nothing you're involved with is *right*, you know that,' he retorted, letting go of her foot.

She pursed her lips. 'No, but this is different.'

'Is it? Nothing has been straightforward when the big cases come along.'

'That's a coincidence. You think I'd sign up for this knowingly? Knowing it could put our daughter in danger every time a call came in for an SMT case?'

'No, I suppose not.'

'Well, then.'

Len stood up. 'I just don't—'

Ellie's work phone rang by her side. The timing was impeccable. She wondered what must be happening for her phone to be getting a call this late in the day.

'You'd better get that, hadn't you?'

'Yes, but—'

'Answer it.' He turned away with an irritable wave of his hand.

She reached for the phone. 'DS Wilkinson?'

'Ah, Ellie Wilkinson.' The voice was dry and crackling, and her heart skipped a beat. The voice. It was him.

She sat up straight. Len turned back, sensing the sudden change in atmosphere.

'Who is this?'

'There you go again,' the voice laughed. 'Pretending you don't know me. Pretending you don't know what you *did*.'

'*But I don't know!*'

Len's eyes widened in realisation as he watched and listened to her.

'All will become clear in time, I'm sure. Don't think moving house is going to help you,' the man said. It sounded as though he was smiling.

Ellie's mouth formed an 'o' shape. She couldn't think straight. This man had to be watching them. He must know where they are.

'What is it you want? What do you want from me?'

'Everything that you hold dear . . . one way or another.'

'Wait, please! Leave my daughter out—'

The call ended.

'Was that—' Len demanded.

'Yes.' Her mind raced as she tried to think of how to resolve the situation. What could she possibly have done to warrant this?

'What do we do?' Len sat next to her, his head in his hands.

Ellie threw her phone down. 'I . . . I don't know. What *can* we do?'

'Surely there's something you guys would do in a situation like this.'

'We already have someone on the door, Len.'

'So, what, we just have to wait for this guy to make his move?'

'Something like—'

Her head snapped toward the sitting-room door. There'd been a noise, like an object dropping to the floor.

'Wait, did you hear that?'

'No.' Len froze. 'What was it? Please tell me that's not him?'

Ellie stood up, motioning for him to be quiet as she listened intently.

No, there couldn't be . . . She could have sworn she'd heard movement. Another creak. Maybe it was just the house expanding or contracting, or whatever old houses were supposed to do.

'Go to your parents. Now,' she said, waving him in the direction of their bedroom.

'No, Ellie. I'm not leaving you. Jesus, I'm not leaving Bella either!' he hissed.

'Just go, Len. Please,' she whispered back.

'Okay, but I'm coming back. Once I see they're okay.'

She huffed. 'Okay, fine. But *be* quiet and find something to arm yourself with.'

They made their way to the kitchen, remaining together for the moment and padding along the thick carpet in their socks. They tried to make sure they made as little noise as possible, but it was proving difficult with the old floorboards.

Perhaps it was just Bella getting out of bed? But perhaps it wasn't. Ellie had to be sure.

Ellie retrieved a black-handled knife from a knife block. Len did the same, but with one much too big to be easily wielded, should the situation arise. He peeled off toward his parents' bedroom, a look of regret on his face as he left his wife.

She composed herself and started towards the stairs, which also appeared not to be made for stealth, the increasingly loud creaks and cracks becoming too much to bear as she rounded another corner on the way up.

Another thud sounded, then another. Then silence as she reached the dark hallway on the first floor. Ellie didn't honestly know what she'd do if there *was* an intruder in the house, and she hoped she wouldn't have to find out. She certainly didn't fancy adding further scars to her burgeoning collection.

Bella's bedroom was the furthest to the right from the stairwell. It was the room set aside for her frequent visits, and it was like a second home to her.

Moonlight shone through a crack in the hallway curtains just beyond Bella's door. A few too many horror film scenarios ran through Ellie's mind while she made her way cautiously towards it, expecting someone to jump out at any moment.

'Mummy!'

Bella came out of the bathroom, her eyes shining in the darkness.

'Bella!' Ellie startled, the relief pouring out of her as she secreted the knife behind her back. 'What are you doing out of bed?'

'I needed to go. I can't reach the light though, or the toilet thingy.'

Ellie rued the old house's quirks. It wasn't exactly five-year-old friendly.

'I'll sort it. You go back to bed, okay?' she said, kissing her forehead.

'Okay, Mummy.'

'Goodnight,' she said, flushing the chain-action toilet and closing the door behind her.

Better check the rooms anyway, she thought. *For my sanity's sake.*

She padded down to Bella's room and checked in on her. The little girl waved from her bed. 'Sleep tight, you.'

Bella giggled.

'Everything okay?' Len said, making her jump.

'Jesus Christ! Don't do that.'

Bella giggled again at her reaction.

'I think it was just our little monster going to the toilet. Crisis averted.'

'Thank God for that,' he said, looking visibly relieved. 'I didn't wake the parents, but the coast was clear there too, I think.'

'You *think*?' Ellie frowned.

She halted outside her daughter's room and turned to open the door opposite. It revealed another spare bedroom, containing a single bed, bedside tables and a built-in wardrobe.

Len followed her to the next door on her round. 'You know, we could just turn on the hallway light.'

'What, and miss out on the adventure?'

She grabbed the handle of the next door just as she heard the sound of movement.

'Len, I—' She looked back in time to see a dark figure swinging an object at her husband's head. 'Len!'

The attack sent him to the ground in a heap, unconscious before he even hit the floor.

Ellie gasped. Seemingly the same person from Alex Ludner's flat stood before her, dressed head to toe in black, a hood and a balaclava rather than a face mask covering their face this time. A club or cosh brandished in a gloved fist.

Ellie backed away, trying to lead the assailant away from her daughter's bedroom.

'Please, don't hurt him,' she whispered. She held a scarred palm up in front of her, keeping her knife hand behind her back, her eyes as big as saucers.

The masked face looked down at Len out cold on the ground and casually stepped over him.

'Whatever you're going to do, you're going to be caught, you know. There are police outside.'

The figure shrugged, its stare unblinking. Then it moved again, stepping forward slowly, creeping ever closer.

'Please, just leave now, while you still have a chance.'

The figure cocked its head mockingly at her. She could sense hatred burning in the intense brown eyes as the intruder played with the weapon, bouncing the weighted head in a gloved palm.

The attacker lunged at her, then pulled back sharply, making Ellie step back quickly. Then lunged again, causing her to react for a second time.

'Please, just leave,' Ellie said, her voice catching as the figure toyed with her.

In the blink of an eye, the figure charged, and Ellie whipped out the knife in response. The assailant barely paused, swiping the weapon to one side as if it was nothing and clubbing her to the ground with a whack to the temple. The impact of the club sent her vision pure white as she hit the floor, her knife tumbling away.

She gasped, unable to move as her sight slowly returned.

'No . . .' she croaked.

The figure picked up the knife and stood over her, wagging a finger. Without warning, the masked attacker swung the club once more, pounding Ellie's kneecap. She let out a pained yelp, clutching at her injured leg. The pain was excruciating, and she did her best to hold back a surge of bile, her insides churning. Her head continued spinning, and she knew she was on the brink of blacking out.

Still fighting to get a grip on herself, she sensed the figure coming back.

'Mummy!' came a cry.

No!

It had her daughter in one arm, the club in the other, and there was a gag around her girl's neck.

'No, Bel – no!' Ellie tried to move, to react to the person taking her daughter away from her.

'You hurt my Mummy!' the girl squealed, before a gag was pulled roughly into her mouth. As Bella wriggled in the assailant's grip, Ellie took advantage of the distraction to swing her uninjured leg at its ankle. But she couldn't put enough strength behind the blow, and her foot rebounded uselessly.

'Bella, I'm . . . coming, baby!' Her eyes rolled as she tried to snatch at the masked figure's legs, the acid still strong in her throat.

The kidnapper kicked her hands away and started down the stairs just ahead of Ellie's head, with Bella still struggling. Slowly and assuredly, they started walking away with their prize.

'N . . . no!'

Ellie took a deep breath and focused her energy. She had to regain control, or she was going to lose her daughter. She clawed her way laboriously to the stairway. Grasping at the banister spindles, she managed to pull herself up.

I can't let them take her. I can't!

Ellie took another gasping breath and stumbled down the stairs, tears streaming down her face. She was terrified of slipping and knocking herself out, and she could feel sweat pouring off her.

A commotion came from the front of the house.

No! Len's parents!

'Stop!' she screamed.

'Mummy!'

Bella, the gag loose around her shoulders, bounded round the corner away from the front door before the kidnapper caught up and grabbed her once more. The little girl's legs flailed as she was pulled her up and away.

The attacker wrenched the front door open and ran.

'No!'

Ellie staggered for the door. Her leg gave out mere feet away from it, causing her to stumble into the thick wooden door at full speed. She grabbed the handle and clung on, her momentum carrying her forward before she managed to hoist herself back upright.

Looking out the door, the sweat stinging her eyes, she caught the outline of a further encounter in progress.

The fluorescent shape of a police officer was on the ground, and another figure was fighting with the masked assailant.

It was Dave.

Bella had somehow got free from her kidnapper once more and had attached herself to his leg. Dave had a hand on her while he attempted to keep the assailant at bay. Ellie watched on helplessly as he seized the attacker's wrist.

She couldn't believe it. He'd got hold of Bella and was winning the fight.

'Dave!' she screamed. 'Stop them!'

He looked over at the sound of her voice, distracted for a split second. It was just enough to give the attacker an opening. The masked figure batted away his flailing hand and thrust Ellie's knife into his chest.

Dave's eyes bulged at the impact. The assailant struck again and again, causing him to stagger to his knees. Pulling Bella in front of him, Dave shielded her with his body, trying to put as much of himself between Bella and the kidnapper as possible.

'No! Dave!' Ellie screamed again. She scrambled to her feet, staggering towards him.

The attacker threw the knife to one side and tried to snatch Bella away, but Dave held the little girl fast.

The sound of police cars sirens wailing in the distance caused the masked figure to pause and stare at Ellie.

'No! I won't . . . let you—' She stumbled over, gasping. Ellie hadn't even made it halfway to her friend and daughter when her leg gave way and her injured knee connected with the solid concrete of the driveway, blinding her with pain, leaving her unable to move.

The attacker made their decision. They gave up and ran, leaving Dave slumped over on the drive, Bella beneath him in his bloodied grasp.

46

Drake couldn't believe what he'd heard. The kidnap attempt, Ellie and her family injured, Dave stabbed . . . He had no idea how severe it was. Melwood had little chance to relay the information before Drake had run down the stairs from his flat and lost the signal on his mobile.

He burst through the doors of the A&E department of St. George's hospital in Tooting and bounded over to the person at the desk, shoving a hospital porter to one side to get an answer.

'David Bradfield – where is he, please?' he demanded. 'They brought him in an hour ago by air ambulance.'

The bespectacled woman peered up at him, her face less than impressed. 'I'm sorry, sir. You're going to have to calm down.'

'Don't tell me to calm down,' he growled, flashing his ID. 'Tell me. Now. He's a police officer. He's been stabbed.'

The woman's eyes narrowed, giving him a curt tut before looking up the details. Finally, she gave him the directions to the major trauma department.

Drake ran through the maze of polished corridors and patients lining the halls. Groans and cries emanated from the various beds and cubicles dotting the hallways. It had been a busy night by the sounds of things. His friend was just another number amidst the carnage.

What if he was too late? What if one of the few remaining good people in his life was going to be taken from him? How was he going to tell Judy, Dave's wife? They'd been together for thirty-five years, and now this.

Drake reached the major trauma department, his shoes squeaking as he took the turn to the entrance. He spotted Miller in the reception area. She was wearing a chic full-length black dress, a clutch bag and her phone in her hands, her grey hair falling to below her shoulders. The sight threw him. He didn't think he'd ever seen her dressed up like that before.

'Laura, how is he? Will he make it?' he blurted.

'John, slow down. He's in theatre now.' She put a hand on his shoulder, doing her best to assuage her old partner.

'How could this happen? What the hell is going on?' His thoughts were running away with him.

'As I said, he's in theatre now. Stabbed while stopping the intruder from taking Ellie's daughter. Ellie is here too.' She paused. 'John, she was also injured. Her husband took a beating as well.'

'Jesus, what? Why did nobody tell me?'

She took a step back, her eyes narrowing. 'The world doesn't revolve around you, you know – and you're here now, aren't you?'

'She's on my team, damn it, Laura!'

'Watch your words, DCI Drake.'

He was about to go into a further tirade, but he collected himself. 'I . . . I'm sorry. I'm just worried. Aren't you?'

'Of course I am. Dave's a good man. Judy knows there's a car on the way to pick her up. She was distraught – so close to retiring and this happens, for God's sake.' She pinched her brow. 'What was he doing there? It's not his case, nor his responsibility.'

'We spoke, and he asked to look out for her. He felt he should.'

'And you let him?' Her eyes burned into him.

'He was quite adamant.'

'John, John . . .' She exhaled heavily through her nose and looked up at the ceiling.

Drake didn't respond as she shook her head and walked off.

* * *

'Chief,' Ellie said meekly as Drake entered her room. Her knee was heavily strapped and elevated. 'How's Dave? Is he going to be okay? Please tell me he'll be all right!'

'I don't know, Ellie. I don't know. He's in surgery. Miller said he was stabbed. What the hell happened? I knew moving houses was a bad idea as soon as I heard about it.'

'Dave . . . he saved Bella. He wouldn't let her go, even after he was hurt. He's a hero, Chief. She'd be gone if it wasn't for him.' She forced her head up as tears formed in her eyes.

'But it's my fault he's hurt. The attacker caught me out, got one over on me. I was stupid. I couldn't protect my family, John.' She hung her head again. 'Two hits and I was fucking useless. I couldn't even help him. And that PC Malik guy is injured, too – he was out cold.'

For her sake, Drake tried to move on from her part in the attack. 'Is Bella okay? Is Len? I heard he had quite the knock.'

'He's got a concussion, but he's going to be fine. Bella is shaken up. The in-laws have her in Len's room. They kept her with him. They're not . . . best pleased with me. Think I brought this to their house,' she croaked.

Drake knew that feeling, the persecution, having had similar with Becca over the years.

'Don't blame yourself. You can't – you didn't decide for this to happen. You weren't keen on involving them. We know that, they know that really. But there's no point blaming him either. That won't help either of you. What's done is done.'

'I know that, but it seems they're less *accepting* of that truth right now. But I know them. They'll calm down in time, you're right,' she said, studying him. 'You know . . . I think I can understand how you feel a little. It's hard, you can't do right for doing wrong. I see that now.'

Drake nodded, but said nothing.

'I'll be back working tomorrow – I'll have crutches if I have to. No-one is stopping me from catching this fucker, not now. They're going to regret it.'

'Ellie—'

'I don't care. They nearly got my daughter.'

'Just rest,' he pleaded. 'Please.'

* * *

Drake woke sharply. He'd slept in the relatives waiting room, and his eyes were groggy from sleep and the nightmares. The sparse surroundings and the NHS posters about various illnesses plastering the walls did little to lift his melancholy.

He winced as he sat up. He didn't know what ached and what didn't. Looking at the clock on the wall, he realised Dave should be out of surgery by now. For all he knew, his friend could have died, and he'd just slept through it.

He left his makeshift bedroom in search of a nurse or doctor who could give him some information. It wasn't long before he found a petite, dark-haired doctor with a serious expression on her face to give him the answers he needed. Drake hoped that the news was good and belied the mood she was giving off.

'Your colleague had successful surgery, but I can't tell you how long it'll be before you can see him or before he's well enough to speak. He has a punctured lung, and one wound narrowly missed his heart. We're talking millimetres. This, along with age and his health . . . We're still in dangerous territory, so we have to see how he responds.'

Drake winced, realising his friend really had been through the wars. 'Jesus . . . thanks.'

He spotted Dave's wife, Judy. She looked like she hadn't slept a wink. Her white hair was tied up roughly, and her kindly face, devoid of makeup, stared into the middle distance. She was toying nervously with her hands when he approached.

'Judy, I—'

'He was only looking out for his friend. How could this happen, John?'

'I'm sorry.'

'He saved that little girl, I hear.' A faint smile flickered on her lips. He felt like the woman was going to chastise Dave when she next saw him. 'He's a stubborn fool, but he's my fool.'

'Can I sit with you?'

They sat and chatted until finally the doctor came to let Judy see her husband. Drake left her and grabbed a coffee. He hoped it would be his turn soon. Visiting him was the least he could do, the man having listened to his bleating enough these past months.

Judy came back out and waved him over.

'He's all yours. I'm just going to get a drink and I'll be back. He needs rest, John. Remember that.' She gave him a look, then took her leave.

He entered the room. 'Dave, what have I told you about standing in the way of knives? It never ends well,' he joked weakly, pulling the door behind him. An oxygen mask and various devices, monitors and intravenous tubes were attached to the man's frail-looking body. Drake's face dropped as he took it all in. The sight of his friend in such shape hit him like a train. He'd never seen the man even have a paper cut, let alone this.

He took the chair beside Dave's bed and pulled it close, clasping his friend's hand.

'You hold on, bud. You're through the worst of it now.' He raised his eyebrows in good humour. 'I know you wanted to retire, but there are easier ways of getting it done, you know? You're going to have to pay for that helicopter ride too.'

There was no reaction to the mention of money, which was unusual for Dave; only his continued, laboured breathing.

Drake sat for a time, his eyes growing darker with each passing minute.

'I'll get whoever did this to you, Dave. You mark my words . . . I'll get them.'

47

Drake packed up his things, stuffing the few articles he'd brought with him into a duffel bag. He'd decided he was done with the place, and he'd understand if it was done with him too. This time round, there was no management to throw the key in the face of. He'd just be posting it back unceremoniously when he got round to it.

A few shards of sunlight penetrated the murk while he packed. Maybe the building's way of seeing him off for the last time and a sign that things could only improve from here on in?

He noted the distinct lack of music emanating from beneath his feet. That was one less problem for him and for whoever was unfortunate enough to take the place on. The world needed less shitty neighbours.

Finished with his packing, he slung the bag over his shoulder and picked up his tattered briefcase. He cast one last glance up at the loft beam, and found the sense of dread it usually exuded was gone. Looking at it now, he felt nothing but anger . . . Anger, for it to have come that close for him. Anger at himself for ever having contemplated the unthinkable. It wasn't him. It never would be, he knew that now. He'd be fighting for his daughter, fighting for the few family and friends he still had in his life. It just might not be in the most conventional of ways occasionally.

Drake huffed at the loft beam and gave the room a last scan after opening the door, then slammed it shut behind him.

* * *

'Right, everyone,' Drake said, grim-faced, coming out from the side-office. Chambers entered the investigation room moments later, her eyes shadowed and groggy. 'As you know, Ellie was attacked last night, her daughter the target of a kidnapping attempt. We just have to thank whoever resides up there,' he pointed at the ceiling, 'that Bradfield was around to save the day and stop her being taken.'

'How is he?' Chambers stuttered, cutting a forlorn figure.

'He's in awful shape, but supposedly through the worst of it.' Drake put his hands in his pockets and attempted to lighten the mood. 'All being well, I hope I'll be able to get some sense out of him – probably for the first time ever – in the coming days.'

'Thank God,' Chambers said.

'Indeed.' Drake nodded. 'Whoever did this will rue the day they were born, believe you me.'

'Amen to that,' Melwood said with a nod of his own.

Strauss remained quiet, his eyes flitting between Drake and his laptop.

'So, what's on the menu for today?' Drake asked. 'Anyone have any leads? Anything on the guy on the school CCTV?'

Melwood swivelled in his chair. 'I'll be going to take a look at where Clare Baker used to live.' He clapped his hands to his knees. 'We've located it – the house she had with her ex-partner.

The place she was living when those payments were made. Fancy coming along, Drake?'

'Sounds like a plan, Inspector.'

'Glad you think so,' Melwood said, smiling.

'I'm chasing the final outputs from her murder scene, sir,' Chambers said. 'It's not looking good, though.'

'Got it, Gemma.' He gave her a nod. She always seemed so downbeat, and Drake was running low on ways to encourage her without taking hold of her and giving her a shake. She shouldn't need it, not on this team. She should be annoying him with her enthusiasm if she was looking to get anywhere in this line of work, bowling him over with new angles and takes, but there was nothing.

'Strauss? For our star investigator, you're strangely quiet.'

He looked over his shoulder at Drake from his desk. 'Nothing to report right now, sir.'

'Really? Nothing on our police colleague, Peter?'

Now it was Strauss' turn to swivel in his chair. 'No, it's so unusually *empty*. It's as though he purposefully kept a low profile.'

'I sense an alarm bell.'

'You would be right to think so.' The German said. 'Meanwhile, I'll keep on it with the analysts to continue our search for CCTV man. See if we can get a positive ID on the system. Going to be checking sex offenders registers, the works.'

'Well, do what you can. Hopefully, you'll have something for us when we get back. I'm counting on you – same goes for you, Chambers.'

Melwood stood up. 'Okay, if we're done, it's time to go. Got a bit of a drive ahead of us.'

'Oh?'

'Yep, Maidenhead, place in Berkshire near Windsor. That's near your old neck of the woods, isn't it?'

He was almost right. It was southeast of the village of Barndon, where his house was situated, on the outer reaches of Oxford.

Drake humoured him anyway. 'Certainly is. Lead the way.'

* * *

He regretted letting Melwood drive and take his own car the moment he'd opened the passenger door.

The vehicle was a pigsty, and this was coming from someone who had lived out of their car for the better part of a week. Coins, food packaging, crumbs, bottles, anything that had seen the inside of his car, had seemingly ended up discarded in said car. Drake pulled a face as he sat in it. For a man who so obviously cared for his appearance, the contrast between Melwood and his car was surprising.

'Sorry, meant to get it valeted,' Melwood mumbled. He starting the engine and the car sputtered into life.

I was thinking more of an exorcism, Drake thought. He immediately wound down the window to rid himself of the smell of feet.

Small talk ensued as they progressed in a westerly direction from London. Melwood navigated the extensive traffic caused by roadworks and idiot drivers before it gave way to the delights of the M4 motorway. He sat in the right-hand lane, his foot planted on the accelerator, the old BMW sounding like it was going to give up the ghost at any second. Cars undertook in the left-hand lanes, the occasional obnoxious horn coming their way. Melwood took it in his stride, giving a few of them the finger.

'Do you think we'll ever get to the bottom of this, Drake?'

Drake pondered the question. When he didn't answer right away, Melwood shot him a look.

'I wasn't expecting war and peace, you know. Just a yes or no will do.'

'All right, Andrew. Cool it,' Drake snapped. He stuck his elbow on the edge of the car door and watched the world go by as he spoke. 'I think we will. I feel as though it's escalating, and last night only proves that. They'll make a mistake, and when they do, we'll be there. Don't you worry.'

'I wish I had your confidence; I really do.'

'Oh?'

'All we have is that this lot are linked somehow. No idea on the Wilkinson connection. That's basically it.'

Drake frowned. 'No, that's not it at all. I don't agree.'

'I see why you are where you are then, and I am where I am,' he said bitterly. 'I bet the bosses lap up that positivity.'

Drake arched an eyebrow, giving Melwood a look. 'Me? Positivity? Really?'

'Okay, maybe that was a step too far,' he back-pedalled. 'But you know what I mean. They like to hear about progress, you know?'

Hang on a second. 'Wait, was it you speaking to Miller behind my back?'

Melwood looked genuinely aghast. 'What? No, of course not. I wouldn't do that. It's not my style.'

'Hmmm.'

'It's not. God's honest truth,' Melwood insisted, looking over at Drake and drumming the knob of the gear stick with his left hand. 'It's not like they'd listen to me anyway,' he added. 'I'm in their bad books.'

That piqued Drake's interest. 'About that—'
'One for another time. We're nearly there now.'
'How do you know?'
'Unlike you, I don't need satnav. Got a memory for it.'

48

Drake and Melwood pulled up by the crescent-shaped verge rimmed by pavement on one side, a series of large house driveways on the other. The side road was quiet, the houses overlooking a series of fields shielded by trees.

Melwood looked around. 'Looks nicer than her new place. Roomier, bit more of a view. She clearly downgraded after sodding off on her own.'

'Yeah, think you could be right.'

Drake didn't want to strike up further conversation as he took in his surroundings. He got out of the grotty car in a hurry, happy to stretch his legs after a near two-hour journey.

The houses stood silent in the early afternoon gloom. What little sun had warmed him in the morning was a long, distant memory now. The further west they'd travelled, the more overcast it had become. Building work was being done on the house on the end, a metal fence cordoning off a mound of bricks and dirt. The rest looked like a little work would have done them some good, too.

Melwood looked at him. 'You want to lead, or shall I?'

'No, you go for it. I'm aware I've been stealing a lot of the fun, so fill your boots,' Drake said.

'Thanks,' Melwood replied, though he didn't look too happy about it. He took the steps leading to the door and rung the bell, while Drake stood back.

A solitary pneumatic drill started in the distance. Drake couldn't tell if it was coming from one of the nearby houses or somewhere else.

The door opened. 'Yeah? What is it?'

A thin, rakish man with a hooked nose and long hair trailing down his back answered the door. He was the type that looked like no matter how much they ate, they were permanently thin. Veins bulged on his bare arms and neck, not from muscle but from the lack of fat.

Melwood showed his ID, and Drake half-heartedly did the same.

'Police, can we come in?'

The man turned his nose up. 'Depends what it's about, doesn't it?'

'Murder enquiry.'

'Oh!' The man's tone changed immediately upon hearing the magic 'M' word. 'Come in, come in.'

He showed them through to a sparse lounge, the type that shouted 'new rental, no money to furnish' rather than having been done through choice. The carpets seemed roughed up and coming away at the skirting boards, like a cat or dog had been at them. Drake was surprised, based on the exterior and how long the man was supposed to have lived in the place.

'Can we take your name?'

'It's Gregory. Gregory Pulver.' He gestured for them to take a seat on a dilapidated brown leather sofa.

'Okay, Mr Pulver. How long have you lived here, please?'

Melwood continued, perching on the edge of the seat. Drake took a similar position on another chair, clasping his hands together.

Gregory pondered the question a bit, sitting down in a matching leather armchair as he did so. 'Twenty . . . nigh on twenty years, give or take? I'm running out of fingers and toes to count.'

'Right, so you must have been with a woman called Clare Baker in this house at some point then? Is that correct?'

'Clare? Woah, that's a name I've not heard in a long time,' he said, rubbing an arm. 'But, yes, we were . . . together around that time, I think, yeah.'

'Greg? What's going on?' A voice called, the sounds of heavy footsteps coming down the stairs.

'Oh, sorry. That's my friend, Jorge,' Gregory told them, as the man entered the room. The face peering round the door frame belonged to someone who had been to one too many tanning salons in his life. He had an overly wide mouth and heavy, dark eyebrows that Drake swore had to be obstructing his sight.

'I see we have company,' Jorge's soft voice noted. There was only a hint of an accent, implying someone who had not lived in their home country for a long time.

'And you are?' Drake asked.

'Jorge Martinez, the man from España,' he replied. 'Sorry, is this a meeting I've crashed?'

'Sort of Jorge, they're police officers.'

'Police Inspectors . . .' Melwood corrected him. 'Well, and a Chief Inspector actually.'

'Right, I see, I see. How . . . *different*.'

Melwood looked at him. Drake judged he wasn't a fan by his expression. 'And you – were you visiting or staying here, all those years ago?'

'Oh, probably. Me and Greg here go way back. Best buds, ain't that right?'

Gregory didn't seem to agree, judging by the look on his face. 'Erm, yes. Suppose so.'

'I see, well, I regret to inform you that Clare Baker died recently.'

'Died?' Gregory retracted his face into his chin. 'And you mentioned this was a murder enquiry. You're saying she was murdered?'

'That's correct, yes.'

Gregory made another strange face. Drake couldn't tell whether it was grief or something else. Guilt, perhaps?

Jorge, by contrast, remained unmoved. 'She was a bit of a bitch anyway, let's be honest. Let herself go, I hear,' he said, gesticulating to imply her size.

'Jorge! Come on, the woman's dead. Have a heart.'

The man shrugged in response, still standing at the door. 'So, what's this got to do with us?'

Melwood pushed on. 'We'd like to understand more about her. What she did back then, what her frame of mind was.'

'Not much to say really, she was just . . .' Gregory picked at a thumbnail while he searched for a word.

'Average.' Jorge supplied.

'Not engaged in any *unusual* activity at the time?' Melwood said, retrieving a notepad from his pocket.

Gregory's eyes fixed on it. 'Unusual?'

'Sexual games? Parties?'

The man appeared flustered at the question.

Jorge jumped in again. 'Oh, *that*. Yes, we all messed around a little back then, fun times. Oh, what it was to be young.' He tittered.

'Messed around?'

'Yeah, just some *swapping* . . . sex games, nothing illegal, officers, I assure you,' he said, lingering on the word 'illegal.'

Drake let Melwood continue with his line of questioning. The pneumatic drill had started once again and was getting on his nerves.

'And was there money involved?'

'Yes, we invited all sorts round. It was great fun. Shame it ended.'

'And . . .' Melwood looked decidedly uncomfortable. 'Did anyone else live here back then?'

'No, no. Just us,' Gregory stated.

Melwood made a show of jotting a note down on the pad and put it back in his jacket pocket. 'And what is it you do, Mr Pulver?'

'I work in religious studies at a school. Have done for many years.'

'And you, Jorge?' Drake asked ahead of Melwood, feeling Jorge was the more suspect of the two. He gave him the creeps, either way.

'I'm a relocation officer.'

'Relocating *what*, exactly?'

'Adults. Social care, victims of domestic abuse. That sort of thing.'

'I see. That your whole career?'

'Yes, I'm good at it, and I derive some enjoyment from it, I suppose. Making such positive changes to people's lives.'

Drake frowned. He changed the subject, directing the next question to Gregory. 'And why did Clare leave?'

The man shrugged. 'Just ended, nothing major. We drifted apart.'

'Found a new model more like,' Jorge laughed.

Gregory gave his friend a look. 'Jorge . . .'

'Sorry.' The man didn't look sorry. His lips curled into an ugly smile.

Drake needed to do something, create some space between them. 'Apologies for asking, but do you have a bathroom I can use, please?'

'Yes, sure. It's down the hall, by the kitchen doorway.' Gregory pointed towards the back of the house.

'Thank you.'

Drake got up and edged around Jorge, who didn't move an inch to let him pass. He could smell stale sweat and cigarettes oozing off the man. He made a face when Drake got past and made his way toward the kitchen.

Nothing stood out from what he could see of the house. It was a little moth-eaten, and not a lot of care had gone into decorating. There were scuff marks on skirting boards, thread-bare carpets, but there was nothing criminal about that.

Opening the small door under the stairs, Drake was greeted by one of the grimiest toilets he'd seen in a long time. He didn't know whether to laugh or cry. It looked as though it had somehow decayed. Perhaps this was the only thing the pair were guilty of. He knew he'd feel guilty if this were his.

He pulled the door behind him, doing his best to ensure his clothes didn't touch anything. There was further chatter coming from the sitting room, the smarmy tones of the Spanish man setting him on edge.

Drake thought about what they'd been saying, how casual they, namely Jorge, had been about what they'd got up to in the past. There seemed to be no love lost between them and Clare. He could sort of understand why; the little he'd seen of her, he'd not taken to her either. But she'd been involved with them. There had to have been a bond of some kind, a bond over something. But what?

He took some toilet roll and wrapped it around his hand before flushing the toilet and chucked it in after. Upon exiting the chamber of horrors, Drake spotted a feature at odds with his knowledge of the place. There were marks on the inside wall of the kitchen, denoting heights, and names – though rendered illegible, having been scribbled out. He'd done the same for Eva when she'd been growing up. Had children lived here?

Drake returned to the sitting room as Melwood was wrapping up. Jorge had finally moved into the room and sat where Drake had originally been perched, though Jorge had gone for a more extravagant pose, lounging across most of the seats.

'. . . Okay, well, I think that's everything, unless there's anything from you, Chief Inspector?' Melwood said, raising an eyebrow at him.

Drake looked at him, still distracted by what he'd seen.

'Oh, no. Nothing more for now. Thanks for your cooperation, fellas.'

'Is there going to be a funeral, do you know?' Gregory asked, still sat in the armchair.

'I'm sure, but we don't have the details. You'll need to call Wandsworth station and ask.'

'Thanks.'

'Oh, and just want to ask . . .' Drake turned back.

'Mmm?'

'Why do you have kids' measurements on the wall in your kitchen, by the door?'

'Oh . . .' Gregory paused. 'That's my nephew and nieces. My family's been kicking them out like there's no tomorrow, you know?'

Drake forced a knowing smile. 'I see. Nothing but trouble.'

Gregory nodded. 'Yes, something like that.'

49

Melwood honked his horn at the car in front for not keeping up with the traffic as they drove back into the heartland. Drake could see their headquarters' tower block looming in the distance like a building laid to waste in some post-apocalyptic film. He had images of a nuclear blast going off in the background, the heat blast surging over them. The realisation dawned on him that his last moments would be in a car that smells of feet with a man who seemed to have anger management issues of his own. *Jesus.*

'This fecking traffic, Drake. Honestly, surprised no one has got out and gone postal before now. The M25 is a bloody nightmare. Why is it so damn busy every . . . single . . . day?' Melwood emphasised the words by pounding the steering wheel.

'People driving back after their daily commute, at a guess.'

'Mmm.'

Drake couldn't resist. 'You know, you insisted on *not* using any navigation? Only a madman would go via the M25.'

'Yes, all right. I suppose I deserve that,' Melwood conceded.

Drake drank in the smell of success. What a time to be alive.

'You think it strange, regarding those marks I saw at the house?'

'Yes, very much so,' he agreed. 'That story about nieces and nephews struck me as bullshit. Who does that for children that aren't theirs, even if they are related?'

'Agreed. That Jorge guy too. Gave me the creeps,' Drake said, flexing his hands. 'He was *grim*. But they don't strike me as the sort to burn people alive.'

'Yeah, quite . . . Oh, balls.' Melwood realised he was now the one failing to keep up with the traffic and stamped his foot on the accelerator, nearly stalling the car. 'Shit.'

'He kept butting in on Gregory Pulver too,' Melwood continued. 'As though he didn't trust the guy to give the right answers.'

Drake agreed. 'Yep, funny how it serves to bring more suspicion on what they're saying, rather than less.'

Melwood nodded. When he began to get irate at even more people, Drake looked out over the buildings and zoned out from the ensuing rant.

* * *

'You go in. I'll just be a minute.' Drake said, leaving his Inspector to go inside. Slouched against the low brick planters that lined the carpark, he took in the moment of being Melwood-less. Whatever was in the planters had long since died and ended up as a repository for the offices chain smokers and other rubbish.

Drake decided he'd text his daughter, show her he was thinking of her, whether she liked it or not.

Eva, I'm sorry about upsetting you the other night. Just know that I'm here for you when you want to talk. Love, Dad. xx

He pressed send, feeling a slight warmth mixed with a sense of nervousness. His daughter shouldn't elicit that response from him. It was ridiculous, but that's what things had come to.

A black short-haired cat meowed, startling him. 'Where'd you come from?' he mused, stroking it. The cat didn't stick around for long, seemingly deciding he wasn't a fan of him either and running off under Melwood's car for warmth.

Drake looked back down at his phone, opening his message to Eva to see if it had been delivered.

His heart sank. She'd blocked him. His own daughter had blocked her dad from contacting her. A familiar fire ignited.

Jesus, just give me a goddamn break!

'John?'

'Becca?' He looked up with a start.

'Drake, you okay?' asked a Scottish woman he didn't recognise.

'Huh?'

'You looked bereft. I just wanted to see you were okay?' she said, cocking her head while she approached, her hands cupped together. 'Sorry, I didn't mean to surprise you. I just wanted to say hi. Understand you've been working with my old protégé, Ellie Wilkinson? I recognised you from The Family Man days – the most recent ones, I mean.'

'Oh, er, yes. I'm okay. Thank you. Just a million miles away, you know?' He put his phone away, shutting off the image of his daughter from his mind.

'I get that,' she said, before sticking a hand out. 'Inspector Elgin, Phoebe Elgin. Just had a few days up here, and finished as of . . .' she made a show of looking at her watch, '. . . now.'

'Nice to meet you, Phoebe,' he said, geeing himself up mentally as he shook her hand. 'May I ask, was Ellie always so . . . what's the word?'

'Enthusiastic? Blunt? Inappropriate?' Elgin laughed at her own list, her ponytail bobbing behind her head.

'Yes! All *three* of those adjectives are very accurate,' Drake said, joining her with a chuckle of his own.

The police inspector had a friendly, warm smile. Something that he'd not been on the receiving end of lately. He realised he missed it, missed having female company that wasn't directly work-related. Most of all, he missed his wife.

'Afraid to say, she was – *is*, that way. She'll never change.'

'Good to know. It seems to be a case of "your loss, my gain". She's a good kid.'

'That she is. Though, maybe don't call her a kid to her face.'

'Agreed. Likely to get a sore arm for that kind of talk.'

An awkward silence ensued, and she wasn't walking away.

Deciding to get inside, Drake did his best to be as jovial as possible, for her sake, if not for his own. 'Well, it was great to meet you. Don't be a stranger, always good to hear the lowdown on my team.'

'Of course, you too,' she smiled.

He made his way inside while she lingered before walking away.

* * *

'You took your time, Drake. You said a minute,' Melwood sniped.

'All right, calm down,' Drake snapped back.

'Well, anyway . . . We have new info. Hot off the press. Strauss here got back the last of the results from our crispy victims, just as I walked in the door.'

'And? Spit it out.'

It had to be something. He needed *something*.

The Ties That Bind

'It's Robert Spencer, the cat guy. He *is* involved somehow,' Strauss stated flatly from his desk.

'You what? You're kidding me.' Drake could feel his heart rate speeding up. 'How?'

Melwood butted in, his pitch escalating as he spoke. 'They got a partial back off the burnt remnants of the photo found in Clare's throat. Drake, it's *him*. He's involved. Perhaps he's even our guy.'

'But how is that possible? We've footage, logs, etc? The man at the school isn't him.' Chambers frowned at the news.

Melwood shrugged. 'I don't know, but we need to bring him in. Fast. It's the only way we find out. Apply pressure.'

'And you're all sitting here talking to me. Why? Get on with it. Now,' Drake ordered. 'Get uniform round to his address, get anyone you can muster.'

'On it.' Strauss nodded, turning back to his laptop, his phone already to his ear.

Drake's mobile started vibrating in his breast pocket.

More good news, eh?

'Hello?'

'John . . . it's Judy. Dave's awake. He wants to speak to you as soon as you're able.'

Drake breathed a sigh of relief. The old guy had him worried for a moment there.

'Hi Judy. I'm sorry, you've kind of caught me at an awkward time. Is it really that urgent?'

'Well, he says it's important. He won't tell me anything more, so it must be. He's not one for keeping things to himself.'

'I see.' Drake pursed his lips. He supposed he could get over there soon. They'd let him know if anything further cropped up.

'Now, I don't want you coming really late. They won't let you see him in his condition. He needs rest.'

The way she was talking, Drake could imagine her nagging Dave. He would get a lot of help, requested or otherwise, over the course of his recuperation. He could tell that much.

'Okay, I'll do what I can. I'll let you know soon.'

'Thank you, John.'

* * *

'Jeez, Dave, you look a right state,' Drake joked feebly as he entered the room. Not much had changed since his last visit. The man still had on an oxygen mask along with the same devices, monitors and intravenous tubes as before, though he had covered his modesty a little more since Drake last saw him. Small mercies.

He thought he detected an infinitesimally small movement, perhaps a slight chuckle, but Dave's eyes were mere slits. He gestured again with a minute raising of his arm and monitored finger, indicating that Drake should sit.

Drake smiled. 'Is this what it takes to shut you up? Am I going to be able to moan at you without the chance of you running off now?'

Another twitch of the man's face.

'Joh . . .' Dave motioned with his finger for Drake to come closer.

'What? What is it?' he said, leaning in closer, his ear near the man's oxygen mask.

'It's . . . ahhh . . . it . . .'

'Seriously, you're worrying me. Should you be exerting yourself like this? Take it easy, you can tell me another time. I'll get you some water. There's a jug just there.'

Dave tapped his hand, trying to keep his attention. He stopped fussing and sat, letting the man try and speak.

'It . . . Joh . . . It . . . was.' He caught his breath, wheezing as he stuttered. 'John, the attack, it was . . . it was a wo . . . woman.'

50

Punishment was a word I'd never heard before that time.

But it was one I soon heard again and again and again.

It wasn't something I understood, at least not initially.

The reasoning . . . the *why* it had to happen.

It wasn't fair.

I didn't think I deserved it, certainly not to the level they meted out.

I wouldn't say it was a struggle for me as such. I just switched off to it after a while. Numbed myself to it after those first few terrifying times.

It wasn't right. I *knew* that.

In fact, it still makes me tremble when something happens that reminds me of it. It draws me back in, back to that time, those feelings.

The numbness returns, the world becomes distant.

Strangely, I almost feel free, looking back down at myself.

Ethereal.

51

The heavens had opened up on Drake's drive back to the house in Barndon, the place where his fall from grace had started.

He squinted his eyes at the glare of the cars in his view. The litany of lights refracted and shimmered across the puddles and soaked roads along his journey home.

He couldn't believe what he'd heard from his friend; the person who had threatened Ellie, attacked her, attempted to kidnap Bella, and damn near killed Dave, was a woman.

Some of what he'd seen made sense now. The person they'd attempted to apprehend that day at Alex Ludner's flat, there *was* a femininity to the person's bearing he hadn't taken in. His experience had clouded his judgement, making him immediately assume it had to be a man.

There was good reason, though, truth be told. It was a well-known fact that women weren't renowned for being serial killers or attackers of such brutality. They certainly weren't known for attempted kidnappings of detective's daughters. Female kidnappers were usually involved only when it was family-related; either trying to retrieve a child from an abusive partner, family member, or attempting to take a child of their own from a mother if they themselves were unable to have children. Drake rued his tunnel vision.

And Robert Spencer, was he really involved? Perhaps he'd been near these photos. Maybe he'd even taken them. But did he know how they were to be used? Or were he and the woman working together? It was too much of a coincidence; him being picked up by Ellie's place like that, surely? So many unanswered questions. It made Drake's head spin.

Shit!

A car flew by, a series of angry beeps baying at him. Swerving back onto his side of the road, he pulled over for a second to catch his breath. 'Jesus Christ, John.'

* * *

Drake slowed the car to a halt outside the dark house. The rain created a cacophony on the roof and windows of his car, the heavier drops from the sodden trees overhead punctuating the steady drum of the less substantial ones. He left the windscreen wipers to thud like a metronome while he sat in contemplation.

The maple tree stood barren in the front garden. It looked as though it had given up the ghost after all these years. As though it had died when his wife had passed. It had never seemed so skeletal.

He yearned for the familiar sight that he'd taken for granted in the past; the warmth of the lights at the windows, that of a house well-lived in. The imagery of the last few times he'd seen Becca ran through his mind. Him opening the front door; her coming to greet him in her well-loved mustard cable knit jumper, her dark hair contrasting against the yellow, her bare feet padding across the floor. Now there was just an empty shell of a house, its dark eyes staring back at him. He felt the same numbing ache he'd had this past year.

But it was now or never. He'd got this far. He had to face it.

Drake took a few deep, calming breaths, following the routine he'd adopted so long ago now. But the process only conjured up the same images that dogged his previous attempts at finding peace: his wife, his daughter, blood and darkness. All swirling together in a sea of helplessness.

Shaking his head in frustration, Drake pulled on the door handle. A hefty gust of wind whipping around him, and he pulled his coat closer. Leaving his things in the car, he hurried through the gate, getting drenched on the way to the front door.

He fumbled his keys to the ground, scrambling for them again before hurriedly unlocking the house. Opening the door, he was met with the faint but disturbingly familiar smell of home, and the sight of the gloomy reception room.

It stopped him in his tracks. Irrespective of the weather, he wasn't in a rush now he was actually there.

Flexing his fists, Drake braced himself and took his first hesitant step into the darkness.

52

Ellie woke screaming, 'Bella! Get Bella, now! Where is she? I need her here!'

'Woah, woah, easy! Easy, now.' Len sat up in bed and turned on the bedside lamp.

Ellie looked around the room, wide awake as her eyes acclimatised to the light.

They were in a hotel room. A kettle, sorry-looking television set and an iron and ironing board stood together as part of the large wooden unit at the foot of the bed.

She brought her breathing under control and wiped away a few beads of sweat from her brow.

'Is this what it's going to be like from now on?'

Len looked at her. 'I hope not. You scared the shit out of me, Ellie. I was only just getting off to sleep, too.'

'But Bella, where is she?'

'She's right here,' a voice said from the floor.

Scrambling to the side of the bed, Ellie saw a masked figure looking up at her from the floor, holding a knife to her daughter's throat. Bella's eyes were cloudy in death.

* * *

'Noooo! No! No! No!' Ellie cried, swatting at the air in front of her, the dream fading to nothing.

'Holy . . . Ellie, are you okay? Calm down. It's me, it's Len,' he reassured her, a hand on her shoulder.

She looked up at him. 'It was . . . it was Bella. Oh God, Len, it was awful!'

Her throat felt as though she'd been fed sand. She grabbed the glass of water at her bedside and gulped greedily.

'She's okay,' Len told her. 'She's under lock and key in the next room with my parents, remember? Breathe, okay?' He rubbed her back. It soothed her, but not enough for her liking.

The room was as it was in her dream. It was still shit.

'When is this going to stop, love? We can't go on like this,' he said, a yawn sneaking up on him.

'I don't know, but I don't think I want a repeat of last night.'

Ellie had spent much of the day resting with her family. The swelling on her leg was beginning to lessen, but not as much as she'd hoped. She'd spent her time trying to console her daughter as best she could. The poor girl had been terrified, still *was* terrified, and kept asking when the bad man was coming to take her away. Asking what it was she had done. Even asking if it was Father Christmas punishing her for being naughty.

If only it was that simple, she thought.

'I can't sleep like this. I feel like I need to be doing something,' she said, getting up and out of bed, pacing (hobbling) in front of him.

'Ellie, it's just gone one in the morning – there's nothing to do right now. Come back to bed. We can watch a film. There's bound to be some shit on at this time of night.'

She waved away the suggestion. 'I can't stop thinking about

what would have happened if she'd taken Bella. Would she be alive right now? She would've been so scared, Len.'

'I know, but she wasn't taken. You and Dave saved her,' he stressed. 'Anyway, at least you had the opportunity. I was out for the count. I couldn't protect either of you.'

He sat in silence, his legs hanging over the side of the bed, his head in his large hands. Her heart broke for him. Realising how useless he must be feeling, how guilty.

'It's not your fault, it's none of our faults. We weren't to know things would escalate like they did. Next time we'll be prepared,' Ellie said, perching next to him.

'Next time? There's not going to *be* a next time.'

'There will always be a next time, Len. Until we catch this fucker, we're at his mercy.'

'Don't say that.'

'I can't think any other way. If I do, it could happen again. And I can't let them take her – I won't. If I get the opportunity again, I'm killing that fucker, I swear it.'

She meant it, too. No one got to do what they did to her family and get away with it.

No one.

53

Drake made a couple of trips to the car during the lulls in the downpour to ship over a few boxes of belongings he'd kept in the car boot. Finally, everything in, he pulled the door up behind him. Now there were no more excuses.

He had only progressed a little past the doorway, having frozen within the first few steps. A sharp contrast to what lay behind him, the stillness of the house was filled with the musty, familiar smell of a place that had stood dormant for the best part of a year. He half expected someone to spring forth from the living room or come down the stairs. But those days were long gone; the place was lifeless, its atmosphere heavy.

Drake knew he had to push past the reluctance and fear he felt and face up to what had happened in their family home. Flicking on the light by the door, the house seemed to grow a little warmer, but not much. More memories came and went. Steeling himself, he grabbed his things and set about hefting them up the stairs. He had work to do, and standing around in fear of his past would not help him.

He nudged open the door to his study with his foot. The room lay in darkness. Dumping the box of files and photos on the floor, he reached for the desk lamp. With it lit, an odd feeling came over him, one that he hadn't felt in such a long time, it seemed almost alien: a feeling of comfort.

Old case notes and books cluttered the room, enveloping him. The stuffed bookcases, the large desk set against the wall overlooking Barndon Forest, the old chesterfield chair inviting him to sit down. The cramped space would have been too much for some, but for Drake it was home. At least there was something about the house that still held a more positive feeling for him, even if it was mired in death.

Drake put away his things in the spare bedroom, then snatched up an old mug from the desk in his study. He wiped it out with his fingers in the bathroom sink, and filled it with water. He was in no state of mind to confront the kitchen just yet.

Back in the study, he looked to his night's work for focus.

Unsurprisingly, they'd had trouble locating Robert Spencer since their discovery of his involvement, and the CCTV man had drawn a blank. It appeared young Robert had upped and left his flat in a hurry. He was not to be found at work and his neighbours had not heard or seen anything of him. It proved the man's guilt in Drake's mind. On the other hand, he'd been surprised to hear there *was* actual evidence of a cat having been there. Not that it was anywhere to be found now, naturally.

As for the man's whereabouts, Drake assumed he was holed up with the woman Dave had fought. It was the only thing that made sense. Either they were working together, killing their respective victims, which would account for the difference in methods, or they were helping each other out in other ways.

Regardless, it worried Drake that they were still out there; two serial killers at large was not something to take lightly. They were increasingly likely to lash out now the net was slowly tightening around them.

He huffed, slumping into the study chair. It emitted the same pained squeak that always set his teeth on edge. Making yet another mental note to fix it sometime soon (it had been nigh on a decade at last count) he picked up a box of photos and notes he'd compiled and emptied it unceremoniously on the desktop. His first job for the night: sifting through and sorting to try and make sense of it all. The rest was going to be his time for mulling over the evidence. Come rain or shine, he was going to find his man, woman and anything else that came up. He had to, for Ellie's sake, if not his own.

* * *

When the noise came, Drake was deep in thought.

Putting down the crime scene photo of Alex Ludner he'd been studying, he cocked his head and listened. The rain had ceased, it didn't sound like the familiar noises the house made, and no-one else was around to make the floor creak. There was only the wind for company. Perhaps the work was playing tricks on his mind?

Thud.

He frowned. There it was again.

Seconds later, a powerful gust of wind battered the house.

Thud.

Had something come loose somewhere? It had to be that, surely?

Venturing out from the study, he checked each of the rooms upstairs. In what had been their master bedroom, the bed was still unmade from the day of the attack.

Drake stuck his head into Eva's room, repeating old habits. It lay half-empty, mostly devoid of her things. A memory of them chatting together on her bed reminded him fleetingly of happier times.

Thud.

If it was coming from that damn kitchen, he didn't know what he'd do.

He listened at the top of the stairs, waiting for another bang. It took longer, but it soon made itself known. It was either the kitchen or the living room. He knew which he hoped for.

Coming down the stairs, an ominous feeling rose slowly in his chest, a tightening of sorts.

You can do this, he told himself. *It's just a house.*

The wind gusted again, slapping the trees and buffeting the house. A breeze wafted round his legs.

Was there a window or something open? Was that it? But how?

The feeling in his chest knotted. He stuck his head into the living room. All the windows were locked fast, a shard of moonlight highlighting the layer of dust that coated the mantelpiece and coffee table.

It had to be the kitchen. There was nowhere else.

Jesus, no. He took a sharp intake of breath as his nerves jangled, reacting to his increasing heart rate.

It would be okay. It was just a house. They'd made sure there were no remnants of the crime left. There would be nothing to see.

Thud!

It would be okay.

The phrase became a mantra as he paced towards the kitchen door.

Drake realised he'd been holding his breath when he gripped

the door handle. Before the events of that night, the door that had never been closed.

He closed his eyes for what he knew must have been minutes, a trickle of sweat running down his back.

It'll be okay.

He took another breath and opened the door.

54

Drake switched on the light, the room stark beneath the sudden brightness. He stood mute at the sight before him. The wind had fallen silent, the air still. But the atmosphere was heavy, oh so heavy. He closed his eyes to the screams echoing in his mind. His family's; his own.

A tear ran down his cheek at the sight of the dining table, the setting where it had all taken place.

Got to focus, he ordered himself. *Sooner you're done, sooner you can close the door again. Shut it out. Get away.*

He saw the source of the noise. It was the door out to the garden, the one that Ellie had kicked in all those months ago. The large glass pane in the door had shattered from hitting the corner of the kitchen unit, such was the force of her kick. A thin sheet of metal had been used to cover it, meant only as a temporary measure. It was flapping on a hinge, knocking against a kitchen cupboard in time with the wind. Drake wondered why he'd not heard it sooner, how long it had been happening. The dried leaves scattered in the corners and recesses of the kitchen diner gave a partial answer.

He immediately felt ashamed of not having respected the space.

Taking hold of the metal panel, he fixed the non-hinged side back into the clip that had once held it in place, thankful to find it took hold and stayed. He hoped it would remain that way, at least for now.

John, a voice whispered.

He gasped and turned towards the dining table, his heart kicking into overdrive.

Nothing there.

'Ho, Jesus.' He shuddered uncontrollably. Her voice had been so close it was as though her lips had brushed his ear lobe. Her breath on his neck.

He had to shake this off somehow. Had to confront it.

Drake inched over to the table. The chairs had been put back in place, the scene sparking a succession of devastating images: his family tied up: the Family Man wiping his bloodied knife on Rebecca's jumper: her funeral, and his daughter bereft. All of it played over and over inside his head.

He tried to steady his nerves, but being back in that room felt overwhelming. Looking down at the tiled floor, he could still see where the Man's knife had impaled his hand. He rubbed the scar on his palm, gritting his teeth at the memory of the sound it had made as it struck the tile.

A shadow flit past in his periphery. Drake's head immediately flicked to the two doorways behind him.

Once more, there was nothing there.

'Stop, Becca. Please,' he whispered, the tears flowing freely. 'Forgive me, please. I beg you.'

He couldn't take any more, the claustrophobia of it, the pain . . . It was all too much. He made a dash for the door, hurriedly closed it behind him, and headed back upstairs.

***

Drake paced the tiny room, knocking a pile of notes to the floor in his unfocused state. He shored them up against the side of the desk once more. The action helped bring him back to the task at hand, enabling him to temporarily push aside his experience downstairs.

He inched around to the front of the desk and stared at the photos he'd laid out. A burst of images from the first scene. Alex Ludner's corpse stared back at him, head bowed, bloodied and beaten.

Wait.

Narrowing his eyes, Drake picked up the picture, rifling through a desk drawer for a magnifying glass with his free hand.

The tree. There's something not right about the tree, I'm sure of it.

He passed the magnifying glass over the image, just above the man's head, to the side. He wasn't imagining things. There was a section of bare tree, as though the bark had been cut away.

Why was that significant?

Think.

He looked at the other photos from the same viewpoint, palming them off into a pile, one at a time. The photos showed the same. A piece of the tree exposed, the bark shorn away.

But why was it bugging him so? What wasn't he *seeing*?

He sifted through the remaining pictures he'd brought with him. Clare Baker, Peter Matthews, Sofia Machado . . . a few more photos from the Alex scene.

It was then he saw. Then that he spotted what it was. He pored over the image with his magnifying glass, the difference clear as day.

Drake kicked himself.

This was just a photo of Alex and the tree. Nothing special if you weren't paying attention.

But in one photo only, the tree bark was intact.

55

Drake arrived early, the office slowly coming to life around him. The hole in the wall appeared to have been mended. Only a sign with a scrawled *Wet Paint* attached nearby gave away its location.

'Impressive,' he murmured.

He'd barely slept a wink, if at all. Then again, sleeping in an old desk chair, slumped over a desk, was never going to count towards quality sleep, was it? His mind had been going into overdrive, orbiting the significance of what he'd spotted.

What could it mean? Was he overthinking things? Maybe SOCO had damaged it by accident?

If it was going to be another SOCO oversight or some other mistake that had impeded their investigation, he was going to go ballistic. Was this a sign of things to come with that profession? Quality work falling off a cliff?

Drake waited patiently for his team to file in: Chambers, in particular.

It pleased him she'd arrived before the others, not that he was expecting to see Ellie for the foreseeable. He'd ordered her to stay away; it wasn't healthy for her or her family.

The Ties That Bind

Gemma, mid-yawn, walked through the door. Her hair was done up in a rough bun, a few strands hanging out.

'Chambers, my office, please,' he requested, standing by the doorway to the SIO room.

She stopped in her tracks, a frown on her face. 'Sounds serious, sir.'

'Drake, please – and don't worry, I'm just trying to understand a situation. One you'll be more familiar with than the others.'

'Sorry, Drake.' She put her bag down on a chair and followed him through into the SIO closet.

He sat down, indicating for her to do likewise while he cleared his briefcase off the desk. He leant forwards, getting straight to the point. 'Chambers, that first scene. How did it go again?'

'The first one? What's that got to—'

'Just humour me, please?'

'Of course. Well, PC Mewton and I arrived at the scene. We'd got the call from Despatch, the alarm raised by those dog walkers.' She paused, studying him. 'Do I have to recount all of it?'

'Yes. Blow-by-blow, please.'

'Okay,' she said, pursing her lips a little, then continuing, 'Adam and I followed them to the scene. They pointed out the general location, but didn't want to come with us all the way – understandably, I'd say. We carried on through the slush and found Alex.'

'Good. And what did you see? Was there anything . . . unusual?' he asked. 'Anything different, that you can think of?'

'Different, how?'

'Like, something that was there, but later wasn't?'

She frowned, her face a picture of confusion and shaking her head. 'Erm, no, si—Drake, I would have said. I know I'm new, and I've probably not come across as *confident* as you'd like, but I'm not that stupid.'

'This isn't a personal attack, Chambers. I'm just trying to establish something.'

'Establish what?'

He brought out the photos from his briefcase on to the desk. 'Why it is that in all the photos, barring one, the tree has a chunk of bark missing by the victim's head? The bare wood's clearly exposed. Yet in one photo, it's all intact,' he said, pointing at the picture.

'What!'

'Now, do you see?'

'Of course.' She looked away for a moment before returning her gaze to him. 'But, how could that have happened? I can't recall the tree being any different, I'm sorry.'

Her face dropped before she collected herself and thought for a moment. 'Perhaps it's worth asking SOCO? Or Adam . . . PC Mewton? Though I guess he'll say much the same as me.'

'Don't you worry, I'll be doing just that.'

'I can do it, if you'd like? It's not a problem.'

'No, no, I'll get on with that,' he said, waving a hand. 'I would like you to see if there're any discrepancies elsewhere, yes?'

'Will do. And I'll ask the others to do the same when they arrive?'

'Also . . .' Drake paused. She'd phrased that last part as a question, but he ignored it. He supposed he should use this as an opportunity to encourage her a bit. 'I would like to commend you for your work so far. You're doing well in what is proving to be a difficult first case. You can be a little quiet, it's been noted. And as you say, you're lacking in confidence . . . but you *are* diligent, and that's needed here.'

'Oh.' Her eyes flitted anywhere but his direction, her cheeks flushing. 'Thank you for saying so, sir.'

'Now, if you would get to checking everything out? I need to make a few calls.'

'Of . . . of course. Thank you, Drake. I mean it.'

* * *

'Dr Kulkarni speaking?'

He smirked down the phone. 'Tanv, that's very formal of you.'

'Sorry, I'm in a meeting. Is it urgent?' It sounded like she was cupping her hand to the phone.

He closed the door to his office space.

'I'd say so, Tanv,' he told her. 'One of your guys, I need to speak with them. Understand a few things.'

'Go on.'

'Who worked the first set of victims? Can you recall? I hadn't worked with them before. I know it wasn't you for that one.'

'It was Daryl Fort and . . .' She paused, getting distracted by someone off call. '. . . Lindsay O'Hare.'

'Right, can you pass me their details, soon as you can?'

'Of course. What's this about, Drake?'

'I need to establish something,' he said, and explained the situation.

* * *

From the details Tanv provided, Drake discovered that Daryl Fort had a seminar that morning in the very same building he was in. He decided to crash it.

Drake burst into the room, a dozen heads turning from their projected slide deck and the speaker running the meeting to see what the commotion was. Three rows of chairs had been arranged, a smattering of occupants, the room barely half full.

'Daryl Fort?' he asked the room.

'Yes?' a muted voice responded from the middle row.

'Can you come outside for a minute, please?'

'Okay.' The man's thin legs stepped over people's feet while he made his apologies to the woman conducting the meeting. Daryl tucked a length of hair behind his ear as he met Drake outside the room, regarding him with a pair of intense grey eyes.

'What can I do for you, sir?'

'It's about the first scene on the SGK case, the one up in the woods at Folly Brook,' he stated.

'What about it? Is something wrong?' he asked. The nasal quality of the man's voice jogged Drake's memory.

'There's a discrepancy. I understand you were the primary photographer?'

'Yes,' the man frowned. His thin lips caved in as he pursed them, crossing his arms in anticipation of Drake's next question.

'What did you do when you got there?'

'Well, I lugged up some equipment, awnings and the like. Then was greeted by the DC and PC – sorry I forget their names, not worked with them before.' He thought hard, looking like he was replaying the events in his mind. Then he put his finger in the air as he relayed the information. 'I started taking photos, then realised the battery was low. So, I went back to the van and grabbed a fresh one. By that time, the other SOCO, Lindsay O'Hare, was ready to accompany me up.'

Bingo.

Drake considered his question. 'So, you're saying there was a time between the first photo and the rest? Where the body was unattended by your team, right?'

'Yes, that would be correct.'

'Who was still there at that point, please?'

The SOCO didn't hesitate. 'Just the male PC, and the detective constable.'

56

Drake hurtled north towards Barnet police station, west of the Folly Brook crime scene. On learning that PC Adam Mewton worked out of that station, Drake had dropped everything to reach him. Drake needed to know, needed to understand what he'd seen. More importantly, Drake needed to look the man in the eye when he answered his questions.

He pulled up to the tired-looking building not long before midday. The sun was struggling to break through yet more thick cloud, the roads still drying from the previous night's barrage of rain. He passed the front and took a turn into a side entrance before being greeted by a blue-barred gate. He got the attention of someone to open the gate and rolled into the car park, one side of which was fully lined with fluorescent Response-liveried vehicles.

Drake hoped he wasn't leading himself up a blind alley. He yearned for his hunch to pay off, for this all to finally lead somewhere. There had to be significance there, *surely*.

He spotted the constable smoking a cigarette by a set of stairs leading into the station, and got out of the car to greet him.

PC Mewton put out the cigarette and made his way over to

Drake, the man's thick brow and small eyes at odds with each other. He wasn't wearing anything to protect his head from the wind this time, so the sight of Mewton's pinkish shaven scalp greeted Drake. He could understand why the man kept it under wraps when it was cold.

'Sir, good to see you again. Happier circumstances this time, I hope?' Mewton said, offering a hand and a warm smile.

'Unfortunately not.'

The man regarded him for a moment. 'No? Not caught the person who did those awful things yet?'

'Nope. Killed two more, in fact.'

'You're kidding . . .' he said with a look of dismay. 'Sounds like you've got a task on your hands, sir.'

'You mind if we talk in my car?' Drake asked, tapping on the roof. 'Bit cold out.'

'Er, yeah,' Mewton said, considering him again. 'Sure, sir.'

Drake got back in the car and turned the electrics on, the heater coming on louder than he liked. He turned it low and turned to the constable. In the confines of the car, the smell of the man's cigarette smoke almost made Drake's eyes water.

'Appreciate you seeing me at short notice.'

Mewton shrugged it off. 'As I said to the desk sergeant, it's not a problem. Really hope I can help in whatever way possible.'

'What I need to ask is simple, really. Can you recount the scene and what you did that day for me?'

The man raised his eyebrows. 'I'll do my best, sir.'

'That's great.'

Drake wondered whether this was really worth his time. Was he getting worked up about nothing? Maybe it was just a wild flight of fancy, and his instincts were wrong.

'Okay, so I arrived at the scene and met with the walkers,' Mewton began. 'The discovery had really shaken them up. It's not often you see . . .' He scrunched his nose up. '. . . It's not often you see something quite as nasty and vindictive as what was in those woods, and they thought there was only that one dead guy at the time, right?'

'Exactly.'

'So,' Mewton went on. He was becoming more animated with his gestures. 'The DC and I, we went up to the woods. The snow was getting real slushy and trodden in by that point and we came across the scene. Nobody else there. It looked undisturbed, barring the dog having made a little mess of the snow. Running about and such, I suppose.'

'I see. Go on.'

'Well, SOCO soon appeared. We ensured there was a cordon, and so on. I went down and waited by the gate to the field, me being uniform and all. I went about keeping anyone at bay while SOCO did what they needed to do along with the DC.'

'So, did you notice anything strange while you were up there?'

Drake studied the man. He didn't give the impression of falsifying anything, or covering for anyone, or for himself. Nothing struck him as untoward about Mewton. His detective sense was well and truly not tingling.

'Strange, sir?'

'Such as the tree. Spot anything unusual there?'

'Can't say I did, sir.' He shrugged. 'Just a tree with a guy tied to it, you know. That was a pretty strange thing, in and of itself.'

'Okay' Drake leant over into the back seat and retrieved a file of the photos. 'So, did the tree look like this?' He offered the intact tree picture. 'Or did it look like . . . this?'

'Definitely like the first one. I don't remember any bare bark near the man's head, at least I don't think so. It was a while ago and it's quite a minor detail. Maybe why I'm not a detective, eh? Sorry, sir,' he added after a moment.

Drake sat and pondered the constable's answer, long enough for the sun to disappear back behind the clouds. He drummed the side of the driver's door with his fingers. Something wasn't ringing true; it was nagging at him, pulling at a thread in his mind. What was it? What wasn't he seeing?

'Sorry, sir. I don't mean to push, but will that be all?' Mewton queried tentatively. 'I've got a shift I'm supposed to be on.'

A shift, wait... Hang on, one second. He hoped it wasn't what he was thinking. There had to be a mistake.

'Constable, back up a bit,' he said, turning in his seat towards him. 'You said at the beginning, "*You*" arrived at the scene. Don't you mean "*we*"?'

Mewton frowned. 'Sorry, sir. I don't follow?'

'You arrived at the scene with DC Chambers. She was on shift with you, so you were showing her the ropes – what you guys do, the day-to-day stuff, yes?'

The man pulled his head back, the frown setting further into his thick brow.

'I think you're mistaken, sir. The first time I saw the DC, she was at the scene already.'

Drake inhaled a sharp breath.

'I see. Was she alone at any point when you were there? Like, were you and SOCO at the gate, and she was at the scene after SOCO had arrived?'

'Hmmm. I think so, sir.'

'Jesus Christ,' Drake muttered. It couldn't be, could it? Gemma couldn't be involved, surely? There had to be a mix-up somewhere. But she'd stated quite clearly that she was with PC Mewton that day. Why would she lie?

Scenarios and ideas played through Drake's mind as he groped for understanding. She had to have toyed with the scene when the SOCO man, Daryl, went back down to get a new battery for the camera. But why do that? What was she covering up? Had she messed up the scene somehow? Was she covering for herself or for someone else?

His eyes darkened, his thoughts raging at the deception. He'd persevered with her, only just praised her for her damn diligence that very morning, and this is how she'd repaid him? By lying?

'Sorry, sir? Are you all right?' Drake heard Mewton ask.

'Yes, yes. Apologies. All good. Appreciate your help, Mewton. Been very . . . *enlightening*. You're free to go.'

'Thank you, sir. Good luck with the case. Me and the guys will be rooting for you.'

The man left the car, slamming the door a little too hard and making him wince. But the movement didn't shake Drake from his thoughts.

The thought that the young detective constable may not be what she appeared, after all.

57

Tentatively, Ellie set her legs down on the floor and pushed off from the bed.

'Argh, fuck!' she exclaimed, sucking in her breath.

She didn't let herself lean back on the bed, reasoning that if she could do it after waking from one of her nightmares, even if she'd been pumped full of adrenaline at the time, she could damn well do it again. Plus, she was done with this hotel room.

She needed to work.

Len entered the room, wearing a natty pair of white slippers to go with his stripy old man pyjama bottoms. All he really needed was a pointed hat with a bobble on top to become a black Christmas Carol Scrooge for the modern age.

He brought the brunch tray over while he chastised her, 'What're you doing up and on that leg, Ellie? You were told to rest. Come on, get back into bed and rest it on the cushion like they told you to.'

'No, Len. I'm calling Drake. I need to be up and about. This is killing me.'

'Ellie, for God's sake. Just stop, would you?'

'No. I'm going in, whether you like it or not.'

Her husband studied her. She could tell he was close to giving up his resistance. He knew what she was like, how stubborn she could be. Determined.

'All right, but call ahead, yeah? Maybe your boss can knock some sense into you,' he said, snagging a rasher of bacon and eating it in one go.

'This will all be over soon, I promise.'

He swallowed his last mouthful. 'I don't doubt it. I just want my wife back afterwards, please. Your daughter needs her mother, too.'

'I'll do my best.'

Ellie picked up the phone and dialled Drake's number.

* * *

Ellie watched her boss pull up to the hotel. Her surroundings while she waited had given her little cause for excitement. The place reminded her of a rundown service station, grey buildings, cars everywhere and little else. There was a glare to the grey skies overhead that irritated her almost as much as her knee. By the looks of her chauffeur arriving, Drake was not happy either. Ellie hobbled over to his car while he jumped out and opened the passenger door.

'I'm not happy about this, Ellie,' he said, confirming her masterly suspicions.

'Sorry, Chief. But I've got to do something, and you left me hanging on the phone. What's got you worked up?'

Drake gestured at the open door. 'Get in and I'll tell you. If you can get that low down, of course.'

'I'll manage, don't you worry. Had worse in my time.'

Ellie hobbled down into the seat and he closed (slammed) the door behind her. She wrinkled her nose immediately; she couldn't ever recall him smoking. What had he been up to?

'Started smoking, have we?'

'What?' he said, snapping on his seat belt. 'Oh, that. No, just the guy I had in my car . . . PC from the first scene. Looks like we've got a dodgy policewoman on our hands, Ellie.'

'Me? What have I done?' she said, taken aback.

'No, not you. Gemma,' he said, his face carved into a deep frown.

Gemma? Where did that come from?

Ellie looked aghast. 'What! No! You're kidding me? She wouldn't say boo to a goose, let alone kill people.'

'Steady on. I've not said she's killed anyone. But she's gone to ground since I've found out she's been lying to us this whole time. Her phone is off, and she's not at the office.' He started the engine and pulled off. 'She's vanished since this morning. It's a long story, I'll fill you in on the way.'

* * *

Ellie struggled to keep up with her boss as they weaved through the corridors to the investigation room. She nearly toppled over when someone knocked into her as she hopped along behind him like a deer that had lost a fight with a car.

He was really irate at what he thought Chambers had done, Ellie could see that. But what had Gemma *really* done? Had she concealed evidence? Why had she already been at the scene? It didn't make sense to Ellie, and she didn't believe it was Gemma who'd attempted to take her daughter from her that night. She was too slight, for starters. Something didn't feel right.

'Melwood, any luck in getting hold of our DC yet?' Drake asked as he strode into the room. Ellie gripped the doorframe, wiping away a thin layer of sweat that had formed on her forehead.

Melwood spun on the chair and Strauss followed suit, both appearing strangely chipper.

'No, nothing. I thought it was odd,' Melwood said. 'She was acting stranger than normal earlier. On edge, twitchy, you know? Upped and left without saying a word. Never would have thought she'd be involved somehow,' he finished. No one had asked for his opinion, but he offered it anyway.

Catching sight of Ellie, he raised his eyebrows at her. 'Wasn't expecting you in for days. Good to have you back, though. Sorry about what happened to you and your family.'

'Thanks—'

'Strauss, anything from your side?' Drake interrupted. 'Can we link Chambers to any of our victims – Gregory or Jorge, even? The CCTV man?'

'Nothing so far, Drake.'

Ellie's turn to jump in. 'So . . . we have payments to Clare from Alex, with Sofia, on behalf of Sofia even, or both,' she summarised. 'We know Clare lived with Gregory, maybe Jorge, and this Peter Matthews was involved with Clare somehow. CCTV guy is involved with the killers somehow, too. Robert Spencer is missing. We have a missing DC and a mysterious female attacker, or killer, who attacked Dave and my family.' She shook her head. 'There must be something going on that we're missing? Something they all must have been involved in all those years ago.'

Strauss burst up from his seat like a thousand volts had struck him.

'Drake, sir—'

'What is it, man? You look like you've seen a ghost.'

'We've wasted a lot of time,' Strauss stated. He ran his hand through his thick hair.

'What? What do you mean?'

'I think I know who's next.'

Ellie saw the precise moment when Drake had the same realisation.

'Idiot!' He berated himself, cutting Strauss off. 'How could I be so blind?'

He snatched his car keys up. 'Gregory Pulver and Jorge Martinez,' he said grimly. 'We need to find them. Now.'

* * *

Drake raced through the office. Time was of the essence. More people were going to die, if he didn't—

'Drake! In here, now.' Heads turned to watch the drama unfolding in front of them as Miller's order rang out across the office. Her icy stare all but froze him in his tracks.

'Ellie, I'll meet you downstairs.' Drake waved her off as he made his way to Miller's office.

She'd had left the door open. He closed it behind him, his boss having returned to her desk chair. He moved to close the blinds and make it less of a goldfish bowl, but she put up her hand to stop him.

'So, were you planning on updating me before disappearing for the day?' When she looked up, her expression was etched with weariness. 'What's got you racing through the office?'

'Sorry, ma'am. It's just . . . it's urgent.'

'Oh? That we have a rogue DC that you can't get hold of, you mean?'

Who was undermining him this time?

'What? How did—'

'Nothing sinister, John. Bumped into DI Melwood and he'd

asked me if I'd seen her, then one thing led to another. You know he likes to talk.'

'Laura, I don't know what to say. It's a bit of a curveball.'

'You got that right. And it makes sense now.'

'Ma'am?'

'She's been the one that's been giving me updates in your absence, mostly unsolicited. It strikes me she was trying to undermine you somehow, don't you think? She didn't paint you in the best of lights – disappearing randomly . . . drinking . . . erratic behaviour.' Miller shrugged.

He couldn't believe that the young woman he'd worked with could do such a thing. But what else could she have done to muddy the waters? She'd likely tampered with the evidence once already.

'I've prioritised her apprehension,' Miller said. 'I can't imagine she'll be underground for much longer, Drake.'

'Thank you, Laura.'

She nodded. 'And where were you rushing off to so urgently?'

'We think that the SGK – or SGKs, God knows – are going to strike again and soon,' he told her.

'So, what are you standing here for? Get a move on. Call in backup as soon as you ascertain the situation. I do not want you going in alone. I mean it, Drake – we've already had two officers hospitalised, I don't need another. And certainly not you.'

Drake nodded and rushed for the lift. Her office blinds billowed noisily as he slammed the door behind him.

58

Luck was on Drake's side. It took him half the time it had taken the previous day to get to Gregory's home in Maidenhead. On the drive over, he'd filled Ellie in on his meeting with the men. He was kicking himself for not realising they could be next on the list. Heck, the person sat next to him in the car could still be in danger, for all they knew.

'Are you going to be okay on that leg of yours, Ellie?'

'Don't worry about me. Just stiff, is all. It'll work itself out the more I move it. It's much better already,' she said. But her face was telling him differently.

Drake pulled up at the familiar crescent of houses. The sunlight had burned away the clouds of earlier and made it seem almost picturesque, belying the battered internals of the house they were honing in on.

'Nice place,' Ellie commented, absently rubbing her working leg.

'Not so much inside, I'm afraid.'

She stopped. 'Oh?'

'As I said, they haven't kept the place ticking over. You'll see.'

'Great. Seen some shit holes in my time, so it will have to go some way to beating any of those.'

He switched the engine off. The space suddenly seemed very quiet.

'Right, you ready?'

'As I'll ever be,' Ellie replied, pulling on the handle.

Drake opened the car door and stretched his legs, the bite of the wind niggling at him. Ellie hoisted herself out, ungainly in her movements.

'Did the door look that battered, the last time you were here?' she asked.

'What?' He stared at the door. There were several marks present that hadn't been there on his previous visit.

'Shit, they've beaten us to it,' Drake hissed. He put his finger to his lips for her to keep her voice low.

Drake wished he had a weapon of some sort, if only to give his hands something to do. This wasn't America, but he felt a little helpless without anything; hell, even an old-school truncheon would do.

'Ellie, you take the right side. I'll open the door.'

'Got it.'

They flanked the door. Drake looked through a window, noting nothing out of the ordinary in the hallway.

'Ready?' He saw Ellie wince as she crouched as low as she could.

'Yep.'

Drake spotted that the door wasn't fully closed, so he nudged it open. He listened carefully for any sounds of movement, but there was only silence.

'Police. Show yourself.'

He waited for a response. None came.

Creeping into the house and past the stairs to his left, he

could see the makings of a struggle further in. The kitchen area, where the children's measurements were, had several items scattered about the place from an upturned drawer. Some of the cupboards stood open, and a spattering of blood speckled on the floor.

He looked backed at Ellie who had entered behind him.

'I think we're too late,' she whispered.

'Yep, but let's be careful,' Drake told her. 'We've not had the best of luck. Check upstairs, and I'll check the back. We might have another scene on our hands, for all we know.'

'Got it.' Gingerly, she ascended the stairs to his left, the treads squeaking in spite of her best efforts. Drake edged through to the kitchen proper.

Knives lay scattered on the floor, together with utensils from drawers, forks and spoons, measuring implements, the works. He scanned his surroundings. The faces of Jorge and Gregory and others he didn't recognise stared back at him from photos on the fridge, held on by fruit-shaped magnets.

Drake proceeded to the back room, which doubled as the dining area. A wooden dining table lay splintered in half on the floor, a couple of chairs scattered around. An old fireplace took up a lot of the wall space, blood spattered on the dirty white stone. More photos stood amidst further blood splatter on the mantle and a bookshelf stuffed in the room's corner. The far wall had a patio door opening out on to an overgrown garden, similar to Clare Baker's house. The door was ajar.

They had to have been surprised in the kitchen before running through into the dining area and possibly out into the garden beyond, Drake surmised. There was another smattering of blood on the wall next to the patio, as though someone's head had been shoved against it, possibly busting their nose.

'Nothing upstairs, Chief,' Ellie called down, the thump of her impaired footsteps following shortly afterwards as she traipsed down the stairs. Evidently, she'd given up on the stealthy approach. 'I looked out onto the garden too. There's nobody there.'

'All right. Anything of use upstairs? Signs of a struggle?' Drake asked.

'Nothing, just an unmade bed. Maybe someone ran down in a hurry, but that's just guesswork.' She jammed her hands in her pockets and looked around the room. 'Looks like you've had more fun, though.'

'Yes, definitely looks like a struggle in here. And Gregory, maybe Jorge too, didn't win either.'

'Oh?'

'They'd still be here otherwise.'

'Of course,' she said, throwing up her hands at her own stupidity. 'But where could they be? Maybe they fled?'

'That's the mystery.'

Ellie took out her phone. 'I'll call it in.'

'Good, I'll be in the garden. See if there's anything useful there.'

While Ellie spoke on the phone for what seemed a long time, Drake looked round the overgrown outdoor space.

It appeared to have been undisturbed for a while. Wild grasses were nearly up to his shoulders in some places and there were the remains of a swing set towards the rear, a solitary tyre hanging from a rope on an oak tree. No bodies were waiting for him in the undergrowth, no further signs of struggle. He wondered why they'd been dragged out there, only to have been dragged back in through the house and whisked away to another location? Wouldn't there have been ample noise to attract neighbours?

Ellie stepped out onto the patio.

'Anything?' he asked.

'Nothing major. Though Strauss did say Jorge owns a property by a nearby town, you might know it? Outskirts of Reading? Like a big wooden shack or a retreat or something.'

'A retreat?'

'Yeah, big place, supposedly. Has a balcony, and it sounds like the property sits within a basin. As in, you drive down into it.'

Why does that description sound familiar? He thought. Seconds later, it dawned on him. 'Wait. You said a wooded area, right?'

Ellie focused on him. 'Strauss said it was, yes.'

Drake dashed back through to the kitchen. The fridge pictures stared back at him. Gregory and Jorge standing in front of a white-washed wooden structure that had seen better days.

'What is it, Chief?' Ellie asked, catching up with him.

Drake yanked the picture off of the fridge.

Oh, my God.

There, staring back at him behind a smiling Jorge and Gregory's shoulders, was a structure. A structure with a set of stained-glass circular windows on the ground level facade, beneath a balcony. The windows depicted a red sun with orange rays set against a blue sky and green grass, amongst a medley of other shapes and colours around the main image. The glass from the first scene had to have been taken from there. It had to.

Ellie, standing next to him, must have been thinking the same thing, judging by her expression.

'Ellie, we have to hurry!'

59

'Slow down, Drake. We won't get there any faster if we're dead,' Ellie pleaded as they flew down the A-road.

Drake glanced at her as she gripped onto the passenger door. 'We're out of time and out of luck, Ellie. They could be already dead, and I need to know at least I tried,' he growled, crisscrossing the mid-afternoon traffic with surprising ease.

Dusk was setting in, the haze of the sun on the horizon bringing an ominous swathe of red to the sky. He hoped it wasn't a sign of things to come.

'We nearly there?' Drake asked.

'Yeah, just take the next exit and there should be a dirt road further in that leads down to it,' Ellie said, casting a glance at him before turning back to her satnav app. 'What if they're still there, Drake? What are we going to do?'

Drake thought back to Miller's comments about going in alone. He had to admit he'd not thought it through, but it was too late to go back now. Every minute he delayed was a minute the two men didn't have. He couldn't bear the thought of more deaths on his conscience.

The Ties That Bind

Images of Dave danced in his mind. His friend hooked up to all those monitors. The man's wife looking bereft. Ellie's child being threatened. Drake gripped the gear stick, his knuckle turning white, his mouth a thin line, trying to quell the fire in the pit of his stomach.

'We stop them, Ellie. We bring them in. It's what we're paid to do. We don't have time to wait around.'

He took the exit off of the A-road and slowed at the roundabout traffic lights.

'I'll call for backup—'

'No. Wait until we're there. We can't have them raining down on the place if there's nobody there and our hunch is completely wrong.'

Drake imagined an apoplectic Miller back in her office, the thought of calling in a team only to find an empty old shack. He needed to get this right. It could be the last straw for him otherwise. He wouldn't be any good to his daughter if he was out of a job.

'Okay, whatever you say. Who knows what we're going to find.'

'Indeed,' he said, putting both hands on the steering wheel.

'Just ahead now, slow down. Take that road, just there,' Ellie pointed over to his right.

Drake rammed on the brakes and pulled over into the sideroad once the chain of oncoming traffic had passed.

Fir trees lined the rough track on either side, blocking out more and more of the retreating light the further they travelled inwards. The only sound was the crunching of the stones and branches under tyre as he slowed to a crawl.

'This is all getting a little sinister, isn't it?'

'We're chasing serial killers, Ellie. I'm not sure how much more sinister you can get.'

'True. But did it have to be in a wood, you know? *And* when it's near dark?'

Drake didn't answer, trying to steel himself. He wasn't sure what they'd find. It could be completely empty, or it could be a crime scene. The closer they got, the more he wasn't sure which he'd prefer.

The fir trees continued to obscure any view other than what was directly ahead of them, the odd skeletal tree punctuating their evergreen dominance. He rounded a bend, and it continued. More bumps, more crunching of gravel. The car's headlights came on automatically as they sidled slowly round another bend.

'Shit, I've got no signal, Drake. You?'

He pulled his phone out of his coat pocket. His phone showed no bars.

Crap.

'You and me both. If we see anything, we'll go back. All right?'

'All right.'

Ellie nodded at the something up ahead. 'There, that looks like an entrance to me. The app's directions have died too, but looks like it could be the right one.'

Drake stopped, the headlights' glare picking up a rickety sign. White paint still caked the edges, but the elements had penetrated and done its work long ago, leaving nothing legible.

'Looks right to me. Let's do this,' Drake said, gritting his teeth and pulling into the entrance.

The car bobbed and jerked as they navigated the rough track that was even more bumpy than what came before. They'd started their descent into the basin Ellie had described earlier and he hadn't even realised. Old tree branches and debris littered their path as they continued down the road.

'Is that . . . ?'

The Ties That Bind

Thick mud lay ahead, a set of tyre tracks embedded in them. They seemed fresh.

'Yeah, looks like it.' His frown deepened. 'We may have been right, after all.'

They rounded a final corner, and Drake's bad feeling was confirmed the instant the headlights lit up the building before them.

Drake stopped the car.

The building owned by Jorge Martinez lay ahead of them, the car's headlights illuminating the entire, white-stained structure. It reminded Drake of communes from seventies America, and it looked just as old and dilapidated, the remnants of white paint still peeling away.

The building stretched over a large area and was surprisingly tall, comprising two floors. The front was adorned with a stout steeple, complete with a weather vane on top. Several thin-paned windows were visible, and an entranceway bulged to the side of the property on the right side. The sight of it made Drake think of old prairie house porches. All it needed was a rocking chair and an old man with a shotgun on his lap. The stained-glass of the circular windows they'd so desperately tried to pinpoint lay shattered on the ground, with only a few coloured shards remaining around the edges.

A rickety balcony poked out of the exceptionally high first floor towards them. A balcony on which Jorge and Gregory both stood, gagged and blindfolded, high on the balustrade. The headlights revealed their blindfolds soaked in blood, their hands bound behind them. And crucially, the large nooses round their necks.

'Oh, Christ, no,' Drake cursed.

'What the . . .' Ellie gawped at what she was seeing.

The two men in front of them stood frozen, terrified to move an inch in case they fell and hung themselves. Behind them stood two figures obscured by the men's shadows.

'We've got to call this in, Drake!' Ellie said, grabbing at her phone.

'Ellie, we have to try to talk them down from this. What else can we do? We can't leave, not now.'

'Fuck!' She turned her nose up in disgust at her phone. Evidently, phone signal was still nowhere to be found. 'Drake, I'm not sure I'm ready for this sort of shit again . . . Are you?'

'Only one way to find out,' he said, and exited the car.

'Drake!'

60

Drake got out of the car, leaving the headlights on, and raised his hands above his head. The building was encircled by a thick set of fir trees, the sound and movement from the wind making them seem alive and as though they had a sinister audience. An old estate car was parked to the side of the retreat, the boot still open, the engine off.

The welcome sound of a car door popping open and shutting came from his left. Glancing over, he felt buoyed to see Ellie had joined him.

'The two of you have timed your visit well. You'll have front row seats,' a steely voice projected from the balcony, the sound echoing around them. It was a woman's voice, but not one Drake recognised.

The two men squealed behind their gags at the voice, their muffled cries creeping up in volume as they tried to shy away from the source of the sound behind them.

'Please don't do this. It doesn't need to go this way. You can stop the killing, here and now. No more people need to die,' Drake called towards the silhouettes. His deeper voice boomed and echoed while he moved to the front of the car, standing between the headlights.

No response came. The headlights and the noise of the men added an unwelcome extra layer to an already tense, thick atmosphere. Dust danced in the headlights while the seconds ticked by.

A figure yanked on the men's nooses and hissed something to them. They stopped their muffled pleas immediately.

'If you understood, you'd know we can't stop what we're doing. That we *shouldn't* stop. They deserve everything that's coming to them,' a man's voice finally replied.

A familiar voice. Robert Spencer. Only, he wasn't as calm as he'd been during his interview, his voice now laced with anger and spite.

'That's not for you to decide, Robert,' Ellie said. She stood next to Drake, her movement not giving away her injury.

'Ah, here she is. DS Ellie Wilkinson. What a pleasant surprise,' the woman said. 'How's the leg? How's your daughter? Is that guy I stabbed dead yet?'

Ellie twitched at the remark, but controlled herself. Her self-control impressed Drake. He didn't know what he'd do if confronted with the person who'd terrorised his family again. The last comment regarding Dave caused him to flex his hands and recall the time he'd choked the man speaking to them.

'Who are you?' Ellie called up.

Silence.

'Answer me!'

The two silhouettes looked at each other before Robert stepped forth. The headlights revealing his face, the shock of unruly dirty blonde hair.

'This here's Fiona, and I'm Jack,' he answered.

The Ties That Bind

Ellie frowned. 'Jack? But you're Robert Spencer, we have it on record.'

'Only on the records I've allowed you to see,' he said, sneering at her, the lights painting a sinister gleam on his features.

'But, how . . . ?'

Jack waved her question away. 'The question has never been how, but "why?" And you have all been so hell-bent on finding us, you've not looked past the crimes. You've been blinded by seeing these people we've killed as "victims" when they're anything but.'

'Then tell us, Jack. Tell us why.'

Drake looked around, willing for an opportunity to present itself that could help their situation and stop these killers from carrying out the men's death sentences. He was failing to see a way forwards. If they rushed into the house, Jorge and Gregory were dead. If they stayed put, the same would inevitably occur.

There must be something we can do, something we can say that could prevent this.

Fiona stepped forwards into the light. 'You think we're just going to spill our guts to you before the main event? Come on, we're not that stupid. Don't take us for fools.'

He was expecting Gemma Chambers. However, this woman was similar in age to Jack: late twenties, perhaps early thirties. Nearly six feet with close blonde hair, a thick neck, and broad shoulders. She wore a black tank top vest, despite the weather, which revealed the remains of a curious large gash on her upper arm. The woman was strongly built, more so than her male counterpart. It was no wonder they'd both mistaken her for a man when they'd encountered her.

The pair turned to each other and said something out of earshot.

'Okay . . . How about this? We hang this one,' Jack called,

pointing to Gregory, a knife having made its way into his hand. 'Then we'll give you a little story. Deal?'

Fiona gave Jack a hard look when she heard the last part.

Drake took a step forward. 'You know we can't agree to that, Jack. We can't let you just kill these men in cold blood.'

'Oh, believe you me, these men are not cold right now. I think this one's pissed himself more than once. And the other, well, I honestly didn't know shit could smell like that. It fucking stinks.' He held his hand up to his nose. 'Makes me dread to think how that pig, Clare, smelt after we'd barbecued her,' he said and laughed.

The killer's face dropped in disappointment. 'I'm just sad I wasn't there to experience it. Fiona here had all the fun, but needs must, I suppose.'

Fiona piped up. 'You're forgetting the other pig too, the policeman – an actual piggy, brother.'

What? They're brother and sister?

'Oh yes, sergeant Matthews! How could I forget? Forgot about that little piggy.'

Fiona laughed.

'He squealed like a piggy too! Piggy, piggy, piggy, oink, oink, oink!' she squealed.

'Anyway, I'm getting carried away . . . where were we?' Jack paused theatrically for a second, the knife handle under his chin in a display of thinking. 'Ah, yes.'

He shoved Gregory in the backside.

'No!' Ellie and Drake shouted in unison.

The man let out a muffled noise of surprise as he fell from the balustrade while Jorge shrieked. The rope unravelled and snapped taut with a sickening crack as Gregory met the end of the rope mere feet above the ground. The noise echoed around the vicinity, the man's neck contorting at an unnatural angle, while Drake and Ellie looked on in shock.

61

Drake surged forwards, only for Jack to point the knife at Jorge, stopping Drake in his tracks. Gregory's body continued spasming in its death throes as he looked on helplessly, the balcony creaking like an old boat in a storm.

'Ah-ah-ah. Don't do that, DCI Drake,' Jack shouted. 'You don't want *yet another* death on your conscience now, do you?'

'Look at him twitch, brother. Ha-ha, he's like a fish!' Fiona said, her voice full of glee. 'Let's do another one!'

Jack put his head down, and spoke quietly, 'Let's not get ahead of ourselves now, Fi. We need to stay focused.'

Now Drake was closer, he could just about make out their discussion.

'What about the other one? Please?' He heard her say.

'No, not yet. They *need* to know our story.'

Fiona scrunched her nose in annoyance as Jack looked out at them once more.

'So, deal's a deal, eh? Story time . . . so, why would we be doing something like this to all these people? Maybe the answer will make you look at us both a little differently, eh?'

Drake felt like he was in an out-of-body experience. This couldn't be happening in front of him. He tried to push his gaze past the body of Gregory. The man's blindfold had fallen around his neck, revealing the ruinous wounds where his eyes had been.

A wave of nausea washed over him. What could possibly be driving this?

'So, I'll say it plainly enough that I think even you'll get it. Please understand we've tried telling you before, but you've never listened. If you had . . . well, none of this,' he pointed at Gregory's corpse and Jorge, 'would have happened, nor the other stuff. Anyway, I digress.'

He paced the balcony, causing it to creak and groan beneath his feet.

'The word you're looking for, brother, is "abuse". Oh, and murder, let's not forget that!' Fiona shrieked, before Jack had a chance to speak.

Jack frowned at her. 'That's a mild description, don't you think, Fi?'

The man appeared to be fighting back tears as he collected his thoughts, 'So, you see, this is what happened . . . Our parents went missing. A day turned into a week, yet still they didn't come back. Do you know what it's like not having any money for food when you live out in the middle of nowhere? To not know where your parents are? The feeling of abandonment? I was only twelve years old.'

He paused, lost in thought. 'Anyway, eventually we were taken into care at a children's home. I thought we were safe. That's what you're supposed to be in that sort of place, right? But it turns out, we weren't. We were anything *but* safe.'

He paced the balcony, getting more wound up at every step, clenching his jaw.

'We were told our parents were dead,' Fiona took up where

he'd left off. 'That they weren't coming back for us. But they never did find the bodies, and we never got to bury them or have a funeral. We got placed in a foster home soon after that.'

Jack continued, 'Yes, a home. But it wasn't a home, not like you'd think. Oh, no. They had rigged it somehow. Rigged, so that they could take us to live with Gregory and Clare.'

The markings in the kitchen, Drake realised. *That was him and Fiona?*

'This thing.' Jack pointed at Jorge, speaking through gritted teeth and tears. 'This *thing* had played the system somehow, using his job to move us to his depraved friends.'

Jorge shook his head hastily, more muffled protests and screams coming from beneath the gag.

'Let me give you a taste of our daily lives for you, what we've had to *endure*. The punishment meted out to us, day after fucking day . . .' Jack stopped and gripped the balustrade, his eyes bulging as he spoke through gritted teeth. 'How would you feel? Drake, Wilkinson – you both have daughters. How would you feel having them farmed out to strangers to be sexually abused for money, eh? To be punched, sodomised, beaten into unconsciousness for fun by groups of men and women? Made to watch while it happened to your family? To see that kind of thing happen in front of you?'

Drake baulked. It couldn't be. These supposed victims they'd been investigating, attempting to save, they'd been abusing Jack and his sisters? It couldn't be right, surely? It didn't bear thinking about.

'It all happened down there.' He pointed down at the stained-glass windows beneath. 'I still see those windows in my nightmares, Drake. In that room. The sun hitting the glass. The warmth of the glow on my face, the colours on my siblings as they were abused.'

Drake blurted. 'How do we know what you're saying is true? Do you have proof?'

'We *gave* you proof.'

'A blurred photo and some glass aren't enough, Jack. You know that.'

'How about our *word*? We were children, for fuck's sake. Is it normal to have those kinds of stories, those kinds of memories . . . those experiences, Drake?'

Ellie crept towards Drake. 'But how could you just be taken away like that?' she asked.

'I told you. This fuck here,' he said, pointing again at Jorge. 'He worked the records, gave us new identities, manoeuvred us into his friend's clutches. He joined in . . . We've got more proof, anyway. We don't need to justify ourselves to you, you bitch! You're just as bad as they are. We were *kids!*'

What? Why is she just as bad as them?

'Holy . . . Ellie, what did you do? Tell me!' he hissed to her.

She gave him a bewildered look. 'Nothing, Drake. Honestly, I've never seen either of them before in my life, I swear.'

Jack went on, 'If you want more proof, we have it. Remember your run in with my sister at Alex's flat? The hard drive? It's got hundreds, if not *thousands,* of photos of them with us. We were with Clare and Gregory for years, Drake . . . *Years!*'

Jesus Christ.

Those poor kids. He couldn't comprehend what they must have been through. It was beyond vile. He realised he was understanding their viewpoint more and more, why they'd done what they'd done. But it was how they'd butchered their abusers . . . Their young minds broken by their experiences; their thoughts bent on exacting their own reckoning. What they had done was beyond the realm of reason.

'Jack, what you've done . . . It's still cold-blooded murder. You can't rationalise killing human beings like that, no matter how much you try. It's not right. Surely you can see that?'

'How about we subject Eva and Bella to it, and see how you think about our *actions* then, Drake?' Fiona retorted.

The morals of his head played against the anger in his heart. He knew he'd kill whoever touched Eva in a heartbeat, but he wouldn't torture someone, and he certainly wouldn't admit it to two deranged killers.

'But, why Ellie? Why her? She's got nothing to do with you!'

Fiona said something in Jack's ear, so quietly Drake couldn't catch it all. 'Show . . . Just . . . it'

'All right. Since you've been so . . . *calm*, Drake. This is why . . . I'll give you this. One more thing, eh?'

Jack looked behind him and back into the house, motioning for someone to come out.

A new figure appeared in the headlights glow.

It couldn't be.

'No!' Ellie gasped.

It was Chambers. The woman winced at the light, her face seemingly full of shame as she stepped further onto the creaking balcony.

Jack motioned with his knife at Gemma. 'Show them, sister. Show them why . . . show Ellie.'

Sister? So she's been their inside man all along? This is just getting worse and worse.

Gemma nodded meekly and pulled on a rope.

Yet another figure came into view.

Drake's eyes were agog. Inspector Elgin . . . Phoebe Elgin, the woman from the car park? Her hands were bound behind her, and she hadn't been given a blindfold, her face still intact. The woman's body quivered at the sight before her. She spotted Drake and Ellie, and began pleading pitifully through her gag.

Fiona grabbed the noose length from Gemma and yanked it hard, causing Elgin to stumble forwards to the front of the groaning balcony.

'Phoebe!' Ellie cried. 'What the hell? What . . . What has she done? Let her go! Gemma, stop this, before it's too late!'

'I can't. Don't you see?' Gemma raised her voice. 'We . . . We flagged you down when they took us to London for one of their clients. Spoke to you both about our abuse, our *punishments*. But she did nothing to help us. *You* did nothing! You believed whatever these bastards told you when they caught up with us. Oh, how we suffered after that.'

Tears started streaming down Gemma's face. 'We're supposed to trust the police, and the one opportunity, the *one time* we had the courage to say anything, you . . . you didn't *listen*. We waited and waited for you to come and save us, but no one ever came. *You* never came.'

Drake looked at Ellie.

She gawped, her eyes shimmering with tears as she brought her hands to her face.

'Oh . . . my . . . Oh my God, I'm so sorry. Please. I didn't know. I didn't *know*. You've got to believe me!' Ellie blurted, her hands shaking.

'Why didn't you help us?' Gemma screamed. 'Why!'

'I . . . I was told not to. That it was nonsense. Just kids being kids.'

Inspector Elgin shook her head in shame.

'How . . . even now, could you not even have the decency to recognise any of us? We meant that little to you?' Jack asked.

'I was young . . .' She stumbled on her words. 'Inexperienced! I must have been, what, twenty years old? I wasn't to know! I was just following orders! You were kids!'

'That's no excuse and you know it, you fucking bitch!' Fiona shrieked, screaming as she lunged forward and shoved Jorge.

'No!' Drake yelled.

The man screamed through his gag as feet met empty air and he plunged to his death, the length of rope snapping tight with a grotesque crunch.

Mere moments later, a loud splintering groan emitted from the building. The force of the second body caused a chain reaction as the balcony buckled under the strain. The twisting, grating and snapping of wood flared from beneath the platform and the balcony collapsed. Elgin and the family disappeared amid a pile of wood and debris, before the whole facade of the structure and steeple sheared off, collapsing in on top of them.

62

Ellie couldn't believe what she'd been told, the effect her inaction had wrought on the family before her. It was disgusting and pitiful. It was shameful. *She* felt ashamed. But killing those disgusting people, not bringing them to justice? Taking her daughter, hurting her friend and Gemma, betraying them? It didn't make what they'd done right.

Seconds later, Ellie watched in stunned horror as the balcony collapsed before her. Mere moments after the death of yet another man.

'Drake, we've got to help them! Please!' She grabbed at the air where his arm had been milliseconds before, but he was already steaming ahead into the wretched pile of timber.

Ellie hobbled over to the wreckage and immediately found Gemma and Elgin. Gemma appeared to be unconscious, battered and bloody, her chest pinned by a beam from the balcony. Elgin was crying out in pain, her mouth still gagged, her arms behind her back. There was no sign of Fiona or Jack.

Drake tried removing some of the debris from Gemma with no luck.

Ellie waved him away. 'Drake, you go on. I'll help them both. Go, find them!'

She stepped gingerly through the debris to Elgin, narrowly avoiding the remnants of a beam spilling from above and slamming into the ground. She twisted and turned until she reached Elgin, her knee throbbing from the abnormal movements she'd had to make.

'Phoebe, you hang in there, okay? I've got you.'

She worked at the woman's bindings, pulling at the knots at her wrists, while Elgin writhed to allow her a better angle.

Suddenly, her old boss screeched.

Ellie stopped and yanked the gag down in time for Elgin to scream, 'Watch out!'

It was too late. Ellie dropped like a sack of potatoes.

* * *

Drake darted around the side of the building and spotted a figure rounding the far corner in the hazy darkness. Following carefully, he crept through the overgrown grass and foliage against the side of the retreat.

Seeing a small wooden post on the ground, he decided he'd need something with which to defend himself and picked it up. It was half-rotted, but better than nothing. It would slow down any would-be assailants, if nothing else.

Drake's heart pounded in his chest as he approached the far corner. Rounding it, he saw an open door a couple of metres ahead. Whoever he'd seen must have gone inside. Drake checked his surroundings once more; the last thing he wanted was to be led into a trap. But he saw nothing except the outlines of trees and murky gloom.

He creaked up the few shallow steps and entered the property, bathing himself in a sombre glow amidst the deadly quiet. The car's headlights shone a hazy beam through the gaping hole where the balcony had been. The windowed doors which had led to it from the first-floor mezzanine were ruined, the left hanging off one hinge and the right completely shorn off.

A couple of lamps punctuated the large, open space on the ground floor, with sofas and recliners dotted around. Several large rugs carpeted the uneven space, while a kitchenette was set off to the side. A door to his immediate right was open, a bathroom contained within. The final and furthest doorway led to the room at the front of the property, the one he assumed was the bedroom from the polaroid, where he assumed Jack and Fiona were hiding.

His eyes followed a set of steps to his left that led up to the mezzanine floor. It rimmed the left-hand side of the interior, and round to the collapsed external balcony, but no further.

Drake hefted the wooden post in his hands, trying to maintain a grip on the decaying matter. 'Jack . . . Fiona, come out. Stop this.'

No reply.

He crept forward, heading into the main lounge area as a muffled scream sounded from outside. Then nothing. He hoped to God it wasn't Ellie. Inside, there was no movement, no noise, just shadows playing on the wood.

Moving across the room, he came across a blood-soaked plate on a side table. Two sets of eyes looked back at him. Drake's stomach roiled at the sight. He turned back in time to see a flutter of movement at the presumed bedroom door.

'Stop!'

He rushed to the doorway.

'Jack? Fiona?' He angled his head to get a view of the room.

As he suspected, it was the one from the photograph retrieved from Alex's throat. What Jack had said was right. They'd been shown the evidence, shown the scene of the crime, right from the beginning.

The upper reaches of the front of the room had been destroyed by the balcony collapse; timbers hung by a thread, the high ceilings beams shorn away, the cursed windows no more. The ruined room held the remains of a log burner or stove in one corner, a steel-framed bed set against another. All that was missing was the shape on the bed in the photo. Drake realised now it had to have been one of the siblings cowering under the covers. His stomach lurched at the thought of how scared they must have been.

Distracted by the room, he didn't react to the sound of someone rushing in from behind. He turned too slowly, leaving time for an arm to wrap around his throat.

'Now it's your turn, Drake,' Jack hissed into his ear while tightening his grip. 'How does it feel, huh?'

Drake choked, pulling at the man's arm with his free hand and stumbling back as the man dragged him. At the last moment, he remembered the weapon in his other hand. He swung it back, clomping Jack's knee and causing the grip to fall away as the man yowled in pain.

Drake swung round to face his attacker.

'Jack, stop,' he pleaded. 'We don't have to do this. I understand why you did what you did, but just stop. Please!'

Jack scowled, taking a few steps back at the sight of the post-wielding DCI. 'You're just saying that, Drake. I'm nothing more than another criminal in your eyes. Another one to go on that long list of yours. There's no turning back now. I'm fucked either way, and you know it.'

A flash of concern came and went. 'I won't let my sisters go to prison. Fi could probably handle herself, but Gemma . . . a detective in prison, she'll be torn apart. I won't let anyone touch her again.'

Drake needed to know what Chambers had done. If he was to get out of this alive, he would need to answer for her actions. She couldn't have taken part, could she?

'What did Gemma do, Jack? Wasn't she just an unwilling participant? She doesn't seem the type to kill . . . not like you and Fiona. Did you manipulate her?'

Jack pursed his lips. 'Manipulate her? She's my *sister*, Drake. She did it willingly. Removed evidence.' His eyes narrowed. 'The tree at Folly Brook. Fi realised her blood was on the tree after that bastard Alex struggled and fought back. Roughed up her arm, but she didn't think there'd been any blood left there until we got Gemma to the scene. Then those damn dog walkers appeared, and Gemma had to remove it when she had a moment alone.'

Jack kept going, the words flooding out. 'I've seen the documentaries – I know how DNA can be used. Family tree databases, familial lineage matches. We couldn't take the chance. I only planted her to be a backup in case things went wrong, nudging her into your boss's path. As disappointing as it is for me to admit it, you're right – I didn't mean for her to be actively involved, not really. We were actually proud of her when she told us she was becoming a detective. Can you believe it?'

He looked away before turning back. 'Prison . . . I can't let you put her there. I just can't.'

Drake tried once more. 'It doesn't have to end like this. You can stop now before the situation gets any worse.'

'Worse?' Jack gave an incredulous laugh.

'Jack, we can work things out. Ellie has a daughter. I've a

daughter. Do you want them to be without a mother? Mine without a father?'

'Come on, Drake. I've been monitoring you – you barely have a relationship with Eva. If anything, judging by what she puts on social media, she'd be happier without you, anyway. I'd be doing her a favour.'

'That's not true,' Drake snapped. 'Stay away from my daughter!'

'Make me.' Jack sneered. 'Speaking of staying away . . . Maybe I'll pay your mate a visit, have him die of 'natural causes' in the night, eh?'

Drake's heart skipped a beat. The man was twisted. 'We've nothing to do with your fucking retribution. Leave us out of it.'

'Drake, the only way out of this now is with one of us dead. You know that.' Jack lunged at him, grabbing for the post.

Drake ducked to one side, holding it up defensively in front of him.

'Jack, I don't want to hurt you.'

'Wanna bet? You enjoyed choking me when you caught me. Admit it – I've seen men like you before. The men they farmed me out to, the enjoyment they get from pain.'

'No, I—'

'Admit it!'

Jack lunged at him for a second time. Again, Drake ducked. But this time, he caught his foot on the steps leading down to the living area. He wrenched his ankle and stumbled headfirst into a chair, the post clattering to the floor.

'Whoops!' Jack mocked, kicking away the post. 'Geez, you're sort of pathetic, aren't you? I read Eva's mother died because of you.'

'No,' Drake gasped. The fall had knocked the wind out of him.

'How is it, knowing you're a failure to your only kid?'

'I'm not . . . I'm not a failure!' Drake got to his feet and lurched forwards. Jack bounded to the side, but Drake caught his jumper and reeled him in.

'Do it, Drake. I dare you. Do it for your daughter. Protect her for once in your miserable life.'

Drake roared. He punched Jack square in the face, feeling the crunch of bone beneath his knuckles. Blood gushed from the man's nose and he fell to the ground.

His teeth smeared with blood, Jack laughed. 'That's more like it, Drake! But you're going to need to do more than that. You know I'm going to find your daughter!'

'No!' Drake straddled the dazed man on the ground. 'No! No . . . You . . . Won't . . . !'

The red mist descended, the fire burning fiercely in Drake's gut. Balling his hands into fists, he bellowed as he rained down blows on the man, finally letting out all the pent-up feelings of the past year.

'I won't let you . . . ! I won't let you hurt her!' Blow after blow, one after the other. Drake pounded the man's face and body, cracking his head against the floor repeatedly. The images of the Family Man kept coming to the fore: Becca dying in front of him, the screams and tears of his daughter, his inability to protect them both. His friend laying in hospital. Everything surged out of him in a flood of rage.

Jack abruptly stopped laughing. A heavy blow knocked the remaining sense from him, his face becoming a mass of swelling and blood beneath the beating.

Drake, tiring with each blow, finally came to a stop. Regaining some degree of self, he looked down at his bloodied, shaking hands, the reality of what he had just done becoming clear as he looked down at the ruined face before him.

'Jack! No!' Fiona screamed. She hurtled towards them, striking Drake in the temple.

He fell to the ground, his body senseless and numb as she descended upon him, her eyes aflame.

Now it was his turn.

63

'Ellie... Ellie, wake up. Please, Ellie... wake up! It's me.'

Ellie heard the distant voice, pleading, willing her into being. The words felt like a dream floating in her mind. Then the pain hit.

Her eyes flew open, but something wet immediately ran into them. She raised a leaden arm and attempted to wipe whatever it was away. It felt warm on her fingertips.

'Ellie, get up. Please!'

Phoebe?

'Yes, that's it – wake up! Get us out of here. She's gone, but I don't know for how long. Please!'

'Uhhhh,' Ellie groaned. She pulled herself up to her knees, the injured one causing her to cry out.

'Hurry, I think she's gone inside to help her brother. I think Drake was fighting him.'

'Huh... John?'

'Yes!'

'I've got to... help him,' Ellie gasped. She swallowed a wave of bile.

'We can both help him. Please, I need to do this! I need to make amends.'

Ellie looked down at the woman amidst the planks of splintered wood. She was in no fit state to help anyone. Her ankle turned at an angle that wasn't natural. Ellie looked at her own hands, covered in blood; her own blood, she realised, as she raised a tentative hand to her temple and wiped at her eyes once more.

'Jesus, my head.'

'She gave you a massive whack,' Elgin told her. 'I'm surprised you're even alive.'

'I don't feel alive.' Ellie swayed in place. 'I've got to help Drake.'

'No, you'll be killed.'

'I've got to help him!'

'No, Ellie, don't. It should be me!'

'What do you mean?'

'They . . . those kids, the reason they're the way they are. I think I'm to blame. The policeman that died, Peter – I was in a relationship with him. I brought it up at the station when I wasn't sure what to do. He told me he'd sort it out. That's why I didn't follow it up.'

'It was *you?* Jesus, Phoebe!'

'I'm sorry, I didn't know! It was stupid of me. How was I to know he was involved?'

Ellie ignored her. Getting to her feet, she hobbled to the side of the building, approaching the porch entrance.

'Don't leave me,' Elgin begged her. 'Please!'

I'll deal with you later, Ellie thought.

She couldn't believe her former boss had been involved with this shit show. That poor family. Being mistreated like that and for so long; they'd been failed by the police and even abused by one of them. She was furious. No wonder Peter Matthews was anonymous. He'd kept himself that way to avoid drawing any attention to the activities of himself and his 'friends'.

Stumbling around the side of the building, she tried the closed, curtained door of the porch entryway. It was locked, and wouldn't budge.

'Urgh. Come on,' she muttered.

Breathing heavily, sweat pouring off her brow and her knee and temple pulsing, she continued on.

'John . . .' She turned the corner and saw an open door.

I've got to stop them; it has to end now. It has to.

She stopped amidst a fit of coughs, trying to mask the sound as best she could. Peering cautiously into the building, she saw a shape kneeling by two others who lay face up on the ground. Fiona was clasping the hand of her brother, and Drake lay nearby.

'John!' she whispered, shocked at the sight. He looked like he was out cold, his face battered and bruised, blood streaming from a gash on his face. It took all her strength not to go in all guns blazing, and fight Fiona where she stood.

Ellie worked her way into the building, taking a half-crouched position next to the mezzanine stairs. She couldn't get any lower, her knee was failing her again.

Fiona's head twitched round, sensing a presence. Her face fixed in a sneer as she set eyes on Ellie.

'Oh no you don't!' Fiona shrieked. 'You're the reason my baby is dead. It's you!'

Ellie didn't stick around to confront her. She half-rocketed, half-leapt up the stairs as she tried to get away, only realising her mistake upon seeing the collapsed balcony doors ahead of her.

There was no way down. She was cornered.

Shit.

'Looks like I've got myself another little piggy,' Fiona said, slowing her pursuit. 'I'll kill you in place of your daughter. An eye for an eye. How's that sound?'

'I haven't killed anyone!' Ellie retorted. 'I know now that I made a terrible mistake. Fiona, I'm sorry, I truly am. But I've not killed anyone.'

'Yes . . . you did. Granted, it wasn't you directly. But you may as well have.' Fiona paused, as though she was unsure of how to phrase her next sentence. 'I was pregnant.'

'What! But you must have been, what, fourteen?'

'Why the surprise? Am I not pretty enough?' Her face twisted. 'I was the most popular one.'

Ellie didn't want to think about what the poor girl had been through. Becoming pregnant by one of her abusers. It shocked her to her very core, bringing on waves of sympathy, despite what the woman had since done.

'But why try to take my little girl? She's done nothing wrong!'

'Neither had mine.'

'What happened?' Ellie edged away from Fiona as the crazed woman approached. She tried desperately to think of a way out of the situation that didn't result in death.

'I gave birth here. She was so beautiful. Then, they . . . they took her away when she wasn't making any sound.' Fiona's face contorted as she relived the memory, the sheer horror of it clear to see. 'They threw her in the log burner. I think she was alive . . . I begged them to stop, but they didn't. And they . . . they scattered her remains here, at this lodge. Like she was rubbish.'

Ellie felt sick to her stomach. That poor, poor child.

'Clare took her from me and discarded her, just like that.' Fiona's face twisted into a wicked smile. 'You see, that's why I had to burn her in return. She had to pay.'

Ellie backed into the banister of the mezzanine floor next to the shorn off balcony door. The other door squeaked in front of her, hanging by its hinge. She was out of space. She had nowhere to go.

She could see Drake below. He was still out cold, and he'd been so badly beaten, she couldn't tell if he was even alive. She prayed he was.

'This is why you have to die,' Fiona said. 'If it wasn't for you and your old boss, Elgin, my daughter would be alive. She would have got the care she needed.'

'No. Don't you see? They manipulated her . . . That man you burned, it was all his doing. We can make this right. You have to trust me.'

'Trust you?' Fiona howled. 'Her being manipulated doesn't mean a thing. You still could have followed up on it.'

Ellie's eyes dropped. In a way, the woman was right. But where would it end? She couldn't follow up on everything that came her way, it just wasn't possible.

'Can you bring my baby girl back? No . . . ? Then shut up. I'm done talking to you. Fucking pig, you failed us.'

Fiona drew closer to within striking distance. The woman snarled as she lunged and withdrew, toying with Ellie the way she'd done when she'd tried to kidnap Bella.

'Maybe I'll find your daughter after this, eh? Sell her off to the highest bidder, put her through what I went through. How about that?'

'No! Don't you dare! That won't change what happened to you. Don't you bring my daughter into this.'

'Or what?'

Ellie took a deep breath. Knowing she had to stop Fiona, had to subdue her somehow until she could get help, Ellie did the only thing she could. She charged at the woman. But her knee gave out almost immediately, and she stumbled into Fiona's outstretched arms.

Fiona grinned, lashing out with a punch to Ellie's swollen knee.

Ellie screamed in pain, her vision blasting white at the shock.

'So pathetic. I guess you'd have been no help after all, you piece of shit.'

I can't let her win, she thought amidst the agony. *I can't let her take Bella from me. Can't let her hurt my family.*

Ellie grabbed the balcony's ruined frame and hauled herself back to her feet, the sweat dripping off her nose. Her heart pounded in her chest as she stood to take on Fiona one last time.

Ellie didn't get a second to think before Fiona decided it was her turn to charge, screaming as she barrelled into her. The blow knocked Ellie into the balcony frame, her foot meeting nothing but air, while her other teetered on the edge. Ellie's arms flailed, scrambling for something, *anything*, to grab on to. Fiona was in reach, as was the door frame. She knew she had to stop her own fall, but also that she had to put a stop to Fiona's violence. In an instant, Ellie had a hold of a stunned Fiona's arm. She knew what she had to do.

Ellie fell, dragging the woman with her as they plunged into the debris below.

64

Drake woke to the kind of devastating headache he'd not experienced in a long time. He attempted to force his eyes open, but only one would budge. They felt sticky as he struggled to adjust his one apparently functioning eye to the bright lights.

He flinched violently as the memories came flooding back; he'd been mid-fight with Jack. Drake twisted himself round in defence, expecting the next blow at any moment, and groaned at the pain shooting through his body.

'Dad! You're awake!'

Eva?

A familiar face coalesced in his vision at his side. An expression on her face that he'd not seen for such a long time. Eva was smiling at him.

'Eva?' he said, incredulous.

A look of total relief was etched on her face.

'Dad, don't you ever do this to me again, or I'll finish the job myself.' Her beaming face was completely at odds with the threat. 'I thought I'd lost you too, you absolute bastard.'

He blinked away the remnants of blurriness in his eye, seeing he was in a hospital room.

'Oh, Eva.' He tried to hold out his arms, but another shooting pain flew through his chest. Were his ribs broken?

Seeing him struggling, she came to him and hugged him where he lay.

Drake finished his sentence through the pain. 'I'm so, so, sorry. You have no idea.'

'Dad, I thought you were dead. We all did,' she said, speaking over his shoulder as he continued half-hugging her as best he could. She stood back. 'You're completely battered. Your eye is still swollen shut. You've a twisted ankle and the doctor said you've broken a few ribs. And for a while, they suspected you had a fractured skull too. I was so scared.'

Her face turned from a look of worry to one of irritation in an instant, as only she could do. 'Did you seriously go to a cabin in the woods with Ellie to catch some serial killers, *and* all by yourselves? Are you actually beyond stupid?'

'Well, er, when you put it that way . . .' He smiled, his mouth sore. Then it dawned on him: 'Shit, Ellie! Is she okay?'

'Yes, I think she saved your arse again.'

He raised his eyebrows. 'You're kidding me?'

She smirked. 'Nope.'

A tentative knock came at the door. Melwood wheeled in Dave, who was wearing a hospital gown that left little to the imagination once again.

'I can confirm that Ellie did indeed save the day,' Melwood said, much too loudly for Drake's liking.

'John, are you and Ellie seriously trying to steal my thunder?' Dave croaked weakly, smiling beneath his moustache. 'It's not on, you know. There's only room for one hero here.'

Drake was pleased to see his friend had come on leaps and bounds since he'd last seen him.

'What . . . what happened? How long was I out for?'

'I'll get you a drink, Dad,' Eva said. 'We need to talk though, okay?'

Drake nodded. 'Got it, love.'

Melwood closed the door after she left and brought up a chair. 'Miller and I were getting nervous that we'd not heard from you since you called in the crime scene at Gregory's house. And we couldn't get through to you – Strauss gave up trying, and it was getting ridiculous. Eventually, we made the executive decision to come with backup to this retreat you went to investigate.'

A look of disbelief spread across his face as he went on. 'I don't know what the hell you did there, but the place was in a right state, Drake. A woman was impaled on a damn stake, for God's sake. Chambers is in a coma. There was a police inspector with a broken ankle. All while Ellie was laying there unconscious with a swollen knee the size of my head. Seriously, what in blazes happened up there?'

Drake grimaced. 'It's a long story . . . and not a pleasant one, at that.'

'Well, we're not going anywhere, eh? I got stabbed more than once as part of this nonsense, remember?' Dave said, stern-faced.

'Okay, okay.' Drake started. 'The victims – they weren't innocent, Dave. They *abused* the SGK killers. Robert – actually called Jack – Fiona and Gemma. They'd abused them for years. They were at the mercy of these *people*, and God knows who else. That's their motive, that's what they told me.'

'Aye, and turns out one of them got pregnant by them.' Dave paused, taking a breath. 'John, I can't believe I'm saying this. Clare and her "friends" . . . they killed the baby, literally threw it in the stove. That's all that Ellie would say before she passed out again.'

Drake couldn't believe it, as if the tale couldn't get any darker. They'd killed a child too? That poor woman. No wonder she was so hell-bent on revenge.

Dave continued. 'A team is checking out the grounds of the retreat for any evidence.'

'And Fiona? Jack?'

'Fiona's dead, died from massive blood loss. Robert – or Jack, whatever – is in intensive care. He really took a beating, John.'

The implication as to how he came to be that way hung in the air between the three men, Dave and Melwood pursing their lips.

Drake could only recall flashes of what happened. The room, the struggle, the threats. Him falling, him punching the man in the face, breaking his nose . . . but intensive care? Holy shit.

He stayed quiet. It was self-defence. It had to be. However, the sight of his knuckles made him think otherwise.

'It's okay, John. Don't worry, you've been through a lot. We've got your back.'

'That's not what I . . .' His eye pulsed. 'I . . . I don't remember much. Just him attacking me.'

'Don't say anything more.' Melwood said, cutting him short.

The men sat in silence. Melwood then spiked it as only he could. 'By the way, Strauss said he would come by later. Despite appearances, he was really worried about you both. Heck, even I was.'

Drake raised an eyebrow pointedly.

Melwood continued on oblivious. 'He's been doing some digging into Jack and co. Turns out their original surname *is* Chambers. He'd somehow forged new identities for himself and Fiona. They were Robert and Meghan Spencer, for all intents and purposes. Strauss only tracked them by looking into Gemma more and following up on her siblings. Then it all started coming together.'

Drake sighed. 'Jesus. And Gemma . . . Jack told me she was planted.'

They sat in silence, his swollen eye pulsing further. 'What about the CCTV man?'

Melwood sighed. 'We still have nothing there. He could be anyone. Did they say anything to you, Drake?'

He frowned, which proved challenging. 'No, nothing. Who could he be?'

'A nobody, maybe?' Dave suggested, his voice hoarse. 'Perhaps they paid someone to do it. It's not beyond the realm of possibility.'

'Mmm, sounds like a stretch to me. We need to find him,' he said, before pausing again. His ribs were really throbbing, even with the medication he must be on. 'Is Ellie still here? Can I see her?'

Dave nodded, his voice becoming steadily weaker. 'I think so. Her family is with her, but if you can walk, I think it'll be okay. They said you've just got concussion, other than the ribs and eye – you're a lucky man.'

'I don't feel it,' Drake said.

Dave clapped his leg gently. 'You're alive, that's what matters.'

* * *

Drake let Eva know he'd be another minute or two before limping down the corridor in the general direction Dave had given him. He saw Ellie's husband leaving the room with Bella, who waved. Len stopped her, giving him a stony look and guiding Bella away down the corridor in the opposite direction.

Guess I deserve that.

His head was still pounding as he reached her hospital room. Jack, or Fiona, whoever it was, had done a real number on him. He ached all over.

Still, despite it all, it may have been worth it. Eva was actually talking to him again. He'd take the hit a thousand times more if he'd known *that* was going to be the outcome. Things were looking up. Finally.

Drake stood at the doorway to the room. His partner lay on the bed, heavily bandaged and with her eyes closed.

He tapped lightly on the open door.

'Can I come in?'

She opened her eyes groggily. 'We really must stop getting hurt like this,' she groaned. 'I mean it. You look like shit.'

'I know. But hey, at least this time we weren't stabbed. No matching scars, at least, eh?' He pointed to their hands.

'Matching concussions count?' A faint smile touched her lips.

'What the hell happened up there?'

Ellie hesitated for a second. 'Fiona charged me. I lost my footing and grabbed at her, and we both fell. Last thing I remember was thinking, "this is it" as the ground rushed towards me.'

'Well, thankfully for us, it wasn't. You saved me again. I'm going to have to start paying you monthly myself –you're turning into a form of life insurance.'

Drake's phone rang.

He took the call, a concerned sounding Strauss on the other end. He relayed to Drake some information that he couldn't believe he was hearing.

'Okay, thanks, Strauss. I'll let her know,' he said, ending the call, his temple pulsing.

'What? What is it? You've got that look.'

The Ties That Bind

'This keeps getting better and better,' he snarled, scratching the back of his neck.

'What?' Ellie tried to sit up in bed, but her leg prevented her.

'You're not going to believe it. This family – the mother and father. Strauss got a hit on them when he dug around some more. They're two of the Family Man's victims, a couple they've identified recently from his kill room at the farm.'

Ellie shot Drake an incredulous look. 'What!'

'I know . . .' He flexed his hands at his sides. 'That bastard is the reason for Jack, Fiona and Gemma going into care. Is there anyone whose lives he hasn't ruined?'

65

'Dad, I'm just going to say this now. I don't think I'll ever truly forgive you for what happened to Mum.'

'Eva—'

'No, let me finish please,' she said. Her tired eyes locked on his as she stared him down in his hospital bed.

'Okay,' he nodded.

'But getting that phone call from your boss lady, I felt that panic like when we were in our kitchen, when that . . . *man* did what he did to Mum. I thought I couldn't feel that kind of panic again . . .' She cast her eyes down to the bed, seeming to gather herself. 'But I did, and I felt like I couldn't lose you too, no matter how I've felt about everything since. You're my dad.'

His heart skipped a beat. Could this be what he'd wished for? What he thought was impossible for so long?

'Oh, Eva.'

'So, I'm . . .' She stopped again, fidgeting with her hands as she tried to find the words. 'I'm going to *try*, okay? I want us to be whatever fucked up version of a family we can be. Please? I can't lose you too.'

'Eva, I understand. I promise, I will always be there for you.'

She gave him a pointed look. 'Don't make promises you can't keep, Dad. Seriously, don't.'

A reply stuck in his throat, causing him to pause. Thinking better of it, he held out his arms to her, his ribs protesting, and she embraced him.

'Oh, and you're *cordially* invited to Christmas dinner with Aunt Rachel and Anna,' she said with a mock butler accent. Then speaking faster. 'And if we live together again, Cari's coming with us. Deal? Okay, good!'

Drake raised his eyebrows.

'Deal.'

* * *

Drake howled with laughter at the joke Eva read from the Christmas cracker they had pulled together. She joined him. Her face lit up in a way he hadn't seen since before her mother had died. It warmed his soul.

'Jesus, John. I knew there was a reason we didn't allow Christmas crackers in this house before now,' Rachel remarked.

Anna laughed, while Cari smiled quietly as they passed around the remaining crackers.

He couldn't believe he was spending Christmas with his daughter. He truly never thought it possible. His girl back with him. It had only taken the threat of death, a head injury or two.

He smiled to himself, taking in how happy she seemed, if only temporarily.

* * *

'Thank you for doing this, Rachel,' Drake said, putting plates away in the kitchen cupboards while she dried some of the remaining cutlery. The action brought back memories of Becca.

'I didn't do it for you, John. Remember that. She might have gone some way to forgiving you, but I *never* will. Once this charade is over, I want you as far away from this house as possible. The sooner the better.'

'Rachel, I—'

'I don't want to hear it.'

'But . . .' He stood, struggling to find the words.

Eva called from the other room. 'Dad, your work phone's ringing. Do you want me to answer it?'

'No, I'll get it, love.'

Rachel gave him a cold look as he limped back to the living room, where Eva was talking with Anna. He grabbed the phone from the arm of the sofa and moved to the hallway, itching his stubble with his free hand while he paced.

'DCI Drake?' He answered, smiling at the noise of his daughter in the living room.

'Hello? Drake? This is Miray. Andrea's mother.'

BLOOD LINES
DCI JOHN DRAKE BOOK 3

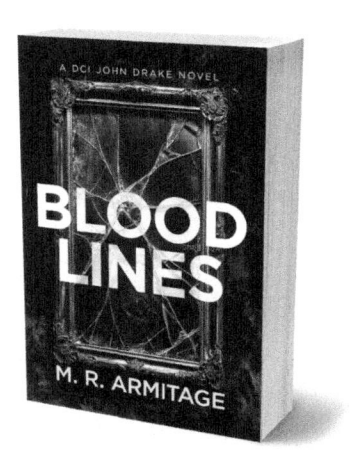

The killer's behind bars. But his legacy lives on.

Life is looking up for DCI John Drake. His relationship with his daughter is back on track and together, they're dealing with the trauma they suffered at the hands of the Family Man.But their respite doesn't last long.

Unknown to Drake, his partner, DS Ellie Wilkinson, has her own demons to battle in the aftermath of their most recent case. And when they're called to a gruesome crime scene in a London underpass, the brutal truths they're forced to confront will test them to the very limit.

ACKNOWLEDGMENTS

I used up all the ways to express my thanks when writing the acknowledgements for my first book, but I'll give it another go.

Thank you again, Mum and Dad. Your support has been as brilliant as ever. May we have many more years of discussions over a Sunday roast – no lamb, thanks!

Thank you to Jon, Naz, Caroline, Andrew and Kit for your continued support and positivity, despite my grumbles.

Margaret, once again, your editing has made this monstrosity into something resembling a coherent book. I seem to have made fewer mistakes this time, perhaps some of your expertise is cementing itself in my brain.

And thank you to all my readers. Seriously, I wouldn't have had the confidence to release the second in the series without your kind reviews, comments and support. I can only hope you enjoyed this one as much.

ABOUT THE AUTHOR

M. R. Armitage is an author hailing from Reading, England. Surrounded by a distressing number of unread books, he hopes one day he will read them all rather than just buying more.

Visit my website:

www.mrarmitage.com

And keep in touch on Facebook:

facebook.com/MRArmitageAuthor

Printed in Great Britain
by Amazon